NOWHERE

THE EDGE OF NOWHERE

A TEXAS BLUE NORTHER WESTERN

WILLIAM W. JOHNSTONE

AND J.A. JOHNSTONE

PINNACLE BOOKS

Kensington Publishing Corp.

www.kensingtonbooks.com

PINNACLE BOOKS are published by

Kensington Publishing Corp.
900 Third Avenue
New York, NY 10022

All Kensington titles, imprints, and distributed lines are available at special quantity discounts for bulk purchases for sales promotion, premiums, fund-raising, and educational or institutional use.

Special book excerpts or customized printings can also be created to fit specific needs. For details, write or phone the office of the Kensington Sales Manager: Kensington Publishing Corp., 900 Third Avenue, New York, NY 10022. Attn. Sales Department. Phone: 1-800-221-2647.

PINNACLE BOOKS, the Pinnacle logo, and the WWJ steer head logo Reg. U.S. Pat. & TM Off.

First Printing: November 2024
ISBN-13: 978-0-7860-5119-9
ISBN-13: 978-0-7860-5120-5 (eBook)

10 9 8 7 6 5 4 3 2 1

Printed in the United States of America

CHAPTER 1

"I just reloaded this pistol with six fresh rounds." The speaker had his hat brim pulled low on his forehead and a blue scarf over his nose. "If you move, I'll use them all to blow you off that stage."

A line of dark blue clouds was almost upon them. The norther promised rapidly falling temperatures and ice or snow, which was unusual for the Red River that time of the year. Five men spread out in front of the stage headed for the boomtown of Blackjack.

"Why would I move?" The driver raised both hands. "None of this belongs to me, so have at it."

A second highwayman wearing a faded cotton scarf almost devoid of pattern reined around to the side. "Everybody get down out of there."

Bobwhite quail called around them, gathering together in response to the changing weather as four men climbed down. Two wore suits and the others were dressed similarly to the stage robbers, in hats, trousers, and vests. Faded Scarf flicked his Colt at them. "Guns on the ground, slow."

Only the two wearing Stetsons were armed with

pistols tucked into their belts. One held a hand close to his revolver. "If I drop this, it'll likely go off. There's a round under the hammer."

Red Scarf nodded and spoke in a voice made gravelly by intention. "You're a good man. Shake them shells out, but be careful."

The cowboy emptied the cylinder and dropped it and the loose shells on the ground as the other man did the same.

The businessmen almost shook out of their shoes. "We don't have guns."

One of the highwaymen, with an abnormally long neck, laughed. "What kind of men don't go around heeled?"

The man in a derby answered. "The kind who don't want to get shot."

The five outlaws laughed.

Red Scarf turned his attention to the stage driver as a chilly gust of wind threatened to snatch the hat from his head. "Cashbox."

The squatty driver reached down and picked it up from under his feet. "It ain't heavy. I doubt there's much in here."

"What's in there'll do. Pitch it down."

The box hit the rocky ground with a crunch. The long-necked highwayman stepped down and, seeing the wooden box was already cracked, picked it up and slammed it back down. The wood exploded and he picked up two canvas sacks that spilled out.

Handing them up to Red Scarf, he swung back into the saddle.

Red Scarf put his Colt back in its holster while the others kept the passengers covered with their revolvers. "Is there anything of value in the boot?"

The stage driver shrugged. "Beats me. You'd have to ask these guys. Luggage that belongs to them in the back there and a few boxes somebody's shipping to Blackjack."

"Climb down and open 'er up."

"For luggage?"

"You don't never know." Red Scarf's voice cracked with the effort of trying to make it lower. "One of you boys get what the passengers are carrying." He waved his pistol. "Y'all turn out them pockets and dump 'em into Fat Boy's derby."

The driver climbed down and walked around to the back while the others kept their guns on the passengers as they dropped everything of value into the larger man's hat. Hard currency, pocket knives, a gold watch, and a buckeye carried for good luck was all they had.

Once around back, the driver untied the canvas cover and set out valises, small grips, and two carpetbags. Becoming impatient, Red Scarf waved his pistol some more. "Empty 'em out."

"Me?" The stage driver was incensed. "That's against company policy. It's illegal for me to open passengers' luggage."

"Legal won't matter if you wake up dead in the morning. Shake 'em out."

One by one, the driver opened the valises and dumped out clothes onto the sandy ground. Lighter garments lifted in the stiffening wind, spreading across the grass and scrub vegetation. As the sky darkened under thick clouds, he did the same with the remaining luggage with the same results.

Satisfied there was nothing of value hidden back there, Red Scarf returned to his men. "This is all we're gonna get. Shoot the two lead horses and let's go."

Scattered raindrops thumped off their hats as Long Neck rode around and fired a shot into each of the leader's foreheads. The horses fell where they were, legs thrashing. The two behind could do nothing but rear in their traces and fight the harness holding them in place.

The passenger who'd donated his hat to collect their loot produced a little pocket pistol and fired at the long-necked outlaw. The bullet missed by a wide margin, but the gang's return fire was a swarm of bullets. One found the dude just below his heart, and he collapsed with a groan.

With the stage anchored until the driver and passengers could unhook the horses' bodies and get underway, the outlaws-turned-murderers rode off to the south, yanking off their scarves and tossing them to the wind as they made their escape.

Icy rain began in earnest only minutes later as the blue norther arrived with a roar of wind, wiping out their tracks and threatening to take the lives of the driver and his passengers as the temperature plummeted.

CHAPTER 2

Almost frozen into his saddle, Ridge Tisdale was cold down to the bone and questioned his intelligence for being out in the icy wind howling across the open Texas prairie. Falling snow whipped in tornadolike swirls and settled on what had already collected. Drifts formed on anything that caught the flakes. Many of those drifts resembled ocean swells, while others were sculpted into sharp, solid waves.

He'd rather have been inside a nice warm building somewhere, or at the very least sheltered by something substantial beside the life-giving heat of a mesquite campfire. Instead, he was headed for the town of Blackjack.

It was difficult to see through the falling weather that isolated his world, and he relied on Rebel to get them there. The buckskin's hooves landed with a soft plop on the snow and the gelding had so much bottom he'd walk without complaint as long as his rider wanted.

Ridge did little but huddle inside his thick sheepskin coat and wish for a glowing stove, a cup of steaming coffee so hot it could scald a hog, and a beefsteak that was still bleeding.

A yellow-and-black silk scarf protruded from under his hat, covering his ears and disappearing inside the coat. Pulled low on his forehead, the stained felt hat stopped just above his eyebrows and collected snow. A second scarf covered his nose and lower face, making him look like a road agent in search of victims.

He reached out with a gloved hand and patted Rebel's neck. The deerskin gloves had been one of his only splurges before leaving Austin. The old men sitting in the late summer sun that day were discussing the aches and pains of rheumatism that awoke with the coming weather. The oldest, with hair down to his shoulders and a white beard reaching nearly to his waist, held up one hand full of knobby knuckles and told the others how his hands had barely survived the winter of 1840, protected by a pair of deerskin gloves he'd gotten in a trade with an old Caddo woman.

Something in the man's story told Ridge to hie on over to a leather shop and pick up a similar pair of gloves. He thanked the old man's stories and his gnarly hands for the inspiration. The only part of Ridge's body exposed to the harsh elements were his squinting eyes, and he wished for something to cover *them*.

The buckskin pretty much had his head, at first following a game trail until it disappeared under the snow. Once enough had fallen, there was little to mark the trace, and the only way Ridge knew they were going in the right direction was the wind blowing hard out of the north.

A week out of Gainesville, Texas, he adjusted the thick collar protecting the back of his neck and felt the horse hesitate. Ridge studied what little he could see in front of him and realized they'd intersected a wagon trace leading off in the general direction they were headed.

It wasn't completely smooth and covered in snow. At least one wagon had been by much earlier, creating small ridges that would be drifted over in the next little while. Once he satisfied himself they'd found signs of civilization in the immediate area, Ridge squeezed the horse's sides with his heels and Rebel started again, but without much spirit.

Riding down the road in the early winter afternoon was no different from the trail they'd previously followed. It was only the illusion of safety that changed things in Ridge's mind. Drained of energy by the cold, he did nothing but ride heavy in the saddle and hope they'd come across some habitation so he could spend the night in relative warmth.

It really wasn't fair to Rebel to ride that way. A man in the saddle does his part of distributing weight and moving in rhythm with the big animal standing fifteen hands high. A good seat surrounds a horse with a constant stream of information, and he senses changes in a rider's body. Simply tightening the thighs can transfer enough sensation that the animal will walk differently, so just sitting there like a lump was probably draining Rebel's confidence and enthusiasm.

Pulling up his coat collar, Ridge sat straighter and looked for lights of any kind. A farm would do. The offer of a barn for the two of them would be enough, and if the little frontier house was welcoming, he could look forward to a warm meal before a fireplace. He dared not hope for a bed inside, but rolling up in his bedroll in a barn would be enough.

He dozed in the saddle, only rousing when the horse's pace changed, and that happened infrequently. When he was awake, the man he was after filled his mind. Clyde Wilkes McPeak was somewhere ahead, running from the law and destined to hang, as far as Ridge was concerned.

He intended to use the badge on his shirt as authorization to take McPeak back to Paris to face Judge Harry L. Forrester for the brutal murder of John Stevenson and his wife, settlers in Blossom Prairie, east of Paris. According to witnesses, McPeak spent the night with the Stevenson family as he passed through Northeast Texas over two weeks earlier. The next morning, after slaughtering the couple who'd given him shelter and food, he took what little they had of value, fired their cabin, and rode on, convinced the fire would destroy any evidence he'd been there.

However, he hadn't known that another traveler spent the night in the woods only half a mile away and heard the screams of Mrs. Stevenson early that morning. When the stranger went to investigate, he saw McPeak pouring coal oil out the front door and across the porch. The witness told the sheriff in Paris that he saw McPeak light the fire and ride away, whistling.

As horrific as it was, the thought of a house fire right then made Ridge shiver with the anticipation of warm relief. Rubbing his nose, he paused when Rebel's determined pace changed and both ears pricked forward.

"Me too." Ridge's soft voice surprised even him when he realized he spoke out loud to no one.

There was nothing to indicate anything different in the land around them. The wind still blew icy pellets into his eyes and the gray world around him looked the same as it had for days. Tilting his head to listen, Ridge strained for a sound that was different, but there was nothing but moaning wind and the squeak of dry snow under Rebel's hooves.

A hundred yards later, Ridge saw drifted-over tracks of a single wagon's wheels that angled off the trace and toward a thick stand of shin oaks barely visible in the distance. As he reached the point where the wagon left the lane, the tracks of a horse turned in also. He wondered if they led to a cabin.

He reined up, studying the almost hidden trail that meant nothing to him, but was interesting all the same. Ridge had always been one to puzzle out the tracks and paths of animals, learning from his father, who was a scout and a tracker for the army. The more he studied the area, he was convinced the rider met the wagon or saw the tracks, followed it off to the bare-limbed shin oaks that weren't much more than a dark smudge in the storm, and then rode back out and returned the way he came.

Something caught his eye: an unnatural straight line that shouldn't be there. The longer he looked, the more the rear of the wagon defined itself. This was very unusual, for there was no reason for a wagon to veer off a reasonably clear road and stop in such weather. For some reason, his gut told him something wasn't right.

Already cold to the bone, a few more minutes to satisfy his curiosity wouldn't matter. He gave Rebel a nudge and the horse grunted like an irritated old man. The trail pointed them due north and right into the teeth of the storm. It seemed colder with the wind in his face, if that was possible, and Ridge had to grit his teeth as the horse pushed forward.

A hundred yards away, the wind lessened as the short thicket of shin oaks blocked some of the storm. A gap provided access into the thick cluster of small trees barely ten feet high. The tracks were more distinct, and he quickly came upon a freight wagon piled high with snow.

Ridge's stomach sank at the sight of four mules dead in their harnesses. It was impossible to tell how they died, but he suspected they'd been shot. His eyes scanned the wagon and came to rest on a figure slumped sideways in the seat. He urged Rebel forward, but the buckskin hesitated, likely smelling frozen blood.

Despite the horse's reluctance, Ridge urged him close enough to reach out and touch the snow-covered corpse. The body was stiff. Leaning into one stirrup, he took off one glove and reached over to touch the man's frozen face. Sliding his hand into the collar, he encountered no sense of warmth.

Satisfied there was nothing he could do, Ridge wriggled cold fingers back into the glove and sat in the windbreak to ponder what might have happened. Four mules dead in their tracks spoke of outlaws and robbery. Had they still been standing, Ridge might have thought the driver had died from exposure and the team had simply veered off the road, but that idea didn't hold water. The wagon hadn't been in the thicket long enough for the cold to kill all four mules, and they wouldn't have died at the same time.

The body lay on its right side, so the killers hadn't robbed him. If they had, the man's clothes would have been in disarray and the body likely sprawled as they went through the limp man's pockets. Even his hat still covered the corpse's head, indicating he'd fallen sideways from the shot and hadn't moved.

Though he was, for the most part, temporarily out of the hardest gales, Ridge was still bone-cold and tired of it. He thought about going through the man's clothes for some kind of identification, or maybe a bill of lading that should contain a name of some kind, but he preferred to let the local constabulary do that.

Just as he was ready to go, he caught sight of a paper sticking up from under the driver's coat collar. Something in the inside pocket had worked its way up and was held in place when it caught the edge of a scarf around his neck. Feeling like a thief, he once again removed his glove and, using his thumb and forefinger, unbuttoned the top of the corpse's coat to find a packet of letters tied with string.

Ridge envisioned the driver sticking the packet into his inside coat pocket and being tormented with the envelopes constantly working their way upward from the movement of his arms and the wagon's motion. Simply holding reins in their hands wasn't the way teamsters drove. It took work and much arm movement to handle four sets of reins, and all the while that coat was moving around and the packet with it.

He took the banded envelopes and stuffed them into his lefthand saddlebag, making sure the latch was secure. Mail was important to folks, and he felt it was better to take them with him than to leave the letters behind. The rest could wait for the local marshal.

Unable to do anything else, he returned to the road, grateful the wind was at his back. His own tracks were already filling in, and those of the rider who'd done the killing were almost indistinguishable. From that angle, he saw he'd returned on his own trail when he reached the road. He turned right into his original direction and fell in to follow for the next mile, alert for trouble, though he didn't expect it.

The tracks soon joined others at the edge of a growing town that materialized around him and were lost in churned-up snow that was fast smoothing over. Completely blanketed in more than two feet of snow, the main street of Blackjack looked empty.

Smoke rose from a variety of shops and houses. Empty lots that were black gaps between the false front stores reminded Ridge of missing teeth. The town looked to be growing at a right smart pace, but it would be a while until all the vacant lots were filled in, both on the main street and a dozen narrow residential and smaller business areas on either side.

Yellow light spilling from windows along the single main street illuminated plank walks, empty hitching racks, and a couple of wagons parked along the street. The first building was a livery, promising comfort and a relatively warm night for Rebel. The business's main door was drifted shut.

He dismounted, hammered with one fist, and kicked some of the snow away. "Anyone inside?"

"Do I hear somebody out there?"

"You do. Customer." Ridge tried to open the door that stuck. "I'll be a customer if I can get in."

"Back up a mite. I'll give her a kick from this side."

A thump and a mighty shove forced the door open wide enough for Ridge to lead the buckskin inside. The barn was built solid, and the heat from several animals made it feel almost comfortable. The strong odor of manure, hay, and horses was as comforting as a fire.

The liveryman had a broad forehead and a ruddy face that hadn't been shaved in a while. His smile went from ear to ear. "Think it's gonna get cold out there?"

Ridge fell into the time-honored discussion of strangers. "Might."

The liveryman's grin widened further. He adjusted his britches over a big belly that forced them right back down again. "How long you here for?"

"That depends on the weather."

The stable owner nodded. "Name's Kingman. Mitch Kingman. Will it be you and the horse?"

"Depends on if there's a room here in town. If there is, then it'll just be Rebel."

"You shouldn't have no trouble getting a room at the Reynolds Hotel at the way far end of town. You'll think you've missed it, but she's there. If they're full, you can come back and roll up there in the office. I keep the stove going all the time. Come on."

"I'd have to walk all the way if I left him here."

"That's a fact."

"Is there a livery stable on that end, too?"

Kingman frowned and rubbed at the stubble under his chin. "There is—a small one on the other side of the Red River Saloon—but it's owned by Jim Barlow, and if you want to hire someone like me who's honest as the day is long, this is a better place."

"Well, I'd rather deal with an honest man. You'll have to tell me that story later."

"Sure enough." Kingman led the way down the hall to an empty stall. "Put him in here."

He leaned against a support post. "My office wouldn't be a bad place to sleep. I'd only charge you two bits. I hate to be cold at night, and there's plenty of firewood comes in. I don't even have to pay for it. We have an old man here in town that dearly loves to cut blackjack oak and don't ask more'n a mouthful of food or a drink over at the saloon. I swear, I never saw anyone who loves to chop and hates blackjack so much. Says that particular tree offends him and he intends to cut down all he can find."

All the time Kingman was talking, Ridge was taking the saddle off Rebel and listening, for there was no way to get a word in edgewise with the stable owner talking.

"You here on business or just passing through? Now, it's none of my business, mind you, and I don't intend to pry, but if you're looking for work, I can point you in the right direction. If it's whiskey you want, well, like I said, hie on down to the Red River. It's as good a place as any to cut the dust, even though Barlow owns it.

"Hell, what'm I saying? There ain't no dust today. A good swaller of whiskey'll warm you up, though. I swear. It's colder than a well-digger's ass out there, and I ain't seen snow like this in a month of Sundays."

"It's cold all right."

"I 'member the winter of '62, now that was a cold one, too. I got to thinking of that when you mentioned your horse's name was Rebel. My daddy fought for the south . . ."

The man's words drifted away when Ridge noticed one of the stall doors leading outside moved ever so slightly. It could have been the wind, but the wood didn't slap the frame as he would have expected. It was almost as if someone had been listening for a moment.

Ridge swung his wet saddle over a well-chewed wooden stand and slid the Henry from the scabbard. Eyes still darting to the door from time to time, he draped the saddle blanket over the stall's side and hung his saddlebags on a nearby peg.

Tired of waiting for an opening, he interrupted, "You got a marshal in this town?"

"Sure do. Good one, too. Been marshal here for several years and ain't no one shot him yet. Name's Runt Carpenter. It's a good first name any way you want to say it. Runt. He won't take no offense, 'cause he's been called that since he was born. Smallest of ten kids, he always took hind tit and they called him that from the time he could walk."

"Where's his office?"

"Just cross the street and go on down past the Red River Saloon, 'bout four doors more and you'll see it."

Kingman thought for a moment. "In fact, he's almost directly across from the Great Western Restaurant. You can find him in there sometimes, too, 'cause they serve purty good food in the restaurant that's part of the building, and they have a little parlor in there where you can get a drink, too. I like to say it's the best of three worlds."

Ridge rested the Henry across the crook of his arm and handed Kingman two dollars. "Let me know when that runs out."

"I'll do 'er. If you need a good hot cup of coffee to last you till you get down to the marshal's office, stop by the Blackjack Mercantile across the street. Maggie keeps a pot on all the time."

"Thanks. I'll be back when I get back."

"I'll be looking for you, then."

"Oh, hey. You know anyone by the name of Clyde McPeak?"

"Why, I don't recognize the name. He someone to you?"

"Owes me a hundred bucks. I ask in every town I go through."

"Well, I hope you find him. A man who can't pay his debt's a skunk in my book."

"Mine too."

Ridge stepped back out into the cold, intending to get that cup of hot coffee first; then he'd find the marshal.

CHAPTER 3

"My mama says that customers bring more dirt into the store than the wind."

Ridge Tisdale stopped just inside the Blackjack Mercantile and looked down at his wet boots as the little girl standing less than four feet tall glared at him. The leather was dark with moisture and both feet were almost frozen.

He closed the door to block out the howling snowstorm and frowned, taken aback by the youngster's sharp statement, which would have made sense six months earlier in the heat of the summer. "There's no dirt out there right now, Miss Ma'am. It's all frozen mud and ice and covered up by two foot of snow."

The winter skies were so dark and gray, the store-owner lit the interior with kerosene lamps scattered around to chase away the shadows. Blessed heat from a pot belly stove smack in the middle of the structure soaked into Ridge's face as the tiny gal, who looked to be about five years old, continued her verbal attack.

She planted her feet in the middle of the store with both hands on her hips, a doll version of an adult woman dressed in blue gingham. "My mama also says that most cowboys stink like the hind end of the cattle they raise. She's probably right, because when old man Barlow was in here a few days ago—he's a rancher, you know—we had to open the doors and let the place air out, let alone it was about freezing outside."

Ridge's mouth couldn't decide to turn upside down, frown, smile, or open and close like a fish as the tiny girl kept talking without taking a breath.

"I swanny, the last time he took a bath was before I was *borned*, and that was almost six years ago. But he only comes in once a year, so he's tolerable." She kept going and pointed at his feet. "At least *you* shut the door behind you, 'cause half of these yahoos around here act like they was born in a barn, but them boots of yours is wet, and I bet there's mud or horse mess caked in there against your heel. Did you wipe them off outside?"

Ridge swallowed and stifled a wriggling snake shiver down his backbone. He'd fought in more fistfights than he'd care to recollect, endured more than one Comanche engagement, hanged rustlers and the odd bad man or two, and survived more than one gunfight, but this little bundle of sass had him backed against a wall like a fresh colt in a breaking pen.

He wondered if she was going to turn her feathers inside out like a mad hen and rush over to start worrying at his ankles. "I, uh, yeah, I stomped the snow off outside."

The girl shook her head full of blond ringlets. "I *heard* you do that, but I hoped you wiped them, too. Just yesterday a bunch of cowboys from the Three Fork came in here and tracked mud and water all over the floor. Mama had to clean all that up after they left and I had to help her, and neither of us wants to wet a mop again today because it's so cold."

Glad he was well-armed in the presence of such a force of nature, Ridge checked first one boot, then the other. "Yep, just wet from the snow." He looked around for an adult. "You here all alone?"

"My mama's out back, getting wood for the stove."

He hoped someone had already split it up, for no one needed to be out chopping wood in the worst storm he'd seen in years. Then he remembered Kingman said there was a man in town who supplied wood for free, and he wondered if that's where it came from.

Ridge leaned the Henry rifle against a counter, unbuttoned his heavy sheepskin coat, and nodded at the coffeepot on top of the stove. "That sure smells good. My innards are about froze solid."

"It's for paying customers."

A sharp voice with an Irish brogue came from the back. "It most certainly is *not*, young lady!"

Most of the starch went out of the girl at the sound of authority. Her head snapped around, causing her ringlets to whip from side to side. She grunted. "Dammit."

"*What* did you say?" A redheaded woman in an oversize coat came through a door leading from the back, her strongest arm filled with stove wood stacked to her chin.

The girl turned back toward her mama, and Ridge felt safe for the first time since he'd entered the store.

"Said can't *stand it.* I meant, I can't stand it for people not to help themselves."

Ridge hurried forward to take the load from the storeowner, who had snow in her hair and on her shoulders. It reminded him of cream on strawberries. "Here, let me help." He reached out with both hands, expecting her to dump the load into his grasp.

"No, you take them off the top and put 'em into the woodbox there." The woman he took to be the girl's mother used the same tone as the youngster. The woman's blue eyes softened as she supported the split firewood's weight with both arms. "Didn't mean that as it sounded; it's just easier if you do it that way."

"Yes, ma'am." Ridge plucked the sticks from the top of the pile in her arm and placed them one by one on end in the woodbox. When he finished, the redhead wiped her hands together, either for warmth or to sweep them clean.

He straightened and noticed melted snow dripping off his hat, which in turn reminded him he was still wearing it. Snatching the soft felt from his head, he worried at the brim. "I'm sorry 'bout the hat. Forgot my manners."

The corners of her eyes crinkled in amusement. "Not to worry. It's cold outside, and your hands were busy." She turned her attention to the girl. "Now, little missy, you apologize to mister . . ." The redhead raised an eyebrow in question.

"Ridge Tisdale."

She tilted her head as if accepting his name as real and not some moniker worn by a drifter dodging the law. "Well, Mr. Tisdale, I'm Margaret, but folks call me Maggie." She addressed her daughter. "And Miss Josie Ruth will now say she's sorry to Mr. Tisdale for being so precocious."

The little one tilted her head to the side. "But you said some of these waddies come in here to drink free coffee and don't spend a penny, not even for a piece of licorice."

The woman's eyes flashed. "What's said between you and me in private, or any other adult you over*hear*, isn't for discussion in front of company nor customers, Josie Ruth."

Ridge liked the way she rolled her *R*s and felt a little flutter in his stomach. It was the first time he'd felt such a flutter in years. He'd been married once, with two children, all of whom had been murdered by Comanches when he was away selling cattle. Since then, he'd steered clear of women, except for the short time he lived with his brother and his wife and helped them with their small, south-central Texas ranch.

Maggie raised one eyebrow at her daughter. "This coffee is for anyone who comes in to see us. Now, apologize and get your little backside somewhere else away from me before I swat it."

"I was just saying—"

"That you apologize to Mr. Tisdale?" She ended the brief sentence on an up note in order for Josie Ruth to take up and finish.

"Yes, ma'am. I'm sorry for what Mama heard me say, Mr. Tisdale. You can have all the coffee you want, and feel free to get some crackers from the barrel over there to go with it, 'cause Mama says they're cheaper than pickles to give away." She turned away, but he caught the tail end of the comment that came from under her breath. "They're getting stale anyway."

Ridge had to bite his lip to keep from laughing. Maggie's face darkened for a moment, then melted into adoration for her daughter. "I swanny, this child. My little Irish lass says whatever comes into her head."

"She doesn't sound Irish, like you."

"That's because she was born here in America. Not me, though. I'm from Kilkinney."

Ridge was no longer used to being around small children since he'd moved on from living with his brother and his family back down toward Mason, Texas. Their boy and girl who weren't as outspoken or precocious.

For a moment, Ridge wondered how they were doing after he and a since-deceased Texas Ranger rescued the kids from a lunatic, murderous preacher and his wife, who intended to sacrifice them on some pagan altar.

Standing there talking to Maggie, Ridge didn't seem to know what to do with his hands, so he worried at the brim of his hat, which still dripped melted snow onto the mercantile's wooden floor. Dismayed, he used the sole of his boot to rub the moisture into the worn boards.

He smiled at Maggie. "She speaks her mind, sounds like. Back to what I was saying. That smells like Arbuckles'." He nodded at the metal coffeepot on the stove, which radiated warmth and comfort.

"It is, and you're welcome to all you can drink.

When that's gone, I'll make some more." Maggie took down a tin cup down a nail on the store's center support post. "You can put your hat back on before you twist the brim off of it, too, or hang it here."

Realizing he'd been torturing the hat more than necessary, he set it back over hair that needed cutting and washing. "Thank you, ma'am."

She picked up the enameled pot from its resting place on the hot plate using an embroidered dishrag, poured a cup full of steaming coffee, and handed it to him. He blew across the surface to cool it enough to drink, looking around the store, which smelled of smoke, leather, newly milled cloth from a sparse selection of brightly colored bolts on the shelves behind one glass and wood counter to his right, and a wonderful mix of things he couldn't identify.

Another matching counter contained merchandise carefully arranged to make it seem that she had more stock. It was obvious that at one time the shelves running the length of the long, narrow store had been filled with everything from flour and salt to saddles and clothes. Now there were only one or two containers of any particular item.

If anyone cared to look closely, they'd find round circles where cones of brown Mexican sugar once sat next to square salt blocks that were almost gone. The walls all the way to the tin ceiling twelve feet overhead once were filled with shelves loaded with wares, but the sagging planks were now empty, or nearly so.

Realizing she still wore her coat, Maggie put the pot back on the stove and shrugged it off, hanging it on the bare nail she'd offered as a hat rack. She flipped the dishrag over her shoulder. "Did you come in for supplies or to get out of the cold, Mr. Tisdale?"

"Ridge, and I just hit town and needed some provender."

She absently smoothed the dish towel with the longest, whitest fingers Ridge had ever seen. "Most cowboys head straight for the saloon, or Nellie's Place down by the catch pens. They usually drop by here on their way back out of town, or when their heads quit hurting."

He knew she was referring to the social clubs found in most railroad and cattle towns. "Right this minute I'd rather have some biscuit flour, salt, bacon, and a little can of blackstrap molasses before I look for a place to throw my bedroll. Besides, I try to stay out of those places."

"You *try*?" She raised an eyebrow and emphasized that last word in a rolling brogue. "Do you have much luck at it, then?"

Taken aback by her pointed question, he took a swallow of coffee still so hot it blistered the inside of his mouth. Ridge's eyes widened in pain and he considered spitting it back into the cup, but Maggie was watching. Composing himself, he realized where little Miss Josie got her attitude.

He was finally able to swallow that mouthful and blew across the surface of his cup with a little more aggression to avoid scalding all the hair off his tongue again. Stalling for time to come up with an answer, he warmed his hands on the hot container and sipped again, taking in more air and noise than hot liquid. "I was referring to the saloons in that comment."

Maggie's eyes showed her amusement. "Of *course* you were."

"And I'm not a cowhand, though I've worked cattle before." He pulled back the left side of his big coat to reveal a round badge pinned to his shirt. "Texas Ranger, these days."

She arched an eyebrow. "So, you're here on business, are you?"

"I am, but none in Blackjack, unless the marshal has welcome news for me." He thought of telling her about the freighter's body he'd found outside of town but decided the first person who should hear the news should be the law.

Ridge felt a little guilty that he'd stopped off at the store before running down the local constabulary but knew for certain that the body wasn't going anywhere in the storm and there was no hurry to get back out in the weather.

He swung the tin cup toward the front door. "Storm caught me outside of town and drove me in. I figured I'd find somewhere warm to sleep until this norther blows through, before I move on up past Fort Concho."

Using the rag to protect her hand against the hot handle of the heater's door, Maggie opened the front to a gush of searing heat and a bed of hot, glowing coals. Picking up a piece of the icy wood she'd just carried in, she pushed it inside. The wood hissed, and she closed the cast-iron door. "You on the trail of some desperado?"

"There's sure enough plenty to follow, but yes, ma'am, I heard from someone at the fort they saw a man thereabouts named Clyde McPeak, who killed a feller east of Paris. They say he's headed for Cottonwood Springs and I intend to bring him in."

"That's a long way from here. Cottonwood Springs is up close to the Prairie Dog Fork of the Red River. You miss it and you'll wind up on the Canadian."

"You sound like you've traveled some. Most folks don't know where those places are."

"My late husband and I moved around quite a bit when we were first married. We tried to homestead a piece of land north of here before he took a job cowboying for Mr. Charles Goodnight, who owned land from here to yonder."

"Late husband. I'm sorry."

"He died right after Jo was born, and I had no intention of staying in a sod cabin all alone with a baby, even though Mr. Goodnight said he'd take care of us. My dad opened this store a few years ago, so we came here to live with him."

"I bet he appreciates the help."

Maggie's face fell for the first time. "He passed in the fall. Just didn't wake up one morning, so now it's me and Jo running the place."

"Looks like you're doing well."

Something flickered behind Maggie's eyes and vanished in a flash. "We do all right."

Jo came around from behind the counter with a half-full bucket of water that took everything she had to carry. "We do fine when them Three Fork no'counts stay out of the store."

Ridge stepped over and took it by the bail so she wouldn't splash water all over herself. "Where do you want this, Miss Ma'am?"

"I was bringing it to you. There's a dipper right there with them cups, if you're thirsty."

He set down the bucket beside the woodbox. "That's thoughtful of you. I'll have a drink when I finish this coffee."

"Mama says folks don't drink enough water when it's this cold, and they dry out inside." Jo wiped a ringlet from the side of her face. "I don't like to drink a bunch of water this time of the year, though, 'cause it's too cold to run out to the privy every hour or so."

"Jo!"

"Well, we all have to do our business, Mama, just like cows and horses." She turned back to him. "We have a nice privy, though, and it ain't but a few steps from back behind the store. Grandpa built it right, and we use lime to keep the smell down. It's a good thing, too, because I've smelled 'em that are *rank*."

"That is *enough*, girl!" Maggie's face grew red, but Ridge figured it was from embarrassment and not anger. Maggie brought herself an inch higher than what he figured was about five foot five and did her best to build a glower. "You get out of my sight before I take a switch to you, lassie. Ladies don't talk about such things in public."

"I swear, I never know what I can and cain't say." Jo headed for the door to the back, which presumably led to their living quarters. "Let me know if that fool Harlan Davis comes back in. I just might bite him this time."

"Git!"

Jo disappeared into the back, and Maggie turned to Ridge. "That girl. She gets some of her sass from those cowboys who come in here and loaf around the stove. They say what comes to mind and don't care if there's an impressionable little girl listening. They think it's cute when she talks like them. They do it for puredee meanness."

Ridge grinned, knowing most of the hands meant no harm. They simply enjoyed getting the little girl all wound up to get a rise out of her mama, who wasn't hard to look at. Those old boys weren't coming in to visit with Jo, though. Cowboys usually headed straight for a saloon or house of ill repute. Those she was talking about were there to look at Maggie, likely one of the few available women in the area.

He chuckled. "*Some* of her sass might come from them. The rest comes from her mama, I'd suspect."

Maggie busted out with a big laugh. "Aye!"

He drained the last of the coffee and picked up the dipper as the front door swung open, emitting a blast of icy air and a swirl of snow. He turned to see a cowboy wearing a big smirk on his face push inside.

His smirk faded when he caught a glimpse of the badge on Ridge's shirt, and the big Colt riding in a cross-draw holster on his left side.

CHAPTER 4

Broad face partially hidden by a scruffy beard, the cowboy stepped inside the door and stomped the snow off his boots. "Howdy, Maggie."

The smile in her eyes died and the muscles in her jaws flexed. Ridge had seen moods change pretty quick in bars and saloons, or around campfires on cattle drives, when men are hot, tired, and frustrated, but that little gal went from pleasant and happy to a mad, swelled-up coon in the space of a single breath. The only thing she didn't do was lay her ears back like a mad mule.

She remained where she was in front of the glass case containing a smattering of smoking and chewing tobacco. Ridge noticed her fingers flexed for a moment before forming a fist. She gave a tight-lipped response along with a tiny nod. "Judd."

Ridge always enjoyed backing up to a fire to warm himself, and the stove was just the thing right then as a river of invisible ice flowed in through the door Judd had left open. Standing there with his palms to the heat, he kept an eye on the door, and on Judd.

The sorry-looking brushpopper, who hadn't been on the sharp side of a razor for the past week, stayed where he was, working on the chew in his jaw and letting the heat out. He pursed his mouth to spit, and Maggie's voice came sharp and louder than Ridge expected her to use with a customer. "Use the spittoon right there." She pointed.

Judd grinned, and for a moment Ridge through he'd spit on the floorboards anyway. Instead, he leaned over and shot a stream of brown juice at the shiny brass cuspidor, most of which hit the spittoon's wide edge. A few drops missed and wound up on the floor anyway.

Unbuttoning his heavy cloth coat to display the Colt in a low-slung holster with a silver concho, Judd slow-blinked Ridge, sizing him up. Most cowboys carried a handgun, but they were usually strapped into holsters riding on their belts, and occasionally in their waistbands. They usually stayed there, unless they ran across a snake or a coyote, or had to put down an injured cow or horse. For the most part, a cowboy's pistol was nothing more than a tool they occasionally used to shoot horse apples under bois d'arc trees, mesquite branches, or the occasional skunk out prowling around in the daylight.

This feller considered himself a shootist, and over the years Ridge'd run into more than one of those puffed-up peacocks. They always left him alone, because Ridge never put himself in a position to brace them, but this time there was a badge between the two of them, and he could tell it put a burr under Judd's saddle.

He hadn't been wearing that Ranger badge for long.

He rode for Captain Royce Bookbinder for a few days as they tracked a bad man named Hack Long and his gang. Bookbinder wasn't the kind of man Ridge wanted to partner with, and after disagreeing with the man's tactics in the small West Texas town of Angel Fire, he resigned and rode off. Only hours later, he and Long tangled at an abandoned homestead, and Ridge shot him dead.

When he returned with the body, he learned that Long had killed Bookbinder before leaving town. Shouldering more than his share of guilt over the captain's death, Ridge pinned the badge back on and took up a career in protecting the citizens of Texas.

In Maggie's store, the air thickened with tension as Judd slipped off his coat and draped it across a nearby wooden barrel of pickles. He made sure the lawman could see the cutaway holster and tried to lock eyes with Ridge, but the Ranger wasn't on the prod and turned his attention to the cowboy's mount, tied just beyond the boardwalk. It was covered in snow, evidence he'd ridden a ways.

Maggie pushed past Judd and closed the door before they all froze to death. Judd turned sideways so he could see them both. "Where's that little yipper of yours?"

Maggie used the sole of her shoe to rub the spit into the boards. The melting snow helped her wipe away the traces of his miss. "You picking up for you, or for Barlow?"

"Mr. Barlow needs a few things, but I have my own list to fill." He emphasized the *mister*, showing tobacco-stained teeth.

"Did he write a list?"

"Sure did." Judd took a piece of paper from his shirt pocket. Unfolding it, he glanced at the page and handed it over.

She read the tight script. "Did he send any money with you this time?"

"Nope." Judd chewed for a moment, then shifted the wad to a different cheek. "Said put it on his tab and he'll pay you next time he comes in."

"He didn't pay a penny on his account last month, nor the one before it."

"He's good for it."

"That's what you say, but he owes me a lot of money, and I owe the teamsters who bring in my goods. They'll be by when the snow melts, and I need to pay them."

Ridge's eyes flicked to Maggie at the mention of freighters. That rig at the edge of town was loaded above the sideboards with crates and boxes, and he wondered if they were destined for Maggie's mercantile or somewhere else.

Judd shrugged and took the top off a glass jar full of peppermint sticks. Plucking out a few with two fingers that looked as if they were strangers to water, he stuck them into his shirt pocket. "I'll enjoy these later. Look, I'm just a hand doing what I'm told."

Maggie shook her head. "I'm afraid I can't fill this bill today. Not until Barlow pays for what he's already taken."

The man shrugged again, and Ridge didn't like that habit, which was already getting on his nerves. Not one little bit. He switched the cup to his left hand and considered her choice of words. *Taken* meant Barlow had done more than put the merchandise on his tab. It sounded like the man had come in, loaded up what he needed, and left without offering to pay.

Or it could mean something completely different, and Ridge didn't want to think about such things without evidence.

Shapes flickered past the windows, and the door opened. Things were getting busy, but all the action was in the store and not on the street. Three young cowboys stomped inside and shook snow off their coats and hats. The trio hesitated at the sight of Judd. When they saw Ridge backed up to the potbellied stove, their cheerful mood faded even more.

CHAPTER 5

A young man with a red scarf sticking out from under his hat and covering both ears pulled off one glove, then another. "Good to see you, Maggie. Coffee?"

Her white teeth flashed in a smile that once again lit up the room. "Sure enough, Zeke. Help yourselves."

The other two cowboys stomped their feet just inside the door, and Ridge stepped to the side, just in case Jo came roaring around the counter like a little wolverine. He nodded at the trio, who seemed like likeable riders. "Boys."

Cold radiating off their clothes, they gathered around the hot stove, sticking their hands out to absorb the heat. Zeke used a glove held loosely in his hand to pick up the coffeepot and fill a mug.

A slender cowboy plucked a tin cup off the support post and held it out. "Sure is good to see you've found something you can do beside herd cows."

Zeke gave him a grin. "You better be sure what I'm pouring into your cup the next time we're out of Maggie's sight."

They laughed, and the other two held out their tin

cups as well. Zeke filled them and returned the pot to the hot stove. There were several moments of eyeing one another as the young men warmed their insides with good, strong coffee and accepted Judd's presence.

The tallest of the three stepped over to a wooden barrel and lifted the top. Taking out a handful of crackers, he leaned against a glass case full of dishes. "Don't see many Texas Rangers out this way."

Ridge allowed him a grin. "I'm the first one I've ever seen out this way."

The good-natured comment made the others laugh. Zeke blew across the surface of his mug to cool the coffee enough to drink. "Guess he told you, Monahan." Zeke pointed with his chin. "That tall drink of water's Mahan."

Ridge considered the name. "Mahan how much?"

They knew the old Texas way of asking for the rest of the man's name. Mahan shrugged. "Mahan is all. No first name's ever suited me."

"That's a new one. I never knew anyone whose first name didn't stick."

He grinned, showing dimples in only one cheek. "Named after my pa, and he wasn't worth the bullet it would have took to kill him. I left home when I was twelve and took to cowboying so I wouldn't have to listen to him no more. Never went back and just kept the last name."

Judd seemed irritated that he was being ignored. "Maggie was filling a bill for me when y'all came in."

Maggie rounded the end counter and fussed around, organizing cans on a shelf and seeming to have forgotten her earlier irritation. "I was doing no such thing. No cash, no supplies."

Frowning, Judd turned to Ridge. "You've heard all our names spoke. What's yours?"

"Ridge."

"Ridge what?"

He gave Mahan a little wink. "Why, Ridge is enough, just like Mahan's enough for him."

Silence was thick for a moment, until Jo finally came back inside from the living quarters at the store's rear. She walked over to Zeke and hugged his leg. He reached down with one hand and squeezed her head against him. "Good morning, Miss Jo."

She let go and crossed her arms. "You said you'd bring me a purty next time you came in."

"Jo!" Maggie's voice stopped her.

"And I have one right here." The cowboy stuck a hand in his pocket.

"Zeke, you don't have to give her anything."

"I know. I don't have to do nothing except what Mr. Hutchins tells me, but he ain't here right now."

He produced a smooth stone four times the size of a taw marble. "Here you go."

She took it as if it were a diamond. "What is it?"

"It's a madstone."

"What's that?"

He looked at Ridge. "Can you tell her?"

Knowing he was being tested and brought into the conversation at the same time, Ridge took a sip from the already lukewarm cup. "They say madstones draw poison from snake or scorpion bites. I knew a feller once who claimed they'll draw rabies out of a bite wound, too."

Her blue eyes were wide with wonder. "Where'd you get it?"

Zeke nodded to show Ridge had passed the test. "Came from the stomach of a white deer I shot this fall. Comanches say that's the strongest medicine you can have, and a deer with a madstone in him is twice as hard to kill as the ordinary kind. I had to shoot him five times 'fore he'd stay down and die decent-like."

Quick as a wink Jo squinted up at him. "It didn't do much for the deer."

"Well, nothing can fix that many shots from a 45-70," Mahan commented dryly. "This boy can't shoot worth spit."

Zeke's buddies laughed.

Jo rubbed the stone with her thumb, studying hard, as if trying to figure out what would make it work. "Thanks, Zeke."

He rubbed the top of her curly head. "You're welcome, Little Bit."

Maggie walked around Judd as if he wasn't there, and his face darkened. She put her hand on Zeke's arm. "You don't have to bring her something every time y'all come by."

The young cowboy studied Ridge for a long moment. "I know it."

Acknowledging the attention, Ridge poured a dipper of water into his empty coffee cup and swallowed it down. "Any of y'all know a feller named Clyde McPeak?"

The tall cowboy named Mahan shook his head and tilted it at Judd, like he was pointing at him. "There's a feller named Clyde with the Three Fork."

Judd frowned at the comment. "I can answer for my boys, and I don't believe it's your place to say."

Ridge turned his attention to Judd. "Been with y'all long?"

"Year or so."

"Big guy. Curly blond hair."

"Naw. Slender, little drawed-up feller who's poor as a snake."

Maggie spoke from behind the counter. "There's two ranches out here. The Three Fork and the Oarlock. Though there ain't no line, they've all agreed that the two ranches are separated by the middle of town. As you can see, there's no love lost between these riders."

She rested her eyes on Judd, who was outnumbered and had backed against an oak and glass counter full of patent medicines and soaps. Looking like he was surrounded by Indians, his shoulders drooped. "We don't much care for one another."

The third skinny cowboy named Monty pitched in, as if he didn't want to be the only one not in the conversation. "The Oarlock was here first, even before the Comanches was whupped."

Judd puffed up a little, trying to prove his position as a shootist. "They ain't yet. Not completely, and if I run into one on this side of the river, there'll be less of 'em to worry about."

Seeming at ease, Zeke added coffee to his cup. "Just so's you'll know, Ridge, our boss is Mr. Drake Hutchins, who settled this part of the country. Had a big spread that was three days' ride in any direction, but then old man Barlow came in and said half was his."

Judd didn't try to interrupt but crossed his arms as if to hide behind the barrier.

"There was trouble for years, but now Mr. Hutchins is getting old, and he don't particularly want to fight all the time, so he just gave in and let Barlow have this half." He jerked a thumb across the street.

It was an odd exchange between riders for two different ranches who obviously didn't care for each other but had called a truce inside Maggie's store. Ridge figured she had something to do with their mutual tolerance for one another.

Maggie waved a hand. "It's been quiet since then. Runt Carpenter keeps a lid on things here in town, but out there, I can't say what happens."

Ridge saw the look on Maggie's face and understood there was more going on than they were telling.

"I've heard about Runt."

"He's the marshal."

"I'm on my way to see him right now."

Judd's voice sounded impertinent. "What business you have with the marshal?"

Ridge's eyes flicked to Judd. "Personal."

The man's black eyes flashed. "Well, you're asking

a lot of questions about one of my men, and the next thing I know is you're wanting to speak to the marshal. It sounds to me like your personal business is getting into Three Fork business."

The door opened and still another man entered. It seemed to Ridge that Maggie's mercantile was a common gathering place that could sometimes be as warm as a blanket and others as cold and dangerous as a rattlesnake when hands from the different ranches met up.

All humans had a built-in dislike for certain kinds of people. It was something handed down for generations from their ancestors, and Ridge felt the back of his neck prickle when two others pushed inside.

Judd's shoulders squared when they took up positions behind him, and Ridge knew they were riders for his brand. One Ridge instantly thought of as Turkey Buzzard had an abnormally long neck that crooked behind his large Adam's apple. Adding to the vulture effect, his chin was almost nonexistent, covered with sparse whiskers.

Solidly built and big shouldered, the other simply looked formidable and mean.

Judd's eyes narrowed, and an insolent attitude filled the air. "Boys, this here's a Texas Ranger and he's looking for Clyde McPeak."

Turkey Buzzard shrugged narrow shoulders. "He can look all he wants to. I have an idea. How 'bout he waits here and we'll let Clyde know. He can come by for a visit after the weather clears, can't he, Mack?"

The Oarlock riders quieted when he called the big man's name, watching to see what would happen.

"Yeah, but I believe he'll have to wait somewhere's else, like maybe down at Nellie's Place. It won't be here."

Without taking his eyes off the Three Fork riders, Ridge spoke. His face was impassive, and nary a wrinkle gave any indication that he was mad, glad, or irritated. "Miss Maggie. Would you bring in some fresh water while I talk to these gentlemen? This dry, cold air makes me thirsty."

From behind the counter, her eyes flicked from the two camps. "If you'll give me a minute, Jo and I will be glad to draw a fresh bucket."

"But I done brought in fresh—"

Maggie took her daughter's arm, steered her toward the back door, and gave her a little push to get her on her way. Jo stopped in the doorway as Maggie picked up the bail and lifted the bucket. She spoke softly to Ridge. "Please, I can't afford any damage."

He didn't take his eyes off the Three Fork riders. "Don't worry. Nothing will happen in here."

She took the bucket, leaving the fresh smell of soap behind. "Out, little miss."

Backed by his two cronies, Judd smirked. "What're you gonna do? There's three of us, and them boys there don't know you enough to back any play you have."

"All I want to know is the whereabouts of McPeak, but you boys have already rubbed me raw. I've only just met Maggie, but I see that she's struggling here, and your boss owes her money, as well as you. What's your tab up to?"

Judd smirked again, raising Ridge's temperature. "Including this stick candy here?"

"Including that."

He frowned, pursed his lips, and studied the ceiling, as if having trouble ciphering such large numbers. "I 'magine around eighteen dollars."

"Fine, then. Put it on the counter there."

"Don't have it."

"Let me tell you what I see. You came in here to try and spend some time with Maggie, who's easy on the eyes, but I can tell she likes you about as much as she does a skunk, then you're gonna put that freezing horse in the stable, ease on down to the saloon for a few drinks before spending most of your money at Nellie's? Right?"

The Three Fork hands chuckled and cut their eyes at each other.

Off to the right, Zeke was watching Ridge like a hawk. It was hard to tell if he agreed or was offended by him referring to Maggie. Men out West held women to a high regard, and even mentioning her in the same discussion as women of ill repute could get a man shot, or worked over with a quirt at the least.

Ridge hoped Zeke would stay out of their . . . discussion . . . and what would happen in the next few seconds. This was between a lawman and the Three Fork hands. The Oarlock boys had best stay out of it.

"So I figure rasseling with one of Nellie's girls'll likely cost you two to five dollars, and that's after you spend another ten drinking in the Red River, then you'll have to eat a bite, and besides that, you didn't think I saw you take a handful of Henry Clays from that box right there."

Judd's eyes narrowed, and he almost reached for his left-hand coat pocket, containing the pilfered cigars. Instead, he slowly lowered his gun hand.

Reluctant to leave the stove, Ridge sighed and took his wet hat from the peg. He set it just right, trying not to flinch at the cold band, and took a step forward. "Hey you, Turkey Buzzard. Open that door, please."

Knowing who he was talking to, the cowboy twisted the front door's knob and swung it open. "What for?" Turkey Buzzard's eyes swept the store. "You get too hot huggin' that stove?"

Ridge had no intention of answering as a river of freezing air flowed inside. Talk was done. Pushing off on one foot, his left arm darted out like a striking rattler. He grabbed Judd by the throat and, keeping his arm stiff, pushed the startled cowboy backward, at the same time squeezing as hard as he could.

Off-balance at the outset, the self-styled gunslinger forgot the Colt on his hip and grabbed at the hand squeezing his neck. Judd stumbled backward as Ridge shoved him through the door and onto the boardwalk, which was slick with ice and snow.

His face already getting red, Judd struggled for balance as Ridge used their momentum to shove him all the way into the street. The cowboy reached the edge of the walk, and there was suddenly nothing under his feet except five inches of air and a fluffy quilt of snow.

He fell backward and out of Ridge's hands. The force it took to shove Judd into the street was hard to overcome, and Ridge stepped off into the street before stopping his forward movement. The moment his feet landed, he felt someone coming fast and hard from behind.

He ducked as a fist brushed past his head, a coward's attack. Throwing an elbow back, Ridge caught Mack in the stomach. The stocky ranch hand's breath expelled in a rush of white vapor as he doubled over from the pain.

Ridge did something no common street grappler had ever seen. He reversed himself and swung his left fist backward, using the force of his swinging body to almost take the man's head off with the back of his fist. Mack staggered backward and would have fallen if he hadn't slammed into a support post that almost snapped in two.

The force of his body hit so hard, it shook the entire cover over the boardwalk. Angled to repel water into the street, the snow collected on the roof slid off in a mini avalanche that nearly knocked the combatants off their feet.

Ridge recovered first and grabbed two handfuls of coat and used it to throw Mack into the street to drop beside Judd, who was holding his throat and gagging. Not a believer in fighting fair—because in no way of thinking is any fight equal—Ridge kicked the cowboy in the chin.

Mack went out like a light.

Hands held in plain view, Turkey Buzzard stepped into the street and stayed just out of reach. "Easy,

Ranger. We were just having fun. You didn't have to kick Mack to death."

"Then you can enjoy picking up those two and getting shut of me." He pointed. "And he ain't dead, just missing a couple of teeth is all, and that's payment enough for trying to hit a man from behind. What's that feller's whole name? I like to know who might be trying to shoot me in the back later."

"Dixon. Mack Dixon."

"And yours?"

"Turkey Thompson."

Ridge tried not to laugh as Judd stood, holding his throat. Like most other bullies, he preferred smaller adversaries or needed his men to back him up. "We have every right to go in there." His voice was full of rasp.

"You can come back when you've paid your bill."

"You don't own that place!"

"No, but I represent the law and say for you to stay out."

"Runt Carpenter's the law in this town."

"I'll talk to him about this."

"You'll talk to Son before this is over."

"I don't know who that is, but you need to stay away from Maggie's store and out of my sight. I'd get on back to the ranch and Barlow if I was you."

"By God, I won't be treated like this!" Judd reached for the pistol on his hip and stopped at the sight of Ridge's big .44, pointed at his nose.

"Don't." Ridge gave Judd a little smile. "You'll stain the snow."

The man struggled with his own fury and instincts. It was obvious he wanted to draw so bad he could taste it. His hand trembled, and telltale facial expressions that appeared and disappeared as he glared at Ridge.

The Ranger had had enough. "Calm that hand and reach into your pocket. You've changed my mind and I intend to see your tab paid up right now. Twenty dollars'll do it, because I know you have it. You won't be drinking in the saloon, but you'll be square with Maggie, and with me, too." His eyes flicked to the side. "And Turkey, you and that other feller leave that iron on your hip where it is."

Judd's eyes flashed. "I'll be damned if I'll let you rob me right here in the street."

"Not a robbery. I have every right to shoot you for starting to draw on me, and you would have if I hadn't been faster. Twenty dollars, now!"

Judd's hand closed in a fist before he relaxed and slid it into the front pocket of his trousers. He came out with a handful of coins.

His eyes gave away what he was about to do, and Ridge cut him off. "Nope. Don't throw that at me. I won't flinch and I'll shoot you where you stand. I don't intend to dig through the snow to find that money, neither. Use your foot to scrape some of the street clear and lay them down."

"This ain't no schoolyard."

"Nope. That ended when you started to shoot me. Do what I said and get gone."

Though the snow was deep, it was easy to move.

Judd scraped a section clear with his boot, and the coins jingled onto the frozen ground.

Mack rose and crabbed away to brace himself on the hitching post.

Watching him, Judd shot lightning bolts with his eyes. "Turkey, you get Dixon and let's go."

CHAPTER 6

For the first time in weeks, Zeke had some time with Maggie all alone, and neither knew what to do with it.

He looked around the store and stepped closer to Maggie. "Let me help you around here."

"You can help by bringing in some more wood."

He nodded and stayed where he was, as if thinking the project through. Maggie picked up a rag and wiped the counter, which was spotless.

Shifting his weight from one foot to the other, he finally decided to do something other than leave. Zeke picked up a couple of pieces of stove wood and fed the fire. "Where's Jo?"

Maggie flipped the rag toward the back. "She went in there to get away from me. I swear, that child's going on fifteen instead of six. She's gonna be the death of me with that mouth."

"I 'magine you're looking at a little version of yourself at that age."

"Not hardly. My mam woulda washed my mouth out with soap and warmed my backside until I couldn't sit for a week." She glanced back at the curtain. "But after my husband passed, I can't do it. She gets a smile and a little whack is all."

Seeing Zeke look uncomfortable, she passed and gave his arm a pat. "That's in the past."

"What about the present?"

Turning her back, she opened the cigar display to rearrange what was left in there. "What about it?"

"Well, you know, I was wondering about us."

She paused and looked him straight in the eye. "Is there an *us*?"

He shrugged. "I don't know. We don't usually get much more time than this, and you know how it is when you're cowboying."

"I wouldn't know about that." She built a tiny smile. "What're you getting at?"

"You know as well as I do." He looked back at their living quarters as something fell to the floor. "We don't get much time alone."

"We'll never have time alone, whether we're a couple or you're a customer. I have a little girl back there I love and am responsible for. She always comes first, and I don't see much chance for any sparking between you and me."

Zeke looked surprised. "Well, I come around as much as I can."

"That's what I'm talking about. You're in here when Mr. Hutchins says you can come by, but there's a steady stream of customers coming through here, and more than a couple hang around to talk."

"Why do you want to tell me that? You know I don't like it, and how I feel."

"Do I?"

He looked at the back curtain again, sure Jo was listening. "It's hard to talk about such when little ears are listening."

"Little ears will always be listening." Maggie's eyes twinkled, causing Zeke to flush.

"What I mean is, I'd like to talk to you, just the two of us."

"How?"

"We can go down to the hotel for supper one night."

"And leave my child alone?"

Frustrated, Zeke took a breath. "Of course she can go with us."

"Then we won't be alone, will we?"

"You beat all I've ever seen. You know what I'm getting at."

"I do, and it makes you uncomfortable. You've walked around in here and touched everything in the store. You're nervous as a cat."

"I just don't know what to do or say."

"Just do it, sir. Or say it."

"Say what?"

She threw back her head and gave out with another laugh. "You beat all, Zeke Frazier."

"That's the first time you've ever said my last name."

"I've thought it a couple of times."

He fiddled with a latigo hanging on the wall. "Are we going to dance around this all the time we have to ourselves?"

"You don't think we're alone now."

"Good gosh almighty, woman. You know how to twist a man into knots."

She grinned. "You're doing a pretty fair job of that by yourself."

"All I'm trying to do is talk to you while we have the chance."

Maggie cut her eyes at him. "This is a fine talk. I'm having a wonderful time."

"I'd have a better time if you'd quit flitting around like a butterfly in here."

"You're doing a considerable amount of moving yourself, mister."

He crossed the room and went around behind the counter. Maggie watched him come with a small grin on her face. She didn't back up, but she didn't meet him, either.

"Maggie, I'm trying to say something here."

"You're not having much luck."

"Help me, then."

She leaned forward. Her lips parted, and she grinned. "Jo's peeking around the curtain. I see her feet."

Zeke grinned back. "I guess we know where this is going."

"We do, Mr. Frazier, if you have the patience."

"Mom!" Jo came around the curtain. "Zeke, you know you're not supposed to be back there."

He stepped out from behind the counter. "Thanks for reminding me."

"Mama, I need to go outdoors."

Dreading a trip to the outhouse in such cold weather,

Maggie tried to put her daughter off. "Can you wait for a little bit?"

"No. My stomach's messed up."

"I'll walk her out," Zeke said.

"You know it's not proper until y'all are married." Jo picked up an old rag and flicked it at him, then threw it over her shoulder in an imitation of her mother. "You old people are gonna be the death of me."

CHAPTER 7

"I don't believe it's right for you to go through another man's belongings." Mitch Kingman stood outside Rebel's stall, as if stepping inside would be some form of trespassing.

Runt Carpenter, a small, compact man standing barely five one, had no such idea. He didn't look up from digging through the stranger's saddlebags. Wearing a bulky buffalo robe, he knelt on the ground. "There's been a lot going on around here, and this man ain't no brushpopper. He looks like a gun hand."

"You seen him?"

"Heard he was here."

"Said he was huntin' you, Runt. He has something to tell you."

Runt hated to be questioned and, due to his diminutive size, had always been forced to use nothing but pure will and determination to gain and maintain his authority.

Melting snow dripped off the huge brown mustache that covered his entire mouth as he worked. The only thing others could see of the lower part of his face was his blocky chin. Conversations around whiskey glasses more than once turned to what the man really looked like, and a few of the regulars down at the saloon agreed that no one would recognize him if he shaved it off.

Because of his size, some opined that if Runt scraped his face clean, he could likely enroll in the school at the end of the street if he didn't open his mouth. Though he was small in size, the man had a deep baritone voice that should have come from the roughest buffalo hunter in the land.

The marshal was as busy digging in the Ridge Tisdale's twin leather satchels as an armadillo burrowing into a creekbank. "Ed Dumas saw him ride in."

"In this storm?"

"You're damn full of questions, ain't you?"

"Well, I haven't been out much, and for Ed to be out enough to see a rider—"

"He was coming out of the Red River when he saw this feller." The truth was that the town woodcutter was staggering drunk and had forgotten where he was going once he went outside in the storm. He'd stumbled toward the livery, intending to sleep it off next to Kingman's stove but stopped short when the stranger dismounted and hammered on the door.

Runt found nothing but extra clothes, a shaving kit, a book of Shakespeare, ammunition, and an extra pistol in one side of the saddlebags. "It's my job to keep this town safe."

"Why'n't you just ask this feller? He seemed like a decent kind of man to me."

"I will, when I see him." Runt flipped around the set of bags. "Have you ever watched a lawyer work?"

"I ain't never been in a courtroom. I'm a law-abiding citizen, so help me God, and I never needed no law like that."

Runt's eyes flicked upward. "Well, I have. They don't ask any questions of a man on the witness stand without already knowing the answer."

"If they know the answer, why would they ask in the first place?"

"To trip up the witness, that's why." Runt unlatched the second buckle. "To make them lie, or to get 'em off-balance. I intend to find out as much about this man as I can before I get him hemmed up."

The first thing he found on that side was a bundle of mail, tied with string. The envelope on top was addressed to Maggie McBrayer in flowing script. "Well, here's something."

The stableman's interest got the better of him. "What's that?"

"Our friend has unopened mail addressed to Maggie."

Knowing how mail moved throughout the West, it wasn't unheard of for travelers to carry letters to strangers upon request, Kingman shrugged. "Somebody back East might've heard he was coming this way and sent it with him."

"The stage mostly brings the mail nowadays. Naw, I smell a rat somewhere."

"It ain't much of a crime to carry letters."

"It is if they was stole in a robbery."

"Who do you think he robbed? The stage won't be

by for a couple of days. Runt, that man's no thief. I reckon he's as honest as the day is long."

"And you can tell that from just talking to him? Desperados ain't always what you think. I've arrested a couple of dandies dressed as fine as Boston lawyers who've stole money and murdered men."

"Well," Kingman scratched at the bristles on his chin, "he takes good care of his horse and his clothes. That says a lot about a man, in my opinion."

Runt returned the pack of letters, closed up the saddlebags, and hung them back over the top board on the stall where he found them. His mustache twitched as he absently ran his hand down Rebel's neck and gave him a pat. The horse, full of oats, hay, and water, turned his head to sniff at the man's hat.

"You can tell a lot about a man by the horse he rides." Kingman rubbed the buckskin's nose. "This is a good-looking animal. Someone used to this part of the world is gonna see to his mount. That can mean life and death. Might need the horse for a quick getaway."

"There won't be nothing quick about such in this weather."

"A horse can run in deep snow."

"Why're you always so argumentative?"

"What does that mean, *arglementive*?"

"It mean's *irritatin'*." Runt pursed his lips, pointing much of his mustache at the liveryman, giving the impression of a porcupine rattling its quills at a threat. The marshal picked up the short, double-barrel coach gun he always carried and laid it in the crook of his arm.

"All right, then. I don't understand all I know here, but it's a start."

"You going to find him?"

"I intend to."

"Uh, Runt . . ."

"What?"

"I'd be careful with that rascal. He don't look like no common brushpopper."

CHAPTER 8

Instead of going back into the store and facing Maggie and Jo, Ridge ducked his head so his hat brim could keep the snow out of his eyes and crossed the street to the other side, where the cutting wind was broken by the buildings there. Judd's coins heavy in his left-hand pocket, Ridge pulled his coat closed and watched the Three Fork boys swing into their saddles and walk their horses down the street.

Though the saloon was only a short distance away, no cowboy ever walked when he could ride. Instead of stopping off at the stable to quarter their mounts out of the weather, the hands rode on to the saloon. Just on the other side, they turned at a snow-covered sign advertising the Sagebrush Corral. The gate was open and they rode on through.

Kingman had told him about the other, smaller livery in town, and it made sense. Cowboys in from a ranch or drive usually headed straight for the saloon, and a small stable provided by the same business kept their customers close so they could spend more money, and have their horses cared for and in out of just such weather as this.

The door to Maggie's mercantile was closed, and he figured Zeke was in there to make sure she was all right. They were probably huddled up to the hot stove and talking about what had just happened. A moment later, Maggie walked to one window and looked out, peering through the falling snow. Standing still against the wall, he was in the gloomiest part of the street and likely out of sight.

She turned back inside and he walked down the boardwalk, thankful for the cover over his head. He opened the small door beside the livery's big double doors and stepped in out of the weather. Kingman paused in shoveling manure and grinned.

"I saw that."

"Saw what?"

"Why, I was closing the door behind the marshal, who's just now heading for the Red River, and glanced down toward Maggie's. Saw you shoving Judd out the wrong way around like he was backing away from the ol' Devil hisself. Why, I never saw anything so purdy as you spiking Dixon and then drawing down on Mr. Gunslinger himself."

Ridge glanced at the door as if the marshal would come pushing through at any second.

"The marshal didn't see any of that," Kingman said. "Likely snow'd already caked up on that brush pile of a mustache all the way up to his eyes. He'd already hoofed it over to the saloon after you, anyways. Figured that's where you'd be, since most of these old boys make a beeline for the watering hole the minute they hit town."

"It don't sound like a bad idea."

"No, sir, a little firewater in the belly's just the thing for a day like this." Kingman reached into his coat pocket and pulled out a pint of Old Overholt. He pulled the cork and took a swallow. "You want a little of this coffin varnish to warm your innards?"

"Probably later." Ridge had an idea. He still needed to report the body he'd found out of town but had a better notion. The murder had piqued his interest and the wagon was beyond the town limits, out of the marshal's jurisdiction. Ridge wanted to investigate on his own for a while before bringing the marshal in on it.

"How about I rent a team of mules and you take a ride with me?"

"Out in this weather? Why, if you want to kill yourself, just give me your horse and gear and go lay down in the corral out back. You'll freeze soon enough, and I won't be out a good team."

"I need you to help me. There's a freight wagon out there with four dead mules and a frozen driver."

Kingman took another swallow and stowed the bottle back into his pocket. "You don't say."

"I do say, and there's a packet of letters over there in my saddlebags that came off the driver. Somebody shot him and the mules but left everything out there." Ridge passed Kingman and kicked through the soft dirt and loose hay to Rebel's stall.

"Shot the mules? Wonder why."

"Right in the head. I figure that's so they wouldn't

wander into town. Whoever killed him wanted that poor guy to stay out there for a while."

Ridge went in and came back out with the packet.

"There's a bill of lading in here that I expect will match the load." Ridge flipped through the packet, barely noting the names and addresses on all the envelopes. He stopped at the one he was looking for. "Here it is."

Ridge thumbed the envelope open and pulled out the contents. A smile crossed his face as he read. "Just as I thought." He turned the papers so Kingman could see them. "Can you read?"

"Why, I went clear through the sixth grade. Finished all the McGuffey Readers." He waved one hand and rubbed his protruding abdomen with the other. "A good business sense and reading got me this livery stable."

"Then you can see this is an order made out to Maggie McBrayer. I expect this is a supply order she's expecting."

Kingman took the papers and studied them. "Dan Franks is the freighter on here. I know old Dan. You think that's him dead out there in the cold?"

"Can't say his name, but that's why I need the team."

"I'll do you one better. We'll take a team and a wagon out. We'll have to unhitch the traces from those dead animals and pull the wagon back to get my mules in place, then we'll lay old Dan in the back and pull his wagon in tandem. Ain't no need to mess with the dead team."

Kingman ran a hand over his mouth, thinking. "Now I got to tell you, Runt went through your bags while he was here. Saw that packet of letters, and he has a sneaking suspicion you might have stole 'em. A-course he don't know nothing about that freight wagon or old Dan."

Ridge felt anger prickle the back of his neck. Such an invasion of a lawman's privacy was a serious offense in that part of Texas. It was like peeking through a window to watch a man's mama pull on her stockings. Now he really wanted to dig around a little on his own.

"He take anything?"

"Nothing but what he saw."

Ridge put the packet of letters back in his saddlebags. "Well, let's ready that team."

CHAPTER 9

The wind laid by the time Ridge and Kingman rode back into town on the wagon, though the snow was falling so hard it made a hissing sound as the flakes landed. It didn't seem so cold, but the temperature remained the same.

Kingman drove the wagon containing nothing but the body, frozen in a curled position in the back, and Ridge rode beside the liveryman. The four-mule team struggled in the deep snow to pull both the makeshift hearse and the loaded vehicle following in tandem.

"Woah." Kingman pulled back on the reins in front of Maggie's.

Ridge stepped off and up onto the boardwalk. He opened the door, surprised to find the Oarlock boys still inside, sprawled in a variety of chairs around the stove and visiting with Maggie, who was making a fresh pot of coffee. Jo was on Zeke's knee, taking it all in.

They stopped talking when the door opened. Again, Ridge was conscious of the snow he was about to track inside. He remained at the threshold and shook off his coat.

"Maggie, have you been expecting a delivery?" Slapping his hat against one leg, he replaced it, then, realizing he was talking to Maggie again, removed it.

Her eyes brightened and she put the enameled pot on the stove. She looked past him at the two wagons, one piled as high as the boardwalk cover. "How did you know?"

He wiped his feet and stepped inside, handing her the bill of lading and the letter bearing her name. "This is for you."

Her eyes went from the papers in her hand to the door and wagons beyond. "Dan plowed through all this snow? I would have imagined he'd stay in Gainesville or Fort Worth until the storm passes."

Ridge shook his head. "I don't know his intentions, but he would have been here this morning, I believe, if someone hadn't shot him."

Jo slipped off Zeke's knee. "I wish someone had shot Judd, but he's not worth the price of the bullet to do it."

Putting a hand over her daughter's mouth like it was something Maggie did a dozen times a day, she gasped as the boys listened. "Where is he?"

"His body's in back of the wagon." Ridge didn't have to explain further.

He pointed at Monty. "Could I ask you to go get the doctor? I know Danny Franks's dead, but I'd like a professional to look at the body before we take it over to the undertaker. You do have one in this town, don't you?"

"We have both." Monty rose and buttoned his boat. "You bet I'll get him."

"And you. Your name's Mahan, right?"

"Yes, sir."

"I'd appreciate it if you'd go find the marshal."

"Might take a while. He's a nervous critter and don't light in any one place for long. He came by while you were gone."

"I have plenty of time. We have to unload this wagon."

"I'll go with him." Zeke pulled on his own coat. "The two of us looking'll make it faster."

For once, Jo was silent in the presence of death and the sudden flurry of orders. The grim-faced men around her seemed to knock the little girl off her little high horse for a bit.

They were gone in an eyeblink. Kingman disconnected the two wagons and stuck his head inside. "It don't feel right that Danny's laying out there in the weather like that. I'll drive this team to the livery and pull him and the wagon inside. You can explain what happened to Runt or Pribble when he gets here, and they can come on over when they have a mind to."

"Pribble?"

"Ernie Pribble. He's the doctor, though he looks like one of them traveling boxers. Muscled up, with a curly handlebar. Maybe a barber."

"That'll be fine." Ridge looked over at the stove and shivered in the warm store. "Me and Maggie'll start unloading the wagon."

She'd disappeared while they were talking and came back wearing a man's big winter coat and a well-used, stained hat. She didn't have to tell Ridge they'd belonged to her late husband.

She tucked a rogue strand of hair back behind an ear. "Let's get started, then. I can't bear to think of poor Dan's body like I imagine he lays in the back of the wagon. I can look at him when he's laid out in his box, all proper-like."

Together, they attacked crates stacked so high, the wagon could have tipped over on a sharp rise. Ridge reached over the tailboard, handing down the lighter boxes and crates loaded in the rear. Maggie took them and tramped a trail through the snow and into the store, stacking them wherever she could find space.

Ridge was surprised that some of the locals didn't come out to help. Maybe they were staying warm by the fire and not looking out or, as he suspected, they intended to stay out of the politics between Barlow and Maggie's business.

Some hope rose when two men arrived. He immediately recognized Doc Pribble by Kingman's description and the gladstone bag in his hand. The man had a distinct, well-modulated voice. "Good evening, sir. I'm Doc Pribble, and this is the town undertaker, Joseph Mayse. Some of the Oarlock boys tell me you have a dead man here."

Ridge looked past them to see if the cowboys had come back, but there was nothing but tracks in the snow drifted on the boardwalk. "Was here. We brought him back in another wagon and Kingman took him over to his place. He didn't want Mr. Franks laying out in the weather anymore."

The doctor glanced at Ridge's gloved hands, then back up to meet his gaze. "What happened?"

"I wasn't there. Found him on the way in."

"Did you tell the marshal?"

"Haven't seen him yet. I imagine we've been missing each other. It didn't seem too urgent since Mr. Franks had been dead for a while."

"This is a legal matter, you know."

Irritation rose like bile. "Doctor, there's a badge pinned on my shirt under this coat. I know what legal matters are. In fact, Mr. Kingman took a good look around, too, so he can testify to what he saw."

Doc Pribble turned to the other gentleman. "Well, Joseph, what do you think?"

The other man, with soft, gray eyes and an infinitely sad expression, finally spoke. "Then I guess this falls to me. Good day, sir."

They struck out through the falling snow toward the livery without another word.

Ridge went back to work, and as he made his way toward the front of the wagon, he came across a box that caused his brow to furrow. Up to then, the freight had been packed tight, with little space between the bags, boxes, and containers. It was stacked so high, they'd tied it down with ropes to make sure the load wouldn't shift on the uneven terrain.

The two-track road leading to Blackjack wasn't much more than old game trails that widened over years of travel. It often sloped left, then right, tilting down on drops leading to creeks, gullies, and low places, then back up at sometimes sharp angles to do the same thing all over again.

Snow was a great cover, coating the world and hiding all its impurities and imperfections beneath a rolling, fluffy blanket. But it also revealed. When Ridge reached a certain point at the front of the wagon, he found the imprint of a missing crate. It wasn't much, just the dim, rectangular outline of something that once was but was now gone.

He paused to study out the problem. Nothing had shifted or slid out of place. Puzzled, he was distracted when six Three Fork riders rode up and dismounted. Once again, Judd Dixon was in the lead and swaggered up to Ridge with a pistol in his hand. "Put down that box."

Taken by surprise, with his coat buttoned over the Colt and the Henry leaning behind the door inside the mercantile, Ridge didn't hesitate to talk. He pitched the box full of airtights at Judd and followed like a lightning bolt.

Instinctively dodging the flying wooden container, Judd slipped on the snow. Ridge's fist caught the cowboy in the jaw, knocking him backward. Turkey Thompson and Mack Dixon charged in, followed by the other Three Fork men in a one-sided battle.

A strong, determined man can handle another pretty easily, two if he's good. An experienced fighter might hold his own against three attackers for a short while in the hopes that one will tire or just the right blow will cause enough damage for him to quit, but more than that is overwhelming.

They'd been building up courage and steam over at

the Red River, and finding Ridge alone gave them the courage to brace the man for a second time in only a few hours. This time they had more of an advantage, because they moved like an organized pack of wolves.

Dixon knew something about fighting. While angry men tend to spend more time wrestling and punching in the dirt, he was proficient and fought with intent. He let out an angry bawl as a fist as hard as granite struck Ridge on his temple, knocking him off-balance.

He staggered, throwing out an arm against the wagon to catch himself. Dixon pressed the attack, swinging a wild left that slammed Ridge on the point of his shoulder. His coat absorbed the blow, giving him a moment of relief. Tucking his chin and raising that shoulder in defense, Ridge launched a hard right that smashed Dixon's nose.

He flew back, most of the fight taken out of him, but two others roared in, striking Ridge down under a flurry of fists. Lying on his side, he used one leg to sweep the feet from under one of the men as a hard kick in the side almost knocked the breath out of him.

A man on his own in such harsh country lived by his wits. Animal instinct kicked in and Ridge went with it. A yard dog can't take on a pack of coyotes, but if they run him up to the house, you can be sure he'll duck under the porch and get his back against something.

Ridge had no porch, but the wagon worked in the Ranger's favor. He rolled underneath, hearing Maggie shriek in fury. Someone reached for him, but the unseen hands clawed at his coat and missed. The move gained precious seconds and, regaining his feet on the other side, the Ranger fumbled with the buttons on his coat in order to equal the odds with his Colt.

The Three Fork boys rounded the wagon and were on him in an instant.

Still too many impediments in the way to reach his revolver, Ridge ducked his shoulder and charged, knocking them back. The slick footing caused one to fall, and a left jab downed another.

Turkey flashed into view. Ridge swung and missed, but he used the momentum to throw a shoulder into the lanky man. Again he was swarmed and went down under a pile of men smelling of sweat, smoke, whiskey fumes, and dirty clothes.

Growling like a mad dog, he fought, kicking and gouging, going for a man's eyes. The gloves were both a problem and a blessing, cushioning his fist and preventing him from getting a good grip on anything.

Someone threw a loop over his head and he felt the rough burn of a rope on his neck. Before it could tighten and strangle him, Ridge had enough presence of mind to slide one arm under the loop. A second loop from the other side of the wagon circled his body, and the next thing he knew, his arms were pinned to his sides as those on the other end threw their weight backward like roping a steer, yanking him back against the sideboards.

Judd appeared, covered in snow and blood. "We got you now, you prairie trash! This is gonna be fun!" Ridge tried to kick him in the stomach, but he was pinned against the wagon. Judd slapped away his leg and threw a roundhouse blow that nearly took Ridge's head off his shoulders. The world spun and went momentarily dark.

A second blow slammed his head to the other side. Fighting to stay conscious, he heard Maggie's scream of fury again. She was a fighter, but there was nothing she could do against so many grown men hardened to outside work. Coherent enough to expect another punch, Ridge wished he could get that coat open.

His Colt would equal things a little.

The next clout never came. Someone grunted, and the snowy air was filled with a flurry of slaps and punches. The sounds of hooves and snorting horses took over, along with whoops and shouts.

Meaty thuds and curses.

Gasps of pain.

Shouts of the sheer joy of battle reached his ears and the pressure on the ropes lessened. Bracing his feet, Ridge threw off the ropes. He was done with it, and with a brawl sprawled out around him, he finished unbuttoning his coat and drew the big Colt.

No matter how he'd been struck, roped, and beaten, this was no killing offense, though it was damn sure over. He pulled the .44, thumb-cocked it, and fired a round into the air. The report stopped the fight, and though the snow was still falling straight down and as hard as he'd ever seen it, he was finally able to identify those around him.

It was Oarlock men against the Three Fork boys. Shaking his head to clear the cobwebs, he found Judd and leveled the pistol at him. "You, sir, are about to breathe through another hole if you don't stand down."

Judd lowered his hands. "Holster that weapon and

we'll see who is who. I'm gonna kill you for murdering Danny Franks."

Ridge spat blood. "The freight driver? I found him shot just out of town and besides, if you'll remember, I'm wearing a badge. Lawmen don't murder freight drivers."

"Well, *somebody* shot him."

"It wasn't me."

A new voice cut through the thick air, one deep and full of gravel. "Mister, I'm about to blow you in two with this twelve-gauge if you don't lower that pistol."

Ridge turned his head to see a short man with a giant mustache holding a short-barreled shotgun with both hammers back. It was almost funny, but he dared not grin. Instead, he lowered the muzzle a mite, raised a left hand, then slowly used one finger to pull back the big coat and reveal the badge on his shirt.

"Easy, Marshal, Texas Ranger here on official business."

The twin barrels lowered, and Marshal Runt Carpenter grunted as he thumbed the hammers back down. "Well, *this* should be good."

Judd pointed an accusing finger. "This man robbed me at gunpoint!"

The marshal tilted his head. "Did he?"

Wiping blood from a split lip, Turkey backed him up. "Me'n Mack and Dee-wight saw it. Robbed him of twenty dollars. Check his pockets."

Apparently unconcerned, Runt tucked the coach gun under his arm. "Do tell."

The Three Fork men looked to Ridge, expecting him to defend himself. He grinned, then winced at the pain in his jaw. "They're partly telling the truth. I collected what was owed to Miss McBrayer, which came to about twenty dollars."

"That's right!" Judd's eyes flashed in indignation. "Four five-dollar gold pieces. Check his pockets!"

Like a dog looking at a new pan, Runt again tilted his head. "Your turn, Ranger."

Ridge pointed. "They're stacked up in there on the counter. Like I said, I was collecting for Miss McBrayer."

Marshal Carpenter saw the doctor standing nearby. He and the undertaker had joined a few other chilly citizens who were curious about the fight. "Doc, would you go in there and look?"

He went inside and they waited, shifting from s[ide to] side in the falling snow. Doc finally came back [out.] "There ain't no gold coins on the counter."

Runt raised an eyebrow, and also the shotgun. "Well?"

For once Ridge had no answer. As they unloaded the wagon, he'd stacked the four coins there for Maggie to find, with a note underneath that said *"Paid in full from Judd How Much,"* a joke, since he didn't know the man's last name.

Runt turned his attention to Maggie, who was still bundled up in her husband's oversize coat and hat. "Maggie, did this man give you any money?"

Her smooth brow furrowed with a troubled look. "He hasn't bought anything."

"Did he give you money from Judd?"

Ridge broke in. "I just put them on the counter. With a note."

She started to shake her head and stopped. Her eyes softened, then went hard. "Just a minute. Josie Ruth!"

The little girl appeared, eyes wide. "Yes, Mama?"

"Where are they?"

"Wha—"

"You know very well what I'm talking about."

Jo faded away and returned in seconds, her tiny hand clasping four gold coins and a piece of paper. Maggie took them with a raised eyebrow.

"I was just playing store. I put them in my cigar box register and was going to surprise you."

Ridge drew a long breath and let it out in a cloud of vapor, along with most of those standing in the street, making him think of what a steam train looked like ⸱ pulled into the station.

CHAPTER 10

Jim Barlow poured himself a whiskey and corked the bottle. He was sitting at the large, rectangular table taking up a good bit of floor space in the kitchen that consumed a third of the first floor in his house. He would have preferred to be sitting on the porch with his drink, but the cold and snow made that an impossibility.

He looked out at the gray landscape and took a swallow. The barn was only a dark, looming shape nearly a hundred yards away. The bunkhouse beyond was all but invisible. He considered the falling weather, and the deep lines in his face smoothed at the thought of his childhood.

His mama was a great one for gathering a pan of fresh snow and bringing it inside. She loved sweets, and was forever making pies and cobblers, but when she had the opportunity to do something different, she added sugar, milk, and a couple of drops of vanilla to the snow, stirred it up good, and divided the snow-cream amongst her seven kids.

Barlow remembered the taste of rich cream and sugar on his tongue. It was one of the few pleasant memories he had from when he was a kid. He rose from the table, opened the back door, and scooped a handful of snow into his whiskey glass.

The amber liquid immediately turned to slush, and stirring it with his forefinger, he closed the door and walked over to the large rock fireplace. The mesquite wood burning there snapped and popped, throwing out waves of heat that took the chill from the big room. He glanced toward the stairs and sipped his drink, hoping it would quiet the constant burn in his stomach.

The floor creaked overhead as his only son moved about. Jim Barlow Junior was a disappointment to his daddy. While the elder Barlow grew up on the plains, fighting for every scrap he could find after his entire family was killed by Comanches during the great uprising that began in 1840, Son had everything given to him.

Growing up fast and tough hardened the man, but the boy everyone called Son couldn't or wouldn't follow in his father's footsteps. The slender man with a mild demeanor constantly annoyed Barlow to the point that he often couldn't stand the sight of his own child.

Barlow considered it his late wife's fault. After losing three girl children, Son came along, and she babied him so much he wasn't worth the trouble it would take to kill him. Sara defended the boy like a she-wolf whenever Barlow tried to take him out to be part of the ranch. Instead, she let the boy stay under her skirts. While other kids his age were making full hands either in the fields or on horseback, young Jim stayed inside, reading or collecting worthless bits of nature.

He was twelve when cholera took Sara, and Barlow put Son to work on a horse, trying to make a cowboy out of him. The boy was so inexperienced in life that everything he touched went wrong. While ranch hands usually took young'uns under their wing, Son's whiney disposition and unpredictable actions pushed them away. He didn't want to learn how to rope or brand. Within months, he was assigned to mucking stalls and doing the work no self-respecting cowboy would consider.

Taking another large swallow of Old Overholt, Barlow backed up to the fire with his free hand held behind him to absorb the heat. He looked around the room, which hadn't felt the soft touch of a woman's hand since Sara's passing. There was nothing feminine about anything in the house other than a single hand-made lace doily on a side table that Sara made.

Skins on the walls weren't there for decoration but to protect them from drafts through the planks that often-times had cracks in them. The bare wooden floors were covered with a scattering of blankets and rugs, and the leather-covered sofas and horsehair-filled chairs were replaced by hard, cane-bottomed, straight-backed chairs that were the only places to sit.

Barlow had to admit, it looked more like the house owned by a man of means rather than the cabin it once was when he found it abandoned on the prairie. They'd added on and upward, so the place was three times the size that it was.

The elder Barlow slept in the only bedroom on the ground floor. Upstairs, Son occupied three rooms that included a wide sitting area where the young man read, looked out, and kept up with the world through a variety of magazines and newspapers. His bedroom was as far away from his dad's as possible.

That was where the sound was coming from. "What're you doing up there, boy?"

It was silent for several heartbeats, as if a startled animal rustling about up there stopped at the sound of a human voice. "What, Dad?"

Even that two-word answer rekindled an ever-present anger in the older man's chest. Son's voice had changed several years earlier, but it never matched the tone and timbre of his dad's. He took another swallow of whiskey. "Come down here where we can talk. I don't aim to be hollering up at you."

More rustling came to Barlow's ear, as if the young man was skittering around like a rat. The anger built as he envisioned Son arranging his collection of odd stones, bird nests, or books and magazines when he should have been attending to those few chores assigned to him in the house or out in the barn.

In Barlow's view, Son should have been with the men in the bunkhouse, learning as much as possible about cowboying and being a man, since someday he'd inherit the huge spread and the town of Blackjack, not to mention all the land spreading west when the Oarlock was his.

He rolled the name around in his mind. The Three Fork Oarlock. It had a nice ring to it, and Barlow was confident he'd own it soon.

Son came down hesitantly, like a young pup afraid of a scolding. Despite growing up on the frontier, he'd never looked as if he belonged there. His clothes always resembled those in the fancy mail order catalogs, and his skin never hardened against the sun. Even his shirt, trousers, and boots seemed out of place, though they were the same ones the ranch hands wore.

"You need me, Dad?"

"This storm's going to be hard on the stock."

The young man paused at the bottom of the stairs, holding on to the newel post as if keeping himself upright. He didn't seem to know how to respond to the statement. Sometimes Son wouldn't even answer a direct question.

"I don't know what to say to that. You have something for me to do?"

He watched his dad with a mildly curious look on his face, then grinned at nothing, like a possum, irritating Barlow even more. That image reminded the old man that his boy had round, close set eyes, just like a possum, and he wished the young man looked more like the new, self-sufficient hired hand out in the bunkhouse.

The man named Clyde was thrown from a horse he was working and broke his leg. Rising up from the dirt, he slapped his pants clean with his hand and walked out of the corral under his own steam. That, in Barlow's opinion, was a man.

Barlow sniffed and rubbed at his large, red nose. "The boys who went into town aren't back yet."

Son knew the answer to that one. "The snow's deep. I suspect they've laid up at Nellie's, or in the Red River, until this weather breaks."

"I don't pay my hands to drink whiskey."

"That's the same thing the boys are doing over in the bunkhouse, 'cept there ain't no women out there . . . that I know of. They've fed and watered the stock in the barn, and there's not much else to do with the snow falling like this."

Anger throbbed in Barlow's forehead. Son was smart. Too smart in most ways, and his calm logic wasn't what the rancher wanted to hear. "They could be out busting ice on the tanks."

"There's enough moving water for the cows to drink. It was warm before this blew in, so I doubt anything's iced over that much, and this ain't no real blizzard. It's just heavy snow."

"You forget who you're talking to?"

"No, sir." Son's attention slipped away from his father and went to the windows, where they could see nothing but a gray world and falling snow. "I was just saying that we have enough hands to take care of what needs to be done here. I have other plans for the boys in town."

"I've given these men over to you to run this place." Barlow finished what was in his glass and crossed to the table. He poured another three fingers and this time didn't add anything else. He returned to the fireplace. "It's been a month since I put you in charge, and now half of our men're strung off to town."

"They're doing what I told them."

"You told them to go to town and drink whiskey?"

"No. I told them to go and wait for me."

"Wait for you to finish doing what? Looking at them little animal bones you have up there? And just where were you yesterday?"

Son looked uncomfortable. "Well, had some things to do. I was in town for a while, checking the Mercantile and the saloon. Picking up a few things for us here."

"By checking on them, what do you mean?"

"I meant I went by the mercantile and told Earl to drop some of the prices on a few things to keep up the pressure on Maggie's place. We've pretty much choked down her supply line, and what she still has on the shelves is working against her. With the drop in prices, more people are going to fill their bills at our place, and what money she has coming in'll be down to a trickle."

Impressed with the idea, Barlow nodded. "Keep going."

"Well, since you put me in charge, we've been getting a lot of our supplies from her, on our tab."

"We're buying from *her*?"

"Didn't say *buying*. Judd and the boys are picking up what they need for the bunkhouse, and it all goes on our tab, which is getting on up there."

A smile crossed Barlow's face. "I see what you're getting at."

"Yes, sir, and the boys lift a few things from time to time. It adds up in the long run. When we get that big new stable built at the other end of town, we'll have Kingman screwed down tight, too. I told you I'd have the whole town sewed up by breakup."

The uncut whiskey was stronger, and Barlow enjoyed the burn as it went down, settling his stomach. "Calving season is gonna be busy. We'll need more men."

A sly look crossed Son's face. "How many are you thinking?"

"A lot. We need hands to help move stock, and guns to keep them."

"How many do you want to hire?"

"As many as we can find. I hear the stage is making more runs. Have some of the boys sew up that Salt Fork road. The tighter things get for other people, the easier it'll be for us."

Son looked uncomfortable. "To tell the truth, I don't know how much of that money makes it back to us."

"Right now, let the boys have it. It'll keep the spirit in 'em, but you make sure none of that leads back here and gets on us. I'll let a posse hang half of these sorry waddies before the law gets suspicious of us."

"You know, we're making good money on cattle. Once we take over Blackjack and absorb the Oarlock, we can let that kind of dangerous stuff go."

"It's money in their pockets that won't have to come out of mine. Let Russ take the lead on the stock, and that new man Clyde can ramrod the night riders, even though he has that broke leg. He's tough, and I like that in a hand. What's his last name again? Mack what?"

"It's McPeak. I don't like him, and he don't want that job; he wants mine, and then yours."

Barlow barked a laugh. "That's what I call ambition!"

"It's dangerous for us both."

Barlow's eyes narrowed and he reached down to pat the Colt in the holster he seldom took off. "Not as long as I got this. Now, hie on out to town before this snow gets any deeper and bring me back a case of whiskey. I don't intend to get snowed in for a week without nothing to drink."

"Whiskey it is, and the rest of the business?"

"Take care of it, and keep the pressure on until we own most of that town and, someday soon, the Oarlock."

"In what way?"

"You wanted a chance to prove yourself, so here it is."

"The boys can handle it without me."

Son turned to go back upstairs when Barlow's sharp voice cut him off. "*You* do it, boy, or the next time you walk out of this house I'll throw everything you own upstairs into the fire and you'll live out in the bunkhouse with the *rest* of the hands."

Son understood the inflection. "All that's mine up there."

"Naw. You're wrong about that. Everything under this roof is mine, and that includes *you*, boy. Don't push me on this."

Son stayed rooted where he was as he considered

his options. He finally turned and headed for the door. "I'll get your whiskey, and me and the boys will put the screws to anyone not riding for the brand."

"Big talk, but I need to see some results, or someday this place will belong to somebody tougher than you."

Snatching his new hat off the rack, Son shrugged on a long riding coat. "One of these days, old man."

"One of these days," Barlow finished his glass and smacked his lips in satisfaction, "will be the one when I don't wake up in the morning."

CHAPTER 11

Under orders from Marshal Runt Carpenter, the Three Fork riders faded back to the Red River Saloon, leaving Zeke and his boys to help unload the rest of the wagon. Taking charge, Maggie stayed in the store, directing the men where to put the boxes, bags, crates, and barrels. Despite the death of the freight driver, she was as filled with light as a kid on Christmas.

What little natural light that still remained in the dark gray sky was going. It would soon be dark and almost impossible to see once full dark descended.

Face and jaw aching from the beating he'd taken, Ridge sat in one of the chairs beside the stove next to Runt Carpenter, who looked as if he'd settled in for the evening. Hat tilted high onto his forehead, coat open, and leaning back on his chair's back legs, the marshal crossed one tall boot over his knee and listened as Ridge told his side of finding the freight driver.

He finished his story at the same time Zeke and his boys carried in the last barrel and thumped it onto the wet and muddy floor. Ridge looked around for Jo, expecting the little scamp to start scolding the men for tracking in such a mess, but she was nowhere in sight, probably still stinging from the spanking she deserved.

Maggie was frowning at her shipping bill and looked up in time to see him looking around. "If you're looking for my little lass, she's supposed to be in her bed. I sent her in right after that little tussle."

Ridge felt an odd relief. Even though she'd almost gotten him shot or arrested, and maybe strung up by pilfering the coins left on the counter, his soft spot for children was still intact. Missing kids were what had originally sent him West from his brother's farm in Mason, and he couldn't help feeling anxious. "You read my mind."

He noticed the look on Runt's face as the sawed-off marshal glanced toward the curtained door at the back. Ridge realized Jo had taken the hearts of nearly every man who came through that door, and he liked the under-sized marshal even more.

Runt twisted his lips in a way that the lower half of his face disappeared behind that great mustache. "That's quite a story. Why didn't you come find me before you went out and moved that wagon? I might need to have seen what was around there."

"Well, you're a hard man to track down, and then me and those Three Fork boys didn't see eye to eye the minute I hit town, so that took some of my attention. Then it didn't feel right to leave that man laying out there. In this weather, coyotes and panthers are on the hunt for something to eat. The body might not have been out there in the morning. And the way this snow's falling"—he waved a hand at the windows—"there wouldn't have been a thing to see."

"You have a point." Runt stood, took a mug off the support post, and poured himself a cup of coffee.

Ridge rocked back and forth on one of the chair's back legs. "It happened outside of town, too, so the jurisdiction fell to me anyway."

"I wish you'd hauled him back to Gainesville and I wouldn't even have to fool with it." Sitting back down, he blew across the surface and took a sip. "Maggie, you make the best coffee I've ever tasted."

"You're very kind, sir, but all I do is throw a handful of grounds into the pot and put it on the stove."

"Must be your hand, then."

The corners of her eyes crinkled as she returned to her list. Her frown returned as she looked over the stacks of supplies around her.

It was just the three of them, and the two lawmen sat in silence for several minutes, pondering what had happened in the past few hours. The store felt different with so much merchandise taking up floor space. Soon the shelves would no longer be empty and the sad feeling of a dying business would be a thing of the past, at least for a while.

Runt took a sip of coffee, soaking the lower third of his brown mustache. He wiped it dry with the back of his hand. "Say you just saw Danny was dead and rode on to town."

Cutting his eyes at the marshal, Ridge considered his

answer. Though they were comfortable together, the marshal still had a hat full of questions he felt needed answering. "That's right."

"Say you didn't touch nothing, maybe turned him over."

"Froze solid. No telling how long he'd been there. So I didn't move him, the first time."

Runt studied on his answer before taking another sip. "Say you didn't touch him the first time."

"Didn't say that. I checked to make sure he was dead, and he was. I get the feeling you're after something, so here it is. There was a packet of what looked like envelopes sticking out of the top of his coat, like they'd worked themselves up from a pocket or his shirt. They looked important, and my thought was the local marshal or sheriff might need them to identify who was out there before they left. I have them in my saddlebags over in the livery. You're welcome to go get them."

"Don't need to." Runt sipped again and stretched his legs toward the stove to warm his feet. Steam soon rose from his knee-high boots, filling the air with the scent of warm leather. His shotgun leaned within reach against a crate Maggie had yet to open.

"It seems to take a lot to satisfy you, Marshal."

"Not really. I just like to know things. Thomas Jefferson said, *knowledge is power*."

"Sorry, Runt." Ridge laced his fingers. "That was Sir Francis Bacon. Jefferson just stole it."

"Well, I'll be damned. An educated man here in my town."

"I just like to read, probably like you. I suspect you spent some time in a class or two somewhere."

"Wanted to be a lawyer. Feller my size has limited options in life. Went to school back in Boston, until one day I looked out a window on a warm, sunny afternoon and realized I didn't want to spend all the rest of my days leaning over dusty books or in a hot office somewhere with a visor on my head. Bought myself a ticket West and wound up here."

"I guess being a lawyer naturally leads to taking a job as a lawman."

"Not at all. The day I got off the stage here in town, Big Jim Barlow shot a feller out there in the street and left him lying there. Just forked his horse and rode off like nobody's business. I expected the local marshal to investigate, and planned to volunteer as a witness to murder, but the last marshal was looking at six feet of dirt over his head. Seems one of Barlow's men killed him in a little dustup in the saloon. The marshal gave as good as he got, and his killer's buried a few feet away.

"I asked around and found out there's a city council here, but they have pretty deep pockets. I got the job, probably for entertainment purposes, and have served ever since." He grunted. "That was four years ago, and I've even outlasted those council members who're either dead, retired, or moved on."

Maggie paused in her work and joined them to gain a little heat from the stove. She shoved a couple more sticks on the fire and considered the papers in her hand. "Well, it's all here except for one crate."

"It might have bounced out on the way." Ridge watched her think. One single crease between her eyes was all that showed she was working on a problem. "What are you missing?"

She shook her head. "It's a crate of airtights, mixed canned gingerbread, and pepper pot stew. That should have been too heavy to bounce."

The word for canned goods brought sweetened condensed milk to Ridge's mind, and he wondered if she had any for the coffee. It was a rare treat for a man who lived on horseback, and cowboys loved the sweet stuff, oftentimes buying it to punch a hole in the lid and drink it from the can.

"Might have slid off," Runt offered.

Ridge remembered the faint imprint in the snow on top of another crate. "No. I saw where it sat." He thought for a moment. "It couldn't have slid off. There were other boxes to hold it in place, but it wasn't there when we pulled up out in the street. Somebody took it after they shot the driver."

Runt stared hard at the flickers of flame through the cracks around the stove's door. "Say it was canned gingerbread."

Maggie nodded. "That's part of what's missing."

"I recall Son likes that gingerbread. I once saw him buy a can here from Maggie, cut the top and bottom out with his knife, and slide the whole thing out in his hand. Looked just like the can it was in, and he sat there on the front steps, taking big bites from it like it was a giant pickle. Damnedest thing I ever saw, up till then."

Ridge looked back and forth between them. "Son? I heard that name earlier."

Runt twitched his mustache. "Jim Barlow's only boy. Calls him Son, and so does everybody else."

CHAPTER 12

Son rode back into Blackjack for the second time in two days, wishing he'd remained there with his one friend, Russ Leopold. The long-haired cowboy was between jobs and stayed close to Son and his deep pockets whenever he was in town.

Russ never had to spend a dime when Son was around. Those dimes were few and far between, because Russ was a drifter. Though he was an excellent ranch hand, he preferred the company of women, who always liked to play with his blond hair, which reached to his shoulders.

Finished off with the same colored mustache, which curved down over both corners of his mouth, Russ was a favorite at Nellie's Place. The young man was so popular with the ladies, Son took to cocking his hat the same way Russ wore his.

The heavy snow didn't dissuade everyone from going out. The closer Son came to town, the more tracks there were coming from that direction. It was as if everyone west of Blackjack wanted to be near civilization.

Harold Burrows looked up from pitching hay into a stall when Son opened the door of the little Sagebrush Corral's stable behind the Red River Saloon. "Got no room."

"You'll find a place." Son led his roan inside and pulled the door closed behind him.

"Oh, hey, Son. Tie him up there to that post. Russ is still inside with Judd."

"How'd you know I was looking for Russ?" It annoyed Son to think he was so predictable. "Maybe I'm looking for Judd."

"You might be, but he's with Russ."

Son pulled the knot tight and turned to leave.

"You gonna loosen that cinch? There's a bucket of water over there."

Embarrassed that he hadn't thought to take care of his horse first, Son turned back. "Thought maybe you'd do that for me."

"I ain't your daddy, nor one of your hands."

Son's eyes grew cold. "You ain't a boil on his butt, but since we *own* the Red River and both corrals out front, I guess you forgot you really do work for us."

Scowling, the stableman closed the stall's gate and opened a wooden box nailed to the wall. He scooped out a can full of oats and poured them into a small feed trough just inside the stall. "What I meant was that you should have tended that gelding first."

Cocking his hat over one eye to make himself look more like Russ, Son adjusted the scarf around his neck to stop any draft that might come down his coat and went outside. A wide pathway tramped by a steady stream of footsteps led to the saloon's back door.

He pushed inside. The air was warm and moist. The bar to his right was fairly busy, despite the weather. Melted snow darkened the boards under his feet and water from customers' boots was everywhere. Cigar and cigarette smoke hung low. Looking for Russ, who was sitting with Judd and a handful of Three Fork riders with cards spread before them, he almost kicked over a nearly full spittoon.

Ignoring the glances they shared at the sight of the boss's boy, Son unbuttoned his coat so that his gun and holster showed. He pulled up an empty chair from a nearby table and turned it backward, sitting with his arms over the back.

"Howdy, boys."

Russ favored him with a wide grin, but the others simply nodded and tended to their game. "I thought you went home. You been over at Nellie's all this time?"

"Had some business to tend to here and there and got to talkin' to some folks."

"And then you hightailed it right back here?"

"I heard there was a feller over at Maggie's asking about one of my hands."

"Clyde." Judd pitched his cards on the table. "He's looking for Clyde. I'm out, boys."

For the first time, Son noticed Judd's bottom lip was swollen. He looked around the table. Dixon's nose was red and crooked, and Turkey sported a dark bruise on his jaw. "What got aholt of y'all?"

Judd's eyes flashed. "That damned Ranger."

"A Ranger? What'd y'all tangle with him for?"

"I don't like him, for one thing."

Turkey swallowed, his large Adam's apple rising and falling. "'Cause he's over there sportin' Maggie."

"It ain't all that." Judd leaned forward on his elbows. "He's the one looking for Clyde, and I think he also had something to do with Danny Franks's murder. Anyway, we was going to settle up with him when them damned Oarlock men waded in, and this is what we got. We were winning until Runt Carpenter showed up with that twelve gauge of his and made us all stop."

Son kept his face impassive. There were a lot of things in this world that concerned him, but personal fights between men were something to stay out of. "Runt getting anywhere on Franks's killing?"

"Naw." Russ shook his head. "Danny's laid out over there at the meat house and word's around town he was shot under his left shoulder blade. Could have been an ambush."

"Robbery?"

"What else is there? Nobody took anything off his wagon. Just shot him and rode off."

Son wiped a hand across his mouth, thinking. He looked across the table and Russ had his hat tilted back. Son unconsciously did the same thing, using his thumb against the brim.

"Runt will find out what happened." Turkey nodded his head, as if in agreement with his own comment. "That little, sawed-off feller's a determined cuss. He's gonna figure out it had something to do with that load he was hauling."

Son perked up. "What makes you think that?"

"Well, I don't reckon I know." Turkey looked perplexed that someone had asked him to explain himself. "But I bet it was robbery, plain and simple."

"He won't know for a while." Son rested his chin on his hands across the back of the chair, then, realizing how that made him look, straightened back up. "Danny was shot last night and this weather ain't helping."

Russ raised an eyebrow. "What makes you say that?"

"Well, look outside."

"No, I meant who said he was shot last night?"

"Didn't you?" A cold chill went down Son's back when he realized he'd given himself away.

"No. I said *where* he was shot. Not *when*."

"Oh. There were some guys talking out front of the corral. I guess that's where I heard it." Son had to get out of that conversation, quick. He stood and jerked his head toward the front door. "Judd, I need to talk to you a minute."

"May as well." Judd rose. "These cards are working against me." He followed Son outside, and they stepped onto the boardwalk. Snow squeaked underfoot as they moved off to the side, staying under the protection of the cover.

Son pulled his hat back down and raised his coat collar. "Dad wants something done about how slow things are happening here in town. He's anxious to own the town, and the Oarlock. I guess being snowed in's got him to thinking."

Judd nodded, keeping his back to the room. "What'd he have in mind?"

"For us to take care of it."

"How? We don't need to do anything with that Ranger in town. That man's tougher than whang leather. He about whipped us all. If Turkey hadn't got a loop around him, I think he could have done it."

"Let's stir things up with those Oarlock boys. Somebody can put a bullet in the Ranger and we can make it look like *they* did it."

"Your daddy's been thinking."

"*I* came up with that idea."

"Sure you did." Judd scratched the three-day growth of beard on his jaw. "There's more of us here than them Oarlocks, but I don't want people pointing fingers at us."

"That's what I've been thinking, too."

Judd turned to see over his shoulder. "You go somewhere else. I don't think you should be part of anything we do. We'll need you to deal with Runt and anyone else here in town that wants to get involved. We'll take care of the rest and you can stay outside of things."

Relieved, Son walked away before realizing he had nowhere to go. He stopped, wishing Russ was with him so he'd have someone to talk to.

His stomach grumbled from the canned gingerbread he'd been eating up in his room before his dad called him down. His guts needed some relief, and the ashpit behind the saloon was so nasty, he needed another place, though the cold would help the smell some.

He had an idea and ducked between the two buildings on his right.

CHAPTER 13

Snow fell so hard, it was difficult to make out any details about the scattered buildings across the street that, in warm weather, would have been humming with activity. Instead, the sight of a horseman going by was a moment of interest.

Content to sit beside the stove and visit with Runt, who still wore the heavy buffalo coat, Ridge took off his own cover and hung it on the back of a chair. It tugged on the badge he wore, and he felt his shirt to make sure it was still pinned properly. Satisfied, he leaned back in the chair just in time to see Jo pulling the curtain back and peering into the store from their living area.

"Mama, I need to go outdoors."

"Again?" She was busy stocking shelves and barely looked up. "We just went. Use the pot under the bed."

"No, not for what I need to do."

She nodded in understanding. "Well, then. Let me get my coat."

"Don't get in a hurry." Jo made a face. "I saw some-body go in there. I bet it was Dwight Grubbs."

Maggie's expression almost made Ridge laugh. "I see something you don't like."

Before Maggie could answer, Jo chimed in. "Grubbs likes our privy more'n any other one in town. He won't use nary other except that'n when he comes to town, and he has the squats so he's in there every time he's here."

All three of them knew what Jo referred to. Young calves often suffered from diarrhea that could weaken them to the point of death, and *the scours* was a common term used to describe their malady.

"Josie *Ruth*!" Maggie raised a hand as if to swat her, though she was fifteen feet away. "You watch your mouth or you're gonna taste soap before daylight." She turned red, a shade that made her hair look even brighter. "I swear, those salty cowboys are gonna be the ruin of this child, and me too."

Ridge and Runt dared not look at each other or they'd both bust out laughing.

Jo defended herself. "Well, the boys say it's true, and Grubbs is just like Son Barlow; they're both little weasels if you was to ask them, at least that's what I hear tell."

Maggie stalked toward her precocious daughter. "That is enough, young lady. You watch until Mr. Grubbs leaves, and then come get me and we'll go out together."

"You just want to make sure he limed it."

"I said for you to hush! There's men in here that don't need to hear such talk."

"I sure wish I knew what I could say around men."

"Nothing would be best."

Ringlets bouncing, Jo disappeared behind the curtain, and Maggie went back to checking her merchandise with her back to the two lawmen. Ridge turned to Runt. "You know what's happening in this town, don't you?"

The man's demeanor changed. His eyes hooded and Runt nodded. "I do, and me and Maggie have talked about it. We know Barlow is obliged to pay his bill, and Maggie has finally cut him off now that she knows what that snake's up to, but it won't do any good. I can't ride out there to make him pay, not against all the gun hands he has working for him. And the truth is, I don't have any jurisdiction way out there. You need a sheriff to serve him, and Matt Larson's as scared of Barlow as I am of a bear."

Ridge lowered his head and looked at Runt from under his eyebrows. The marshal's mustache twitched, indicating he'd tightened his lips. "I know what you're thinking. Find the man when he comes to town and detain him until he pays up."

"That's what I'd do."

"Look at me. I wear a badge, carry a big pistol, and have more growl than a grizzly bear, but if I tried to make him pay, or put him in jail, I'd have to stand up against thirty men at one time. When it's one on one between me and a drunk cowboy, or some usually law-abiding citizen, or a no-'count drifter, I can hold my own. Face it. The fact is, there ain't enough of me to do the job."

Maggie joined them, backing up to the fire to soak up some heat for a moment. No matter that the stove was burning hot, the plank building did little to insulate against the icy cold that seeped in through every small crack in the building. In fact, a small drift of snow had collected under the front door and she'd resorted to rolling up an old towel and laying it along the sill.

Ridge saw that before she caught herself, she almost lifted the back of her dress like his mother did in front of their fireplace when he was a kid, to warm her backside. She stood there, hands behind her, like a schoolgirl reciting the day's lessons.

"I carried a lot of people when times were good, but Barlow wants to own the whole town." She squared her shoulders. "I didn't realize what he was doing until he was into me for so much money. Instead of stocking up from his own store, he was getting supplies from me without paying. That way, I have little cash to replace what I sell. I like people and want to do what's right for them. I was trying to help, and it took a while for me to realize he was trying to drive me out of business."

"Don't take offense," Ridge said, "but you're one little enterprise. Why's he after *you* so hard?"

She licked her lips, checked to make sure Jo wasn't eavesdropping, and ducked her head as if she'd done something wrong. "He's very interested in me. We'd barely settled in here with my daddy when he started coming around."

Runt helped her out as best he could. "For a while, there was a steady stream of men coming through here. A young widow in such a place is unique, and every man who wasn't married made their intentions known."

Maggie blushed. "I tried to let them all know I wasn't interested, and after a while, most of them quit trying to court me. Barlow never gave up, and when I finally had to tell him to his face that I wasn't interested in getting married again, especially to him, he got mad and said that someday he'd own this place, and me too."

Runt's deep voice was a growl. "He wants another boy, one that'll grow up with the gumption to be a man and run his ranch, and someday the Oarlock. He wants an heir, and Son ain't it."

"It isn't just me." Maggie seemed to want to change the subject. "He wants the whole town, too, and when he has that, he can put pressure on the Oarlock and eventually take it, too. His men still come over here, like Judd and them today. They'll buy one thing or another, but I know they're stealing from me when my back is turned. A little bit here. A little bit there. It hurts because it adds up, and they do their best to steer travelers over to Barlow's mercantile when they can. They're drying me up little by little.

"Now I'm having trouble getting stock. I buy from my suppliers in Gainesville and Fort Worth, and every other time, the shipment disappears. It's happened twice, and that took all my available cash, because those loads are simply gone and no one has the responsibility of paying me back. Then, not too long ago, I learned that Barlow has his claws in those shipping companies back there."

"So your money goes out and nothing comes back in." Ridge absently flicked the small rowel on one spur.

"That's right, and I can't borrow from the bank. He owns that, too."

"He's just a rancher who moved in on the Oarlock

and Blackjack." Ridge looked from one to the other. "How does he have enough money or muscle to make such things happen?"

"Nobody knows about his money, but he's ruthless." Maggie looked at Runt, who continued to stare at the hot stove. "I think his crew are also highwaymen. There are robberies all between here and Gainesville, and travelers have been known to disappear."

Runt swallowed the last of the coffee in his cup. "Lots of Oarlock cattle have disappeared. They haven't caught anyone rustling, but there are twice the number of Three Fork men as there are Oarlock riders. I have a sneaking suspicion they keep an eye on where the Oarlock men are, and then come in on the sly and take their cattle that aren't watched.

"That's how it works here in town, too. I can't be everywhere, like today. They slipped in and tangled with you while I was over at Nellie's, settling a disagreement between one of her girls and a customer." Runt paused and swallowed. "I'm sorry, ma'am."

"No need to apologize, Marshal. I'm a grown woman and know all about such things. I've met Nell, and she comes in from time to time like any other customer. She's a beautiful lady, but she's a bit rough around the edges. I suppose she and her girls perform a necessary service."

"I've never heard a woman support those ladies before," Ridge said.

"Oh, I don't support them. I simply let them alone and don't pass judgment like some of them over at the White Chapel do."

"The church?"

"Yes."

"There's no way to prove what Barlow's up to," Ridge added, getting back to the matter at hand.

"That's right." Runt crossed one leg over the other and toyed with the rowel on his spur, unconsciously mimicking Ridge. "I deal with what goes on within the town limits. As I said, anything beyond that is the responsibility of the county sheriff—that's Matt Larson—but some say he's working with Barlow and lining his pockets by looking the other way. If that's true, my hands are tied as sure as if there's a bowknot around them."

Runt's eyes crinkled at Ridge's look of interest. "I know more knots than a clove hitch and a slipknot. My daddy was a seaman."

"You could have gone to sea, then, instead of dealing with outlaws and land-hungry ranchers."

"I get seasick."

They laughed, and as if his chair had grown hot, Runt rose. "You know, that's Maggie's property out back there. As marshal, I'm gonna go out there and run Grubbs out of her privy, whether he's finished or not, so that baby can do her business and go to bed."

He pulled on his coat and set his hat. "I'll be right back."

Leaving his Greener shotgun leaning against a counter, he adjusted the long buffalo coat on his shoulders and disappeared behind the curtain as if he knew exactly what to find back there. Ridge heard footsteps stop and the marshal's voice speaking to Jo. "Get your coat on, honey, your mama's fixin' to take you out."

The curtain billowed when he opened the door, and Ridge saw Jo's feet cross the room. She slid the curtain down the rail as far as it would go and peeked into the store. "I'm ready, Mama."

The outside door creaked, and from where he sat, Ridge caught a glimpse of the snow-covered world out back at the same time a gust of cold air washed into the store. Jo's short figure crossed the bright rectangle, and Runt's slightly taller shape followed as the flat report of a gunshot came from outside. Runt groaned, and the sound of his falling body was loud in the following silence.

"Jo!" Maggie's shriek was sharp with horror.

Ridge jumped to his feet and snatched the Colt from his holster. He and Maggie were almost to the back when Jo raced through and into her mother's arms. At the same time, Runt fell into the room, taking the curtain down with him.

Lying on his stomach with a hole in his back, the marshal's voice was unnaturally deep from the pain. "Out back."

Ridge rushed past and paused at the doorway, looking out into the gloomy weather. Another gunshot slapped his ears, and he realized the open door and light from the store silhouetted him in the darkness. Something broke behind him and Jo screamed.

Knowing he couldn't do anything for the marshal that Maggie or the doctor couldn't do, he rushed back, almost leaping over Runt, and grabbed his coat. "Help will be here soon!"

Ridge plunged into the snowstorm.

CHAPTER 14

Jo sat down beside Runt, who was moaning and barely conscious. "I'll hold your hand, Mr. Runt."

Maggie covered the marshal with a blanket and rested a hand on his head. "Hang on, Runt. Men'll be here soon and they'll go find Doc Pribble."

The town doctor could be in any number of places, but the best way to locate his whereabouts would start in the saloon. Once informed of the shooting, a dozen men scattering around town would be faster than going to the doc's office and finding him gone.

Gunshots in the middle of a snowstorm weren't common, and men appeared on the street, asking questions. A handful hurried down the boardwalk and into Maggie's store.

Of course one was Judd. A wad of his men were scattered behind him. "Maggie! What's wrong?"

Leaving Jo with the blanket-covered marshal, she met them halfway. "Runt's been shot!"

They started forward, but she held out a hand. "No. He doesn't need people patting him on the shoulder and telling him it's all right. Y'all go find Doc!"

"I knew it!" He turned to his men. "It's that damned Texas Ranger impersonator. He did it, didn't he?"

A cold chill trickled down Maggie's back. "No. That's not what I said at all."

A Three Fork rider joined in the accusation. "Probably shot him in the back. Where is he, Maggie? Are you all right?"

"I'm fine. He was in the store . . . no . . . it wasn't . . . Son?"

A cowboy with his hat cocked to the right spoke up. He was Russ Leopold, and one of the few Barlow men she could tolerate. She'd seen Son Barlow following him around town like a puppy, mimicking his habits right down to wearing his hat the same way. "Right here, Maggie. What do you need?"

In shock, she saw Son Barlow kneeling down to look into Jo's face. He frowned in concern. "Are you all right, honey?"

Jo looked him in the eye. "They didn't shoot *me*. Somebody shot Marshal Carpenter."

Maggie shook her head to clear the cobwebs, trying to get a grip on her thoughts. There was too much going on and swirling in her head. "We need the doctor. Can some of y'all go find him? Runt's hurt bad."

The men, most of them half-drunk, considered their options, and a handful scattered to track down the doctor. Maggie looked around, hoping to find Zeke and some of the Oarlock boys, but they were nowhere in sight. She assumed they preferred not to drink in the same saloon as the Three Fork riders, and with good cause.

The Reynolds Hotel at the far end of the street had a

bar, and that might be where they'd gathered, if they hadn't gone back to the ranch. It was hard for them to be away in the first place, but the Oarlock's owner, Mr. Drake Hutchins, usually allowed half of his men to be gone at a time in such weather, knowing that as soon as the storm cleared, his dedicated hands would be out checking the cattle.

But right then, being in a bunkhouse was the same as waiting out the storm in town. She glanced down past the Red River Saloon to Nellie's Place, but the snow was falling so hard she barely saw the glow of lights through the windows.

The front door was wide open as they poured into the mercantile. The undertaker, Joseph Mayse, stepped close and took her arm. "Doc just left me five minutes ago and headed back to the office. Someone'll find him, but come with me. Maybe I can do something if Runt's still alive."

Mayse knelt beside Runt, looking under the blanket covering the man lying on his back. "I'm here, Runt. This is Joseph. Let me see how bad you're hurt."

He lifted the buffalo coat and felt around. "There's no exit wound, but we need to get this robe off of you to see."

"Don't move me." Runt groaned. "It hurts too bad. Hit in the back."

A forest of legs and boots surrounded the two men. Turkey Thompson leaned over for a look. "Mr. Vulture, he ain't yours yet."

The older man's soft eyes flashed. "I studied medicine

once. Didn't like working on the living. That's how I became a mortician."

Taken aback by the usually gentle man's anger, Turkey reared back. "I don't know what that is."

Russ grunted. "A mortician's another word for undertaker, you uneducated get."

Mayse slid his hand under the marshal, who twisted from the pain. "It's all right, Runt. I need to see where you're hit." He felt around and shook his head. "We need to get him over to Doc's, 'cause he sure ain't operating here. It'll save time. Somebody get me a door."

Footsteps receded, and soon two men returned with the back door to Maggie's living quarters, followed by a rush of cold air. A mix of townspeople and Barlow riders gathered around the wounded marshal and lifted him gently onto the makeshift stretcher.

They quickly found that the door they carried was wider than the front and had to tilt it to get him through, almost losing Runt in the process. He had enough self-awareness to throw one arm over the high side until they had him out on the boardwalk.

Two gloved hands appeared and grabbed his belt. "I gotcha, Runt."

He'd regained some of his breath by that time, though the pain had his face twisted up. He recognized the voice. "Don't let me fall, Russ."

"I won't."

Maggie saw Barlow's boy had joined them, though she didn't know when. He held on tight until the six men carrying Runt had him level again. They hurried off as fast as possible without the wounded marshal falling off his door.

Following, Son called over his shoulder, "We'll get this back to you as soon as we can, Maggie!"

As she absorbed all the activity around her, two men came in through the open back door. Both were Barlow riders with guns in their hands, who tromped snow onto the fallen curtain without paying attention to what they were stepping on. She knew them by sight but not by name.

"There's a lot of tracks out there, but we don't see that Ranger. He cleared out after he shot Runt."

Her face flushed with exasperation, and she realized she was nearly crushing Jo's little hand. She loosened her grip. "He didn't *shoot* Runt, I'm telling you."

Voices came from outside. "Runt's been murdered!"

"He's been shot! That stranger who killed Danny Franks has done gone and killed Runt!"

"Spread out and find him!"

"When you do, take him to Kingman's livery! We'll hang him in there!"

CHAPTER 15

As the heavy snow fell and swirled around him, Ridge circled around to the back of the Red River Saloon. Two empty Sagebrush corrals were separated from the building by a small alley, and on the other side was a stable smaller than Kingman's.

Oil lights inside glowed between the vertical plank sides. Pistol in hand, he eased up to the wall and peered one-eyed through a knothole to see the interior consisted of a hall lined with narrow stalls just wide enough to hold one horse each.

They were full, and he figured most if not all belonged to cowboys and other Red River customers. He watched for a full minute but saw no evidence that anyone was inside. Not even a stableman.

Loud voices coming from around front told him the town was awake after the shooting. It was impossible to identify specific people, but they were all upset, and that likely meant a shared anger was building. Such a response always ended badly, especially after Ridge heard his name more than once.

An unseen man called out, "Somebody posing as a

Texas Ranger's done murdered Runt. We're getting a posse together! Get your guns and meet us back here!"

Ridge started out to straighten out those who were gathering, then decided caution was necessary. In his opinion, there was nothing more dangerous than a bunch of angry drunks, and they sounded so worked up, they'd probably string him up before he could explain that it was an assassin who shot the marshal.

They were all going down to Maggie's to see what had happened, and he expected more than a few vigilantes to fan out, looking for the shooter, no matter who he was.

Anyone unlucky enough to arouse their suspicions was going to find themselves straddling a horse under some high tree limb or beam. Still expecting to be ambushed by the assassin, he took care to be aware of his surroundings. He eased forward to look around the edge of the building and saw the snowy street lit from the yellow glow of light coming through a dozen windows.

The bushwhacker was gone, blended in with all the activity around them. Men and horses were moving back and forth on the street. Staying back in the shadows, he heard snippets of conversations.

"It was that Ranger."

". . . shot Runt in the back . . ."

There was a pause and more words came to him.

". . . looking for Doc . . ."

"I heard Maggie's fine . . ."

His original idea of going back to Maggie's was out of the question. If Runt was dead, they wanted immediate justice, no matter who was on the swinging end of a rope. The bottom fell out of Ridge's stomach. Despite the Ranger badge on his shirt, he was now prey.

Gun in hand, he leaned against the back of the building and considered what to do. It was usually in his nature to charge into any problem, whether it was Comanches, outlaws, or something as simple as a bad horse. But this was different. He had a whole town looking for him and few friends he could rely on.

One of his two friends was shot, maybe dead. Maggie was his best chance, but there was no way he could get to her without being killed, and one woman had no chance of holding off a lynch mob until they could calm down and listen as she explained what happened.

He had to find a place to hide out.

CHAPTER 16

Runt was in Doc's chilly office, but his blood still pooled on Maggie's floor. Men were in and out, on errands she didn't understand or care about. Jo was perched on a stool beside the stove, for once quiet and watching with wide eyes.

Russ Leopold was there, hat tilted back to show a curl of hair peeking out on his forehead. He had his eye on the little girl and gave her a wink. Solemn as a judge, she returned it with both eyes.

"You're probably gonna have to put more wood in that stove if these *piloncillos* keep fanning the door."

Maggie rubbed her forehead. "Jo! Watch your language."

Russ grinned. "That's a Spanish word for brush-poppers, and she used it right. It's not bad."

"Well, she don't need to be ordering adults around."

"I took it as a suggestion." Russ put a stick of wood down through the stove's hob and put the handle on the floor, where it wouldn't get lost.

Without the back door, cold air rushed in to neutralize the stove's heat. The curtain that Runt had fallen through was kicked into a corner and the young cowboy picked it up, studying the frame to hang it back up.

Maggie was terrified she'd hear they'd caught Ridge. She knew he had nothing to do with the marshal's shooting, but no one with any common sense would listen. She told half a dozen people what they saw, and that the Ranger was right there beside her when Runt was shot, but their blood was up and some stranger had to pay.

"Russ, you have to tell your friends it wasn't Tisdale who shot Runt. I don't know who it was, but Ridge was right there beside the stove and we were just talking."

Zeke and Mahan pushed inside. Zeke's eyes darted about, rested on Russ beside the stove for a heartbeat, and then found Maggie and Jo. He visibly relaxed and went to her side. "You all right?"

"I am," Maggie answered. "But they're looking for Ridge. Zeke, he didn't shoot Runt. Somebody shot from outside."

"I believe her." Russ stopped talking when two men arrived bearing Maggie's back door. "Good. Maggie, we're gonna hang this back up for you to keep out the cold."

The side of the plank door facing her was stained dark with drying blood. They hadn't taken the time to wash it off, and she found she didn't care. For the moment, she just wanted the cold blocked out. "Fine. You need tools?"

"Don't worry about that. We'll fix it right as rain."

She was still wearing her husband's now soaked hat. She took it off, plopped it on a clear spot on the counter, and used her fingertips to fluff her hair. Zeke's eyes on her made Maggie sad, and she wished she was ugly as a mud fence.

The pool of blood on the floor was congealing and she needed to get some water to clean it up before someone put their big foot in it. The men with the door had to step wide to pass, and she didn't want bloody footprints all over her place of business.

The draft she'd been feeling soon stopped and Jo looked up at her. "Mama, I still need to go outdoors."

Maggie almost laughed but caught herself. They'd forgotten what started everything. "Come on then, little missy." She replaced the hat. The drying blood would have to wait. "Gentlemen, we have business to attend to out back."

They immediately understood and didn't look her in the eye. Monty turned to Mahan. "Maybe we ought to go out and look for Ridge."

Russ came back and added more firewood to the box. "Maggie keeps saying it wasn't him."

Tilting his hat back, Zeke took a measure of the other cowboy. "I heard her."

Taking Jo's hand, Maggie helped the little girl off her stool, and Zeke caught her eye. "Maybe I should go out with you, to stand guard."

"No one is after me or Jo. You stay here where it's warm and keep an eye on my stock." She looked at Dixon. She was tired of all the cowboys from opposing ranches fighting every time they ran into each other. "Mack, there, came in to keep an eye on us."

She saw Zeke understood what she was saying. "Y'all

stay with him and mind the store. I'll lose everything if it all disappears in this confusion."

Before he could answer, they went through the curtainless entry to their living quarters and found the good Samaritans had finished. One held the door open for them and closed it after they left.

The snow hadn't lightened up any, falling just as hard as it had when they were unloading the wagon. The prints Ridge made were already smoothed over and would soon be covered. She suspected that there'd be another foot of snow on the ground by morning.

Following the trail broken through the fluff made walking easy, and she was glad to get there with little snow in her shoes. Maggie opened the door and peered inside, not expecting anyone to be there, but to put Jo's mind at ease.

"It's empty. In you go, and don't dawdle."

"My dawdle'll freeze off if I take very long. Don't close it all the way, please. It's too dark without a lamp."

Maggie hadn't considered bringing a light, but the night was uncommonly dark and they could have used one. Even something as primitive and distasteful as an outhouse seemed soft and more pleasing in its attractive blanket. Hunching her shoulders against the cold, Maggie turned her back on the little building covered in snow to keep an eye on her surroundings.

The street blocked by the buildings was still loud with voices. Enough people were up that the lamplight through the windows she could see provided a soft glow that defined the indistinct edges of her roof.

Footsteps squeaking in the fresh snowfall made Maggie catch her breath. She wished she'd picked up the little pocket pistol she kept behind the counter. She'd never felt afraid in Blackjack before, but after what she'd seen in the past hour, it would have soothed her nerves.

The steps stopped and a soft voice called, "Miss Maggie. Is that you?"

She tensed at the familiar sound. "Dwight Grubbs."

His answer was an apologetic confirmation. "Yessum."

"What're you doing back here?"

"Back here? I don't know what you mean."

"Come closer so I can see you."

The young brushpopper's shape materialized through the gloom and falling snow, and he stopped only a couple of feet away. His head and shoulders were covered, and both hands were stuffed deep in the pockets of a canvas coat. "That better?"

"A little. I asked why you came back. Do you need my privy again? Or do you intend to shoot someone else from there?"

Despite the gloom, she saw the surprise on the cowboy's face. "Why, how'd you know why I was here?"

"'Cause the boys say you have the scours, that's why." Jo's voice came loud and clear from inside the outhouse.

"Quiet, missy!" Maggie slapped the flat of her hand on the partially opened door with a sharp crack. Snow fell off the roof with a soft plop. She gave the door a little shove to make the opening smaller. "I don't want to hear another peep out of you."

The cowboy seemed to have shrunk in the past few moments. "I didn't think you'd mind. Most of these other . . ." he swallowed, trying to find the appropriate words for their situation.

"My privy. You like to use this one when you're in town."

He swallowed. "Yessum."

"Were you here earlier tonight?"

"Why, no." He looked around, as if expecting someone to sneak up on them. "I haven't needed to."

She studied him with hard eyes. "Do you know what happened tonight?"

"Sure do. The whole town's looking for that lying, backshooting stranger who says he's a Texas Ranger. They say he shot Runt down in your store when he wasn't looking."

Any fear that Maggie had felt melted like the snow in her hair. She softened, but another thought came to mind. "Do you have a pistol on you?"

"Yessum."

"Where do you carry it?"

"Tucked under my belt. Why? We ain't in no danger out here."

She held out her hand. "Let me see it."

Grubbs shrugged and opened his coat. He took out a revolver and held it up.

"No, hand it to me."

"Sure, but be careful. It's loaded."

"All guns should be loaded, else they wouldn't have any use other than as a hammer." She took it, fumbled with the barrel for a moment until she found the cylinder rod, and snapped it open. Only then did she bring the barrel to her nose and sniff.

"What're you doing that for?"

"Do you smoke?"

"Yessum. I have the makin's here if—"

"Matches."

He dug a wooden Lucifer from one pocket and handed it over. "I got some more if you need 'em."

"Wait here for a moment." She reached for the warped door without turning around. "Jo, I'm coming in for a minute."

"I ain't done yet."

"Don't matter. I've changed your diapers." She slipped inside and pulled the door closed. Striking the match, she waited until the flame settled and lowered it close to the pistol to reveal five fresh cartridges and one empty cylinder.

It wasn't Grubbs who shot Runt, as she'd suspected.

She turned to Jo. "Stay right there till I call for you."

"My backside's like ice."

"That's your fault. Stop eavesdropping and tend to your business so we can go inside."

"And for Grubbs to come in. It's a lucky thing for him I've sat here long enough to warm this seat for him."

"You better *close* that mouth." Maggie shook out the match, closed the cylinder, and stepped outside. She handed it to Grubbs. "I doubt I have the hammer down on that empty. You'd better check it before you drop it."

Without looking, he took the pistol, opened the cylinder, and used his thumb to find the empty chamber. He adjusted it by feel so the hammer rested on air and clicked it back into place. That way the pistol wouldn't go off by accident.

"What's this about, Miss McBrayer? You don't think I shot the marshal?"

"Not anymore. You say you weren't here? Jo says she saw you before the shooting."

"I sure did!"

"Finish up!" Maggie waited.

"I'm sorry. I fibbed to you. I have some kind of problem with my insides and have to go a lot. I did come by earlier, but I figured the snow would cover my footprints and you wouldn't know. It's embarrassing to talk of such things with a lady. That's why I misspoke the truth."

"Did you see anybody here?"

"No'm. I just came and went. Back to the Red River."

"You didn't pass anyone back here?"

"Saw a feller on a horse coming down the alley over yonder, but it was too dark and snowing so hard, I couldn't make out who he was. Rode all huddled up. He went on over to the Red River livery, though. Didn't stop."

Jo finally pushed the door open. "I'm done."

"Good. Mr. Grubbs you're welcome to go in now, and thank you for talking with me."

"You bet." He stood rock solid as they trailed back to the mercantile.

Holding her mama's hand, Jo couldn't resist getting the last word she threw over one shoulder. "There's a can of lime in there, you know."

CHAPTER 17

Despite the weather, the town of Blackjack was a red ant mound of activity. The street that had been quiet an hour earlier was filled with armed men who prowled up and down the boardwalk, between buildings, and in the alleys behind the sprawling community.

Thankful for the gloom, his coat pulled up high and hat drawn low, Ranger Ridge Tisdale blended in. He'd rewrapped his scarf and pulled it up to hide his face, mimicking those ducking their chins into their own wraps to escape the cold.

Few people had seen him, and most of those were Three Fork men. From his appearance, no one was likely to point fingers and shout. For a while, at least, he could move about and try to find the assassin. He thought about going to Kingman and the livery stable to work things out, but it would be the first place they'd look, since his horse was there.

He also didn't want to put the man in danger. He was sure Kingman would help him escape, but if the emotional lynch mob found out, he'd likely be just as dead, or at the very least run out of town, his business destroyed.

What Ridge wanted more than anything was to find the shooter, but investigating the attempted murder right then would be fruitless. One thing was for sure: He had to find someplace to get in out of the weather before the cold sapped his strength and addled him.

At first, he thought of heading back to Maggie's. No one would suspect he'd go there to hide out. Not at the scene of the crime resting on his shoulders.

Two men on foot appeared in the snow and walked past without anything more than a nod in greeting. Ridge nodded back. "Gentlemen." No one would expect a man running from a posse to speak like it was a normal day.

Keeping his head, the pistol in his coat pocket felt good in his hand, calming. He realized only one gun against so many was useless, but the smooth handle gave him the illusion of at least some control in all the chaos.

Everyone around him was armed, too. If their weapons weren't in hand, they were either secreted in pockets like his, or in their holsters and buttoned up tight under coats. Two or three carried rifles, and there was a scattering of shotguns; the long weapons were awkward to handle through thick gloves, though.

That was why his deerskin gloves were carefully tucked away, his bare hands free to react in any way necessary. He thought of the hotel standing at the outskirts of town, imagining the warm interior. He could try his luck in there. Maybe the bar was so full no one would notice, but he couldn't take the chance.

He kept walking toward a white, two-story house

with a sign reading NELLIE'S PLACE. It was odd for the owner to use her own name. Most madams were secretive sorts, preferring to stay to themselves and run their houses like small kingdoms. That would work, except Runt might have been a good customer, or she'd paid him off so the law would leave her alone. He couldn't stay; someone might send up an alarm and a posse would come running.

Alone on the boardwalk, he looked across the street to see an ornate sign hanging close overhead so pedestrians could read it as they walked along the street. J. T. BARLOW & SON MERCANTILE. The building stood alone on the street, flanked by two, wide open lots on each side. Workers were framing another building farther down that stood without walls. The skeleton of a future business had no roof to protect the stacks of rough-cut lumber waiting for nails and hammers.

Looking at the false front shop, he almost smiled at the plan that hatched in his head. Hiding in plain sight suited Ridge, and he stepped inside, tense as a wound pocket watch, waiting for a shout. The long and narrow store was exactly the opposite of Maggie's business. Some shelves were stacked to the fourteen-foot ceiling with canned goods and wares. Others sagged under merchandise, and the oak and glass cases lining both sides of the store were filled with anything the people of a frontier town could imagine.

Carefully arranged tin cans of everything from peaches to corn were displayed in pyramids and walls of colorfully printed labels. Harness and leather goods hung from racks like drying meat over a fire, and there was little floor space that wasn't taken up with burlap sacks of potatoes, kegs, boxes, and barrels.

One entire section halfway down on the right was long guns of all sorts standing in vertical racks with boxes of ammunition stacked below. Another counter and glass case separated customers from pocket pistols to new Colt revolvers.

Only one salesman, with a skinny mustache and long, thin brown hair was helping a brightly dressed lady near a stack of folded material. Her calf-length, gray frock coat lay draped over a display of shirts.

The man looked up from his business. "Be with you in a shake, sir. Expedite your selections. We're closing in a few minutes."

"That's good to hear," Ridge said and walked straight over to the section of tobaccos, where he turned his back to the door and appeared to peruse the display of cigars, cigarette makin's, and plugs, just another customer there to satisfy his habit before the store closed.

The salesman, who seemed to have one eyebrow permanently raised and the other frozen downward into a frown, returned to his business with the lady. "So, how much do you need of this?"

The woman studied Ridge for a long moment before returning to their commerce. "Oh, only a couple of yards. My girl's a proficient seamstress and there's little waste. She asked for me to pick up a couple of needles and some thread to match the color."

"Sure enough, Miss Nellie." The man's voice lowered and he cut his eyes toward Ridge. "I got in those wool sheep rolls you wanted."

Ridge noticed the salesman's debauched look and put two and two together. If it was the same Nellie, she owned the house of ill repute, and wool rolls were a necessary item in a house full of women, along with various powders, soaps, and the occasional patent medicine for a wide variety of real and supposed ailments.

Nellie stared him hard in the eye until the slimy little man ducked his head. "It's about time. Wrap all that up for me, please, and have it delivered in the morning." Nellie drifted away from the material and in Ridge's direction, as if drawn by a magnet. "How are you today, sir?"

Ridge kept his back to the door and windows, figuring it was safer to be seen talking easily to another person. He was surprised to see she was dressed like any respectable lady in town, with a high-cut shirtwaist that was buttoned at the neck. A Camay pendant pin closed the neck.

"I'm just fine, ma'am. I didn't intend to eavesdrop, but I confess I overheard your name's Nellie?"

Her eyes twinkled. "I am. I'm the proud owner of that establishment right over there. Have you dropped by yet?"

"I have not. Had some business as soon as I got to town and it's kept me tied up ever since." He watched the proprietor wrap the material and tie the package with a piece of string. Despite concentrating on his task, his ear was tuned to their conversation.

She frowned indulgently. "I'm sorry to hear that. Will your business keep you here long?"

"I hope not. I intend to collect a package and leave soon."

"Not in this storm, I hope. Why don't you come over for a drink by the fireplace? I have the most comfortable place in town, and if you don't yet have a room at the hotel, I reserve two at my place for special travelers. Clean sheets and not a bedbug in sight."

"Special?"

"Those who catch my eye."

Ridge had no intention of going there. The social club was an obvious place the vigilantes would look. If they didn't get there within the next hour, they'd surely search it at some point as they swept the town. They weren't going to look in Barlow's own store.

The door opened and a brass bell jingled above. A man holding a rifle leaned in. "Everything all right, Earl?"

The man looked up, surprised. "Why wouldn't it be, Jonas?"

"Well." The man's eyes flicked over the three of them standing casually at the counter. "I meant, we're still looking for that feller who shot Runt."

The clerk's mouth gaped open. "Shot dead? That's hard to believe."

"That's what they say. Shot in the back by a Texas Ranger. There's a posse forming up and the rest of us scattered out to find the assassin. We intend to hang him."

"Well, why would a Ranger murder the marshal?" Nellie rested a hand on Ridge's forearm.

"Someone said they were in Maggie's and got in an argument over her."

"I can see why. She's a looker." Earl raised his eyebrow even higher.

Jonas waved a hand and closed the door. He disappeared into the darkness.

Ridge turned to Nellie, pretending not to know. "Who's Maggie?"

"Storekeeper at the other end of town. Where's your horse?"

"Tied a ways down right now." Ridge kept his face impassive at the second lie. "Just got to town here and came in to pick up some supplies."

She smiled. "This is the place, all right. They have *almost* everything a man needs, don't you?"

"We do." Earl placed the wrapped material with a stack of other purchases and picked up a pencil. "Will that be all tonight, Nellie?"

"It is." Dismissing the clerk, she turned her attention to Ridge. "What about you, sir. Is there anything else you want, or need?"

Ridge pretended to consider her question. "I'm not sure, Miss Ma'am. Like I said, I just hit town." He emphasized that statement again, just to be sure the store clerk wouldn't get suspicious. He'd dodged a bullet with the vigilante a moment earlier and wanted to make sure the man across the counter wouldn't start thinking and raise the alarm.

Besides, the slimy little man kept leering at the two of them, titillated by their conversation.

"That's Miss *Madam* to you." Nellie winked.

"A little late to be out shopping in such weather, isn't it?"

"I do my shopping late, when most of the other people are off the street."

"I can see that. Cuts through a lot of chaff, I bet."

She threw back her head and cut loose with a laugh that came from deep inside. "Chaff. I never thought of it as that. Earl, this gentleman's a real professor. What's your name, Professor?"

"Funny, that's really what people call me."

"Well, that's grand. Why don't you escort me across the street and let's get on with this conversation, Professor?"

"I have an idea, if you'll allow me to lay it out."

"*Lay* it out." She came down hard on the word. "Why, have at it."

Ridge turned to Earl. "I'd like a bottle of that Beechtree sipping whiskey up there, and a couple of glasses, if you have them around here."

"Mister, this ain't no saloon. I'll sell you the whiskey, but you can drink it somewhere's else."

"I'd rather sit in that little back room I see through there, the one with that Spark stove." He pointed at a small office at the back that was heated by a fourteen-inch-high grey iron stove. "See, my old mama has one of those little fellers, and I've been on the road for months. This snow has me thinking of when I grew up in West Virginia and we sat and talked all night through storms while she sipped a little medicine and told me about when she was a kid."

Nellie tilted her head. "Medicine?"

"You know, homemade popskull that she got from my Uncle Erasmus."

She raised an eyebrow. "Usquebaugh."

"Why, yes. The old Gaelic term for whiskey. Mama never taught us that one."

"Some of us receive our educations in different doses."

"I can see that." Ridge turned back to Earl. "Well, sir, I'd like to be alone with Miss Nellie here and share some stories, like her knowledge of the Gaelic language. If we go to her . . . parlor, there'll be a lot of people listening in.

"I'd just prefer talk and peace and quiet. You said yourself you were about to close up. Well, then, lock the door and leave us in here. I'll allow you know and trust Nellie enough to leave her here with me."

Earl bristled. "Why don't you go on over there with her? She has everything you need and then some."

"Nope. Then she'd be at work and every time we'd get to a teary-eyed moment together, someone would come knocking at her door, or a customer would want to see her, and all I want is her company and conversation. You get that, don't you, Miss Nellie?"

"I'll understand better if you'll just call me Nell."

"Well, there you go, Earl. We've come to an agreement here between the two of us, so let's make it unanimous. I reckon all I need to do is compensate you for the time and space."

Nell raised that eyebrow again, an acknowledgment that she wanted to know what Ridge was up to.

That was simple. He was banking on the man's greed

to seal the deal. "Look here. I bet you had to split a lot of that wood stacked back there. I know that's hard. A man sweats when he cuts the tree down, sweats when he's splitting it, and again when he's stacking it. My old daddy used to say that firewood warms a man at least three times."

Earl's eyes narrowed as he listened.

Ridge pictured the old woodcutter he'd heard about, delivering the very wood that was burning in the stove because he simply loved the work. All Earl did was shove it down the hob, but he let Ridge believe he'd done all the work.

"So here." Ridge opened the big coat, and turning so Earl couldn't see the empty holster and slid a hand in his pocket. "I'll give you this ten-dollar gold piece that you won't have to put in the till for Barlow. It's yours to spend, free and clear, so me and Nell can get to know each other and not be bothered by other people's troubles."

He placed the heavy coin in Earl's hand, and the man weighed it in his palm, considering. "So, you two are just going to sit in there by the stove and talk after I lock up? Mister, I'm responsible for everything within these walls. Guns, ammunition, expensive chocolates over there, and all this food, and especially the whiskey sitting on them shelves. How will I know you won't steal me blind?"

"Well, you don't." He turned to the brunette woman beside him. "Nell, you're an experienced woman of the world. Have you ever known a professor to steal?"

"I have not."

"And Earl, don't you trust Nell?"

"Of course I do."

"So there you go." Ridge reached into his pocket and produced another coin. "There. I just doubled your money as insurance. I won't even take as much as a cigar. How's that? I'm just renting that little bitty space back there and the heat held within."

The coins disappeared as quick as a drop of water on a hot stove. Earl glanced at the front door. "Nellie, you're part of this, so you're just as responsible as he is. Anything comes up missing, you're gonna be the one to pay, and you know Barlow'll collect."

"Oh, I'll be responsible all right."

He seemed to run out of arguments. He took a bottle off the shelf and placed it in front of Ridge. "That'll be two-fifty."

Ridge matched his permanently raised eyebrow. Instead of commenting that he'd already given the man twenty dollars, he grinned. "Barlow's prices, right?"

"I have to charge for the merchandise."

Ridge put the money on the counter, and Earl made it disappear like a magician. "There's two glasses in the office back there. Use them." He pointed a forefinger at Ridge. "And you, Professor Whatever-Your-Name-Is, lock up when you leave. Put the key on the top sill out there and I'll get it in the morning. Don't you forget, Nell, or Barlow'll put me in a shallow grave, and I mean every word I said."

Gathering up his coat and hat, Earl scurried around like a rat, blowing out all the lamps except one. He turned around the sign on the door to read CLOSED and stepped outside. For a moment, he had a little trouble locking the door and held up the key so they could see it, then reached up and hid it on the top sill.

They watched him walk away, and Ridge drew a long breath as he picked up the lamp and checked the level. It was almost full, guaranteeing several more hours of light. He led the way to the safety of the back room, the floor creaking under his feet. Such sounds shouldn't come from a new building and illustrated the cheap construction Barlow paid for.

The cluttered little office contained a desk, three chairs, and a small woodstove. Ridge set the lamp on a stack of papers and chuckled. "That man knows Barlow will have him killed if anyone comes in here and steals as much as a bag of cornmeal, but he just sold his soul for a few gold coins."

"Money is the root of all evil." Nellie slipped past him, getting close enough he could get a faint whiff of perfume.

Ridge breathed in her scent, closed the door, and they were safe and alone, for the time being. "No, the accurate quote is from Timothy, *For the* love *of money is the root of all evil.*"

"Love is a wonderful thing." She took off her coat and draped it across the back of a chair. "We sell love across the street."

"No, you don't. Your girls just rent out some time."

That huge laugh coming from the small, slender woman filled the warm little room. Nell dropped into a straight-backed, cane-bottomed chair and settled into a most unladylike position with her knees spread, almost encircling the little stove. She pulled up her dress close to keep the material away from the hot metal.

"Damn, Ridge. It's good to see you again!"

"You too, Nell. How's my little sister?"

CHAPTER 18

Cold and tired of being in the snow, a handful of Three Fork riders led by Judd gathered in Kingman's livery. Full of whiskey, Turkey Thompson, Mack Dixon, and Dwight Grubbs were joined by three others from the Red River Saloon. When Russ Leopold announced he was staying there with them, a disgusted Son disappeared through the swirling curtains of snow, heading for the far end of town.

Four townspeople were in there out of the weather, too, friends of Kingman. A bank teller named Donovan, Jerry Wayne Halpin, Larry Williams, and Gary Reeves all huddled up to discuss Runt's near murder.

The door from Kingman's office was opened to the grand hall, wide enough for two wagons to pass. Heat from his woodstove rolled into the barn, making it comfortable for the men to converse out of the weather.

Kingman didn't much like having Barlow men in his business, preferring they use the Red River's livery instead. He was as anxious as anyone for the Barlow's new stable to open at the other end of the town. He figured all the riffraff would go down there, and he'd be left alone to serve better folks, such as the four townspeople there, worrying about Runt.

Judd's hands were deep in his coat pockets. "I'd bet my wages for a month it was that Ranger who shot Runt in the back. We never were friends, but no man deserves that."

"I bet he shot him and ducked out the back." Dwight Grubbs couldn't stand still, swaying from foot to foot, trying to bleed off energy.

Russ appeared to be thinking hard about something and not interested in what the men were saying.

Williams, a short man with dark brown hair, chewed his bottom lip. "Now, we don't know any such of a thing. The law says a man's innocent until he's convicted by a jury of his peers."

"Somebody needs to find him and bring him in," Turkey said. "I'll do it if I get the chance, but he won't be walking."

"What's he look like, anyway?" Halpin asked. He was a stout man who worked in the land office with Williams.

"Can't say." Williams stamped his feet like a colt, keeping the blood flowing. "I'm not sure anybody but Maggie and Runt knows. None of the Three Forks men gave any indication they knew."

"I do."

They all looked at Kingman, who pointed at the far end of the barn. "He stabled his horse here when he got to town."

Dixon's head snapped in that direction. "Why didn't you say so?"

"Didn't need to. He just left his horse here with his saddlebags—"

"Goddlemighty!" Dixon took off down the hall. "His things are back there?"

"Now, don't be messing with them!" Kingman reached out and took Turkey's arm as the slender man followed his partner. "That there's private property, same as it would be in a hotel room."

Dixon stopped at the buckskin's stall and rested one hand on top of the stable gate. "This the one?"

"Stop it!" Kingman pushed through the men and held the latch. "Runt's done looked in there. The rest of what the man has in there's none of your business."

Dwight Grubbs grabbed Kingman's wrist and yanked the man's hand away. "Stay out of this!"

Russ Leopold shook his head. "Y'all leave that alone. If he comes in here and sees y'all messing with his things, or his horse, Tisdale's likely to start shooting. I take him for a man who won't be trifled with."

The livery's back door swung open and a shape stood in the doorway with a long object in his hands.

Grubbs suddenly came to life. "There he is!"

Wound tight from their trespassing in the Ranger's possessions, Judd mistook the new arrival's intentions. "He has a rifle!" He whirled and snatched the revolver from his holster, snapping two shots in a roar of thunder as the figure fell backward and out of sight.

Turkey jerked a worn navy revolver and thumb-cocked the hammer. His thumb slipped, and the .36 caliber pistol went off, striking Gary Reeves in the leg.

Standing six foot tall, the man who made a living

making saddles yelped and went down hard on the ground. "I've been shot! What'd you shoot me for, Turkey?"

"It wasn't me! It was that Ranger!"

"Behind us!" In the dim interior, Grubbs saw Reeves fall and, thinking he'd been shot from behind by an assailant, he whirled and drew a Remington from his belt. Hampered by his bulky coat and thick gloves, he also fired too fast and hit Dixon in the back. The cowboy grunted and stumbled forward, his own pistol going off into the floor.

Thinking they were caught in a crossfire, the others also produced firearms and fired at anything that took their fancy. A string of gunshots rang, sounding like Chinese firecrackers until the guns quieted. They crouched behind cover, waiting to see who was going to fire next.

"Hold it!" Kingman shouted, still on his feet. He held both hands outward, as if to keep everyone apart. "That wasn't Tisdale back there! It was Barney Taylor, the butcher! Y'all put them guns down! There ain't nobody else in here, neither!"

Kingman's breath caught at the sight of still another body on the ground. Blood pumped out of a hole in Russ Leopold's neck.

Horrified, Kingman raced to the entrance and into the street to see Doc step out of Maggie's and onto the boardwalk. He rushed toward him for help.

Standing beside one of the thick support posts rising high in the stable, Judd watched the two land men apply a compress against Reeves's leg, while Grubbs worked on his own buddy he'd shot. Judd recalled the conversation between himself and Son.

The Barlows wanted confusion, and a war. It was all right there in Judd's hands, and all he had to do was add more wood to the stove that was already burning hot. He'd reloaded the Remington revolver that had started the gunfight and put a sizeable hole in Russ Leopold's neck, taking Son's good friend out of the way.

Their friendship had the potential to get in the way of Judd's plans. The young men were too close, and Judd was afraid that if old man Barlow died in his sleep someday, Son would take over and make Russ his foreman. That wouldn't do at all.

He glanced at the door, knowing someone was soon going to come rushing in, and he hoped it was Zeke, or one of the other Oarlock riders.

It didn't matter which it was. One would be all it would take to start the dance.

The first shape that came through the door was who he expected. Doc paused for a moment so his eyes could become accustomed to the dim interior. "Who is it? Who was shot?"

"Over here, Doc!" Donovan shouted and waved one arm.

Doc saw the tall man and rushed forward. The moment he was out of the way, two others in Stetsons paused at the door, looking in. Judd cocked his revolver and aimed at the door, sensing those around him were twisted tight as Dick's hatband. It wouldn't take much to get them started.

"It's Tisdale! Shoot!"

Despite the fact that two men were silhouetted in the doorway, the surviving Barlow riders fired at the same time. No sooner than the bodies fell, Judd holstered his pistol and rushed toward the back door.

He stepped over the butcher's dead body and cut left, into the heavily falling snow, leaving his own men to suffer whatever came their way.

The war was on, and Three Fork had plenty of men to spare back in the Red River Saloon.

CHAPTER 19

Hours later and groggy from lack of sleep, Maggie put away the bucket and brushes she'd used to scrub the blood off her floor. Josie Ruth was deep asleep in back, under the weight of a pile of patchwork quilts that seemed to press her into the cotton mattress they shared. When she looked in to check on her precocious daughter, all she saw were ringlets on her pillow.

She returned to the front and found Zeke looking out through the frost-covered glass in her door. He turned to Mahan and Monty, who'd stayed with them all night. "Man, it's coming down again. If this don't slack off, we're gonna be stuck here in town for another day."

"I've never seen snow like this." Leaning back in his chair, Mahan opened sleepy eyes.

Monty chuckled. "All you've seen is the back of your eyelids for the past couple of hours."

"Weather like this has happened before, and it'll happen again." Zeke turned back into the room as his breath clouded the pane. "We're gonna lose a lot of stock if this keeps up."

"Mr. Hutchins is gonna have our hides for being gone so long," Monty said.

"We can't help we got snowed in," Mahan responded. "He'll understand, but when we get back, the rest of the boys in the bunkhouse are gonna want their turn here in town and you can't blame 'em. That'll be double the work for us."

The pair of cowboys had wandered in a year earlier, looking for jobs. Of course they stopped by the saloon as soon as they drifted into town, and then made another stop, at Nellie's, asking around at both places if anyone knew of work around.

Some bar rats had suggested the Three Fork outfit, but the stories Mahan and Monty heard about the old man made up their minds for them. Almost broke, they saw Maggie sweeping the boardwalk out front and came in to talk with the attractive redhead. Seeing they were out of money, she fed the young men and suggested they ride out to the Oarlock ranch and talk with Drake, who put them to work on the spot.

"Wonder how Runt's doing." Maggie's mind had been on him all night, especially while she cleaned up the stain from where he fell. The boards were still discolored, but it was not as noticeable now, and it was all she could do not to weep the entire time. Overwhelmed, she'd required Zeke to scrub the door they'd carried the marshal on.

"We're about to find out." Zeke turned the knob on the door. "Here comes Doc."

The snow was knee deep in the street, with drifts

against the buildings up to four or more feet. Doc kicked his way through until his pants were covered from the knees down, and when he stepped inside, the eight-inch drift against the door collapsed inward.

He stopped just inside, looking down in dismay at what he'd wrought. "I'm sorry, Maggie."

Zeke closed the door, using one foot to kick the rolled-up towel back into place against the threshold. Maggie crossed her arms and leaned against the counter. "Don't worry. It's just snow. It'll melt. How's Runt?"

Doc filled a cup from the coffeepot on top of the stove. "He's one lucky man." He took a sip. "That big old coat of his did something I've only read about."

Mahan barely opened his eyes. "What's that?"

"The bullet did some damage, but it wasn't as bad as it looked." He looked around. "Have y'all ever heard of Samurai warriors?"

"Is that one of them northeastern tribes?"

Doc chuckled and poured himself some coffee. "Eastern is right. The Far East, though, across the Pacific Ocean. They're Japanese."

"Like them Chinese men back there who take in laundry?" Zeke jutted his chin across the street.

"No. You don't see many Japanese over here, and almost none take in laundry. It's a little country, but they fight one another all the time. Warlords is what they call their chiefs, and hundreds of years ago they started wearing capes into battle. They're tougher'n Comanches, and I daresay if they were as tough and organized as Samurai, we'd all still be East of the Mississippi."

"Capes? Like women wear, or those playactors who come through throwing over their shoulders?"

"Pretty close. You have the concept, but not the true idea. The robes weren't invented as decoration but were designed to be held on to their upper bodies by a series of straps that caught air when they were on a horse and billowed out from the sides and front."

Despite being worried, the discussion caught Maggie's interest. "What for?"

"They learned long ago that the robes made of silk were better than armor at turning arrows. All that flying material was loose, and when the arrows hit, they wouldn't penetrate and almost bounced off, or if they didn't, there wasn't enough resistance, and they'd get caught in the silk and do little damage."

Monty leaned forward with a hand on one knee. "What's that got to do with Runt?"

"Well, it's a combination of things. He must've been turning when he was shot, and y'all know how thick those buffalo hides are. It was likely kind of flowing out and there wasn't much resistance. The bullet penetrated some, but it lost a lot of power."

Doc grinned. "I ought not tell this, but he also wears a . . . I guess you'd call it a corset . . . no, a brace. I ordered it for him about a year ago, when his back was giving him fits. It has whalebone stays in it, and that bullet hit one of 'em and skittered off. Broke a rib or two, but it probably saved his life. Though it was a good lick, he'll live. I expect he's gonna wake up sometime soon, and knowing that little man, he'll be a bear for a while."

"Has he come to himself to say what happened?" Zeke stayed where he was, keeping a lookout, as if expecting a war party of Comanches to come riding up.

"He has not." Doc threw a look out at the gray world beyond the windows and changed the subject. "I see there's still a bunch of people looking for that Ranger."

"They're just wandering around to scare him up, like a bunch of hunters trying to kick up rabbits," Zeke said. "No one's caught him yet, as far as I know."

"Probably lit out in that storm." Doc took another sip. "That's what I'd do."

The words had barely left his mouth when the rattle of muffled gunshots filled the air. They rushed outside, ignoring the snow, and looked toward the livery. The small door to the stableman's office burst open and Kingman ran into the street, struggling against the snow that held him back.

Doc stepped to the edge and waited until he got to within calling distance. "What's the matter?"

Vapor puffing like a steam engine, Kingman gained a few more yards before he stopped, out of breath. "Doc! We've had a bad shooting over here. Folks are hurt, and I believe one or two're dead."

Maggie's stomach dropped. "Anyone else?"

"Yep, another feller."

"The Ranger?"

"Naw, Barney Taylor."

"The butcher?"

"Yeah, came over to deal with a steer I have out back. He walked in, and one of them idiot cowboys thought he was the Ranger. They all took to shooting at

Barney and killed him stone dead, but none of 'em paid any attention to where they were all standing. Shot one another, and a couple are down. One's bleeding pretty bad, though with a bullet in his leg, but the others are just scratched."

"Now these fools are trying to kill one another on their own side." Doc sighed and looked down into his steaming coffee mug. He took one last sip, flicked it empty into the street, and handed it to Maggie. "Thanks for the coffee, what there was of it I got to enjoy."

Monty buttoned his coat and set his hat. "I'll go with you. I need to check on my horse."

Mahan reached back and closed the door behind him. "I'll go, too. I've been cooped up for too long anyhow. You going with us, Zeke?"

He tried not to look at Maggie, but it was obvious he had another idea that involved female companionship. "Naw, y'all go on. I'll be along shortly."

They stepped along behind Doc, who walked with determination fueled by anger and a duty to be executed. Arms crossed against the cold, Maggie watched him open the small door on the livery and step inside. Several steps behind, the Oarlock boys paused, probably to let their eyes adjust to the dim interior, and three more shots rang out from inside.

They twisted and fell where they stood, like doves shot from a branch. Both were obviously dead by the time they stilled. Maggie screamed and rushed off the boardwalk and through the trail they'd broken only moments earlier. Doc came boiling back out by the time she reached the two cowboys.

"You damned fools!" he shouted over his shoulder. "Put down them damned guns! You've done killed two innocent men!"

She stopped at the horrific sight of the dead boys she'd just been talking to, hands against her cheeks at the bloody wounds. Her voice was soft with shock and grief. "What happened?"

"Those fools inside are insisting they thought it was the Ranger coming in behind me."

Mahan suffered a shot to his forehead and Monte had two bullet holes in his coat, right over his heart.

"But there are *two* of them." Maggie's voice was a whisper. "What made them think it was Ridge?"

Doc knelt beside the cooling bodies. Monte still had both hands in his coat pockets. Mahan wore a surprised look on his white face that was stark against the bright red blood. The sad-faced doctor glanced at the dark interior and turned so his back was to the door.

As Zeke joined them and put a hand on Maggie's shoulder, Doc spoke soft and low, so only the two of them could hear. "They knew good and well who this was. It was murder plain and simple, Mags. The Three Fork boys have started a war against the Oarlock ranch. I've been expecting this for a long time, and now it's here under the guise of finding that Texas Ranger. They're going to use that excuse to start killing our friends."

CHAPTER 20

The night was uncommonly cold outside, but the small office in Barlow's mercantile felt snug and warm, with no cracks in the walls and floors to allow drafts. It was so frigid, the wooden building contracted, popping and groaning from time to time. The cheap construction was a testament to shoddy work.

The Beechtree whiskey bottle was empty, and most of it in Nellie, who seemed unaffected by the liquor. In the warm glow of a lamp turned low, she took a tiny sip of what remained in her glass and looked at Ridge over the rim. "So, my big brother's a Texas Ranger. What happened to ranching with Oscar? They're all right, aren't they?"

There were three kids out of six that survived their childhoods in the Tisdale family. Ridge was the oldest, with Oscar only a couple of years behind. Nell came along late, a hard-headed baby sister they all doted on until she left home one day to become an *entrepreneur*, in her words, but without any idea of how to go about it. He hadn't seen her since.

"They're fine now, as far as I know. You haven't heard from him?"

"Lordy, my line of work don't lend itself to much conversation with family. He'd have a rigor if he knew what I do for a living, and we haven't exchanged letters more'n once in the last five years."

"Oscar always was one to judge, but he's a good, solid man. I lived with them for a while on that little spread outside of Mason. It's going good and they're comfortable, but a few months ago a crazy preacher and his hay-head wife came through while we were out working cows in the north pasture. When we got back to the house, they'd taken both his little boy and girl."

Nellie gasped. "Stole his kids? Did they hurt Ruth?"

"Stole them, sure enough. No, the little ones were playing down by the creek and she didn't know anything about it at the time. Found out later that those two intended to murder them kids for some religious reason. Before we found that out, though, we lit out after them and came up on the damnedest collection of wicked people you ever did see. To this day, I'm not sure who was completely on which side of the law, but we knew where *we* stood. There happened to be a Texas Ranger there at the same time and we got the kids back and sent those two crazies straight to hell. There's a lot more to tell, but it don't make no difference.

"The kids are safe, and they're with Oscar and Ruth again. The Ranger swore me in to help, and after that I rode with them for a little while before he and I got crossways about our different interpretations of the law. I left and ran into a bad outlaw we'd been chasing.

He tried to kill me, but I did the same for him, and I pinned the badge back on and took in his body. I've been a Ranger ever since."

"Even when we were kids, I knew you'd wind up wearing a badge. You were never cut out to look at the south end of northbound cattle all your life."

"Not sure I'm cut out for this, neither, but I'm doing the best I can." Ridge rose and cracked the office door, listening for anything on the street that might reveal what was going on outside in the early morning snow. It was quiet. He secured the latch and fed the fire.

She watched in silence until he settled back into his chair. "You want to tell me what's going on out there?"

Nell had every right to know why Ridge was on the dodge only hours after reaching town. He told her all that had happened, what he found out under the snow and the dead man in the wagon, and what he suspected. He also talked about Maggie's situation, and was surprised at the tone in his own voice.

She absently used the chewed nail on her little finger and scraped at the corner of her mouth, something she'd always done when thinking. "So, you just took it upon yourself to take up for a woman you don't know."

"I was kinda thrust into that position, if you want to look at it that way. There's a little girl involved, too."

The whole family knew how Ridge felt about children. He'd seen his brothers and sisters lowered into the ground, and it had always affected him to the point that he would disappear for a couple of days before returning and not saying another word about it.

"What are you gonna do?"

"Try and stay alive, for the most part. The only way I can get into the clear is to find whoever it was that shot Runt and bring him in. I have a sneaking suspicion it'll be the same person who murdered that freighter outside of town, though I can't say for sure why."

"There's only one backshooter in Blackjack, and I can tell you right now who it is."

"Go on ahead."

"Son Barlow."

"What makes you say that?"

"Because we hear a lot of talk in my place. Son's a good customer." She chuckled. "Some of the girls call him Rabbit."

Ridge felt his face flush and Nellie laughed. "Big brother! Wipe that look off your face. When I say *customer*, I mean he's someone who comes in to visit the *other* girls."

Uncomfortable with the conversation, he shifted his position on the chair that matched hers. She threw back her head and laughed again, sliding a few inches back as the stove grew hotter. "I have a confession to make."

He held up a hand as if to keep her back. "I don't need to hear anything about what goes on over there."

"You need to hear this. I own and run the place, but I'm not like the girls who work for me."

"What does that mean?" His voice was filled with doubt.

"It means I make money off what the girls will do, but I've never been in the business in a personal sense. Not once."

He grunted, looking around the cluttered office so

as not to look him in the eye on such a subject. "That's the biggest load of horse fertilizer I've ever heard."

"It's true. I'm like Earl out there, and Maggie."

His eyebrows rose.

"I just sell what people want, but I'm only the proprietor." She grinned wide again, showing bright white teeth. "Speaking of horse fertilizer, what was all that about West Virginia and Mama? Our great-grandparents came from there, but we were all raised outside of Mason, right here in Texas, which is one of the best reasons I can name for being up this way. If I never see another rocky piece of ground, it'll be too soon."

He ignored the first part of the question, not wanting to confess he'd just made up the story to throw Earl off the track. "So, you prefer the prairie, outlaws, and Comanches." He thought for a moment. "And snowstorms and ice storms that'll freeze a man to his saddle."

"I've not seen one Indian, and the prairie's pretty most times of the year. Hell, we had outlaws in Mason, highwaymen and renegade Mexicans up from the river. I like this country and I like being away from our family to live my own life as I see fit. I never gee-hawed with any of them, anyway, other than you."

Ridge went back to his confab with the salesclerk. "I didn't want Earl out there to know anything about me, or you. Talking about West Virginia sent his thoughts that way, and sometimes I like to misdirect a man when I'm questioning him, or looking for information."

He paused and returned to their original discussion, though it was uncomfortable. "You're telling me you came all this way from home, and instead of finding a husband or opening a seamstress shop like you always wanted, you set up a . . . a brothel, and never . . . participated yourself."

She grinned at his struggle to find the right words. "Not as a professional, like the girls. I saw that making a little bit of money sewing for other folks wasn't a life, and then one day in Austin I ran into a couple of gals who worked out of the Austin Social Club over in Guy Town. We got to talking, and they told me about the business, and how they didn't like the woman they worked for. Her name was Ann Howard and she was a hellion who had been arrested more than a dozen times.

"I had a little cash and asked if they'd come to work for me, and we hatched the idea to start our own business." She sighed. "I didn't realize how much politics there was in this profession. It got so bad, all the bagnios had to pay off the police, who were as bad as any rowdy customer. Then some of the girls started turning one another in for prostitution just to get them arrested, so I gathered up my own little herd, the best gals working Austin, and we came here."

"Why Blackjack? Why not Dallas, or Fort Worth?"

"Because there was no competition in Blackjack, and because it's just us, business is booming. By next year there'll be a rail line through, and I plan to build a bigger place just out of the city limits, not far from the station." She finished the last sip in her glass. "I'm thinking of a big hotel with everything a traveler could want, a good bed, food, whiskey, and female company. And I tell you what. This is a business Barlow can't horn in on. He can own everything outside of Nellie's House, but not what we have to sell."

"He'll just bring in his own girls. Start his own place."

"I have better quality. Clean sheets, and we also offer something most social clubs don't. Companionship. I don't charge for dancing like they did in Austin, and my whiskey's as pure as this we've been drinking tonight.

"It costs three dollars to be with one of my girls, but I don't insist on time limits, and the boys know that. Sometimes the cowboys who come in only want somebody to talk to for a few minutes, and women who'll listen but won't nag."

They grew silent when voices came from out back. Ridge quickly leaned over the lamp, cupped his hand behind the chimney, and blew it out.

Men were right outside the door. "There ain't no tracks out here."

"There's smoke coming from the stovepipe up there, but the sign on the front says they're closed."

"Hell, Arthur. That little peckerwood Earl probably stoked up the stove to keep the place warm overnight when he left."

The latch rattled as someone gave it a shake. Ridge waited with the Colt in his hand, hoping he'd engaged the lock properly when he looked out earlier, and the door wouldn't pop open. Nell's breathing was fast and shallow, loud in the quiet office.

"Buttoned up tight. Let's make a swing around to Nellie's Place. If I was hiding out, that's where I'd be."

A harsh laugh from a different person told Ridge

there was three of them out there. "I know why you'd be there, all right."

"Hey, I got a little cash in my pocket to jingle at them. I wonder if Ivy's interested in entertaining a customer so early."

The men left, and Ridge realized he'd been holding his breath. He let it out and settled back. "Well, I guess I won't be going to your place anytime soon."

"Sure you can. They're gonna look and then leave. You said yourself earlier, most of 'em won't recognize you. This is perfect. Keep that badge out of sight, and when they're gone, you can hole up in one of those rooms I told you about, and that'll give you time to figure out what to do. They won't come back to check again, but if someone comes in asking questions, I'll tell 'em you're my brother and here visiting."

"I'm not much for hiding like a rabbit. Runt will clear me, if he pulls through. I know good and well Maggie's told them I was right there beside her when he got shot, and maybe once everyone cools down they'll believe *her*."

"You know how Barlow works." Nell produced a wooden match from somewhere Ridge didn't want to think about and struck it on her thumbnail like a man to light the lamp again. "He's the kind who'll tell a lie over and over until someone believes him. Then, that someone'll repeat the lie until others come to their way of thinking, and before long, they'll say it so much, the lie will become the truth. Once that happens, they'll convince everyone that you shot Runt and they all saw it."

"You're right. That's the way people like that work."

"So, what are you going to do?"

"Find the man who did it and make them hear it right from the horse's mouth."

The voices came back in the alley behind them. "Earl's coming down the street. He's gonna let us in so we can get warm. I hear Son told him to open up."

Ridge rose and listened at the back door. They only had a few moments to act. "Grab your coat. When they come in the front, we're going out the back and around to your place after all."

He cracked the door and peered into the predawn morning. Snow was piled high, and he was relieved to see the men who'd been out there had left uncountable crisscrossing tracks and paths. Their passing wouldn't be as noticeable. He stepped out and motioned for her to come.

They stayed in the fresh trail left by the others leading around the side of Barlow and Son Mercantile. Taking off his hat, Ridge peered around the corner to see the three men from the alley follow Earl into the store.

"Come on." Once again setting his hat low, Ridge offered his arm and Nell slipped hers into his. Breathing deep of the clean, cold air, they walked like an old married couple through the falling snow and across the imprints left by the searchers and up her steps.

CHAPTER 21

Muffled sounds came from down the street as the town woke up, despite the snow. Ridge's back tingled with the thought of a shot coming from one of the vigilantes sure to be out looking for them. Holding his left arm, Nell leaned her head against his shoulder like a couple out for an icy early morning stroll.

Thinking ahead, he wore his sheepskin coat open so he could reach the Colt on his hip. He and Nell were soon cloaked by the snow that filled the air and he hoped the men who'd just entered the cold Barlow and Son Mercantile were concentrating on warming their hands at the woodstove and not looking outside.

He and Nell were on the street at the bottom step leading up to Nellie's Place when the front door opened and Judd stepped out laughing, along with another man Ridge didn't recognize.

Nell gasped, and the four of them froze into place as if the already frigid temperature had dropped fifty degrees and cold froze their joints. His laugh cut off, Judd's eyes widened in surprise at the couple standing down below, but the other cowboy, in a brand-new, wide-brimmed Stetson, simply looked confused.

Maybe it was the way Ridge and Nell were standing arm in arm, as if posing for a photographer with a winter-draped scene behind them. While the young stranger without a line on his face tilted his head to consider the two people standing below them, Judd's immobility didn't last long. Encumbered by his coat, he reached to unfasten the lower buttons.

Ridge threw a look down the veiled street to find no one was yet in sight. Their only danger, besides the two in front of them, was the possibility that someone in Barlow's Mercantile would look out the window to see the four of them squared off.

The Colt seemed to come unbidden into Ridge's hand before the other two could react.

"You boys lace them fingers across your bellies before you do something stupid."

Shocked by the situation, they exchanged glances, and the tone of Ridge's voice changed. "Nope. I'll cut the two of you down where you stand. Lace them fingers, I said!"

He wanted to glance around to make sure others were occupied on the street and no one was coming for them with guns drawn, but the real threat was standing four feet above him.

"Judd. Son." Nell's soft voice calmed all three men. "This is my brother. He's the one you're looking for and not the man you think he is, but he'll for certain kill you both if you give him a reason to. Lace your fingers like he says."

Judd glanced down the street, but all the activity down there was still veiled by the falling snow, which refused to stop. His eyes flicked to Barlow's Mercantile, likely knowing he had men in there, but they were all probably hugging the stove right then to warm up and were of no use in the situation that had blown up in an instant.

As one they laced their fingers as Ridge had ordered, looking like fawning councilmen waiting for the mayor to join them. Without having to be told, Nell raised her skirts enough she wouldn't trip over the hem and almost danced up the steps. She stayed to the side and reached under Son's riding coat and plucked a pistol from his holster.

Holding the revolver at ease and proving she knew how to use it,, she spoke to Judd. "Don't try to grab me. Ridge is good enough to shoot you in the forehead from that distance, and if you touch me, I'll use Son's pistol to blow a hole right through you. Now, I'm going to cross between you. Stay still."

"Nope." Ridge's command cut through the still air. He didn't like what he saw on Judd's face. "Wait a second, Nell. You two take one step forward."

As one, they did as they were told, and Ridge nodded. "Okay."

Nell stepped behind them. Eyes burning hot with fury, Judd locked his glare onto Ridge as she bent at the knees to pull back his long coat far enough to reach under and take his revolver.

While Son couldn't take his eyes off the big .44 pointed at them, Judd's anger subsided and he looked at her with a smirk. "That usually costs me three dollars in here."

"Keep talking and you won't have anything to wiggle at the girls." Nell spun and opened the door.

Ridge was already on the way up the steps, the Colt now held low alongside his leg. "Back inside, with your hands just the way they are."

They obeyed and followed her into a large, ornate foyer filled with heavy drapes and carpets. Curtains that hadn't been opened in months, if not a year or two, were pulled tight against prying eyes on the outside. Relieved they were inside, Ridge reached back and closed the door without turning from them.

"This way." Nell disappeared into the parlor on their right, and they followed. A hard-looking woman in filmy clothes darted past with a squeak. Another with the soft, dreamy face of a child rose from a couch, her wares almost spilling out of a loose blouse.

She had what Ridge considered early morning hair, tousled and hanging down over one shoulder. "Oh my."

Nell barely acknowledged her. "Go put on some clothes, Gertrude."

Gertrude moseyed over to a cased entrance and stopped there to watch.

"Excuse me, ladies." Ridge used the muzzle of his Colt to point at two upholstered chairs against one wall, separated by a small table bearing a lantern turned low, dirty glasses, and an ashtray filled with ashes and cigar stubs. "Over there. You two kneel in front of those chairs and fold your chests over the seats. Lace your hands behind you."

Judd spat on the floor. "I won't kneel to you!"

"You'll be facing the other way, stupid." They turned, and Ridge kicked the Three Fork foreman hard behind the knee. He gasped from the pain and dropped. Ridge swung the pistol toward Son. "You need the same encouragement?"

Fear flickered through the young man's eyes, and his gaze slipped from Ridge's face. "Uh, n-n-no, sir."

With the two men bent over their chairs, Ridge felt a little better. He addressed the woman with olive skin and black, bedroom hair. "What's your name again, miss?"

"Gertrude."

"Are there any other customers left?"

"You counting those two?"

"Consider them as customers no more."

"Then no."

Three more wide-eyed ladies of the evening joined them. Nell stopped one by taking her arm. "Livvy, where's Sam?"

The plump, auburn-haired girl pointed toward the back. "He's sleeping."

Ridge raised an eyebrow in question and Nell answered, "Sam's our fighting man."

Most sporting parlors had a hired hand to deal with rowdy customers. It wasn't uncommon for disagreements to break out between the soiled doves and their customers, and like as not, at least once a week, gentlemen with their eyes set on one particular lady might find himself out of luck when a previous customer, flush with pay, laid out the funds for an entire hour or evening.

The fighting men hired to keep the peace were typically large and rough. The bigger the better, the less chance there was of an altercation and the resulting appearance of the law.

Ridge noted the information. "Make sure somebody tells him what's going on so he don't get the wrong idea."

Girls were arriving from all directions. Nell spoke to a tiny, sleepy-eyed woman who couldn't seem to find her tongue. "Egypt, are there any more customers left that Gertrude missed?"

"Not that I know of."

"Good. Go find Sam."

"Yessum. He went to bed an hour ago and thought they'd already left."

Nell picked up a glass, sniffed the contents, and drained it. She spoke to her brother. "This late in the morning, business slows down."

"Good." Ridge tried not to watch the girls around them. "Y'all have any piggin' strings?"

Nell rolled her eyes. "This is a cathouse, not a barn."

"Cord, then."

A skinny, dark-haired girl darted into the parlor and came back with a handful of slender braided cords. "Will these curtain tiebacks do?"

"A little soft, but it's a good idea." Ridge nodded at one of their pistols still in Nell's hand. "You still know how to use one of those?"

"We'll have to find out, won't we, boys?"

"Be still." Ridge holstered his pistol and made a loop in one of the cords. "You two keep them fingers laced and cross your ankles. Either one of you raises a holler, I'm gonna apply the butt of this Colt against the back of *both* your heads, no matter which one raises it. Got it?"

They nodded, and he drew a knot tight around each man's wrists.

The fallen angel who'd gone after Sam returned with a mountain of a man with mixed-blood skin, long, black hair in ringlets down to shoulders that could carry a bull, and, in direct opposition, soft, blue eyes. Nell sat on a nearby red settee and crossed her legs. "Sam, this is my brother, Ridge."

The man's calm voice belied his size. His deep voice sounded like boulders rumbling downhill. "He accustomed to tying up customers?"

"He just started doing that a few minutes ago."

Ridge looked up from his work to take the man's measure and grinned. "Mr. Sam. Howdy, Texas Ranger, and these two are under arrest."

"Don't surprise me none. And since you're Miss Nell's kinfolk, the name's just Sam."

When Ridge was satisfied they couldn't work the knots loose, he used the other cords to tie their ankles, and then laced the two of them together in a spiderweb of intersections so neither could work at their bindings without tightening those on the other.

When Judd and Son were secure, Ridge searched their pockets. Impassive, Sam watched. Judd carried a razor-sharp folding knife, several spare cartridges for a pistol, and some coins. Son had a little sheath knife tucked into the small of his back, folding money in his left front pocket, and a small stone in his right.

Ridge weighed the stone in his hand. "This looks like the madstone Zeke gave Jo."

"It's probably similar. That's, that's a chert nodule. I'm an amateur geologist and collect rocks."

Ridge grunted. "Geologist."

"Rocks."

"I know what you're talking about." He tucked the madstone in his own pocket and laid the contents of theirs on a nearby table and went to a front window to peek outside around a heavy red curtain. "You boys and I are gonna have a little talk in a few minutes, once my heart settles down."

What little sunrise there would be that morning grayed the street. The snow was tapering off, and he hoped the worst of the storm was over.

He turned to find the parlor full of women. Most seemed to be in their underclothes. Everywhere he looked was wild hair, breasts, and ankles, and, the most shocking to him, bare feet. He swallowed and turned his attention to the safety of his sister.

Nell's hands were empty once again and she was standing there as casual as you please beside Sam, smoking a cigarette someone had given her. "Now what, big brother?"

The girls murmured to one another at the sudden information.

He started to take off his hat in the presence of women but stopped. It wasn't the time, nor place, for such niceties. "First, lock up all the doors and windows."

Without being told, several of the women followed the orders that were directed to his sister. Nell let out a lungful of smoke through her nose. "You look like you could use some coffee."

"And a bite to eat, if you have it."

"We sure do." She reached out to rub a big-bosomed woman's arm. "Athena Mae here can cook up a storm."

The lady nodded. "I'll fix you some breakfast. What about them other two?"

"I doubt they're hungry." Ridge tried not to look at all the women around him for too long. "Sorry, ladies, for bringing trouble to your door."

Nell took charge. "Girls, my big brother here's the one half the town's hunting."

Gertrude spoke up. "What for?"

"Marshal Carpenter's been shot. The Barlow riders are trying to lay it off on Ridge, who says he didn't do it."

"That's because I didn't."

"See? So, I believe my big brother and I don't intend to let any of Barlow's men have him. His only crime is that he didn't do what they said."

"You didn't shoot Runt?" A flat-faced woman with brushy eyebrows, taking up three times the space as the marshal, spoke up. "I heard Judd say last night that you shot him in the back. He's my favorite."

Ridge hid a grin when the image of the two of them rose in his mind. "No, ma'am. I was sitting in Maggie's store when somebody fired at him from outside. She'll vouch for me."

"He's gonna be fine, Gertrude." One of the girls with

hair black as coal sipped from a fragile china cup. "Price Stewart came through while you was upstairs. He didn't stay, but he said Runt's gonna live. The bullet bounced off a rib or something and gouged along under his skin. Doc loaded him up with laudanum and he'll be out like a light for a day or so, but he'll make it."

The good news washed over Ridge like a wave of warm water. He backed up to a settee and dropped. "That's good to hear. Now all I gotta do is stay alive until he can tell what happened."

"You'll be dead by noon." Judd turned his head to speak.

"What for? You heard the truth."

"Because you're meddlin'. Barlow don't like strangers meddling in his business, and he ain't gonna stand for one of our men to be taken in and hanged."

Ridge had almost forgotten the reason he was in town in the first place. He hadn't yet seen Barlow to tell him he was there to collect Clyde McPeak for the murder of John Stevenson in Blossom Prairie. Was all this just to protect a murdering range rider?

"You'll risk death or a bullet to protect one of your men, despite the fact that he's a murderer?"

"We protect the brand."

Son spoke up for the first time, startling them all. Ridge realized the man who was second-in-command of that outfit had been silent, letting one of his own men talk for his daddy, and himself. It spoke volumes about the man who would someday take over the huge cattle ranch and much of the town.

Son's curiously high voice quavered, though Ridge

didn't know if it was from anger or fear. "You've squared off with the brand, all right. Nobody tries to roll over the Three Fork. My daddy's gonna be here soon, and when he shows up, you'll wake up tomorrow morning under six feet of dirt."

The first thing out of the weakling's mouth was the idle threat from a man tied up like a steer ready for branding.

Ridge caught the odor of frying bacon. His stomach rumbled. "You're second-in-command on your dad's ranch. Let's me and you settle this and leave ol' Judd there out of it."

Son tried to look over his shoulder, but the strain was too much, and he wound up resting his head back down on the seat. That position took all the authority from his words. "My dad runs this outfit."

"I can see that, but don't you have enough huevos to stand up for what's right?"

"You'll see what I got if you untie these knots and give me back my pistol."

Judd licked his lips. "Look, Ranger. I've had enough of this. How about the three of us ride out to the ranch to get Clyde together? I changed my mind. I don't want a man in my outfit that's guilty of murder. Take him with you to stand trial. If a judge finds he did what you say, do what the law wants. If he's innocent, he can come right back here and go to work."

Son couldn't see Judd's face past the arm of his chair, but he shook his head as best he could. "That's a decision for my dad to make, or me. Not you."

The dirty ear Ridge could see reddened in anger as

Judd tensed. "Shut up, boy. I'm trying to work out a deal to get us out of this."

"This is family business when it comes to the ranch. You're only the foreman of this outfit. That's all. Russ'll find out where we are soon enough, and he'll bring enough men to take this stupid lawman."

Judd sighed into the chair's seat. "He's dead."

"What?"

"Oarlock men killed him a little while ago, when they shot up the Kingman livery."

"Oh, no." Son squeezed his eyes closed as tears rolled out.

"Are you two puppies through trying to histe your legs on each other?" Ridge ignored the weakling and walked to one of the front-facing windows and looked out around a curtain for a second time. The snow was falling hard again. "This has gone way beyond Clyde McPeak. I don't have time for him right now, dealing with what's out there in the street."

"I won't be treated like this!" Judd yanked at the knots and shouted into the chair that absorbed most of the sound.

Athena Mae came back into the room with a plate piled high with scrambled eggs and bacon. "Hope this is enough for you."

"Many thanks." Ridge took the plate and returned to the settee. He nudged Judd's foot with the toe of his boot. "You'll be quiet now while I have my breakfast and we'll see what happens next."

CHAPTER 22

In Maggie's mercantile, Zeke picked up the Henry rifle Ridge had leaned behind her door. "I'm going to borrow this."

"No, you're not!" She rushed across the floor and took it from him in a swirl and flurry of skirts. He was so surprised that she had no trouble tearing it from his fingers. "You're not a gun hand. Even with this, you can't go running over there, shooting at Three Fork riders."

"They killed my partners!" Zeke reached out to take it back but hesitated at the look on her face. "I ain't much of a man if I just sit here with you and don't do what's right. It's a man's duty to stand up to wrong!"

"You're one against what, two or three? And how many of their riders spent the night over in that watering hole? Come on. How many of them are in town?"

Some of the steam went out of the cowboy. "Six or eight. I didn't count them."

"And Son. I bet he's somewhere around here. He has that room in the Reynolds Hotel where he holes up."

Zeke bit his lip. "Maybe." He whirled and stomped

across the store to where Runt's coach gun rested on top of a counter. Maggie'd picked it up when he was shot and absently put it above the cigar display.

"This'll even the odds." Breaking the little 12-gauge open to check the loads, he snapped it shut. "I'll owe you for a box of shells."

He rounded the counter to a shelf of ammunition. Thumbing open a box of Winchester buckshot, he plucked out a handful of the red paper shells and slipped them into his pocket.

Maggie hemmed him in with her body. "That scatter-gun won't be enough, either, if they're spread out. Stop and think for a minute. I can't stand the thought of you getting hurt."

"I don't have to think, Mags. Those men over there opened the ball, and with Runt gone, there ain't no law here until someone goes to find the sheriff."

"There is law! Ridge Tisdale's here."

"He's one man, too! And the whole *town's* after him to boot. He can't go sashaying down the street or into the saloon to find those boys and arrest them. He's on the run."

Maggie and Zeke were nose to nose when Jo walked into the room. Hair tousled from sleep, one cheek red from being pressed onto her pillow, she didn't register the tension that surrounded them like a cloud. "Mama, I can't find my magic stone."

Though a dozen other issues took precedence over a little girl's misplaced item, Maggie gave Zeke a pat on his chest and gently took the shotgun from him. She laid

it on a shelf behind her before turning her full attention
to the child's problem. "You sure it isn't under the bed,
or tangled up in the blankets?"

"No, I was looking for it when I went to sleep, but I
was so tired I gave up."

"When did you have it last?"

"Well, it was beside my doll on the table back there,
but then I can't remember. Oh, wait! I took it with me
to the privy. I put it on the seat, against the wall, so I
wouldn't knock it in the hole, or on the floor."

"Well, if you dropped it in the snow, it'll be there
until spring thaw."

"I didn't. I remember just where I put it."

"Get your boots on then; I suspect you'll need to go
outdoors anyway, now that you're awake."

Jo whirled and disappeared into the back. A minute
later, she was in her coat and boots. The door opened
and closed.

"You don't have to go with her?" Zeke had told her
he'd never been around children after he was grown and
was mystified by all they said and got into.

"It's light out, now. She only wants me with her when
it's dark."

Maggie sighed. It seemed so common to sit there
talking about life cycles when two of her friends, men
she'd sat up half the night talking to, were lying cold on
the undertaker's table down the street. She'd felt the
same way when her husband died. One minute he was
there, and an hour later the angels took him away and

the house contained a huge, empty space that would never be filled the same way again.

The pit of her stomach fell when she looked over at the pickle barrel to see one of the men's coffee mugs sitting there, as if he'd come back in from the cold and fill it again. Even the dried, brown drop that ran down the side was somehow so personal she burst into tears.

Covering her face with both hands, she turned from Zeke and wailed. It was the perfect time to give in to her grief, with Jo outside so she wouldn't hear. Despite being so precocious and mouthy, the little girl had a tender heart and would have broken down with her mother, increasing the grief that threatened to take her into the dark depths she'd barely avoided when her husband died.

Unfamiliar with women, Zeke didn't know what to do. He started over to Maggie, but she didn't want him touching her. No amount of arm patting and hugging was going to make any difference in how she felt. Holding him back with the palm of her hand in the air, she continued to cry, leaving Zeke standing there in uncomfortable silence.

Her time was short because Jo wasn't going to take long with her little rear end hanging out in the cold. She might be an extra minute or two while she looked for the madstone, but that was all.

Going around behind the counter, Maggie reached underneath, where she kept a good supply of well-used, ragged towels reserved for cleaning up and wiping down the countertops. She moved a small Smith & Wesson revolver from the top of the pile and put it aside before taking the first rag. She wiped her eyes and blew.

"I'm sorry," Zeke said. "I didn't mean to make you more uncomfortable."

"It wasn't anything you did, and thanks for offering to hug me. I just needed a minute to let it all out."

The back door slammed and Jo rushed in, tears streaming down her face. "It wasn't out there."

Taking a deep breath to regain control, Maggie wiped her nose again and used the thin towel to dry her daughter's eyes. Her voice was again calm and steady. "Don't worry. We'll find it. It can't be far. You were just in the back, and out to the privy."

"It wasn't where I left it."

"You looked good?"

"I did."

"You didn't use man-eyes, did you?" Her question broke the spell and they both giggled.

Zeke frowned back and forth between them. He'd temporarily forgotten his anger toward the other ranch. "Does that have something to do with me?"

"A bit." Maggie used her fingertips on Jo's scalp to tease her ringlets back into shape. "Men can't find anything in a house, even if it's right under their noses. I've seen it time and again when some male customer asks for an item on a shelf, and even after I tell them exactly where it is, they can't find it."

Zeke rested his hat on the back of his head, as if pondering a problem. "When we look like this?"

Mother and daughter again broke into giggles and Jo pointed a tiny finger. "That's what we're talking about."

Men were killed, wounded, and possibly dying, and Zeke found himself in a strange discussion with a little girl. "Look, the next time I shoot a deer, or know someone who's cleaning game, I'll look for another stone for you."

"No, I want that one, because it was such a surprise."

Cold air gusted in from the living quarters. Maggie eyed her daughter. "You didn't latch the back door good."

"I did. I made sure of it."

They all stopped at the sight of two Three Fork riders holding pistols. Zeke grabbed Maggie and threw her to the ground behind the counter. Her hand shot out and yanked Jo down with them at the same time both guns belched flame.

Zeke was no gunslinger, just a working cowboy who carried a pistol for protection, but in that situation, he had no time to draw his weapon. The best thing he could have done was exactly what he did, slinging Maggie down behind the counter as she reached for Jo's hand.

The assassins each fired three or four shots before ducking back out the rear and running. Despite being afraid, Zeke was no coward, and he despised the coward's way of fighting, and he expected nothing more from Barlow men.

They disappeared out back. Protected by the heavy oak counters, he and Maggie were so tangled that by the time he rose, they were gone.

Seeing Runt's shotgun lying on the counter, he

snatched it up and eased out from behind the cover that sheltered the other two. Stock against his shoulder, he crept to the back only to find the door open and two sets of fresh footprints leading away and rounding the building, where they would disappear in the street.

By the time he returned, Doc, Joseph Mayse, and a half dozen other townspeople were gathered around Maggie. Doc knelt in front of the crying little girl. "Jo, are you hurt?"

"No!" the girl wailed, burying her face in Maggie's skirts.

Shaken, Zeke walked around the counter. "Look, guys. Nobody's hurt, and I recognize those two who shot at us. One was a Barlow rider named Turkey Thompson; a few of y'all know who he is. The other's first name is Leon. I'd appreciate it if you'd pass the word for me, and while they're gone, I need to talk with Doc and Mr. Mayse."

Though the townspeople believed in the law, they weren't lawmen, allowing Zeke to herd them out of the way, where they could mill around and discuss the shooting.

When he came back in, he stood there with the shotgun pointed at the ground. "Mr. Mayse, I have a request."

"What's that?"

"I'm going for help." He looked out the window at the group that hadn't yet taken any action. "I need you to take Maggie and Jo down to stay with Nell."

"The owner of the parlor?" The undertaker took half a step back.

"That's right." Zeke met Maggie's eyes, and she nodded and took over.

She took a deep breath to steady her voice. "He's right. I need a safe place and Nell will let us stay there."

Doc absently ran his hands down Jo's head, back, and arms, more a force of habit with patients rather than looking for a bleeding wound. "Why, you can't take this child there!"

"Would you rather we come with you?"

"Well," the undertaker scratched under his hat, "she don't need to be in there with dead men."

"And Runt's unconscious in your office. Doc, would we be safer with you?"

"I can't say, but I have no experience with this kind of thing."

"Nell says she has someone there to help."

"Where's that Ranger? Has Tisdale been back?"

"They're hunting him, too." She waved an arm at the crowd gathering outside. "I've told those people he didn't shoot Runt, but they've all made up their minds. Until the marshal wakes up, I don't have any help from him."

Doc looked sad. "I can't say when Runt will come to, neither."

"Then Mr. Mayse, would you escort us down to Nellie's?"

"I suppose so."

Zeke handed him Runt's shotgun. "Take this with you."

"I've never shot anyone. I just deal with bodies."

"Then you know where to point that thing."

Zeke ducked out the back to get help. There was no telling what those murderers from the other ranch would do.

Mayse put the shotgun on a nearby shelf and walked over to look out the window.

CHAPTER 23

Muffled gunshots drew Ridge to the front window in Nell's parlor. He peeked around a curtain to see indistinct shapes moving in the street. Men on foot and horseback started toward that end of town with a sense of urgency that made the hair on Ridge's neck stand up. There would have been more if the weather was better, but the number was unexpected.

"Lot's going on down there."

He turned back into the room and kicked the sole of Son's boot. "What're you up to out there?"

"Me? I've been here all night, and so has Judd."

Torn, Ridge paced the distance from the parlor to the door and back. The shots might not mean a thing—a few rounds thrown at the sky or a target by men tired of being cooped up inside. Or it could be a couple of men squaring off over some unknown slight or argument. It might not have a thing to do with Son and the Barlow outfit.

It had been him and the two prisoners since he'd finished breakfast. Nell stayed close, but even with the excitement of seeing two of their customers tied up like hogs for the slaughter, the majority of the girls had returned to their rooms to rest after a long night of work.

Nell came back into the parlor with her hat and coat.

Ridge's pacing paused. "Where are you going?"

She wrapped a thick scarf around her neck. "To find out what's going on down there."

"It might be nothing."

"It was something all right, and you know it, big brother. The spacing of those shots meant people are shooting at one another."

"It's no business of yours, and you're liable to get hurt."

"Let's just say I'm naturally curious, especially with those two tied up here in my parlor."

"Somebody'll see you."

"That won't be a treat for a good number of the men in town. They've seen me sitting right there in that very chair Son's laying on when they come in."

"That's not what I meant."

"Ridge, you're the one who's on the run. Not me." She took his arm and led him to the door and leaned in. She whispered, "You're thinking too much. Nobody knows about us, so it won't be any big deal for me to walk myself down to Maggie's for a few things and get a feel for what's going on. The knowledge might help us down the road."

"But you buy from Barlow over there."

"I buy from everywhere. The butcher shop, dough-nuts from W. L. Lane's bakery just right over there, from the Fosters' Goods and Notions, and from Maggie. I spread money around town, and that buys good will."

She gave him a pat on his biceps. "You just stay here out of sight and keep those two pirates company. I'll be back directly."

She slipped out the door smooth as silk, leaving her big brother behind.

Wishing he had the Henry he'd left back in Maggie's, Ridge resisted the urge to pull his Colt and check the loads. He'd taken off so fast after Runt's assassin, he hadn't thought of the Henry rifle he habitually carried but knew good and well the pistol on his hip was loaded and couldn't help himself.

Judd groaned. "Ranger, my knees are killing me."

"Good."

"Good? What do you mean, good?"

"You won't be moving very fast, all stiff and stove-up, if you decide to be stupid, and that's exactly how I want it."

"There's laws against this. You can't just take and tie a man up for no reason."

"How about suspicion of consorting with criminals?"

"There ain't no such law."

"Suspicion of attempted murder, then."

"You're making up those laws and charges."

"Charges. Those are charges, and I'm an agent of the law. You're under arrest, and those cords serve as the shackles I'd use on you if they weren't in my saddlebags."

Son cleared his throat. "I can tell you one thing. When we get loose from these chairs, my boys are gonna track you down and hang you from the highest beam they can find, and then they're gonna burn this place to the ground."

Ridge tamped down his response. There was no need to argue with those two, and he already knew he'd have to take the prisoners with him when he left to stand before a judge.

"You keep talking . . ." He almost used Son's name but couldn't bring himself to speak it. Uttering that moniker would make them seem friendly, or family, and they were neither.

Ridge resumed pacing. He never liked to be cooped up, and with men looking for him, he was twisted up tight. Somehow the house full of women was silent, save for the lonesome ticking of a windup clock counting off the seconds, then minutes and hours of his life.

He was walking a rut in the carpets when the door latch rattled. Gun in hand, he stood just out of sight from the entry hall when Nell slipped inside. She pulled a hat from her head and saw Ridge standing there.

She didn't smile, and he felt a jolt to his stomach. Something was wrong.

Nell took a step forward, and he saw she had his Henry rifle, carrying it muzzle down by the forepiece close to her leg and partially hidden by her skirts. "Thought you might need this."

He replaced the Colt and took the welcome weight from her hand, never taking his eyes off her face. "Thanks, Sis. What'd you find out?"

Grim as a burial, her face was impassive. "There was a shooting in Kingman's livery. Couple of people shot. Mitch Kingman says it was the Three Fork men who got all jumpy and somehow started shooting some locals who were in there. Killed the butcher, too, but some of those I heard talking on the street say it was Oarlock riders who snuck in and ambushed them. I tend to believe Kingman, but when two Oarlock hands went in a few minutes later, they were murdered by Three Fork riders."

"Good God."

"That's not the worst. War's broke out everywhere. Some of Son's hands busted in through the back of Maggie's store, shooting. That's what we heard just before I left."

"At whom?" Ridge stiffened. "Who were they shooting at in the store?"

"They were just throwing lead, maybe at Zeke Frazier, who was there. He grabbed Maggie and Jo and dropped down behind a counter, and they weren't hurt at all."

"You sure?"

"That's what I heard, both girls are all right and Zeke drove 'em back. Not long afterward, somebody came around and left word if she didn't close up and get out of town, they'd come after Jo next."

He felt the blood run from his face and his body grow cold and still. An old, familiar feeling rose up and drew a numb cloak over him, a sense of no longer caring about anything but the fury burning in his gut.

He thought about Maggie trying to run a business on her own.

He thought of little Jo and imagined the horrified look on her face when men with guns were shooting at the little girl and her mother.

He thought of Barlow trying to take everything from a widow woman.

He imagined the men walking into Nell's house and place of business to start shooting because Ridge might be hiding there, and the snake uncoiled in his soul.

Hiding.

Ridge had never dodged trouble in his life, and here for the past few hours he was huddled up like a rabbit in a thicket. Something Son said earlier stuck in his mind. "Nell, go into the other room."

"Why?"

"I have something to do in here."

Both of the trussed-up men tried to look over their shoulders.

Nell put herself between them. "Ridge, this is my place of business, and I live here, too. I stretched my neck out a long ways last night and this morning, but I don't like that look on your face. I saw it more than once when we were younger, and people got hurt every time."

He moved over to the ocher settee and sat down. Jacking the lever on his rifle, he shucked out fifteen rounds that bounced on the seat's tight material. Satisfied the 45-70 hadn't been meddled with, he reloaded the rifle and seated the hammer back to safety with his thumb.

He reached under the coat he still wore and drew the .44 from his holster. As he did, she saw a sheathed bowie knife she'd missed as they talked that evening. He turned the oiled cylinder of his Colt and, satisfied by the oily clicks, replaced it.

"Don't hurt us," Son said.

"Shut up, Geologist." It was the best name he could come up with.

"What're you gonna do?" Judd asked. The fear in his voice made it crack.

"I was gonna cut your damned throats, but Nell talked me out of it. You two can thank her for that later, if you're able. But I want to thank you for an idea you gave me."

He took two doilies from a sideboard and rolled them up. A hat tree beside the door was draped with scarves the women tied over their hair when they went out. He plucked two off the rack and saw an empty shoulder holster someone had likely left after a visit to the parlor.

He straddled Judd from behind, the hardest of the two to bluff. "Open your mouth."

"No."

He punched the man hard in the kidney and he gasped in pain. Before he could recover, Ridge reached around to stuff the doily into the man's mouth and held it there with a scarf tied tight around his head. He turned to Son, who'd watched the entire thing.

"Open up."

Not wanting to get the same rough treatment, the younger Barlow opened his mouth. Ridge gagged him the same way.

He returned to the hat tree and lifted the shoulder rig off the hook. Slipping it on, he adjusted the fit by tugging at a system of leather straps and buckles. Once satisfied with the way it hung, he tucked his Colt into the holster on the left side of his chest and flexed his shoulders to see how it rode.

Satisfied, he dropped Son's pistol into the empty holster on his hip and pulled the big sheepskin collar up around his neck and rested the Henry in the crook of his left arm. He stood behind the men again for a long moment.

"Nell, I want you to leave these two here until I get back. Rap 'em in the back of the head with something hard if they start acting up."

She nodded and drew a deep breath. "Where are you going?"

"To kill some people and burn everything Barlow owns down to the ground."

"Isn't there another way to fight him?"

"Probably, but none I intend to entertain."

"You're a lawman. You wear a badge."

"They tried to turn this into a lawless town. Looked to murder me and shot at a woman and child. What I'm about to do is the only thing they understand."

A rumble from outside startled them both. Nell's breath caught, and she watched Ridge to see his reaction. He glanced toward the ceiling as if expecting it to fall in. The sound came again, and light flickered in the windows.

"Thunder and lightning in a snowstorm." Wondering if it was some kind of sign, Ridge checked the bindings on his captives. "I've heard of this before. It only happens when it's snowing really hard. But the old folks used to say when they heard thunder snow, the weather was about to warm up some."

A couple of the girls came into the room, worried looks on their faces. Nell waved a hand. "It's all right. Just thunder and lightning."

"In a snowstorm?" Gertrude. "I never heard of such a thing."

Sam appeared in the arched opening leading to the back. He wore a pair of striped trousers held up with leather suspenders. "I have."

A soft knock interrupted their conversation. Nell threw a fearful glance at the door. "It's a little early for customers on a day like this."

Sam reached into the pocket of his voluminous pants and produced a five-shot .32 Colt that almost disappeared in his big hand. He stepped around the cased opening as Ridge once again took up a position where he could see from the parlor, resting one hand on the Colt in his borrowed shoulder holster.

Composing herself, Nell took a deep breath, cracked the door, and put her eye to the opening. "Oh!" She immediately backed up, swinging it open to allow Maggie and Jo to rush inside.

Holding her mother's hand, the little girl came in first and stopped in wonder, gaping at the dark draperies and rich carpets. "Why, I ain't never seen anything so pretty!"

Maggie turned back to someone still outside. "Thank you, Mr. Mayse. We'll be safe now."

Nell closed the door behind them, and Maggie removed the scarf from her head. "Zeke sent us here."

She visibly flinched when she saw the big Seminole

guard and pressed her chest for a moment before composing herself.

Ridge stepped out and smiled down at Jo. "You came to the right place."

Surprising Ridge, Maggie threw herself into his arms. "You're all right."

He hugged her back until Maggie stepped back with an embarrassed look on her face.

Jo looked Sam up and down. "That's a darned big Indian."

Instead of scolding her, Maggie put her hand over Jo's mouth and turned to the madam. "Nell, you said if we needed anything . . . I don't know . . . this is the only place I knew to come to."

Jo removed her hand and caught Sam's attention. "Can we hire you?"

"What makes you think I'm for hire?"

"Because you look like you just got up, so that means you don't have a job, and I need someone to find my madstone. I left it in the privy and now we can't find it."

Maggie colored, and this time she pulled Jo tight against her leg and put her hand on the little girl's mouth hard enough to smother her. "Please forgive my daughter. She doesn't know how to control her mouth."

Sam's grin widened, revealing a mouthful of big teeth. "Sounds like what I deal with around here every day."

CHAPTER 24

After sending Maggie and Jo down the street with the undertaker, who said he would escort the pair down to Nellie's Place, Zeke slipped through the drifted alleys until he came to the Red River livery. There were too many Three Fork men in town and he was outnumbered. He had to find help, and the only men he could count on were a handful of friends and the brand riders back at the Oarlock ranch.

Zeke had never been a fighter, had spent most of his life forcing himself to stand up and be a man when necessary. With the death of his friends, he was alone and had no strategy to survive other than to get some help.

His horse was in the rear stall, and after making sure there were no Three Fork riders inside, he saddled up. As he tightened the cinch, Zeke fully expected a gang of men to come boiling into the barn with guns drawn. Finally ready and still alive despite the events unfolding in his mind, he lit out of town.

The snowstorm flickered with lightning, worrying the young cowboy even more. Thunder followed, and he threw a look over his shoulder as if some giant beast was bearing down on him with growls of hunger. He was still shook after the attempted murder in Maggie's store and was afraid the fear that burned in his stomach would never go out.

He was afraid for Maggie, a gal who stayed on his mind pretty much all the time. She was there in the spring, when he and the boys were rounding up stock. Her smile popped up when he was tending to his horse, riding alone, or in the evenings, when the boys were settling in for the night and he stretched out on his bunk and closed his eyes.

Zeke knew he wasn't her only potential suitor in Blackjack. From the moment she arrived, a ripple went through the community of unmarried men. For several weeks, she was the primary source of discussion in the saloon and around campfires, until she made it known she had no interest in finding a husband to replace the one she lost.

His horse pushed through the soft snow without much effort, though it came up to its knees. More than one mounted rider had come this way, so the snow wasn't completely shutting down travel. He pulled his coat up tight, snugged the scarf around his neck, and tugged his hat low.

Had it not been so cold and snowing hard, he would have convinced Maggie to bring Jo and come with him to Mr. Hutchins's spread. Taking her out of town was the best thing, but he was afraid something would happen in the storm, especially with Jo, and that maybe they'd stray off the road, and freeze to death when sundown came.

He wasn't much at finding his way alone, usually had a partner to ride with him whenever they were rounding up cattle. Zeke once got lost on the western edge of the Oarlock spread and spent a chilly night without a fire, worrying about Comanches and rattlers and afraid he'd strike out the next morning and wind up out on the Llano Estacado, lost forever in a sea of grass.

Lucky for him, despite the heavy storm, he found his way back to the ranch, covered in a soft, white blanket that hid all the imperfections in the land. Smoke rose from three chimneys, two from the big house and one from the bunkhouse.

He rode past a corral with half a dozen mounts stomping in the snow. They were still warm from riding, and someone had combed their coats. A trail of footsteps led to the barn, and no doubt the hands who'd been out checking the stock were putting all the tack away.

Tying his mount to a post in front of the sprawling ranch house, he hurried across the porch and inside, not bothering to knock. Insulated by thick logs that were the original cabin, the interior was warm and inviting. He pushed inside to find Mr. Drake Hutchins seated at a great table pulled up close to the living room's crackling fireplace.

The grizzled rancher looked up from a ledger open in front of him and squinted at the snow-covered figure. "Zeke? You forget how to enter a house?"

The foreman took off his hat and slapped it against his leg, scattering melting snow across the split-pine floorboards. A mustached, gray-haired man came from the kitchen, wiping his hands on a damp towel. Wes Callahan was Drake's right hand.

Drake's silent partner on the Oarlock ranch adjusted one suspender. They'd ridden together since they were boys, but Wes preferred to let Drake take the lead on all matters. That left him to do whatever he wanted, whenever the mood struck.

Wes sometimes disappeared for weeks at a time, only to return with more money than he left with and interesting stories to tell the boys in the bunkhouse.

Wes never went more than ten feet without a pistol on his belt and, true to form, despite the time of day and being inside the house buttoned up by a snowstorm, one was on his hip in a cross-draw holster. "Good to see y'all finally made it." He looked past Zeke, expecting the rest of the boys to be behind him.

"They ain't with me." Zeke crossed the wide room and stopped in front of Mr. Hutchins. "Bad news, Mr. Hutchins. Mahan and Monty are dead. Killed by Three Fork riders. It's come to war, Boss."

Drake Hutchins had lived through hard times most of his life. He'd survived the War of Northern Aggression, fought Comanches at the same time he and Wes built the ranch and herd, and had killed rustlers and outlaws until they learned not to mess with the pair of men who preferred to be left alone. His most recent conflict with Barlow was just one more challenge to overcome.

Setting his jaw, Drake laid down his pencil as Wes joined them. "Slow down and tell me, Son."

Hat in hand and with the two battle-hardened old

men listening, Zeke shifted from foot to foot, dripping water on the floor and outlining everything that had happened in town since he and the boys were caught there by the storm the day before. Hutchins listened without interrupting and Wes pulled up a chair to sit nearby.

When Zeke was finished, Hutchins leaned back. "Those were good boys. We'll bring 'em back here to the ranch for a proper burial. Now, tell me about this Texas Ranger. You say he's on the run for shooting Runt in the back?"

"Yes, sir. Runt's still out, but the Ranger didn't do it. Maggie says she was right there and saw it all, but Judd and that turkey-neck sidekick of his keeps insisting he did it. Most of the town's starting to believe them. The whole thing's a mess, with fingers pointing every which way."

Wes rested an elbow on the table and pulled at his mustache, which grew down both sides of his mouth all the way to his jawline. "Maggie's all right, though?"

"Far as I know. I asked Mr. Mayse to escort her to someplace safe." Zeke paused to lick his lips. "She's at Nellie's Place."

"You had an *undertaker* walk her down to the *cathouse*?" Wes spoke more to himself than Zeke, emphasizing the words.

"She'd been talking to Nellie; you know, the woman who owns the parlor. She'll be hiding out there."

Wes shook his head. "She'll be fine with that big Seminole half-breed there. He's much of a man."

"As long as she and that little bearcat she feeds is all

right, it don't matter where they are." Hutchins watched the door, as if expecting someone else to come bursting in. "Wes, it looks like everything's come to a head."

"I've been expecting it."

"How many men do we have here?"

Wes thought a moment. "Twenty. With six out at the far line shacks, but it'll take a while for somebody to bust through the snow out that way and get 'em, if we need to call 'em in."

"We'll take all but two that's here, then. Leave the others out there. We built this place to stand off Comanches. Two good men with rifles can hole up in here and do some damage, if need be."

"Barlow comes in here with a gang, the first thing he'll do is fire the barn and the bunkhouse," Zeke said.

"They can be rebuilt, but the fight won't be way out here. It'll be in town."

"You don't know that." Wes stood and walked to the big front window. "I'm glad we left those big shutters in place. We might need 'em, because I have a hunch we'll be fighting in both places."

Hutchins stood and went to a gun case built into the wall on the right side of the rock fireplace. "Zeke, go out to the bunkhouse and get the boys."

The young man whirled and was gone in a heartbeat.

Drake Hutchins lifted his gun belt from a peg on the wall and strapped it on. Wes went into another room and came back armed to the teeth with two more pistols scattered on his body, along with a sheath knife.

Both men selected Henry rifles from the rack. Each of the weapons were loaded, but Wes checked the loads in his rifle by jacking the lever to see brass in the chamber, a habit he'd carried all of his adult life. "We handling this the way I've been wanting?"

"Not exactly."

Their hats were on the wall beside the front door. Wes set his and picked up a heavy coat. "What do you mean?"

"We ain't going straight to town. We're going to the Barlow ranch to cut the head off that snake; then we'll see what needs doing in Blackjack."

"It's about time," Wes said as Hutchins got ready for the cold, and the war.

CHAPTER 25

Though the sun was up, it was hard to tell inside Nellie's Place. Dark gray clouds absorbed the rays that couldn't penetrate the cover. In six months, it would be so hot the residents of Blackjack could barely breathe, but right then it was dangerously cold.

Since Barlow wanted to run others out of business, Ridge decided to start the dance with the mercantile across the street. When Son popped off and said he'd burn Nellie's Place to the ground if he got loose, Ridge took the idea for his own.

Ridge Tisdale was done with almost everything about Blackjack. Tamping down the hot coals burning in his gut, he was going to take the fight to them.

In awe of the strange world around her, Maggie stood rooted to the floor in the entryway. She put a hand on his arm to hold him still. "I'm glad you're all right, but none of this is your fight."

"The badge on my shirt makes it so." He reached for the door latch to let himself out. "I don't take to people blaming me for something I didn't do. This was my fight, too, from the moment they tried to put the blame for Runt's shooting on my shoulders."

Nell lit a cigarette, inhaled a lungful of smoke, and raised one eyebrow. "It doesn't do any good to talk to this hardheaded broomtail. I learned that years ago."

Maggie's face showed her surprise. "You know each other?"

"Let's just say we're related." Ridge frowned at Nell.

Jo grinned. "Y'all married?"

Ridge tried not to look at Maggie, but she raised a hand as if to touch him. "No."

Nell laughed. "He's my big, ol' hardheaded brother."

Buttoned up against the cold, Ridge jerked his head toward the two tied up in the parlor and frowned. Nell shut up and he put a hand on the top of Jo's head. "You'll be just fine here. Sam—"

"Don't need no instructions." The big Seminole looked down at Jo. "I'll just get my shoes and a little more gun, though I doubt anyone's gonna come in here anyway. These two fine ladies are in good hands."

As the adults talked, Jo stepped around to the parlor and stopped. "Hey! Is that Son and Judd all tied up like pigs there?"

Maggie hurried forward and pulled her daughter back. She frowned at Ridge and Sam. "I don't know why they're like that, but it's none of our business, missy. You stay back from them."

Nell took the little girl's hand. "How about we go get something to eat? We have a lady here named Athena Mae who knows how to fry delicious eggs."

"I don't like 'em fried. Mama usually leaves them in

the pan till they're crispy as ashes. Can Miss Athena scramble them instead?"

"Jo, you'll take what you get." Maggie's face reddened.

"She scrambles eggs like nobody's business," Nell said. "You two come with me."

His badge now in plain view, Ridge stepped out on the porch. A passing horseman glanced up at his appearance and then ducked his head again, continuing on. Just another customer leaving the ladies. Yellow light glowed behind the windows of Barlow and Son Mercantile, and despite the sweat running down the inside, Earl was clear in there, moving around.

It was at that unfortunate moment that three cowhands rode up and dismounted in front of the store. They pushed through the entrance and disappeared inside. Had he not been mad, Ridge might have changed his mind about the first strike against Barlow, but he was on the prod and didn't intend to wait for a lynch mob to go looking for him. He'd learned a long time ago to take the fight to those who deserved or started it.

He stalked across the street and went straight to the mercantile's door. Opening it, he stepped inside to find the three were Barlow men. One was standing across the counter from Earl. "I'll need a box of shells and a couple of cigars."

"Put it on your tab, Leon?"

"Sure, but when we shoot that Ranger like a mule gone lame, I bet he'll clear my account, and the boys here, too."

"You know where he is?" Not paying any attention to the new customer, Earl turned to take a box of .44s off the shelf.

One of the other hands the size of a bull laughed. "Nope, but we've split up. We're starting at this end of town with some of the other boys, and we'll meet the other searchers coming from the other direction. Maybe catch that Ranger in a pinch. Judd wants him bad."

The third stocky cowboy crossed his arms and leaned back against a pickle barrel. "I hope we all find him in the saloon. We'll kill him there and have whiskey right at hand to celebrate."

Ridge had heard enough. "Earl."

The salesman looked up, and his eyes widened at the sight of the badge. "You're back." The man's tone washed over the other three, who weren't sure what to do.

The Henry rifle laying in the crook of Ridge's left arm, he unbuttoned the top of his coat. "If I was you, I'd right now slip out the back door of this place and get gone."

The trio of gun hands finally realized who the stranger was. Leon seemed not to know what to do with the cigars in his hand. He started to slip them into his shirt pocket and then looked at the counter as if wondering whether it was better to lay them down instead.

"You're that Ranger." The bull, just beyond Leon, shifted his position, readying himself to draw the big Colt on his right hip.

Noticing his partner shift to the side, Leon grinned. "You can't kill all of us."

With the Henry's muzzle pointing at the wall to his left, Ridge took stock of where they stood. "I don't intend to. I'll just shoot that big tub of lard who has his hand on his pistol, then I'll kill *you, Leon*. You, the one who's still standing, can decide what to do after that."

Hearing his name spoken by the Ranger, Leon swallowed.

The third man's eyes widened. He had an unusually large nose and oversize ears to match.

With the three of them facing Ridge, they had the advantage of numbers, but when he started aiming at his intended targets, the whole situation changed.

The declaration of what was about to happen took the starch out of Bull, who suddenly seemed indecisive and looked back and forth between Leon and Ridge. "I don't . . . I'm not a gun hand—"

"You were here all the time they were looking for you." Earl decided to be the bearer of all news. "This is the guy y'all were asking about. I didn't know who he was at the time, but he spent the night in the back room with—"

"You need to be quiet, Earl." Ridge spoke soft and low, without taking his eyes off the other three. "A man don't need to tell all he knows, and like I said, get gone."

"Barlow wants to see you swinging." Seeming to recover, Leon puffed out his chest with the confidence of a man who'd rolled over others all his life. "We looked this town over and you were in here all snug and warm, with who, Earl?"

Ridge's attention switched to the salesman, who also

moved. Only one of his hands rested on the counter. His stomach sank at what was about to happen. "Don't."

Leon took half a step toward Ridge, who thumb-cocked the rifle's hammer and shifted the muzzle. "You're number one now, hoss."

Bull's hand closed on the butt of his Colt. When that man's hand touched his pistol, the dance had already started. They were watching the rifle, and when Ridge took his hand off and slid it high inside his coat, they all relaxed. Without hesitation, Ridge drew the Colt from the shoulder holster.

Stunned by what had just happened, they were a heartbeat behind. He raised the pistol and seemed to take his time pointing it at Bull. Ridge learned years ago that most men who fancied themselves a fast draw depended on speed instead of accuracy. They often missed the first shot, bringing the pistol to bear on the second as the startled man they faced hurried his movements.

Bull's thick shoulder rose in preparation to draw.

Well ahead of the shocked men, Ridge squeezed the trigger as his dad taught him. The .44 slug took the man just above the diaphragm. The blast was like a physical slap that dropped the outlaw rider's pistol before he cleared the holster. Knees suddenly weak, he took one step back, rocked for a moment, and collapsed, making the floor vibrate.

It didn't take but an eyeblink for Ridge to thumb-cock the Colt and fire again, this time punching a large hole in Leon's chest. He stumbled sideways and into Earl's line of fire. The counterman raised a pistol and squeezed off a round that hit Leon in the side instead of his intended target.

The man's knees folded and he dropped onto a crate of wrinkled potatoes. The slat-side box snapped, and the vegetables rolled across the floor like marbles. Shooting as if he were firing at tin cans on a log, Ridge fired twice more. One of the slugs punched through the button on Earl's shirt pocket and he went down out of sight.

Ridge didn't remember cocking the .44 again, but he swung the pistol to line up with the third man with the large nose, who stood there with both hands held up, palm out.

"Don't shoot me, Ranger!" His voice cracked with fear. "I'm just a hired hand."

"You're running with murderers, and you wear that iron awful low on your leg."

"I was, and I do. You saw I didn't puff up at you like the others. I just hired on to cowboy for Barlow, and this has all gotten out of hand. I wear my gun like this because these men are a pack of wolves and it's the only way to hold my own with 'em."

The man's whole body quivered with fear that wasn't contrived. He was truly terrified that death was standing there with a smoking Colt aiming directly at him.

"Mister, if you'll let me go, I'll ride off out of here right now and you'll never see me again."

"Where's your horse?"

"Over in the Red River livery."

Ridge noted the man's watery eyes and pointed with

the pistol. "You leave this place and Barlow behind you. If I see your face again, I'll blow it off."

Big Nose wiped his mouth. "I will. Don't you worry. I'm gone."

"Then do it." Ridge stepped to the side, behind a low table full of cans. Without another glance around him, Big Nose passed, turning his body as if trying to slip between two close-set trees. He opened the door and quickstepped it down the icy boardwalk toward the saloon.

Sliding the Colt back into the shoulder holster, Ridge checked the bodies leaking blood onto the floorboards. Both of the Barlow riders were dead, as was Earl, who lay sprawled behind the counter with a smoking pistol lying on his chest.

It wouldn't be long before someone came to check on the gunshots. He looked around at the shelves loaded with merchandise purchased with Barlow money. The man was doing everything he could to run Maggie out of business, and all the stores on those shelves would put her on easy street if she had them to sell.

Ridge blew out three of the four lamps Earl lit to chase out the early morning gloom and locked the front doors. Against his better judgment, he couldn't burn the bodies. That kind of thing wasn't in him. One at a time, he grabbed a handful of collar and drug the two lighter corpses out the back and dropped them in the snow.

Bull was bigger and heavier, and it took longer than he planned, and by the time he was back inside, several men were gathered at the front door, peering into the dim interior. More shouts rose from the street and the sound of hooves came to him. Looking in both directions, Ridge thought about disappearing right then, but there was still something he had to do.

Finding themselves locked out, even more curious townspeople cupped their hands against the glass to peer inside the dark store.

Cocking his hat to hide his face, Ridge picked up the remaining oil lamp, stepped out from behind cover, and threw it toward the front. The glass exploded on the floor, flame boiling up. The men recoiled, shouting. The air reeked of coal oil as he pitched unlit lamps into different parts of the store.

Blue flames rushed across the floor, and in seconds, the interior was an inferno. He darted out the back door and ran straight into two cowboys studying the bodies lying in the snow. They jumped back in surprise.

Capitalizing on their shock, he slammed a fist into one man's chin, and he stiffened like a board and toppled to the side. The other grappled for a gun somewhere under his coat, and Ridge butt-stroked him in the face with the Henry's stock. It was a sharp, hard blow and the man staggered away, clutching at his bleeding head.

Ridge rushed forward and grabbed his attacker, throwing the stunned man's arm over his shoulders. He half-carried the stranger into the vacant lot and raised an arm. "Help! We need somebody to help us here!"

Men rushing to join those in front of the store veered off at his shout, pointing at the pair. Glass broke as someone kicked in the mercantile's front door. With the back door standing open, the influx of oxygen fanned the flames that roared out the opening. People shouted in alarm as most of the would-be good Samaritans recoiled.

Carrying the rifle loose in his left hand, Ridge waved it to catch their attention. "I have a hurt man here!"

They were halfway across the lot when the newcomers met them. Several reached out to help, and Ridge let them take the barely conscious man on their shoulders. "Get him to the doctor! He's hurt bad!"

"We have him." The injured man's knees went out from under him, and they took his entire weight. With nothing more than a glance, they hurried down the street with his toes dragging furrows in the snow.

Ridge judged the wide lots between the burning building and the closest other structures. Everything in town was covered with snow that would insulate them from sparks. It was the perfect time to selectively burn down everything Barlow had built.

Ridge took his badge off once again and headed straight for the Red River Saloon.

CHAPTER 26

Bessie Waggoner had just gotten to sleep after her night's work when a commotion in the parlor pulled her back to consciousness. Voices came and went, something not uncommon in such a public place.

She dozed again for a short period of time before louder men irritated her enough to get up. It was too early for customers, unless some rich traveler came in with a handful of cash and entertainment on his mind. Bessie hoped he was there for one of the other girls; the little dark-haired woman was inherently lazy and wanted to sleep.

Cracking her door, she saw Ivy Ann Shears heading back to her own room. The skinny girl with large, dark eyes was Bessie's age and quite popular with their clients. She was in a tight white camisole and baggy bloomers yellowed with age. "What's going on out there?"

"Some kind of trouble I don't know about. Nell and

some stranger have Judd and Son all tied up in the parlor."

"Tied up?" She grinned. "In the parlor? I knew Son had a wild streak."

In the narrow hall, Ivy Ann leaned on the plank wall and rested one foot against her opposite knee. "I'd think you know more about Judd."

Bessie felt a flutter in her stomach. "He likes to jingle his money at me pretty regular all right, but Son's my man."

"That *boy*?" Ivy snickered. "He spent a while with me a couple of months ago when you had your time, and what he mostly wanted to do was talk about his collections and what he was going to do when he owned Blackjack."

Bessie tried not to look annoyed. Son came to her often, funded by his daddy's money, but after they finished their *rasslin' match*, as Bessie liked to call the act, the conversation often drifted to books he'd read, or his scientific interests. They talked of different bird nests, those on the ground and in the trees, or under the eaves of houses and buildings, of colorful rocks that could be used to make jewelry, and his collection of small animal and reptile skulls and skeletons.

She enjoyed it when he paid for hours of her time, giving the madam downstairs enough money for the entire night and sleeping with her head on his shoulder till the morning. Son wasn't like the rest of the cowboys who came to lay on top of her, grunt, then leave. He had a side most grown men never showed, and it was attractive to her.

Bessie wet her thin lips, thinking. "Why does that feller have 'em tied up in there?"

Ivy shrugged. "One of the girls says he's a Texas Ranger and Nell knows him. They got crossways over something, and I guess him and Judd are under arrest."

"What's Nell gonna do about it?"

"Can't say."

"Where's Sam? He might have something to say about this."

Seminole Sam was a good friend to the girls, and Bessie thought he had something special for her. If there was wrongdoing, he'd straighten things out pretty quick.

Ivy shrugged again and chewed a fingernail, standing there on one leg as if it was the most natural thing in the world. "Sam was in there just a few minutes ago, talking to him like they was old buddies."

That news was concerning. Now the man Bessie considered her beau was tied up like a pig in the parlor, along with one of his friends who worked for him and his daddy, and the parlor's fighting man wasn't doing his job.

Something had to be done, in her opinion, but she was caught between a rock and a hard place. Maybe she could talk to their housemaid. She'd know more, for people tended to forget she was around and talked freely in front of her. "Where's Jenny, then?"

"She's in her bunk. Came down with something last evening and spent all night puking up her guts."

"That's just like her when I need that woman." Bessie pouted. In her opinion, she was the star of the bordello and felt the rest of those living under Nell's roof should kowtow to her every whim. "I hope she ain't got herself pregnant making a little extra money, 'cause if she is, Nell's gonna have to hire us another maid. I ain't washing these sheets every day when I'm not working just to mess 'em up that night."

"You know she won't do that." Ivy found a new hangnail to chew. "None of this has anything to do with me. I'm going to bed."

She padded off, leaving Bessie leaning on her doorframe, thinking some more.

She wanted to be out of the business, and with Son sniffing around more and more, she might have a way out, especially if he owed her for something.

Bessie paced the bare floorboards in her small room in Nellie's Place. She pulled at her clothes, a nervous habit she'd had since childhood. There wasn't a lot to pull on with what the bordello's girls called *brothel gowns*, which reached down to their ankles. The thin, white material was the unofficial loose-fitting uniform of prostitutes across the West.

Most mornings, the girls wandered around the house in their gowns or less, disinclined to put on much more since they had no reason to go outside. Coming to a decision, Bessie picked up a pair of scissors from their place beside the comb and mirror that rested on a small table in her room. Glancing up and down the narrow hallway, she stepped out and walked barefoot down to the parlor.

As Ivy said, two men were trussed like Christmas turkeys and kneeling awkwardly into two padded chairs. No one else was there, but she heard Nell talking to another woman in the dining room. A child's voice interrupted them from time to time, and she cocked her head to listen.

Their words were indistinct, as if they were keeping them low so no one else would hear. It didn't matter what they were talking about. As long as they stayed in there, Bessie could free her beau.

She almost danced across the parlor and whispered, "Son."

He turned his head and spoke softly. "Bessie?"

"It's me. Be still. I'm gonna get you free, but if I do, you're gonna make it up and take me out of here."

"It's a deal!"

She grabbed one of a spiderweb of familiar cords and cut it, taking the pressure off a loop around Son's neck. He sighed in relief.

"Me next," Judd whispered.

"Hush, you two." She worked one of the scissor points under the knot binding Son's wrists and squeezed over and over, the blades chewing through the thick material. After what seemed like an eternity to her, the fibers finally separated, and she went to work on Judd.

As she did, Son stood and nearly fell. Throwing a frightened look toward the voices in the dining room, he sat on the edge of the chair he'd been lying on for so long and worked at the muscles in his legs. Bessie soon freed Judd and stepped back.

Having stronger legs from work and riding, Judd rose and looked around the room. "I don't see our guns."

"We'll get some more from Dad's store." Son stood. "Let's get out of here before that Ranger gets back."

Bessie threw her arms around him and whispered in his ear, "Remember what you promised."

"Now?"

"No, when we can leave."

Son watched Judd head for the door and pushed her away. "We'll talk about this later."

She followed, holding his arm. The scissors in her hand fell, clattering on the only piece of oak floor that wasn't covered by a rug. She snatched them up and flew back up the stairs as Judd and Son fled the building.

Soft gunshots came to Bessie's ears as she darted back into her room and she almost panicked, thinking that someone had opened up on the two escaping prisoners. She dressed for the first time in months, thinking about what her life with Son would be like in that big ranch house he'd told her about.

A soft tap at her door made her heart soar. It was one of the boys, come back to get her. She opened it up and her face fell. It was Ivy again.

"Did you hear what all's going on around here?" She stopped. "Where are you going?"

"What makes you think I'm going anywhere?"

"You haven't put clothes on to go outside for a month. The rest of the girls are walking around in their gowns and unmentionables and you're in a shirt and britches. Thinking of riding somewhere in those shoes?"

Frowning, Bessie wouldn't look her in the eye. "It's cold in here. I figured clothes were better than my drawers."

"I thought you were going to bed."

"You were thinking about me while you were getting dressed. You aren't telling the truth, girl."

"I tried to sleep, but once I got woke up with all that going on outside, I got up."

"Ummm. Humm." Ivy's voice was so low, Bessie could barely hear, but it carried a definite threat. "Girl, I'm about to drag you outside by the hair of the head if you don't tell me what's going on. Should I pack up to leave, too?"

Bessie's chin quivered. "What makes you think I know anything?"

"Because I know you, and sometimes you're a little liar to get what you want." Ivy sat on the edge of the unmade bed.

"I'm leaving, that's all."

"Tell me the truth or I'm gonna tell Nell you're leaving."

Drawing a deep, shuddering breath, Bessie took the makings out of a side drawer and built a cigarette, thinking all the while. Ivy watched as she rolled it, licked the edges, and lit the malformed little smoke.

Bessie drew on her cigarette and blew the smoke through her nostrils. "Judd and Son are gonna take me out of here."

Ivy stifled a laugh. "Both of them?"

"Yeah, I have the two of 'em on a string and they dance whenever I pull it."

"They dance as long as their money holds out, dearie. Where are you and those two no'counts going?"

"Wherever Son takes me. He has the money, and one or both of 'em's gonna marry me and we're leaving."

"In this deep snow all of a sudden?"

"Now's just as good as any."

Ivy snorted in disgust. "Girl, if you think either one of 'em is coming back here again, you're crazy."

She looked up, startled. "Well, why not?"

Ivy pointed at her. "There's a lot going on outside these walls you ain't privy to. Son and Judd are mixed up in something that's taken you completely off their plates. That's why they were all wrapped up here earlier."

"Son said he'd be back when it was safe." Bessie's voice was suddenly soft and full of doubt. "I bet Judd's enough of a man to come get me."

"Hon, they always say they're coming back for us, but they never do." Seeing the hurt, sad look in Bessie's eyes, Ivy drew a deep breath. "You couldn't pick just one to hang a rope on. Where'd they go, then?"

"I don't know. Both of them at different times said for me to be ready. I'm gonna live with them in that big house Son tells me about, and I'll be married to a cattle baron or his top hand. Either way, it'll be heaven."

Ivy took the cigarette from her fingers and inhaled. "Hell, most likely just a different version of the one we live in here."

CHAPTER 27

The confusion created by the fire that was quickly engulfing Barlow and Son Mercantile was the perfect escape plan. Though the snow was still falling, it had lessened somewhat but not enough that Ridge didn't duck his head, as if preventing it from getting into his eyes. Voices shouted in alarm as a dozen men flowed from the Red River Saloon to join twice as many converging on the Barlow and Son Mercantile building.

He ducked past the Sagebrush Corral, separating the Red River Saloon from the adjacent building. The horses that stamped down the snow were gone, and he paused to open the gate leading into the street. The opposite gate at the far end stood open to the barn. Ridge slipped inside the livery and was relieved to see he was the only one there.

Horses in stalls on each side hung their heads into the hall and snorted at the stranger. Breathing deep of the warm air scented with hay and horse manure, he made his way to the far end and peeked out through the wide double doors.

Two buildings out back and a hundred yards away

were dark and apparently unoccupied. He couldn't tell if they were houses or more future commercial structures. No tracks led to them, and the lack of smoke rising from their stovepipes told him there wouldn't be anyone coming from that direction.

"Can I help you?"

The gruff voice coming from behind almost made him jump. Ridge turned slowly, hoping there wasn't a gun pointed at his middle. The stableman with long gray hair scratched his beard. "You have a mount here? I don't remember you."

Ridge leveled the Henry. "Hands up."

The man's expression told him there wouldn't be trouble from that quarter. "Don't shoot me. Hey, you're the man they're all looking for."

"Maybe." He jerked his head. "Come this way."

The man's face turned stubborn as a mule. "No."

"Look, you're going with me out to one of those buildings back there and you'll be just fine. I have things to do here you won't like."

"No, I said." The stableman crossed his arms like a petulant child. "And you can't make me do a damned thing."

Ridge saw movement behind him and shifted his aim. "Hey!"

Before he could fathom what was happening, the man flew forward, accompanied by the crack of an axe handle against the back of his head.

"The man said come there." Seminole Sam tapped the handle against his big palm. "Shoulda listened."

"Thanks." Relieved that he didn't have to shoot

someone who might not have been working for Barlow, Ridge lowered the rifle's muzzle.

"You won't thank me when you hear that them two you left back at Nellie's are gone."

"How the hell did that happen? Those knots were tight."

"One of her girls is sweet on Son. Cut 'em loose while I was getting my shoes and coat. They skinned out of there like a couple of rabbits."

"They're going to raise a holler before long."

"They already did." Sam leaned the axe handle against a stall. "Barlow's mercantile's on fire, and they told the Three Fork men who were there you had 'em hogtied inside. They quit fighting the fire and headed here to the saloon to tell the rest. I saw two ride out of town toward Barlow's ranch. They'll have two dozen riders here looking for you before long."

Ridge rubbed his chin, thinking. "We need to get rid of this guy and turn out the stock."

Sam grinned, his dark Seminole eyes twinkling. "You the one set that fire to burn down Barlow's store."

"Yep. With all this snow, it'll burn down without spreading to the rest of the town."

"And you intend to do it here, too."

"You read my mind. Before I'm done, everything Barlow owns will be ashes when he gets here."

"Then what?"

"I'm gonna take him in, if he'll have it."

"And if he don't?"

"That undertaker here in town's gonna be pretty busy."

CHAPTER 28

Doc Ernie Pribble unbuttoned his coat and slapped his snow-covered hat on the Red River bar, much to the annoyance of the man with bad teeth and oiled hair who poured drinks back there. The bartender had been standing with a group of townspeople outside, watching Barlow's mercantile at the far end of town burn to the ground and had to come back inside and miss the entertainment.

There wasn't the usual sense of urgency about a fire in town. The thick layer of snow and the building standing by itself kept the blaze contained. The town well was flowing, despite the cold, and a bucket brigade stretched from there, across the street, and to the burning structure that was already fully engulfed.

Knowing he could do nothing to help, Doc returned to his original errand. Runt was still out, and some of the other patients were either home or, in the case of those wounded in the Kingman livery shooting, still where he'd patched them. Since there were no other medical facilities in town, they'd stay where they were until it was safe to move them.

"I'd expect such behavior from these waddies," the bartender said, pointing at the hat covered with melting snow. "But you're an educated man, Doc. That's why we have hat racks over there."

"I won't be here long enough to hang my hat." Opening his frock coat, Doc reached into an inside pocket for the cash he kept there. "I need a bottle of whiskey, and don't give me that snakehead rotgut you pour for these other people."

The barkeep opened a lower cabinet behind him and plucked out a bottle of Old Overholt. "Those folks you're talking about would rather not spend the money for expensive whiskey. They just want to get drunk, and fast. What we sell in here ain't half bad. What you call rotgut does the job. You want a glass?"

"This isn't for here. I'm taking it back for when Runt wakes up. He'll need a dose, and I intend to have one with him."

"I heard he was dead."

"He most certainly is not."

"You expect Runt to live after what that Ranger did to him?"

"I've said it a dozen times before and I'd appreciate it if you'd help me pass the word. Maggie says it wasn't the Ranger who shot him, though she don't know who it was. Runt'll tell the truth when he wakes up."

"He's gonna make it?" Son Barlow's voice cut across the saloon.

Doc turned, cursing himself. He hadn't seen Son or Judd over there with a couple of their men. He immediately regretted being forthcoming to the barkeep. "Son, you look like you've been rode hard and put away wet. You come in from fighting that fire over there?"

"Your Ranger kidnapped me and Judd here. Had us tied up over at Nellie's Place."

Doc waited for more, seeing Son rub at his wrists. They looked somewhat red and swollen. "He let y'all go?"

"We got away." Judd swept a finger around the table at his men. "We're about to go find him when the rest of the boys get here from the ranch." He moved his arm for Doc to see the borrowed six-shooter stuck in his belt. "He just murdered two of my boys over in the mercantile. Shot 'em in the back before he burned it down on them. I have men looking at the other end of town, and we're about to go out, too."

Doc felt a cold chill go down his spine. He'd left Runt alone in his examination room, sleeping soundly, but he hadn't considered that Three Fork men were prowling around. It was hard for Doc to think like those others who walked a darker side of the line. It wouldn't take but a minute for someone to slip into his office, smother Runt, and walk out free and clear.

A figure stood in the dim corner near the back. "You're mistaken, Judd." He walked the length of the bar to join Doc. "Your two men are dead all right, but the holes I saw are in the front, and I had men carry them down to my office."

Judd frowned at the undertaker, annoyed. "Well, I'm just going by what I heard. What're you doing in here, anyway? You should be down at your meat house, tending to my dead boys."

"I had an errand to run, and when they brought your

hands down the street on the buckboard, I took one look at 'em and decided I needed a drink before getting started. You people are killing everyone you can find and it's wearing me out."

"He's right." Doc rested an elbow on the bar. "I've been patching people up left and right and there ain't no reason for it."

"That Ranger shot my men!"

"Once again, Joe here tells it different. That seems to happen a lot with you Three Fork boys, reciting a different version of the truth." Doc's fingers fiddled with the bottle's cork, as if he were considering a drink. "You didn't say why the Ranger arrested you two."

"Didn't say arrested us. He just took us at gunpoint and forced us into Nellie's for no reason. Tied us up there and had that big, half-breed Indian of hers watch us."

"Umm hmm." Doc studied the bottle in his hand. "How'd you get away, then? Sam tends to stick to a task."

"He left the room for a few minutes and we worked loose." Judd turned his attention back to his men. "Maggie and her kid are in there."

They accepted the news as if, to a man, they'd been waiting on hearing of her whereabouts. Joseph Mayse stiffened and exchanged looks with Doc. He'd been charged with taking Maggie down to Nellie's Place but had gone straight to the saloon afterward. Neither of them liked that Judd was talking about where she'd gone after the shooting in her place of business.

They especially didn't like seeing two of the Barlow men rise without a word and button up to leave the saloon. Doc turned himself to watch which way they went, expecting them to go in the direction of Nellie's Place and the fire, but instead, they turned to the right.

"Runt!" Alarmed, he grabbed the bottle by the neck and rushed outside. The men, walking at a determined pace, stopped on the boardwalk when a shout reached them.

"The livery's on fire! The Barlow livery is on fire out back!"

The brand riders whirled at the alarm, pouring out the front. Doc followed them off the boardwalk into the middle of the street and turned to see black smoke rising behind the saloon. He stood there a minute, watching the cowboys run around through the corral to rescue their ponies.

They hadn't been out of sight for a second when, from the opposite side of the saloon, more than a dozen unsaddled horses raced into sight. The wild-eyed leader turned right and the rest followed, throwing up great clods of snow and disappearing down the street as lacy curtains swirled around the retreating mounts.

Mayse joined him with a smile on his face now that Maggie's whereabouts were no longer of interest. "I believe they've cornered a boogerbear. That Ranger's mad." He chuckled and pointed past the burning mercantile. "Look yonder."

Doc squinted into the snow. "What's that?"

"The Barlow livery they've framed up. It's burning like hell."

Doc stifled a laugh. "I need you to help me."

Mayse tore his eyes from the sight. "Do what?"

"I think those two Barlow men were heading for my office. We need to move Runt to somewhere safe, and I can't do it by myself."

"How do we do it?"

"Bring your funeral wagon over to my office. I'm gonna pronounce Runt dead, and you take his body over to your place."

"Then what?"

"I'll get the word out that he's passed on from his wound, and we'll care for him there until he wakes up."

"If he don't open his eyes pretty soon and tell us what he knows, that Ranger's gonna burn the whole town down."

Doc walked off. "Might not be the worst thing that ever happened."

CHAPTER 29

"The livery's on fire!"

Shouts from outside once again emptied the Red River Saloon. Judd Fletcher and Son Barlow walked out the back, casually following a crush of men who'd stabled their horses in the livery close to the saloon. Judd, Son, and a dozen others were caught up in the excitement as a herd of horses boiled out the side door, running from the fire.

Judd grabbed one of his cowboys' arms and almost threw him toward the burning livery. "Make sure the rest of our horses aren't in there, Matt!"

The man in a slouch hat hesitated. "If it's that Ranger, he might still be in there." He turned to the handful of men who lived in Blackjack. "Y'all come with me."

One of them shook his head. "I'm a carpenter, not a gunfighter. I'll build this place back when the fire's out, but I ain't going in there right now."

Instead of checking the barn, they stood there listening to the townspeople, who were furious, frustrated at the fact that the range war that had been smoldering for months had finally broken out. They had no marshal, and some lawman who'd ridden into town saying he was after a murderer was said to be the one doing it.

The carpenter turned to an acquaintance standing close by. "This is the second Barlow business to go. Whoever's setting these fires ain't mad at the rest of us."

"Third. I think that's the new livery burning down there, too."

Son pushed him like an angry schoolboy. "You don't know what you're saying. Stop that talk and get a posse together."

The carpenter shook his head. "I'm not a lawman, neither."

Son whirled, flinging his arm at the onlookers gathered around him. "Do something! Get some men and put this out."

A gruff voice barked a laugh at the back edge of the crowd. "It'll only start again, I reckon."

"How?"

Two strangers pointed at the Red River Saloon and the black smoke boiling out of the windows on the corral side, and the open back door. "'Cause this is gonna be a bigger fire."

CHAPTER 30

After spreading the contents of several oil lamps and lighting the third fire in the saloon and sneaking out, Ridge and Sam saw Doc and Undertaker Mayse standing in the middle of the street fifty yards away. Recognizing them, Sam hurried across the street.

"Sirs, our Ranger friend is at the mouth of that alley over there. He'd like you both to join him."

He led them away from the growing conflagration, where the four of them huddled together, hiding in plain sight as men rushed up and down the street.

Doc's thin mustache twitched, and he grinned. "You two've stirred up a yellow jacket's nest."

Sam grinned at the ground. "They made this feller here mad."

"I see that." Doc took Ridge's arm and turned him away from the growing fire that threatened to illuminate his face. "Walk with us. Nobody'll notice you with me."

Keeping his head ducked low, Ridge pulled up his collar once again. "Where are we going?"

"Down to my office to move Runt." They walked for a few seconds against the slowing tide of men running, walking, and riding toward the burning buildings. "Y'all just missed Son and Judd."

"Where were they?"

"In the saloon a minute before the livery caught fire. They must've headed out the back while y'all went in . . . the front?"

"Naw." Sam chuckled. "The window on the side. Place was empty when we got in."

"I wish we hadn't missed those two," Ridge said. "I should have killed them when I had the chance."

"You aren't that kind," Doc said. They walked four abreast, away from the three burning buildings behind them. "You'll shoot a man in a fair fight but not murder."

Reaching the doctor's office, he unlocked the door. Mayse gave them a wave. "I'll be back with the funeral wagon in a second."

They stepped inside. Doc pulled down the paper shades over the windows and went to the stove to add a piece of wood. His office area had cooled more than he liked it. Sam took up a position to keep an eye on the room as Ridge leaned his rifle against the wall beside the door.

He glanced around, seeing a door flanked by two cabinets full of medicine and medical equipment. "Runt's body back there?"

"For the time being, but he's as alive as we are."

Ridge waited. "What's the funeral wagon for?"

"An idea to keep him that way.

"He's still unconscious," Doc said, "but I'm afraid some assassin is going to slip in here and kill him to keep him quiet. We're moving him down to the funeral parlor. Mayse is gonna pass the word that Runt died. I'll finish taking care of him there and nobody'll come looking for him."

Sam chuckled, a sound like a panther's growl coming from deep in his chest. "That's good thinking."

Ridge admired the man's plan. "Can I talk to him?"

"When he's awake. He was in quite a bit of pain when he came in. It was hard to stop the bleeding, and I had to chloroform him to clean his wound. Some people don't take to it very well, and he's one of them. He went under hard, and then, when he roused up still hurting, I gave him a dose of laudanum. I have no worry that he won't wake up, but it might be a while, and when he does, I suspect he'll come up fighting when it wears off."

Ridge remembered Zeke's gift to Jo. "You needed Jo's madstone to stop the bleeding?"

"Old wives' tale." Doc shook his head. "That'd work just as well as cobwebs, and let me tell y'all something, I've never seen enough cobwebs in any one spot to stuff into a wound."

They chuckled, but something tickled Ridge's brain and he tried to get a grasp on a thought that flickered like a firefly at the edge of his memory. Feeling the warmth coming from the stove, he absorbed the heat as he remembered emptying Son's pockets. What was the connection to Jo?

The madstone. She'd lost it and was upset . . .

. . . and when he emptied Son's pockets after tying him up, he found another madstone.

No. Wait!

It wasn't another one. It was the *same* madstone. They couldn't be common enough for two people in a matter of hours to have one. Son insisted it was only a chert nodule, but that one wasn't the first madstone Ridge had ever seen, and he knew the difference.

Jo said she left it in their privy.

Afraid he was going to lose his train of thought, Ridge crossed his arms and stared at the flue's screw on the pipe disappearing in the metal-tiled ceiling. The other two saw him concentrating and grew quiet.

Runt was shot from the back.

"Doc, that bullet that hit Runt." Ridge tore his eyes from the keylike screw. "Why didn't it kill him?"

"Couple of reasons I was explaining to Zeke and Maggie right before those two cowboys came in the store, shooting. That big, old, loose buffalo coat of his turned the bullet. Then he wears a whalebone corset for his back. The slug was slowed down enough when it hit one of the stays to angle off."

"What kind of bullet was it?"

"Wasn't a rifle. That's for sure. Pistol, I'll allow, but it wasn't a .44. Something lighter. I suspect a .36 or a .38."

"Runt's a short man. The shot must have come downward to angle off the stay."

"Not at all. It looked like it came straight. Parallel to the ground."

"Somebody stood in the door and crouched, maybe."

"I don't think so. Why would a shooter do that? But come to think of it, that's the other thing about his wound. I think whoever shot him was standing at a distance."

"Didn't walk up and shoot him point-blank." Ridge's statement served no purpose other than to flick through the ideas in his mind.

"Well, yes." Doc scratched his head. "What're you getting at?"

"About how far's the privy out back from the back of Maggie's place?"

"Twenty, thirty yards? A ways farther than some folks might put it."

"Somebody sitting in the privy would have a straight shot."

Doc's eyebrow lifted. "I get your drift. An assassin sat in her privy and out of the weather, waiting for Runt, or someone, to come out."

"Someone who wasn't particularly after the marshal but me." Ridge finally looked up from the flue's adjustment screw. "Someone who was there long enough to see Jo's madstone she lost and took it with him."

"Someone who likes to collect things."

All three said it at the same time.

"Son."

CHAPTER 31

The Red River Saloon blazed, snow fell, and water hissed as it turned to steam. Snowflakes coming too close to the flames melted in the air and landed in a soft, icy rain on those trying to put out the fire in the soupy mud mixed with ashes.

"This is gonna finish killing your daddy." Judd stood with Son in the street, feeling the warmth of the fire as it destroyed still another Barlow building.

Son's stomach fluttered with fear. He'd have to tell his dad about what had happened, but at the same time everything that was falling around them had the capacity to accelerate the old man's decline.

He recalled the last time Jim Barlow was in town the week before, when he came back with a twinkle in his dulling eyes and poured whiskeys in their house for him and Son. "It won't be long until the rest of the town's mine."

"Ours?"

The old man took off his hat in the house, revealing a splotched bald head full of liver spots. "Yours and mine, boy. By the time that rail line comes in, I'll have everything in place. Here's what I need for you to do: find a way to run Mitch Kingman out of business or buy his stable before ours is finished. That way we'll catch people coming in from either end of town. I have more money in the bank than anyone else, so it's already ours. We just need to make it faster, before that rail line pushes through.

"With Maggie's store out of the way, we're gonna put another saloon in its place. That butcher shop going up next to our mercantile is gonna be a gold mine because we'll have run the Oarlock out of business."

He grinned at his son, a rarity, since the old man had no use for his boy, who wasn't much of a man on his best day. "The railroad will make this a boomtown, and we'll be able to ship our cattle right from those pens I intend to put up out of town once Drake Hutchins is dead and the Oarlock's mine. Then we'll own everything from here to a hundred miles west of town."

With that conversation from a week ago in his head, Son decided to accelerate things in town. He didn't want to wait anymore for his time in the sunshine. His dad didn't think much of him, and he wanted to prove himself to be Judd's equal. Barlow always praised his foreman, and Son was afraid he'd give him a significant stake in the ranch.

Son wanted it all, and he would have gotten it if Russ Leopold was still alive. He'd seen a problem at the outset when their newest hand, Clyde McPeak, came to work for the Three Fork and the big blond cowboy took up with Judd. In only a few days they'd spent way too much time together, talking quietly and casting around furtive glances.

Barlow started going downhill about the same time, and Son could see they were taking advantage of the situation. The only thing in town standing in their way was Runt Carpenter. Though he was small in size, the marshal had proven to be formidable.

He stuck his nose in everything, watching every time Son came to town. He almost screwed up their takeover of the saddle shop. When the owner, Cecil Braddock, was starting to crack under the pressure of the bank leaning on him to pay off a five-hundred-dollar loan, Son went to the saddlemaker with a plan. He'd buy him out at twice the value of the shop. Cecil could take the money and not have to work for years.

Runt came in as Son was talking with Cecil and butted in, explaining that the Barlows owned most of the bank, and any money they slipped into Cecil's pocket was fake. It was a maneuver where they moved numbers around until it all looked good on paper, but Cecil would get nothing after his loan payment was canceled.

He would lose his business.

Runt loaned him the money out his own pocket, and Son had to crawl under the porch and lick his wounds when the old man split his lip for him when he heard how they'd been outmaneuvered and sent Judd and McPeak in to deal with the saddlemaker.

When Cecil went to Doc's to sew up his hand the next day, he told him a leather knife slipped and laid his left hand open, severing tendons and putting an end to his career. A single man, he had no other ties in Blackjack, and once Doc sewed him up as best he could, Cecil drifted out of town to find work fit for a man who would finish his life with a crippled hand and never admitted he'd been crippled by Judd and McPeak.

Standing there in the street, watching the three structures burn when they'd been on the edge of success, Son felt his anger rise. He needed to do something that would earn the old man's faith. "I have an idea."

Judd merely raised an eyebrow. "I did, too. I sent Dick Schaker to the ranch to bring back as many of the boys as he could. I have a feeling the lid's gonna blow off this place and we're gonna have a showdown with those Oarlock riders. By the time the snow melts, this town's gonna be called Barlow."

Wondering how he knew that's what Son wanted to call the town when the railroad arrived, he felt a flush of anger that Judd had once again overstepped his bounds. "That was my call."

"Sorry. I was just doing what I figured Mr. Barlow— and you—would want." He waited with a crooked grin on his face. "What was your idea?"

"I'm a-doing it."

Judd stood there with both hands in his coat pockets. "With these fires, wouldn't it be a shame if Maggie's place caught fire, too?"

"She's about out of business already."

"Hell, half the town's on fire. We can light her place and blame it on either that Ranger or the Oarlock men. The way the town's turned right now, they'll believe us."

Annoyed at the man's insolence, Son turned his back on him. "Well, we need to wait until the boys get here, then."

"Let's go down to the hotel bar."

"Naw, too many people down there fighting the fire, and I don't want them to see me . . . us . . . doing nothing. Besides, the place will be packed once they get it out, if it's not already full."

Judd turned and struck off down the street. His move took the power from Son who, not wanting to be left alone in the street, hurried to join him. He hated to walk, but their mounts, which someone had released from the livery, were probably already back at the Three Fork barn. "Where we going?"

"I don't know if you care, but we have boys shot up there in Kingman's stable. Let's wait with them for your daddy to get here."

Annoyed with himself that he hadn't thought of that, Son saw that it looked like he was following Judd. Appearances were important, so he took half a dozen long steps to catch up, and they walked shoulder to shoulder past Doc's office.

A black funeral wagon turned out onto the street. Joseph Mayse had a large corral and a barn out behind the undertaker's storefront where he kept and maintained the hearse. Mayse held the reins on a team of mules and passed the two men with a nod.

Son stopped. "Where you headed? To pick up our boys down at the mercantile?"

"Already sent a wagon down there to get them." Mayse frowned. "Y'all didn't know that?"

Not wanting to admit the truth, Son stepped forward to place himself in front of Judd. "You didn't take this?"

"Two men and maybe more? This is more for formalities. Nope. Sent the wagon."

"Where you going, then?"

"To get Runt Carpenter's body."

Relief washed over Son. "Gone, huh?"

"Yep. He's mine now."

"Well, all right, then." Son nodded, as if giving the undertaker permission to go on about his work.

The funeral hearse rolled on and they continued to Kingman's stable, snow squeaking underfoot.

CHAPTER 32

Doc's office was warm and packed with medicine cabinets, medical equipment both on the floor and on shelves, and his examination table. Runt was awake and not having it. Coming to, he tried to get up, and it took Doc, Ridge, and Sam to hold him down long enough for his head to clear.

Ridge was afraid the man was going to open his wound again and Doc surprised him by slapping Runt's cheek to calm him down. "Be still or you're gonna rip them stitches out. I spent too much time to make 'em good and tight and I won't appreciate you ruining my work."

Now lying on his stomach in the room off Doc's office, Runt glared at the men gathered around the table. They'd explained that he needed to be moved for his own sake, but the little marshal who'd fought all his life to prove himself had other ideas.

"You're not putting me in that meat wagon." His deep voice rumbled like the earlier thundersnow as he cursed everything from Doc to the assassin to the table he was lying on.

Doc shook his head and scratched behind one ear. "You damned fool. There's men out there hoping you're gonna die, and Undertaker Mayse passed Son and Judd on his way over here. To top it off, Ridge, here, suspects it was Barlow men who shot you. Besides Maggie, who's hiding, too, you're the only one who knows it wasn't Ridge who did the shooting."

Runt laid his head back down. His huge mustache seemed to be laying by itself in front of his face. "Just write out a statement and I'll sign it. Then I can stay here."

"We don't have anyone to show it to right now." Ridge leaned against the wall amid the smells of astringents. To him, some of the odors in the doctor's office had the sharp bite of horse liniment. "I wouldn't put it past those Three Fork men to burn anything you sign and put a pillow over your face. They're all so worked up, they'll shoot first if they see me or you on the street."

"Because you supposedly shot me."

"Nope." Sam laughed, deep and loud. "They're mad as hornets because he's burning half this town to the ground and shooting Barlow men whenever he sees one."

Runt squinted through one eye. "Is that you, Sam, standing over there?"

The big man rumbled. "It's me all right. How're you doing, Marshal?"

"Not worth a damned." He closed his eyes. "Who's watching Nellie's?"

"A little three-foot wolverine named Jo."

"Y'all can tell me that later over a beer. What'd they shoot me with, a buffalo gun?"

Doc chuckled. "I bet it feels like that, but it was a pistol."

"Hurts like hell."

"Wait'll you try and really sit up instead of all that thrashing around you're doing." Doc jerked a thumb at the undertaker. "That's why Joe brought a stretcher."

"I ain't dead yet."

"Not by a long sight. We can cover you up and carry you out of here to someplace safe. I hear there's parties searching buildings, and probably houses, too. They'll come looking in here for Ridge before it's over, and it wouldn't surprise me none for a band of Barlows to kick the door in. It wouldn't take much for one of them to knock you in the head while they're here."

Runt turned his head and made a wounded sound in his throat. "I may be laid up, but I'm still the marshal of this town. Tell me what you know, Ridge."

Ridge unraveled the story from the moment Runt was shot until they walked into Doc's office minutes before. Runt lay there breathing deep. Ridge started to think he'd dozed back off. He'd been shot himself, and for a week afterward all he wanted to do was sleep and heal up without anyone bothering him.

Runt licked his lips, rustling his mustache. "Has anyone wired for the sheriff?"

"It's been snowing so hard, the lines are down," Doc said.

Ridge took the news by surprise. "Y'all have a telegraph?"

"Sure do. Went in a month or so ago. Paid for by the railroad."

"I wish you'd told me. How do you know it's down?"

"I went over this morning and talked to Percy."

"He the telegraph operator?"

"He is, Percy Witherspoon, and he sent two men down the line to find the break. I doubt they're moving fast with all this snow."

"How long would it take for someone to get here if he can get word to the county sheriff?"

"Day after tomorrow, I reckon, maybe two days with all this snow on the ground."

"That won't be soon enough." Runt moved an arm and winced.

"You're right, and that's why we need to keep you hid, Runt."

He finally gave in. "All right. Where's my shotgun? I want it close."

"The last time I saw it was over at Maggie's."

"Somebody go find it and get me a gun in the meantime."

Sam stepped close and reached into one of his pockets. He came out with a little Remington revolver and laid it near Runt's hand. "This ain't but a .32, but it'll stop a man."

Runt's hand slid forward and grasped the butt. He

seemed to relax a little. "Go ahead and do what you have to do."

Doc put his hand on Runt's shoulder. "All right. It's gonna hurt like hell when we pick you up." He stepped to the side and pointed with one finger. "Boys, slip your hands under him and space 'em out to keep his body supported. All right. When everyone's ready, we're gonna raise him up and walk him around to the litter. Lay him down easy on it."

Despite their care, Runt groaned when they lifted him off the table. Moving in the small room was awkward, but they finally laid him on the stretcher. "Goddlemighty! That felt like my ribs were grinding together."

"Probably were. The bullet broke at least one of them, and there's not a thing I can do but keep you strapped up until they heal." Doc checked his patient's bandages. "You can't put a splint on a rib, and you holding that revolver didn't help much."

"You're lucky I didn't shoot one of y'all. I might have, if I hadn't been afraid you'd drop me."

The undertaker spread a sheet over Runt's body, covering him from head to toe. "Lay still until we get you in the hearse."

"'It's a funeral wagon. I never thought I'd be breathing in one of those."

"You'll get another chance someday," Doc said. "Be quiet now."

Ridge and Sam stayed inside as Doc and Joe Mayse carried the litter outside to the waiting funeral wagon. Windows stretching along the black vehicle's length and in the rear gate would allow anyone outside to see the sheet-covered body.

Doc spoke softly. "Don't you move. There's people watching."

He set his end at the edge of the open door at the rear. Mayse shoved it forward, and a soft moan came from under the sheet. He closed the back and jumped when someone spoke nearby.

Bud Campbell appeared and squinted in through one of the hearse's side windows. "That Runt?"

For the first time, Doc pretended to notice the other men standing nearby, drawn by the actions of loading Runt. "It is."

"That sawed-off little man had an attitude." Campbell glanced from the hearse to the front of the Doc's office.

Doc shook his head. "I wouldn't speak harshly of the dead, Bud. Superstitious folks might say a man's spirit could hear it and attach itself to you."

"Well, I don't mean no disrespect. But that's how Runt was. He had that little-man insolence that made him hard to like sometimes."

"Just because he locked you up a time or two for being drunk don't mean you should insult him."

A soft chuckle came from one of the other onlookers. Doc couldn't help himself. "I can guarantee you that Runt can hear you. My mama said the dead don't depart right off the bat. They sometimes hang around for a few hours before going on to their reward."

"That little feller's gonna be held back from his reward by that big old mustache." The other man almost slapped his knee at his own wit. "I wonder if it's gonna get in the way of going through those Pearly Gates. He might be short, but he's liable to have to turn sideways to get inside."

Ridge heard them through the window glass and knew that Runt was doing the same inside the funeral wagon. He hoped the marshal could keep his temper until later. He'd have plenty of time to remind those gathered around the hearse that they should watch what they say.

He peeked around the shade and saw the undertaker climb up on the seat. He seemed in a hurry to get a move on and snapped the reins a little too hard. The mules jolted the funeral wagon at first before Joe turned them in the street and headed back the way they came.

Bud Campbell turned his back to the funeral parlor to watch the wagon roll away. "I swear, I thought I heard a grunt from inside that wagon."

Doc slapped him on the shoulder and walked past to his office. "Gasses escape from a body long after a person's gone. That's likely what you heard."

"Naw, it was Runt growling at us one last time with that raspy voice of his. That's what it was."

Doc stepped onto the boardwalk. "You ain't a-woofin."

CHAPTER 33

Runt was safe with the dead people, Maggie and Jo were safe in a house of ill repute, and Ridge Tisdale wasn't good at doing nothing. With the knowledge that people were out looking for him, he paced from frosted window to window in Doc's office.

Standing close to the stove, Doc and Sam watched with interest. Doc rubbed his dry hands together. "You know, Sam, I might have to chloroform Ridge, there, just so we can get some rest."

"I can knock him in the head, but I never know how hard. I know how to push in on the sides of his neck, though, to put him to sleep." He side-eyed Doc and paused. "But there's been a time or two when they don't wake up. I think I either push too hard or too long."

Doc frowned. "Too long. If you cut off the blood to the brain, they likely won't come back."

"I been meaning to ask you. If they're fightin' when they go out, they always come back up swinging. Why's that?"

Ridge took off his hat to scratch. "There's men out

there looking for me right now. I'd rather worry about that."

Doc picked up the bottle of whiskey he'd bought and poured them all a drink. He passed them around. "And you're safe in here."

"Until they come beating on the door. Then you'll be in as much trouble as me."

Ridge remembered several months earlier, when he turned his Ranger badge in because the captain he served under was doing the same thing as the Barlow men, kicking in doors and looking for someone.

Captain Bookbinder and his Rangers were after a dangerous outlaw in the far west Texas town of Angel Fire. Determined to find Hack Long and kill him, Bookbinder insisted the Ranger company go door to door, pushing their way inside until he was found.

Believing people had rights, Ridge argued against the search until Bookbinder would hear no more of it. A shouting match ensued, and Ridge took off his badge and rode out of town, a civilian once more.

But only hours later, he rode straight into Long, who'd eluded the search parties. His sense of right and wrong was tested on the plains that day, when the outlaw recognized Ridge and drew down on him. Ridge killed Long, pinned the badge back on, and crossed back to the right side of the law.

It was Ridge's opinion that people should be safe in their homes and places of business, without having agents of the law or government come pushing inside. That went for outlaws, too, and the thought of Barlow's men kicking in the doors of innocent townspeople almost made the badge on his shirt grow hot.

"I'm not good at waiting for trouble to come to me." Ridge joined them to warm his hands at the stove.

Sam showed his teeth in a wide smile. "You're fixin' to take the fight to them, ain't you?"

"That I am. I don't want these animals pushing their way into anyplace trying to find me. They'll eventually be at Nell's, and I can't let that happen to Maggie and Jo."

Ridge slapped the doctor on his arm. "Doc, you stay here. I might need you later to dig out a bullet if one of those Barlow men gets lucky."

"Stay here and wait for the sheriff."

"It's all you can do." Ridge picked up his rifle. "Sam, this isn't your fight, neither."

"I made it mine when I cracked that yahoo back there with the axe handle."

"He didn't see you, and neither did anyone else, so you're in the clear."

"Judd and Son know after you had 'em trussed up at Nellie's."

"That they do, but I'll take care of it pretty fast."

"You don't know where they are."

Ridge grinned. "I know where they'll be in a few minutes when the shooting starts."

Doc held up a soft, white hand. "You can't just go out there and start gunning people down."

"That's not my whole plan. There's a jail here, right?"

"Of course. Runt has an office down there."

"Well, then, I'm going to arrest those Barlow men

for shooting the two Oarlock boys I met, Mahan and Monty. Some of those that did the shooting are probably still in the Kingman livery where you worked on them, right, Doc?"

He wiped a hand across his mouth. "That's where they were when they shot one another, and I doubt they've gone far. Wounded men don't tend to move far if they don't have to, and I wouldn't let them bring anyone in here. I offered that empty house I have over on the south side of town, but they refused."

"Then I'm going in there to do my duty. I'll march them down to the jail and lock them up."

"You're forgetting, half the town is after you for shooting Runt. I'll allow there's a posse already formed, whether they're behind a lawman or not. All it takes is for a man to holler loud enough to follow him, and there's weak or misguided men who'll do it."

"I'll just have to convince them. Putting shackles on some of Barlow's men will make them stop and think." Ridge stopped, thinking. "Hey, Doc. I do have something for you to do."

"What?"

"Do you think the telegraph operator will believe you if you tell him that Runt's alive and will say it wasn't me who shot him?"

"I've known Percy since I came to town. He's a reasonable and honest man."

"Good, though I hope he's not too honest. I'd like for him to write out a telegram saying he just got word from the sheriff that a company of Rangers is headed here to join me in settling all this mess."

"You remember, the line's down."

"You said yourself, men are out looking for that break. Nobody knows it isn't fixed. Have him write it out and nail it to the front of the marshal's office, where people can read it. Then I'd like you to send a telegram to Texas Ranger Captain Will Armstrong in Austin that I need that company of men as soon as they can get here."

"It's a long way from Austin."

"There's men closer if he can get word to them. Just one more badge will help, and a man who'll vouch for me behind it."

Ridge put his hand on the latch. "Get ready, Doc. I might be sending some business your way in a few minutes."

"If they're Barlow men, I'd rather they surrender, or go over to Mayse's embalming tables."

"Don't matter none to me."

CHAPTER 34

Ridge knew only one way to complete a task, and that was to meet it head on. Back outside on the boardwalk, with his hat once again pulled low, he headed down to Kingman's livery through the snowfall that showed no signs of slacking off. To make visibility even worse, smoke from the fires hung close to the ground in a thick fog that worked in his favor.

Most of the street's activity was at the other end of town, concentrated around the three burning buildings that had collapsed. Feeling as if everyone was looking at him but confident that the air was so bad they couldn't make him out, Ridge kept up a determined pace, hoping not to draw attention. When he came to the Kingman livery on his side of the street, he saw a man bundled up against the cold and leaning against the boarding stable.

The Barlow guard was more concerned with staying warm and performing whatever duty had sent him out there. Head down, scarved and gloved, the only thing Ridge saw when he approached was a Winchester lying in one arm and the man's dead-fish eyes that watched him approach with disinterest.

"Livery's closed," he said without moving out from the wall and spat a thick stream of tobacco juice into a wide, brown stain by his feet.

"Good." Ridge drew the Colt from his new shoulder holster and shoved it into the man's chest. "Turn loose of that rifle."

Jerked from boredom and cold, the man's face tightened with fear as he released his hold on the Winchester and Ridge yanked it away. "Darn it.! You're that Ranger. Don't shoot me."

"You're under arrest. If you don't try anything, you won't wake up tomorrow morning with any new holes in you. Open that door, and don't make one sound when you do it."

The guard opened the door and did as he was told. He entered the livery's wide hall and paused. Ridge leaned the Winchester against the wall and followed. It didn't take but a second for Ridge to see why. They both had to wait for their eyes to adjust to the dimness.

A voice came from the other end. "You freeze out, Bob?"

"Sure did." Ridge answered for him, using the man as a shield. He held the Henry in his left hand like a two-by-four across the man's back and nudged his prisoner forward, making sure the Three Fork rider felt the Colt pistol's muzzle against his spine.

Despite the weak light outside, they were silhouetted against the open door, and the men on the other end of the barn weren't able to make out their features.

"Who's that with you? The rest of the boys make it?"

Ridge recognized Turkey's voice, which didn't yet sound alarmed. He pushed Bob forward and followed, continuing with the charade as long as possible. "Still waiting."

Two men were lying propped up against the hay stacked behind them. One had his leg wrapped in a bloody bandage and elevated on a sack of grain. The other was still and gray, resembling a corpse. It was hard to tell from a distance whether he was breathing or not.

Because of the cloud cover outside, there were oil lamps scattered on the ground nearby to provide illumination. They'd scraped away the hay and rested the wide glass bases on the dirt floor. Two lamps in holders on the building's support posts also helped push away the gloom.

Ridge and his prisoner were halfway across the wide hall when Turkey finally realized something was up. Rising from where he was sitting on a keg, he rested one hand on the butt of his pistol.

"Bob!"

Instead of answering, the man simply stopped. "He was on me before I knew what to do."

A trio of slump-shouldered men were huddled inside the open stall beside the man who looked dead. Dressed in town clothes, they stood with the others, looking hopeful but resigned to their fate. The only one tied up, Mitch Kingman, was with them and spoke up. "They won't let us leave."

"Shut up," Turkey ordered.

Ridge recognized two other Three Fork men who'd been in Maggie's. They tensed, still not sure what was going on with Ridge and their friend, who remained rock solid in front of them.

Turkey planted his feet. "Bob. Step to the side."

"He's going to stay right where he is for a minute." Ridge kept the Colt against Bob's spine and the Henry pressed lengthways down his back. He could see Bob's demeanor made them nervous. There was no telling if he had a pistol hidden there behind the man, or a coach gun. At that range, a shotgun would be devastating.

Unconcerned with the townies in the stall, Ridge kept his eye on Turkey. "Name's Ridge Tisdale. We've met. I'm a Texas Ranger, and this man's under arrest, along with the rest of you. Put down your guns."

One of the men chuckled, and Turkey addressed him without taking his eyes off Ridge. "He's funny, ain't he, Dick?"

Any hope of an arrest vanished in the instant Dick Schaker yanked a six-gun from his holster and fired. He wasn't even close to fast, and his aim was just as bad. The slug whizzed past Ridge and the man he still held in front of him. A faster thinker, Bob threw himself to the side.

The muzzle blast in the dim light was blinding. Seeing the flare wherever he looked slowed Ridge's response, but he knew exactly where the man stood the instant he pulled the trigger.

Still holding the Henry in his left fist, Ridge swung the Colt to the left, and three quick lances of flame shot from the barrel. Dick grunted and made a little crow hop, spinning to the side. Blinking his eyes clear of the first muzzle flash, Ridge looked away from the next man he didn't know. It was a trick he'd learned early in life, not to look directly at what he wanted to see in the darkness, rather looking to the side. He had no idea how that worked, but it did.

With half a second to get ready, that Three Fork man had a chance to end the shooting, but he fired too fast also, and the round struck a board somewhere behind Ridge and whizzed away.

Looking to the left of the shooter, Ridge shot at a dark shape and hit him square in the chest. The six-gun in the dying man's hand fired into the floor and he fell backward toward Turkey, who had to jump sideways or get knocked down.

The air seemed thick as molasses and full of smoke as guns went off everywhere, the flashes like monster lightning bugs in the barn. The bright flashes temporarily froze the men in bursts of light.

Turkey extended his arm and was lined up on Ridge when a dark streak shot from the stall, and one of the unarmed townspeople knocked him off his feet.

The first man Ridge shot was Dick Schaker, who was on the ground but still in the fight. Though seriously wounded, Dick was game. Propped on one elbow, he raised his pistol. Ridge shot him again and dodged to the side, hoping the movement would throw off the other's aim.

Turkey was in a fistfight with a tall feller who'd knocked him to the ground. Holding Turkey's gun hand in one fist, the stranger hammered at his face with the other.

The next thing Ridge knew, he was on his back as Bob used one leg to sweep him off his feet. He landed hard, his head bouncing on the thick mat of hay covering the ground. Lying prone on his back, Ridge cocked the Colt and barely raised the revolver a few inches above the ground and shot Bob from point-blank range. The muzzle flash sparked his cloth coat, which glowed around the edges and sent up tendrils of smoke. Angry that he'd been bested for the moment, Ridge shot him again and felt the hot burn of a returned bullet that plucked the coat covering his chest.

The wounded man who was propped on a sack of oats used two hands to cock his pistol and steady it again. Ridge's six-shooter was out of bullets. He twisted to put himself behind Bob's still corpse and struggled to get his rifle into action. Another bullet thumped into the body lying between them, and Ridge laid the long gun across Bob's now still body and fired, striking the shooter at the base of the throat.

All around them, frightened horses snorted and pawed at the ground, shoving against the stalls to escape the smoke, flashes, and noise. The fight wasn't limited to firearms. Turkey was buried under the three townspeople who hammered him into silence.

Shaken, Ridge let them have at him and rose to one knee, keeping an eye on the last wounded Three Fork man, who lay still as death against the hay. With no threat from that quarter, Ridge spun and ran to the barn door to drop the security bar into place. Now no one could come in the front until he was ready.

Keeping the Henry at the ready, he walked up to the men still wrestling in the dust and hay. "You boys can let him up now, and one of y'all needs to go untie Mitch over there."

When they let go and rose, Turkey stayed where he was. Blood ran from his nose and the corner of his mouth. Both eyes already blackened, he groaned and closed his eyes. "Enough."

Ridge saw Turkey's nose was more hooked than before, broken and twisted to the side. "Like I said, you're under arrest."

CHAPTER 35

Drake Hutchins and Wes Callahan led the Oarlock riders across the snow-covered prairie. Knowing that country like the back of their hands, they didn't need to follow the wagon roads cut through what was once Comanche country, which, the last couple of decades, wound around miles out of the way.

Flakes still fluttered in the air, adding to the frozen drifts, waves, swirls, and piles of snow that sculpted the landscape. Bushes and tufts of grass caught the initial blowing crystals that in turn snagged more tiny flakes until it piled in undulating solids hiding rabbits, quails, and sage hens huddling in tiny ice caves until the thaw.

The heavily armed cowboys hadn't seen any other horsemen since leaving Oarlock land. Hutchins fully expected to see a band of Three Fork hands coming their way and was a little surprised they'd encountered no one.

"I'm gonna shoot Barlow as soon as I see him for getting us out in this weather." Wes Callahan tried to settle deeper into his sheepskin coat. "The older I get, the more I want to sit by the fire."

"You used to didn't be so cranky and particular about your comfort."

"That comes from a lifetime of trailing around with you, rounding up cattle for other folks. I thought once we rounded up enough cattle to start our own outfit, I could sit by the fire and give orders."

Hutchins laughed. "You always let me issue orders."

"That's because you took over that job. I'd prefer just to count my money, but it's all in the bank back in Ft. Worth."

"And you oughta be glad that's where it is. Neither one of us ever trusted Barlow's bank."

"I don't trust a thing about that man," Wes stated. "The best thing we can do for him and this country is take him in and let Runt Carpenter put him on trial for all this."

"I don't want to turn it over to the law. This is the way to handle a mad dog, and I figure this is the best idea."

Hutchins settled back in his saddle as they came over a low rise to see smoke from the Three Fork ranch house rise from the chimney and disappear into the low clouds that refused to yield. Both horses and men expelled warm, moist breath that vaporized in thick puffs.

The saddle creaked as Wes shifted his weight in the seat and tightened the scarf around his neck. "I say we ride in there hard and fast before they know we're here."

Zeke rode up beside them. "The place looks deserted."

"Ours does, too, on this day." Twisting his saddle,

Hutchins studied those behind him. "I suspect every-one's inside and out of the cold, like I wish we were. Spread out and don't bunch up. Single men make harder targets."

He'd learned that fighting Comanches. More than once, howling bands of painted warriors swarmed in on him and Wes, and their hands. The Indians always separated during the attack, providing too many targets and confusing inexperienced men who tended to over-think their shots. On the other hand, those same inexpe-rienced fighters tended to simply shoot into a cluster of attackers and their horses, missing more than they hit.

Wes seemed still as a statue. "If these boys start shooting, back out of range and wait for me or Drake."

Zeke squinted at the corrals. "I don't see a single horse."

Hutchins considered the calm scene before them. "Inside the barn?"

"Could be, but I think they're all gone." Wes felt under his coat, looking for a cigar somewhere in his clothes. "I tell you where they are, and it ain't in there waiting for us."

Hutchins waited. "Do tell."

"They're headed for Blackjack, if they aren't already there."

"What makes you say that?"

"Because nobody's here." Wes laughed like it was the biggest joke in the world.

"We might have passed them riding for our place," Zeke said.

"We could have, but they don't want a standup fight.

We all got our bellies full of that in the war." Hutchins was partially disappointed and equally glad the fight was delayed. "They learned to fight the same way we did, and the whole mess is over rangeland and Black-jack, where I suspect it'll end. If they have the town, our goose is cooked. Rootin' them out'll be bloody."

"I'll find out. Y'all wait here until I need you, Wes."

"I still think we oughta swarm them."

"Not until I say." Seeming to be in no hurry, Hutchins walked his horse down the long slope and toward the house as the rest eased their mounts a short ways down off the rise so they wouldn't be silhouetted against the clouds. Another habit from fighting Indians.

Hutchins hadn't gone a hundred yards when Wes rode up beside him. The rancher gave his old friend a disgusted look. "Thought you were going to stay back there with the others."

"You thought wrong."

Arguing with Wes was useless, so he nodded, gave in to experience, and kept going. The old friends took their time and finally reined up where they could see all the buildings. "Hello the house!" Hutchins was startled when the barn door opened instead.

A blond-headed man with a splint on one leg stood there with a rifle in one hand, held by the forepiece and muzzle down. "I see your people scattered out there with guns. You two here to fight?"

"Naw, I ain't in the mood." Hutchins rested one hand over the other on his saddle horn.

Wes grinned around the unlit cigar in the corner of his mouth. "You look like you just lost one yourself."

"Bronc threw me here a while back." He turned his attention back. "You're Mr. Hutchins. Oarlock."

"I am. I have twenty men back there who aren't as settled as me and Wes here, so you might want to put that rifle down. We came to talk with Jim Barlow."

"You're probably right." The ranch hand leaned the rifle somewhere out of sight. "Looks like you brought your army to fight ours. You'll have to find the boss elsewhere. They rode out a couple of hours ago, headed for Blackjack."

To Hutchins's annoyance, the man hit the nail on the head. He'd never run such a big crew on the Oarlock, but when Barlow started building what the man rightly called an army, Hutchins saw what he was doing and began hiring those he trusted.

The only difference was that Barlow hired gunmen, while Hutchins brought men aboard who were tough as the land they lived on and could handle cows, horses, and any other kind of trouble that might arise. Their part of the world was full of just such cowboys.

"That's what we figured." Wes worked the cheroot around into the corner of his mouth. "You the only one here?"

"Somebody had to stay behind. Mister, I'm just a cowhand and I'm kinda glad my leg got broke. I can't fight and don't want to, but Barlow's mean as a snake. He says he'll shoot you on sight."

"He'd better aim true. Do you have a horse?"

"I do, but I can't ride him for long. Leg sticks straight out. You want me to clear out so you can burn the place?"

"Nope. You don't sound like you care much for Barlow. How about coming to work for me?"

"Might as well. From the looks of y'all, I'd say this place is about finished."

"Then hitch up a buckboard or buggy and tie your nag to the back. Go to my place and tell the boys there I just hired you."

"Much obliged. I'll do it, but Mr. Hutchins, this is gonna get bad before it gets any better."

Hutchins reined his horse around. "That's all up to Barlow." Wes followed, and they rode back to Zeke, looking worried.

"They all gone?"

Hutchins nodded. "Yep, to town."

"How many did they leave down there?"

"One." Wes finally found a match and lit his cigar. "He works for us now."

Zeke frowned. "How do you know he's honest? He might just be a scout for Barlow."

Hutchins shrugged. "He might be, but I don't think so."

"Should we go burn them out, if there's no one there? If they don't have a place to hole up, it'll be easier to win."

"No." Hutchins shook his head. "That's a fine house, and I'd hate to see it go."

"Nobody's gonna live in it after this is all over."

"Well, I might just have some men tear it down and bring it over to our place. Might want to add on and use what's here."

"You can't move a house like that," Zeke said.

"I heard they moved a whole *town* a while back somewhere northeast of Dallas. Embree was its name, and when the railroad laid their tracks ten miles away, why, they just up and rolled the whole place right there where the train was."

"I never heard of such a thing."

Anxious to get going, Wes butted into the conversation. "If you two don't beat all. Are we going to Blackjack or not?"

From where they sat, Hutchins watched the young man he'd just hired limp out of the barn, leading a team of mules pulling a wagon. "You know, I forgot to ask that boy's name."

CHAPTER 36

Gun smoke still hung in the air, swirling in cold currents coming through the cracks between the barn's exterior planks. Wounded men and bodies lay scattered on the hay as Ridge Tisdale reloaded his weapons.

A fist banged against the Kingman livery's door, rattling it on its hinges. "Mitch! We heard shooting in there. You all right? Open this door!"

The liveryman stayed back a few feet, breathing hard from fear. "It's fine! One of the men who was hurt in here's out of his head with fever. Grabbed a gun and got to shooting, but Jerry Wayne, Larry, and Donovan got it away from him."

"You sure? They okay?"

"They are."

"Come out so we can see you're all right."

Kingman looked back at Ridge near the far end of the stable, who shrugged. Kingman opened the door and stepped outside. "See? I'm fine."

Not taking that answer, Joseph Mayse and Bud Campbell pushed inside. Mayse saw the bodies at the far end and gave Kingman a pat on the shoulder. "More trouble."

"All this is out of my hands."

Doc arrived next, carrying his bag. "Good God. More dead and hurt." He looked around. "Anyone else in here? Maybe hiding behind that hay?"

Kingman shook his head. "If you're talking about Ridge, he was right there until y'all got here."

"Probably wasn't sure who was with us."

The words were barely out of his mouth when two Three Fork men pushed inside. Les Cobb and Tomas Bragg rushed to the back, nearly knocking Doc down. "Murderers!" Cobb threw an arm wide, as if performing on stage. "Somebody killed our men."

Doc set his bag on the ground and turned to Bragg. "Who are these boys laying here?"

Bragg shouted as if they weren't only feet away. "Barlow men! Mack Dixon! Dwight Grubbs! And that one there's Dick Schaker. It looks like somebody murdered a wounded man while he lay there!"

Cobb raised his voice. "I bet it was that Ranger! He murdered them."

Donovan, the big man who'd fought Turkey, glowered down at them. "It wasn't like that!"

Turkey raised a hand. "Help me up, Doc."

The doctor pointed at Bragg. "Get him up on this keg so I can take a look at him. I need to address these others first."

"I'm hurt! Look at my nose."

"They are, too, and maybe dying, if they haven't gone

on already. Your nose probably hurts, but it won't kill you." For a moment, Doc appeared to be uncertain about who to examine first. He lifted one of the oil lamps from its bracket on the wall and knelt beside the body closest to the door. A huge puddle of blood soaked into the ground and the man's eyes were already drying out.

The others were the same.

Wounded in the leg during the initial shooting hours before, Gary Reeves sat propped against the back wall of the stall he and the others were held in. Doc knelt beside him. "Why haven't they taken you home yet?"

Reeves glanced up at the tall gentleman standing nearby. "They wouldn't let Donovan or anyone take me out of here. Held us, saying I could bleed to death before they would."

Doc shook his head in disgust. "Will you and the boys carry him to my office?"

Jerry Wayne, Williams, and Donovan lifted Reeves to his feet and carried him out. The crowd gathered both inside and out separated to let them pass.

When they were gone, Doc finally squinted at Turkey. "Looks like somebody beat the tar out of you."

"Them men there just did."

Doc used a thumb and forefinger to separate the edges of a wide gash at Turkey's hairline. It had stopped bleeding, and his skull was white against the angry red edges. "I'll have to sew this one up."

"I can walk to your office."

"Nope. I won't have your kind in my examination

room. I'll do it here in the barn, where you're more at home."

Kingman joined them. "I told everyone that it was the Ranger who they were trying to kill, and he returned the favor. I believe they'll pass the word." He considered Turkey's face. "You're lucky they whipped on you, instead of letting Ridge shoot you."

"Keep talking, mister." Turkey glared at him. "And it'll be you and me."

"Okay. The Ranger said you're under arrest."

Turkey's upper lip rose. "Let him come back and cuff me."

"Don't have to." The stableman went to Ridge's saddlebags and took out a set of shackles. He returned to Turkey, who was still sitting on the keg. "Hands behind your back."

Turkey laughed. "You can't arrest me."

"The Ranger deputized me. Said I'm a Ranger now, until he says different. As an agent of the law, I'm telling you for the last time to put your hands behind you."

"Make me."

Doc reached out and dug his thumb into the open wound on Turkey's forehead. He let out a shout of pain and did as he was told. Kingman snapped the shackles around his wrists and tucked the key into his pocket. "There you go, and it was just you and me . . . and Doc."

He and Doc walked into the stall where Ridge's buckskin waited for his owner to return. Doc kept his voice low. "When did Ridge deputize you?"

"He didn't. I saw those shackles in there when they were going through his stuff."

Doc chuckled. "I didn't see him leave. Where did he go?"

"Went hunting."

CHAPTER 37

"This is all going to hell." Judd and Son hurried away from the Kingman livery, almost running down the snaggletoothed alley running parallel to the main street. A scattered line of new buildings back there were evidence that the town was growing and would soon expand to the north.

Small bungalows, a couple of unidentifiable buildings, a Chinese laundry, and dozens of other constructs and tents had sprouted up at the edge of town. Smoke rose from a number of them and drifted close to the snow-covered ground.

Earlier, they'd followed the alleyway and tramped into frozen mud, out of sight on the street, intending to enter the barn from there. Assassins looking for the Ranger, their plan was to peek through the boards until their prey arrived, but their true colors showed when the shooting started: They rushed back the way they came.

Judd's face was flushed red. "I'm tired of this."

"Who do you think that was?"

"I don't care. All I saw were flashes in there, but they

weren't shooting at us or we'd both have faces full of splinters."

A man stepped out of a white canvas tent serving as a Chinese laundry. Startled, Judd snatched the pistol from under his coat and pointed at the frightened laundryman. Holding his hands up palms out, he backed out of sight.

Son hadn't reacted and kept walking. "Where are we going?"

"I know a way to flush that Ranger out."

"It was probably him back there in the barn. Some of our boys were in there. I imagine we had him well outnumbered."

"If there was shooting, then he was ready. I don't intend to get into a stand-up shooting match with him."

"So what's your idea?"

"We know his weak spot. Let's use it."

His feet freezing, Son wasn't in the mood for games. "You might know it. I don't."

"You will if you think about it." The alley they followed was on the opposite side of the street from the burning Red River Saloon. Farther down and directly in front of them was the smoking and still blazing remains of Barlow and Son Mercantile, and beyond that, the ashes of the unfinished stable.

"I still don't understand, but we just came from here." Son waved a hand in disgust. "We're running around like a couple of chickens with their heads cut off."

"We did, but I'm going back to Nellie's and getting Maggie and that little rat of hers. We'll find a place to hole up that'll work to our advantage and send word that we have them."

"Just send word? Nobody's talking to that Ranger! There's people after him, too, because he shot Runt."

"We both know who shot Runt, but he has enough people here in town on his side that he'll find out we have Maggie." Judd's voice was full of confidence. "He'll come running."

"Where are we taking her?"

"The one place we know like the back of our hand. The ranch, and with the boss there to help us, we'll kill that damned Ranger and everything'll be back to normal."

"How can it be normal if we have Maggie and a little girl?"

"She'll come around and work for Mr. Barlow. He can use a housemaid."

"That's crazy. She won't never go for that."

"She will to keep her daughter safe and healthy, and if she don't, the Llano covers a lot of country that people can get lost in."

CHAPTER 38

Ridge was done hiding.

He slipped out the back door of Kingman's livery stable and circled around the big corral there. Someone had already been through and stomped a trail around to the street. He followed the tracks, expecting the worst and ready for it.

He had Bob's pistol in the Colt's holster on his hip. The reloaded Colt was riding in the shoulder holster and, once again stuffed full of shells, he carried the Henry in his right hand.

The Ranger badge was pinned onto the outside of his coat, and in his mind, it no longer mattered if people were looking for him. Ridge was tired and mad, and he walked out into the open, daring anyone to do anything.

When he came around in front of the livery, Ridge turned to face the length of the thoroughfare, which looked as if Sherman's army had marched through it. The fresh snow was churned into a dirty mess. Smoke hung low over the false fronts, both from the burned-out buildings and the fireplaces and woodstoves keeping the residents warm. The remaining small flames flickered on both sides of the street, reflecting off the low clouds that seemed to be only feet overhead.

Once again, most people didn't pay much attention to just another man on the street, assuming he was merely a stranger in town, or another cowboy on some errand. He quickly came to the bank owned by Barlow and went inside.

Directly in front of him was an ornate wall with two teller windows. Dark, expensive paneling and an opulent desk to his right made Ridge shake his head at the waste of money. Grinning to himself, he wondered if they spent as much money on the safe.

An elderly woman behind one of the barred openings smiled when she saw him. "How can I help you, sir?"

"You can start by not screaming." He pointed the rifle to the left of the gaping woman. A man at a desk back there saw him and rose. "The safe is locked!"

"Don't care." Moving fast, he crossed the small space and kicked a Dutch door off the hinges. Stepping through to the forbidden side of the bank, he leveled the rifle at the man who was reaching for a desk drawer. "This isn't a robbery, but don't you draw no gun on me."

Looking down the rifle's muzzle, the banker raised both hands. "Don't shoot me."

"I don't intend to. Y'all get out the back door now, while you can."

To emphasize his point, Ridge picked up an oil lamp and threw it against a nearby wall with the crash of glass as the thin-walled chimney shattered. The kerosene exploded into flame and the woman yelped. Ridge pointed at the rear exit with the rifle. "Run!"

They fled through the rear, and he pitched a second lamp against the teller cage. A flash of heat prickled his exposed skin as Ridge stalked through the front door and back onto the street, closing the door behind him to hold the smoke in as long as possible.

Barely two doors down, he saw a pair of Three Fork men coming his way from the direction of the fires. One was heavyset and the other wore a wide-brimmed hat. Two others following closely behind and carrying shotguns looked more at home in a shop of some kind.

They saw each other at the same time. Ridge leveled the rifle. "Texas Ranger! Official business. Put down your arms."

The townies disappeared like spirits, but the Barlow men clawed at the weapons under their coats. In such cold, few people were carrying guns in the open, and that was what Ridge was counting on. Weapons were no good if you couldn't get to them.

The Henry in his hands barked, and the heavyset one on the left went down, fumbling at the buttons that held his coat closed. The other was faster and managed to free an old cap-and-ball revolver. Ridge jacked a fresh round into the chamber and the rifle thundered again.

He missed, and the one under a big hat spread his feet and fired. His shot flew wide, and Ridge ducked sideways. He rounded an old broomtail tied to the hitching post, and when he came around the other side, the Henry now at his shoulder fired again.

The cowboy trying to hide behind a support post stumbled back and cocked his pistol again. When he squeezed the trigger, the gun misfired, and he cocked it once more. Ridge took careful aim at the second button on his coat and squeezed the trigger like he was target shooting. The big slug hit true and the guy fell back, arms sprawled like wings.

As smoke roiled from the bank and flames flashed red and orange inside, Ridge looked like an angel of vengeance as he continued past the bodies and down the street, hoping more Three Fork riders showed up.

Especially Judd and Son.

CHAPTER 39

Separated from Ridge by several buildings, the crackle of gunfire reached Judd and Son. The younger man whirled at the sound, a pistol in his hand.

Judd threw him a disgusted look and flung an arm around. "That's coming from over in the street. What're you gonna shoot here?"

"If it's the Ranger, he's liable to boil around a corner at any minute."

"He's involved for sure, but maybe it's the boys doing the killing. No matter, we're still heading to Nellie's."

Son pointed. "We can cut through up there."

Judd felt heat rise into his face. He wasn't much for following orders and answered only to old man Barlow. Being saddled off with this shavetail was almost too much for him. "We could, but I want to go around this fire and come in from the opposite side. There's too many people out there fighting that thing."

Son looked at the glow ahead. "What difference does it make?"

"It's the way I want to do it."

Frustrated that he was being told what to do, Son rebelled. "You go on and take the long way, then."

Judd knew it wasn't a five-minute difference, but he wanted to do it his way. Like two bucks tangling, he wasn't about to let the younger man try to be the boss of their outfit.

Judd stopped for a moment, trying to intimidate his boss's son. He needed to keep his bluff in, and letting the slender man bow up at him would be the first crack in his façade. "You'll get in trouble out there."

Son patted the butt of his pistol. "Nothing I can't get out of."

"If you aren't careful, that thing'll get you into more than you can handle."

"From you, or others?"

Judd glared. "I'm just looking out for you. You know, the way you're acting, I have a sneaking suspicion you might know more about all this than you're letting on."

Without answering, Son ducked between two buildings and disappeared. Giving the burning building a wide berth, Judd circled around to come into Nellie's from the west side like he wanted to in the first place.

Moments later, Son came back around and followed like a puppy.

CHAPTER 40

Circling Nellie's Place, Judd and Son eased up on a side porch and slipped through the door he used to visit Bessie when Son wasn't around. He never could figure if Bessie liked him or Son the most, but each time he came in, she acted as if he were the only man in the world for her.

Low voices came from the kitchen and in an off side of the house, maybe another sitting room, someone was playing the piano. The calming sound was out of place with all that was going on in town, but the player had nimble fingers and the music was as good as any he'd ever heard.

Seminole Sam would have been a problem had he been downstairs, but since there were no customers that time of day and possibly because of the weather, the big breed was somewhere out of sight. Judd breathed a sigh of relief at the realization he wouldn't have to engage the man who fought for a living. Judd's only alternative would be to shoot him, and because he was there to take

Maggie and Jo, if he was caught, a jury would find him guilty of murder if the big man died.

Instead, the only two people they saw were Maggie and Jo. Both were napping on the sofas, likely exhausted from the night before and their escape from her store. He started for them when a whisper from the stairs caught his attention.

Judd whispered in Son's ear, "You go over there in the corner so no one can see you and wait."

"For what?"

"For me to tell you what to do."

Sulking, Son went to the far end of the parlor so he could keep an eye on the mother and daughter, and sat behind a huge ornate pot so that only his feet were visible.

Judd crept upstairs, thankful for the carpet runner to pad the sound of his boots. He reached the top and found Bessie Waggoner standing in her doorway, dressed as he'd never seen her. He put a finger to his lips and she disappeared inside.

Walking on his toes and feeling ridiculous, Judd crept down the hall and into her room.

She closed the door, making sure the latch didn't snap, and threw her arms around him. "I'm so glad you came. Is Son with you?"

"No," he lied.

"Well, I thought we were getting out of here."

"So that's why you're wearing clothes."

"I always wear clothes."

"Not this kind."

"I have to get out sometimes, so this is what I wear."

She fiddled with the top button that was at the base of her neck. "When are we leaving?"

"Not right now."

"But we need to go. It's the perfect time. Sam just went out to do his business, and he takes a long time."

"You've been watching out the window?"

"Of course, silly. I've been waiting on you or Son so we can leave and get on with our new life." She ran the palm of her hand inside his coat and against his chest. "It'll be the three of us, taking the world by the throat."

"The three of us?"

"Why, sure. You know I like you both, and I know y'all've talked about how we can make this work."

Stunned, Judd shook his head. "We're friends, but me and Son ain't that close. Not enough to share one woman."

She licked her lips, shifting ideas. "That's all right. It'll be me and Son, then. Just get me out of here so we can go."

"You think you can ride off in this weather?"

"The stage'll be here soon."

"And just where do you think we can light until then? There's a lot going on in this world, and you aren't exactly welcome after letting me and Son go."

"Where's Son? You can take me to him."

"You're not getting this, gal. There ain't no *us*. There's just me, and I don't intend to swing from a rope for any reason."

Bessie grabbed his sleeve. "Y'all promised to take me out of here. Now's the time."

"When did I tell you that?"

"Well, we talked about going someplace else."

"You're getting mixed up. I believe that's a conversation you had with Son. If I said anything like that, it was the whiskey talking."

"You won't take me with you?"

"You can wait for Son if you want to, but right now I have things to do."

The soft, childlike look on her face vanished and hard edges suddenly appeared, along with black eyes that went cold and crazy. Like magic, a thin knife appeared in her hand and she thrust it toward his stomach. Her eyes and expression gave her away, and he had half a second to realize what was happening.

He caught her forearm and twisted it back, forcing her elbow straight and down. Using his other hand, he twisted the knife from her fingers and buried it to the hilt in her heart. Bessie's eyes fluttered and she gasped in pain.

Leaving the knife where it was, he slapped his hand over her mouth and eased her body backward onto the bed. Bessie blinked a couple of times and died without a struggle.

Pausing to listen, Judd waited to see if anyone had heard the sound, but nothing had changed in the building. He pulled back the covers, rolled her onto her side, and covered the body until nothing but her hair showed. Stepped back, he studied his work and was satisfied it looked like she was asleep.

Cracking the door, he peered into the hallway to find it quiet. He slipped down the hall and then the stairs. He felt his stomach sink when he couldn't find Son. It was only when he moved his foot that he caught sight of the young man behind the pot.

He leaned in and whispered, pointing at Jo and Maggie, "I'll take them out, and you stay behind in case anything goes wrong."

"Like what?"

Judd stifled the urge to punch the imbecile. "Like someone comes down here looking for them in the next five minutes. Wait that long, and then slip out and meet me at the hotel."

It was a simple thing to pick up Jo. The little girl was sleeping hard, and when he laid her head on his shoulder, she barely stirred.

Lying on her side, Maggie's mouth was partially open, and he paused for a minute to admire her look. A laugh came from upstairs and a female voice came to him. "Ivy, have you seen Nell?"

"She's in her room as far as I know."

Afraid they were going to come downstairs, he shook Maggie awake and put his hand over her mouth. When her eyes snapped open, she gasped with fear at the sight of a man holding Jo. Realizing who it was, she sat up and gently moved his hand. She whispered, "Don't hurt my baby."

"Then you keep quiet and do what I say."

Maggie saw the hand supporting Jo. "You have blood on your hand." She licked her lips and swallowed. "Is she hurt?"

"No. This is from one of the girls upstairs who crossed me. Don't let it happen to you."

"Let me have her."

"No. And if you scream or shout out, I'll shoot you and she'll grow up without a mama."

She nodded and saw Son standing nearby before she glanced toward the stairs, as if hoping help would come from that direction. "What do you want?"

"Follow me."

Resisting the urge to reach out and move the curls from her sleeping daughter's forehead, she nodded and rose. Not knowing what else to do, Maggie had no doubt Judd would shoot her.

The side porch they used to enter the house was off the parlor, with steps leading down to a path between the Reynolds Hotel and Nellie's, beaten by hundreds of feet going back and forth at all hours of the day and night. The path was completely buried under the snow, but he knew where it was.

"You keep your head down and don't look at anyone if they pass. Just shrink up and stay under my feet."

The cold was intense, the light dark and flat. Jo tightened her shoulders and slid her arms between her and Judd for the warmth. Coatless, Maggie followed him to the hotel as the sounds of gunfire back in town followed them, sounding like war.

CHAPTER 41

The two Three Fork riders lay sprawled in the street that had quickly emptied during the gun battle. Standing beside a hitching post and taking stock of his surroundings, Ridge dug more ammunition from his pockets and reloaded the Henry.

Breath fogging in front of them, a second pair of gunmen appeared out of nowhere in front of Ridge. One wore a three-day scrub on his jaws and the other a young man's wispy mustache that might or might not come in thick once he was fully mature.

When they saw him, there was no shouting. No orders. Two pistols came up and they fired almost at the same time.

Innocent men who'd reemerged to begin fighting the fires again scattered like quail, seeking shelter wherever they could. One yanked open the door of a closed sweet shop and fell inside the dark store. Others simply ran between buildings, across the street, and toward any kind of cover they saw.

The slugs whizzed past Ridge like angry insects. Scruffy crouched behind a stack of nail kegs stacked in front of a hardware store and rested his arm on the top one like he was taking target practice with a pistol.

Seeing red that he was being hunted and they wouldn't quit, Ridge dodged to his left and then juked to the right, throwing off their aim. His feet slipped on the icy ground and he landed hard on his side.

The muzzle flashes seemed so close he almost thought he could feel the heat. Scrabbling onto one knee and still in the open, he shouldered the rifle and punched a hole in Scruffy. Throwing his hands wide, his smoking pistol flew into the street to disappear in the snow. He fell back, slamming into his partner and ruining his aim.

The kid with the wispy mustache fired at the same time he caught himself. His pistol went off and the slug dug a chunk out of a hitching rail over the Ranger's shoulder. Heart hammering, Ridge took a deep breath and squeezed the trigger. The 45-70 caught the man under the collarbone, dropping him in his tracks.

"Don't you move!"

Ridge whirled to see what he took for a counterman in a white apron from his chest to his knees and aiming a double-barrel shotgun at his middle. He straightened up, holding the rifle like he was hunting. Ridge's mouth went dry, and he expected at any moment to feel the slap of a bullet. "Easy. I'm a Texas Ranger."

The balding man's eyes flashed. "You're the one burning down our whole town and you're gonna stop that right now."

"Take a breath here." Ridge glanced past him to see others coming down the street. "What's burning is

Barlow property. Nothing else. You know it as well as I do."

The twin barrels never wavered. "The whole town will catch."

Fighting the urge to shout, Ridge wanted their stand-off to end before more Three Fork men found them. "I'm on your side. Lower that gun and let me go before more of 'em show up. I'm gonna finish this up and find out who shot Runt."

"I've heard you killed him."

"Look at these bodies. They're not from town. They're Barlow's soldiers who've been trying to take over Blackjack. Look, I know you have me where you want me, but there's a telegram coming in from the county sheriff who says I'm here on the side of the law."

A flicker passed over the man's eyes. "That badge real, then?"

"It is. Doc and Joe Mayse'll vouch for me, and so will Runt."

"Runt's dead."

"Not so's you'd notice it."

The barrels lowered as men converged on where they stood. "Look, I'm—"

Coming from the east, Jim Barlow led an army of his men down the street, pushing other people out of the way through sheer cussedness. The shopkeeper turned at the sound, and when he turned back, Ridge was gone.

CHAPTER 42

Gunfire reached Barlow's cold ears a couple of minutes before they arrived at the outer edge of town. The rattle of gunfire caused his men to tense. They fumbled with coats and reached inside to make sure nothing bound their firearms.

There was more activity in the street than the rancher expected in such weather, and he slowed the big Appaloosa stud he rode more for show than anything else. The glow of a fire against the low clouds looked like someone had opened a door into hell. He expected to find a building or shed burning but was stunned to see what appeared to be at first glance half of the town in flames.

Pausing, he studied the street stretching out before them and noted where the blazes were located. "By God, they're all mine!"

James McClellan, one of his men who'd been with him longer than most, moved up abreast of his boss. "I don't see any of our boys here. They should have stopped all this."

"How many do we have in town?"

"Ten, maybe. Judd's here with Son, too, as far as I know."

Barlow noted that he said Judd's name first. It was another concern the older man had been struggling with, because his boy wasn't passing muster with the men they paid. He wasn't one of them, nor the man next in charge, just a wet-behind-the-ears kid and nothing more.

"When we find them," the rancher clenched his jaw, "I'm gonna kill 'em all for letting this happen."

The Kingman livery was the first big structure on their right as they rode into town. The snow was churned up all around the building, and as they passed, Barlow saw some of it was stained with blood.

The doors were closed, but he felt as if eyes were watching them pass. Walking their horses abreast and taking up the entire street, the crew followed close by. They passed a handful of buildings before reaching Maggie's mercantile on the left. It appeared to be closed up, not even the light of a single lamp pushed back the darkness.

Across and down the street, his bank was burning bright, black smoke roiling out of broken windows and the door. Despite being covered in snow, the buildings on either side were starting to smolder. Ten feet of space wasn't enough separation, but it gave the bucket brigade fighting the fire enough room to continually douse the walls with water. Some were even scooping up buckets of snow and throwing it through the windows.

A sea of icy mud, water, and slushy snow reached almost across the street. Horses' hooves splattered slop that struck anyone nearby. His attention focused on the building, Barlow rode without slowing. "My money."

As if the line of Blackjack residents fighting the fire didn't cross the street, Barlow rode between them, followed by the Three Fork riders. Shouts and curses followed them as the bucket brigade ducked and dodged out of the way.

Looking straight ahead once again, the grim-faced rancher continued down the street to pass his saloon and livery, which had already collapsed but was still burning. Tired men backed out of the way. High above them, Barlow glared at the scene. "Who's the sidewinder responsible for this?"

Sweaty despite the cold, and wet from the knees down, a man with an empty bucket answered. Rivulets ran from under his wet derby hat. "Some Texas Ranger."

"Where is he?"

"Nobody knows, but there's a posse after him and they aren't doing much good. Look in any direction at all, these guys watching us, people who're all bundled up. Hard to tell who's who." Shrugging, the man jerked a thumb down the street. "All I know is that he was just down there killing some more of your men a few minutes ago."

Barlow's eyes flashed, and he thought about whipping the messenger with the lariat rope on his saddle. Rough, work-hardened fingers fiddled with the saddle string's knot holding the rope by his knee. "What do you mean, some *more* of my men? Who're you?"

"Ed Dumas, but you won't know me. I spend most of my time cutting wood, not trying to put it out."

"How many of my people are hurt?"

"Mister, I don't have any idea, but I know that every one of them who went up against that Ranger are either dead or so shot up they ain't got no more fight left in 'em."

Barlow turned to McClellan. "Send somebody back there to find out what he's talking about. Have 'em ask Runt."

Dumas laughed. "The marshal's dead," he shrugged, "or alive, depending on who's telling the story." He flipped his hand back and forth. "You'll have to find somebody else. You could go to the newspaper office, if we had one, but we don't." The woodcutter cackled at his own wit.

Barlow rode on as McClellan pointed at one of their riders. "Go back and find out what the hell's going on around here."

He wheeled his mount and went back the way they had come. The rest of his men followed, silent as the grave at the devastation around them. Farther down the street, the now-smoking ruins of the Barlow and Son Mercantile was a total loss. Most of those who'd been fighting that fire had moved down the street to the Red River and the bank, leaving the blackened timbers behind to burn themselves out.

Only a few doors down, people were gathered around two bodies lying on the boardwalk.

One of Barlow's riders spoke low and sad when he got a good look at the bloody corpses. "That's Hut and Brushy. I figured Brushy could take care of himself, but that kid never was much punkin'."

Barlow spat to the side. "He was old enough to hire on as a gun hand, and he knew what that meant."

A stranger rose and addressed the rancher. "I'm sorry they're still laying here. We sent for Doc and the undertaker to bring a wagon, but I hear they've been right busy today."

"I don't care." Barlow pointed. "What happened to 'em?"

The stranger pulled his coat up tight around his neck. "Tangled with that Texas Ranger."

"How come someone hasn't killed that mutt?"

"Nobody's good enough."

Shaking his head, Barlow led the way through what looked like a battlefield and reined up in front of his store. Farther down and across the street was Nellie's Place, which looked untouched except for all the snow that had melted from the heat. On past there and far from everything else, the hotel still stood, and he wondered why, but his livery, which was framed and roofed, was gone.

It was the last building he owned. Catching movement on the social club's porch, Barlow turned to see Son coming out of the door. The young man's face showed surprise at running into his father so suddenly.

The rancher's face darkened and a rage rose in his chest. Son had been inside entertaining himself in that brothel while his town, his legacy, burned. Someone who carried his name wasn't worth a damn, and it infuriated the old man. Spurring the stud, Barlow yanked the reins and rushed toward his startled son, who came down the steps at an insolent speed.

The Appaloosa's sudden stop threw snow and cold mud onto the slender young man, who reached the bottom step and looked up. He brushed at the spots on his coat and pants. "You're a l-l-little late, Daddy."

Resisting the urge to jump off his horse and beat his only son bloody, Barlow set his jaw. "What do you mean?"

"We've been in a f-f-fight here, as you can see."

"Looks like one you lost."

"N-n-not hardly."

"How so?" He leaned down and slapped the young man with his hat. "Almost everything we own here's burned to the ground except for the hotel, and I'm not sure is ain't scorched where I can't see it."

Hand up to prevent another blow, Son ducked his head. "Judd and I h-h-had an idea."

"Well, it's good to hear *he's* still alive. I hope your idea didn't have anything to do with all this!" Jaw trembling with rage, he jerked a thumb down the street.

"We changed the game. We intend to s-s-stop it."

Frustrated with how his boy was drawing out the conversation, Barlow took a deep breath and let it out in a cloud of vapor. In times of extreme stress, especially when he was talking to the elder Barlow, Son had to concentrate on his speech. Ever since he was a child, he'd get nervous and find himself stuttering.

"Get ahold of yourself, boy, and slow down. You have about one minute to tell me what's happened here before I climb down off this stud and beat you to death."

Son's face blanched. Several times as he was growing up, his father's legendary temper got out of hand

and he'd suffered the results. More than one hired hand who had words with him rode off nursing bruises and broken bones. Two who went so far as to slap leather were sleeping under wooden crosses not far from the house.

Standing in the snow and looking up at Barlow, Son swallowed and related everything that had happened since the evening before, leaving out the parts he was ashamed of.

Barlow listened, jaw clenched and the big muscle in his temple throbbing as his teeth ground together. "I can't imagine what this outfit will be like when I'm gone and you're in charge. All right, what stroke of brilliance is going to solve all this, and first off, what were you doing in this cathouse while our town burned to the ground?"

"I . . . I . . . I was inside with N-N-Nellie, telling her what's going to happen if th-th-that Ranger doesn't give himself up."

"Nellie? What'n hell does she have to do with all this?"

"M-M-Maggie's been hiding here with her."

Barlow tilted back his hat and rubbed his forehead. "Tell me, too, so I'll know. What does Maggie have to do with this?"

"She's hooked up with that Ranger, and I think she had something to do with the marshal's death. We figured that if we took her out to the ranch, we could bargain with the Ranger to just go away and leave us alone. At least he can cool down."

Barlow's voice was flat and disbelieving. "You'd

hold her hostage until he saw the futility of fighting you and just ride off, is that what you think?"

"It sounds a little different when you say it out loud." With the Three Fork crew watching and smirking, Son stopped, squinted his eyes, and screwed up his face to get the words out. "Think of it. We have Maggie and her little girl now. If the Ranger don't give up, they'll never see them again."

"You *stole* a woman and a child." The elder Barlow's words were flat, almost a slap.

Son opened his mouth and his brain misfired. He wanted to speak normally but stuck on the letter *I*. "I-I-I-I-I-I'm not sure that's the word I'd use. We're holding them for r-ransom, I'd say."

"Look around you, Son. The man you're trifling with is the devil, and I doubt he's even mad yet. When he finds out what you've done, he's gonna finish pulling hell down around our ears. Whatever you ask of him won't be enough to save you, or me, or our ranch."

For the first time since he walked outside, Son looked as if he didn't know what to say. "I just t-t-tried to think like you."

"Well, you did a damned poor job of it. You're up against a man who'll walk down a street and *invite* people to try to kill him. From what I hear, you don't know what to *do* with a man like that. To tell you the truth, I don't know if we have enough men to stop him."

"I have some news for you, Boss." McClellan moved his horse up close to the old man. "But let me kill this Ranger for you first."

Before Barlow could answer, the big man grunted

at the same time the flat report of a gunshot echoed off the buildings around them. Already dead before he hit the ground, McClellan landed hard and didn't move.

The riders around Barlow scattered as he ducked low and kicked his stud into a run around the side of Nellie's and out of sight. Son sidestepped, threw a shot where he thought the bullet came from, and raced back up the steps he'd just descended and shoved his way inside as female screams poured out around him.

The Barlow men didn't know where to go. Two broncs forgot their training and crowhopped, forcing the riders to hang on. Guns drawn, the others reined their horses around, looking for a target. A rifle barked again, and another man dropped.

Struggling to get his horse under control, one of the Three Fork men shouted, "We gotta get out of here or he's gonna kill us all!"

He flipped back over the saddle and was still in the churned snow as the rest of them raced back down the street where they came from.

CHAPTER 43

Angry with himself for waiting so long, Ridge Tisdale stepped out of the empty bakery not far from Nellie's and into the street that only moments before was filled with Three Fork men. He'd slipped in from the back and barely cracked the door about an inch as Son Barlow told his dad everything that had happened.

From where Ridge stood inside the shop to listen to the exchange between the two, there was a support post and a horse tied to the rack out in front of the parlor house that prevented him from seeing Son. He suspected the older man sitting high on an Appaloosa stud to be the rancher who'd started all this mess but hesitated to be sure. By the time he was certain of Barlow's identity, a big man with deep creases in his cheeks pushed his horse between them, blocking his shot and declaring he would kill Ridge.

The Ranger knew better than to shoot from a window or open door. They'd be less likely to see him if he stood back. He'd been debating what to do. He wanted Son, and for sure old man Barlow, but when the big cowboy declared he was going to murder Ridge, the

Ranger was enough of an Indian fighter to consider the dance to be open. With the odds so much in their favor, all he could do was take out the big talker, and he did.

There was no regret for shooting from cover. Some might have called it bushwhacking, but Ridge served the law and, as such, had been threatened with murder. Someone was always the better or he was outnumbered, whether it was a bar fight or a Comanche war party. Twenty against one in the street was as unfair as you could get, and he needed to whittle down their numbers as much as possible any way he could.

He knew good and well, too, that his actions would be twisted in the telling, and by those with their own axes to grind and loyalties, into a simple bushwhacking. He didn't care, though. In his opinion, he was in the right and doing what needed to be done.

As Ridge turned to leave, someone kicked in the bakery's back door and came in shooting. It was a long building, and narrow. Ridge ducked down behind a counter. Two bullets ripped great chunks out of the countertop, shattering glass covers and scattering baked goods across the floor. One of the horsemen out in the street must have circled around to come in back. The shots came so quick and fast, all he could do was stick the Colt over the top and squeeze off three rounds to throw his attacker off-guard.

Another pistol back there cracked, and the air was full of bullets headed in Ridge's general direction. A second gunman joined the battle. Staying and fighting wasn't an option. He was about to be caught in a crossfire.

The front door was still cracked open, as he'd left it

to shoot. Throwing two more shots toward the back to keep their heads down, Ridge charged outside and right into more guns of those still out there.

Not all of the Three Fork riders had fled down the street. Three remained behind and were kneeling beside McClellan's body and another man who lay sprawled several feet away. One of their well-trained horses was ground tied in the street between Ridge and the Three Fork men, snorting and rolling his eyes.

Their shots were erratic and completely missed the Ranger. One shattered the window on the bakery door, and another hit an iron hinge, careering off down the street. Whoever was in back was suddenly ducking bullets from his own crew.

"Stop shooting this way! Me'n Caleb are back here!"

Getting shut of that place fast was Ridge's only hope. Hating to do it, he saw only one way to escape all those guns that were aimed at him. He dropped the Henry on the boardwalk to free up his hands. Shoving the empty revolver into his shoulder holster, he raced to the roan between them, grabbed the loose reins, and stuck his left foot in the stirrup, yanking the horse's head around to keep it between him and the guns.

As the two Three Fork men fired, he kept that leg bent and, clutching the saddle horn, he yanked at the bit and the horse whirled. Keeping his head low, he hung off the side like a Comanche, keeping the big animal between him and sure death.

A slug slapped the pommel just before he disappeared between two buildings, barely missing his arm wrapped around the horn. Once out of sight, he rose and swung his right leg across the saddle and did what he hoped they wouldn't suspect.

He rode around behind the burned-out mercantile, and the moment he was out of sight, looped the reins around the saddle horn and kicked out of the stirrups. Staying on the horse would be suicide; those who'd scattered would soon reassemble and take off after him. Slapping the horse on the rear, he headed toward the Chinese laundry some distance back, hoping they would hide him.

"Here!"

The familiar voice belonged to Joseph Mayse. The undertaker and Doc rode side by side on a buckboard, coming to the sound of trouble. Immediately reading the situation, Mayse stepped down. "Give me your hat."

They traded covers. The undertaker's hat was a little large, and it set down on his forehead and ears. Eyes darting all around, Doc stood and took off his long overcoat. "Trade with me."

Ridge plucked the badge off his coat and pulled on the one Doc offered, looking completely different from only a moment earlier. Mayse snapped the reins and they continued on their way around the backside of the street.

Seconds later, Ridge walked between two buildings and onto the main street that was a sea of excited men and horses hurrying on dozens of errands.

No one paid him any attention as he crossed to the other side and headed back to Maggie's. He wanted Runt's shotgun now that his Henry was gone, and needed a few minutes to gather himself and decide what to do next. Besides, right then everyone who was looking to kill him was at the other end of town.

Old man Barlow and Son would have to wait, but he made a vow to himself. He'd kill them both before it was over, if he had to take off that badge to do it.

CHAPTER 44

No one was behind the hotel registration desk when they entered, and Judd went straight up the stairs and to the farthest room in the back. Both he and Maggie left wet footprints on the wooden steps and down the wide hall.

Jo was still groggy when he laid her on the bed. "I'm going to tie your hands for a little while. Hers too. We can do this any way you want, but if you fight or cause a fuss, you'll find yourselves on the hard floor. Do what I say and y'all can be comfortable on the bed."

"No!" She whirled and reached for the door, maybe to escape or to shout for help, but Judd wasn't taking any chances now that he'd crossed an invisible line that would have him swinging from a rope if anyone found out what he'd done.

He balled his fist and cracked the redhead on the jaw. Maggie fell back beside Jo, startling the little girl to full wakefulness. She shrieked and reached for her mother, as staccato gunfire in the street covered the sounds of their struggle. Judd slapped her with the palm of his hand. The blow stunned the little girl, and she threw herself down on the bed, hiding her face in a pillow, wailing.

He drew piggin' strings from his coat. An experienced cowhand, Judd had them both tied before they regained their wits. Remembering how the Ranger had gagged him and Son, Judd snatched two washrags from the washstand and stuffed them into their mouths to silence them. Eyes watering from the blow, fear, and pain, Maggie tried to butt his chin with her head.

Judd dodged her and used a forearm across her throat. "I oughta drag you onto the floor for that."

Maggie glared at him, and when he looked at Jo, the little girl's eyes flashed in exactly the same way as she fought the binds around her wrists.

"You two are a couple of hellions."

Judd used two more piggin' strings to secure the gags and tightened them with solid knots. Finished and breathing hard, as if he'd been running, he backed away from the bed and looked out the window that overlooked nothing on that side but leafless mesquite trees and a gray, old world.

"I think Son's gonna be here in a little while, and when your Ranger friend shows up, we'll finish this up with him and I'll decide what to do with the two of you."

Maggie turned and wriggled closer to Jo, who sniffled and struggled to breathe through her snot- and fear-clogged nose.

For the first time, Judd showed some concern for the child. "Jo, calm down or you're not going to be able to breathe. Take slow, deep breaths."

He took off his hat and hung it on a rack beside the door. "I had my nose broke once, and that's what I had to do this morning when your buddy had me and Son hugging those chairs."

They quieted, and Judd took the only chair in the room. He cut a chew off a plug of tobacco and tucked it into his cheek, watching out the window at the white, cotton world.

Nearly thirty minutes later, heavy footsteps came down the hall and Judd drew his pistol. A soft knock came on the door. "It's me."

He turned the knob and Son walked in, breathing hard.

Judd checked the hall. "No problems?"

Barely glancing at the two on the bed, he walked over to a metal contraption on the wall. Rubbing his hands together, he shivered. "This new steam heat is magic. That's why I like this room. A couple of the others up here don't even have a fireplace."

Judd didn't care about the hotel amenities. "What was all that shooting?"

"Which time?"

"The last one."

Son looked uncomfortable. "I didn't stay inside like you said. There was too much going on, and I left as soon as you did. It was that damned Ranger again. He almost killed me and the old man in front of Nellie's. Shot three others. Ambushed. He don't fight like a white man."

"Why didn't you kill him?"

"Didn't have a chance. I was standing there talking

to Daddy and he shot McClellan right out of the saddle. Two or three rounds just missed my head, and then he hit some others. We all scattered."

"Where'd he shoot from? He didn't come walking down the middle of the street like he did earlier."

"The bakery. This guy's a ghost. Shoots from one place, then disappears and pops up somewhere else. He stole a horse and rode off, and the next thing we knew, someone caught the horse only a couple of minutes later, and now we don't know where he is."

Judd considered the new twist on their situation. Meeting Maggie's eyes, he stared right through her, not registering the daggers she was throwing at him. "Barlow's in town? How many men did he bring?"

"All of 'em."

"He'll find that guy, then, and kill him."

"He'll be here soon. He wants to talk to both of us about this." Son nodded his head at Maggie.

"How does he know?"

Son looked uncomfortable. "I told him."

"When? Where?"

"He caught me coming out of Nellie's, right before the Ranger bushwhacked us."

"Bessie told me y'all's plan." Judd rubbed his forehead. "Were you thinking of taking her with us?"

"Of course. She's my girl."

"She's a whore. She belongs to anyone with a dollar in his pocket and a few minutes of idle time."

Son's mouth tightened. "What does that mean?"

"It means I been with her, too, stupid. And she had

in her mind the three of us were going to just set up somewhere and play house. Was that your idea?"

Son rubbed his forehead, thinking. "It was an idea before Daddy . . . Dad rode in and made me tell him everything."

"Everything! You just stood right there in the middle of the street and announced what we did?"

"I was on my way over here and he surprised me by showing up, asking a lot of questions and talking to beat the band."

Judd slapped the younger man as if he were a woman. Son staggered back against the foot of the bed frame. He launched himself toward Judd, throwing a round-house swing that the more experienced fighter dodged. The fist flashed by and he jabbed Son in the mouth, followed by a hard right that bounced him off the wall.

It wasn't Son's first fight, but he was never good at fisticuffs. Throwing himself against Judd, he knocked the bigger man off-balance. When Judd pushed young Barlow back, Son swung with all his might, catching Judd on the cheek and snapping his head around. He swung again and missed, and Judd regained his balance.

He threw a stiff left into Son's ribs and when he grunted and gave in to that side, he dropped his guard. Judd hit him in the nose, which crunched under his fist. Blood poured, and he hit him again. Son slid down the edge of the bed and onto the floor.

Using both feet to push himself back against the wall, he snatched the Colt from his holster and cocked it. "Touch me again and I'll kill you."

Breathing hard, Judd backed up a step. "You better shoot me now."

"I don't want to. I just want you to quit hitting me."

"I killed the last man who drew on me."

"You won't kill me because the old man'll hang you sure as we're both breathing."

A hard knock came on the door, and they forgot what they were doing. "Open this damned door."

It was Jim Barlow, and he was mad enough to hang them both.

CHAPTER 45

Fearing an ambush from Barlow and his crew, Drake Hutchins and the Oarlock outfit took the long way around to come into town from the west. Wes cut their trail once they left the Three Fork ranch house, but Hutchins had no intention to follow their path.

In places the snow was only a couple of feet deep, but in a few the drifts were high. Picking their way across the flats, Drake and Wes had to avoid short cholla, which could fill their horses' legs with painful spines. They followed a meandering wash that ranged from a couple of feet deep to places where it was impossible to see a man on horseback.

It was at one such deep place that a band of Comanches suddenly appeared, following a game trail leading up to intersect their riders. Drake and Wes pulled up when they saw the first two Indians and quickly moved to the side so the remainder of their party could reach the top.

They spread out, prepared for anything, mirroring what the Oarlock men did.

"Uh-oh." Wes had been carrying his Henry across

his thighs, but several of his men had them in their scabbards and unavailable at once.

Drake stopped on his right, away from the rifle's muzzle. "Boys, take it easy. Don't move fast. This is a hunting party."

A voice came from behind him. "They don't have to wear paint to fight."

One of the long-haired men ahead of them on a gray stud raised a hand. He also carried a rifle across his thighs. There were a dozen men in his party, who were armed with both rifles and bows. A couple even had pistols in their belts, but there were plenty of war clubs and axes in sight.

"You boys sit easy." Drake raised his palm outward and rode forward with Wes by his side.

"You don't see Comanches wrapped up that much," Wes said.

"Them blankets and stolen coats are loose."

Being respectful, and because Drake didn't like to holler across any distance to a man, they waited to talk until they were close. "Name's Drake Hutchins. You speak English?"

The man with a broad nose and dark eyes nodded. "Some."

Drake talked, along with basic sign language. "You're hungry. Hunting?"

The man waved a hand toward the sky and snow. "Yes."

"Wish we had something for you, but we don't."

"Horse."

"Yep, but we're riding 'em all." Wes nodded and

smiled. "If you want a horse, go home and eat one of yours."

The warrior seemed to consider his words. "Trade."

Knowing his partner could be short and smart alecky in his answers and comments, Drake leaned forward in the saddle to show he was the one to talk to. "What do you need?"

"Ammunition."

"Nope." He turned to Wes and grinned. "Dig out a couple of them nasty cigars you're always trying to kill me with and give him a couple."

"You don't know good smokes when you see them." Smiling and nodding, Wes slowly reached into his coat and came out with a pair of cigars. Holding them up, he nudged his horse forward and passed them to the leader.

Refusing to back up, Wes stayed where he was, and Hutchins had to join him, putting them within reach of the leader and another warrior.

The Comanche pointed at himself. "Na'taa." He pointed at Wes. "I shot at you on the Canadian River. I remember your cigar."

"Your English suddenly got better." Wes considered the recollection. "We were in a fight there. You missed."

"You missed, too." The Comanche flicked a finger past his ear.

"We won, though." Wes chuckled. "You remember that fight, Drake?"

"I do." He made a point of counting the warriors scattered in front of them, then he turned to look at his men, making it obvious there were more of them, than the Comanche. "Good luck hunting."

"The weather will break soon. No more snow by tomorrow." Na'taa pointed at the ground. "Deer tracks lead that way, where we will go. Next time maybe we won't be so hungry."

Drake understood the statement. "We'll be ready."

Na'taa handed one of the cigars to a hook-nosed man beside him and turned his horse to follow the trail broken by a deer. "Maybe your Comanche will be better by then, too."

Wes laughed as he and Drake led their men at an angle away from the direction the Comanches traveled.

When they reached Blackjack, Hutchins reined up at the edge of town in shock as he took in the street that men, hooves, and wagons were quickly turning into a dark, nasty quagmire.

The familiar scent of woodsmoke filled the air, clashing with the unpleasant odor of wet ashes. If he didn't know any better, he would have thought Na'taa and his Comanche warriors had raided through town and tried to burn it to the ground. It took a minute to realize the burned-out building beyond Nellie's Place was Barlow's mercantile.

To their right, the untouched two-story Reynolds Hotel stood alone and covered with snow. A crowd of riders sat on their mounts out front, and they stirred at the sight of the Oarlock riders. A couple of figures stepped down and pulled rifles from their scabbards. Others remained in the saddle, throwing looks between the hotel and the new arrivals.

Resting the butt of his Winchester on one thigh, Wes chewed the stub of his cigar back into position. "Well, don't that beat all? We ride all over hell's half acre and run smack into the very men we're both looking for and trying to avoid."

Hutchins unbuttoned his coat to reach his Colt in case he had to act fast. "You see Barlow with them?"

"It's a ways off, but no. With all them sitting there like they're waiting to ride in a parade, I suspect he's inside. Zeke, your eyes are probably better than mine. You see Barlow?"

"No, sir. Son isn't there, either. Judd's the one we need to watch."

"Which one's he?"

"I don't see him, neither, and it bothers me that all three of them are out of sight."

Unsure of what to do, Hutchins considered their situation. "How many riders do you count, Zeke?"

"About the same as us."

Wes found a Lucifer in his pocket and thumbed it alive. Lighting the cigar stub, he flicked the match into the snow. "I don't believe a cavalry charge will be a good idea. We get to shooting, we're liable to lose as many as they do."

"Well, we can't sit here all day acting like we're afraid." Hutchins walked his bay forward, reins in his left hand and his right resting close to the pistol on his hip. "Remember what I told you boys back at Barlow's ranch: scatter out."

Putting a little distance between them, Wes paced

behind Hutchins. "These boys behind us are watching you."

"That's what they need to do." He called over his shoulder, "Zeke."

"Yessir."

"Y'all stay easy back there. Don't start this dance."

"Sir, I thought we came here to settle up with Barlow."

"We're going to, but I intend to be on this side of the grass when we're done."

Wes chuckled and blew smoke at the colorless world around them. "Grass. In the end, that's what this is all about, my friend. Either a whole prairie or a little three-by-six plot."

Hutchins looked up as a few snowflakes drifted down. The sky lowered, and he knew that within the next few minutes that grass was going to be covered even deeper as the back side of the storm pushed through.

CHAPTER 46

The elder Barlow had always been hardheaded and did things his own way, which, according to him, was the only way. Son had learned through the years that any suggestions he made were immediately disregarded with a snort of derision and a firm "No!" Only days or even weeks after the old man had time to consider the proposal and consequences would he come to Son or Judd and make it sound as if he'd come up with the idea himself.

When Barlow pushed inside the hotel lobby, the desk clerk took one look at the fuming rancher. "I had my girl clean your room, Mr. Barlow."

The old man looked confused. He glared at the clerk and snapped, "My *room*?"

"The one we keep for Son and any other Barlow man who has permission to use it." The innocent man swallowed, sweat popping out on his forehead as he realized he'd drifted off into a conversation he had no business being in. "Son says it's for you when you're in town."

"Am I paying for that?"

The desk clerk nodded. "It goes through the bank each month. They have it listed on the ledger as *services*."

"Do I have a room in *Nellie's*, too?"

"Sir, I can't answer that. We have no association with that business."

Barlow spat toward a cuspidor and headed upstairs. "Which room am I paying for?"

The desk clerk cleared his throat. "All the way back. On the right. Number ten."

Barlow stomped down the hallway like a bull rushing through a loading chute. He pushed into the room to find Judd standing between the rancher and Maggie and Jo tied on the bed. Suddenly finding nowhere to rest his eyes, Judd faded away toward the window. Barlow's face first went blank with shock and then darkened at the sight of Son's broken nose and bloody face.

Son stepped forward, and like a rattlesnake strike, Barlow slapped his only boy hard enough to knock off Son's hat. His head snapped back and the young man staggered sideways before landing on the floor for the second time in a matter of minutes. Spitting blood and breathing through his mouth, he crawfished away from his furious father, who followed, red faced.

"What'n hell did you do?"

Taking a folding knife from his pocket, the old rancher snapped open the blade. Judd rested one hand on the butt of his pistol and Son's eyes widened at the sight of the razor-sharp edge that had gelded countless horses and young bulls. Not seeing the reactions of both men, he leaned over the bed and cut the gag off Maggie before freeing her hands.

He handed her the knife. "Get that baby free."

They relaxed as she cut the binds on her feet and then those on Jo. The little girl threw herself in her mother's arms and sobbed as they huddled on the bed, watching.

Son pushed back against the wall. "T-t-things got out of hand."

"I said, what did you do?"

Holding his hands high in case he needed to defend himself again, Son spat again. "What makes you think I d-d-did anything?"

"Any grown man who hides airtights under his bed and plays with butterflies makes me wonder. And stop that damned stuttering. You can quit it if you want to. Get ahold of yourself, boy."

Son swallowed and concentrated on slowing down. It was how he'd learned to control the affliction that brought ridicule and torment from others his entire life. "What," he pressed his lips together and gathered himself, "what were you doing in my room?"

"Throwing out all that junk in there and burning it."

"You burned my collections!?"

"I did, and you live in the bunkhouse now, but I see these two on the bed, so I don't need to have anything else answered right this second. I want to know what you've done here."

"You told me yourself back at the house to *handle it*. Those were your words, to take care of it because I wanted a chance to prove myself. That includes I'm doing my best to deal with the Ranger, and everything else in this sorry, one-horse town." Son found a little backbone and stood. "This war's been going on for a couple of years. I was just trying to end it so we can get on with building our empire."

"Empire." Barlow snorted at the word.

"That's how I think of it." Son looked at Maggie, and mentally recoiling from the hatred in her eyes, he pointed at Judd. "Me and Judd are doing what you want."

Judd pointed his finger across the room. "You don't speak for me."

"I've had enough of this! Judd will get his turn, but I want to know what *you*'ve done. Was this your idea?"

Son licked his lips, tasting blood from a cut inside his mouth and more running down the back of his throat. "Well, yesterday morning when it was snowing so hard, I was on the way back to the ranch and ran into a freight wagon coming into town." He wouldn't look at Maggie, addressing only his father. "I knew it wasn't a delivery for *us*, and when I stopped the driver and asked him where he was going with the load, he roostered up at me."

Maggie found her voice. "Danny Franks."

"I guess that was his name. At least, that's what I heard later. I didn't know the man."

"What about Franks?" Barlow stuck both thumbs into his belt.

"I made him turn off and drive into a big thicket of shin oaks."

"How'd you *make* him?"

Son shrugged, trying to ignore the venom in his father's voice. "Pointed my pistol at him, but I didn't intend to do what happened next. It was a puredee accident."

"Boy, I'm getting tired of this story coming out one piece at a time. You get to talking."

"All right. I wanted to stop the delivery." He jerked a thumb at Maggie. "I figured she was getting desperate for the supplies, and because it was snowing so hard, I was gonna stash the wagon and come back with a couple of the boys after I run the driver off, figuring we'd take the stock down to our . . . your store and let Earl shelve it. But it went wrong.

"He did what I told him and pulled into those shin oaks, but I'd been out there a long time. It was snowing hard and my hands were cold. I had to take off my glove to handle the pistol, and by the time we got stopped, my fingers were numb. I told him to cut one of the mules free and ride on back where he came from, and to never tell what happened."

Barlow snorted. "He was going straight to the marshal's office as soon as he could. They'd have a posse out looking for you half an hour after he hit town."

"I was all covered up. Hat down and scarf up. He didn't know who I was."

Son didn't mention that he and Judd had made a considerable amount of money over the past few months doing the same thing, stopping strangers at gunpoint like highwaymen. Each time they used a different scarf to cover their faces and, more than once, different hats they kept stashed in the barn.

It was part of Son's plan to squeeze travelers for money, forcing them to reconsider stopping in town for any length of time. The Barlow holdings were managing just fine with the sale of cattle to fund their battle over the town, but Maggie and a couple of other store owners who hadn't sold out to them were struggling. Strangers with no money to spend weren't doing much business, and Son's thought was to siphon off as much cash as possible until they surrendered and closed.

"I didn't mean for it to happen. I thought my finger was outside the trigger guard, and when I went to shake the gun at him to get a move on, I accidentally squeezed, and it went off."

He'd cocked the pistol in his hand, but the intense cold stiffened his muscles and dried his bare hand so much, his thumb slipped off the hammer. It went off, catching the driver in the side of his chest and the man fell over, dead before his body came to rest.

It was a common mishap with revolvers, but the man was dead, just as much by accident as it would have been if Son had intentionally shot him. He had no idea of robbing the dead man and ran from the scene.

"I didn't want the mules to come on into town with the body, so I shot them, too, and came back here to the hotel so me and Judd could decide what to do."

Barlow's eyebrows met in the middle. "I know you, and that's not all."

Son wouldn't look at Judd, though he jerked a thumb at him. "Well, him and the boys tangled with the Ranger at the same time I intended to drop in on Runt to see if he'd heard anything. I didn't think so because it was snowing so hard, but it would be a good alibi to see him there in town if he started asking questions. Well, Judd and the Ranger were fighting . . ."

"I told you not to speak for me!"

"I ain't. I'm just telling my side. I went to help when the Ranger started winning. I can't believe a man can fight that hard, but he did, and I kinda stepped back . . ."

"You *hid*." Barlow's voice was whipcrack sharp.

"I didn't *hide*." Son's voice rose high and whiny, like a kid, and it made him hate himself for it. "I-I-I just didn't join in because Runt showed up and everyone cleared out. Everybody went inside, leaving the wagon half unloaded and a case of gingerbread sitting right there in plain sight, and you know how much I like it and pepper soup, so I took the case and left."

He licked his lips, thinking about the case of canned gingerbread stashed in the now burning livery behind the saloon. Son dearly loved that tasty-sweet confection. Now, with their mercantile gone, he would never order anything like that from Earl for fear his dad or the brand riders would make fun of him, again.

"That's the stupidest thing I've ever heard," Jo snapped.

Barlow pointed at her. "And she's just a kid."

Still curled up on the bed with her arm around Jo, Maggie put one hand over her mouth. "My God. All this was over a wagon full of supplies and gingerbread. I've never heard anything so ridiculous."

Barlow turned to Judd. "All right. I have this side of my idiot son's story; what do you have to say for yourself?"

"I was just doing what he told me."

"You're lying!" Though he'd confessed to being in charge, Son expected Judd to accept some of the blame.

When he didn't, Son lost his head and sprang at him. Judd pushed him back like he was an annoying puppy.

"I am not. Mr. Barlow, you told me to stay close to Son and keep him out of trouble. That's a hard thing to do. He's pretty safe when we spend time in Nellie's, but he don't hold his liquor well, and I spend most of my time getting him out of trouble."

Eyes hard as flint, the old man stood with his back to the door, arms crossed. "I'm gonna be dead soon and this is how I get to live out the last of my life."

Son's mouth opened and closed like a fish. "Dead?"

"I feel it in my bones. Something's wrong inside, and when I'm hot, I smell like death."

Jo rose up on her knees and pulled Maggie's hand away. "I smell it every time you come in."

With a shocked look on her face, Maggie put her hand back over Jo's mouth. "Hush, child!"

"I bet you do." Barlow's eyes softened when he looked at the little girl. "Kids see, smell, and hear better than us old folks. Old men smell like dogs and age."

Jo pulled her mother's hand away. "Sometimes you smell like whiskey, too."

Resigned, Maggie sighed but said nothing.

Barlow reached over and turned the knob. "You two get out of here, and Maggie, I'm sorry. I meant to shut down your store, but it was just business. Nothing personal, and I intended to offer you any job you wanted here in town."

She slid off the bed and took Jo's hand. "I wouldn't have taken it."

"Of course you wouldn't. Go on, now. You don't have anything to worry about."

They were out of the door in a flash, and their running footsteps echoed back into the room containing the three men. Barlow closed the door with one fingertip. "Now, Son, I want the whole, true story of who shot Runt Carpenter."

CHAPTER 47

Dog-tired and worn to a frazzle, Ridge Tisdale sat in the back of Maggie's dark, empty store, looking out the open door at the outhouse. There was no spirit in there without the redhead's perky demeanor. It was there the whole situation had spun out of control. He'd been sitting in that exact chair when someone shot Runt, and when Ridge shifted to better see around the stove, it became clear.

The shooter'd been in the privy, just like Ridge thought, waiting. With the back door partially open, it was a straight shot from there, down a narrow gap and past the stove, and right into Ridge's chest.

He leaned to the left and the stove was in the way. When he leaned right, he could look straight inside the little house. As he suspected, Runt hadn't been the target. He'd simply been in the way. Likely the bushwhacker pulled the trigger at the exact time the marshal stepped into the line of fire.

Considering the shot, Ridge figured the gunman felt he was a shootist since he used a revolver. Someone with a little forethought would have used a rifle, for accuracy was important. That led Ridge to wonder who'd picked up his Henry. He dearly hoped he wouldn't soon be looking down the muzzle of his own rifle later that day.

Sitting there and studying how he'd come to be hunted by nearly everyone in town with a gun, Ridge heard footsteps on the boardwalk. Pulling the Colt, he twisted in the chair and was shocked to see Runt Carpenter using one of the awning's support posts to steady himself. A horseman outside saw the marshal and spurred his horse into a run. Ridge figured he wanted to be the first to announce that Runt was alive.

The Ranger rose and quickly opened the door, reaching out a hand to help the marshal inside. He took Runt's arm, and the smaller man, wearing his buffalo coat, leaned on him, shuffling inside. "What'n hell are you doing out there?"

"I don't intend to lay around while my town burns to a cinder." His lips moved, but all Ridge could see was the gigantic, twitching brush pile that hid his mouth.

Runt leaned on Ridge as he helped him to the straight-backed, cane-bottomed chair he was just sitting in. "Ease down there."

Wincing, Runt took the seat. "That hurts."

"How can you be up? Doc said you were hurt bad, and we just loaded you in the funeral wagon a few hours ago."

"It hurts when I lay still. It hurts when I move and it hurts when I breathe. I figure I'd just as well hurt helping you."

"You won't do anything but slow me down if I have

to move. Don't you realize every Three Fork man in town is looking for me? We hauled you over to the undertaker to protect you."

"I had a good nap with all those dead folks and a couple of swallers of that laudanum. I feel a sight better than they do."

"I swear." Ridge shook his head. "And how did you know I was here?"

"Didn't." Face white with pain, Runt took a shallow breath and slowly let it out. "Came to get my shotgun, or one off Maggie's rack. I feel half nekked with just one little ol' pistol." He looked around the store. "Where is she?"

Ridge told him how they'd moved her and Jo to Nell's to keep them safe.

"How'd you get in?"

"Back door's open, and I suspect the front wasn't locked, either. I'm surprised she ain't been stole blind. From what I've seen, most of this town loves her. I doubt many considered coming in here to take what wasn't theirs, if they aren't Three Fork men." Ridge pointed. "There was six dollars laying on the counter from honest people."

"Good to know we have folks like that in town."

"It gives me hope about this place that I really don't think much of. So, tell me, how are you up, anyway?"

For a moment, Runt looked embarrassed. "I guess Doc told you what I wear for my back."

"Your corset."

"I'd ruther call it a back brace. Ordered it from a New York catalog offering medical devices. Doc showed it to me once and said it was worth a try. Sure am glad I did, or I wouldn't be here now after that wicker bill tried to kill me."

"He wasn't after you."

"How do you figure?"

"Look past the stove."

Wincing at the slight movement, Runt moved a couple of inches. "Right out the back door into the outhouse."

"That's right. I was sitting where you are when you were shot. I suspect he was after me, not you."

"Well, it doesn't matter. He shot *me*."

"He did."

"Any idea who it was got things all stirred up?"

Ridge reached into his pocket and took out the madstone he'd picked up in Nell's and pointed out back. "This was supposed to be in there; Jo left it in the privy."

"How'd you come to have it?"

"It was in Son Barlow's pocket."

Their eyes met.

Ridge told him about holding him and Judd in Nellie's Place and everything else that he could think of. Runt chuckled and winced at the pain. "Oh, Lordy. Don't make me laugh." He smoothed his mustache. "That little boy shot *me*?"

"That's what I think, but it doesn't take much to shoot someone."

Runt thought about what he'd just heard. "We need to get all this straightened out."

"That'd help."

"Then hand me over my Greener."

"I don't know where it is. I'll have to look for it."

Ridge tucked the madstone back in his pocket and rounded the counter. With more time to search than the last time he was in the store trying to find the shotgun, Ridge searched the shelves underneath. When it wasn't there, he scanned a different section than where he thought it might be and finally saw an opened box of buckshot. He found where the shotgun had slipped behind some sacks of salt.

He brought it back and handed it to Runt. "Here you go."

The marshal broke it open and checked the loads. Seeing the glint of brass, he snapped it shut. "Now, you might be a Texas Ranger, but this is still my town, and I need to settle all this once and for all. Take and get me a buggy from over there at Kingman's."

"Then what?"

"You and I are going to be like that woman over in England who rode a horse naked through town."

"What?"

"I'll tell you the story. It's the same idea as I remember it, but this will be different. Her name was Lady Godiva and she didn't want anyone to look, but *I* want to catch every eye in town."

CHAPTER 48

"This is gonna get one of us killed," Ridge Tisdale snapped at Runt, who'd virtually disappeared in his great coat. They'd already gathered a small group of onlookers, who were astonished to see the marshal alive and well, climbing onto the buggy.

By the time he'd taken his seat, the town marshal had broken out into a cold sweat. "Climbing up here damned near killed me." He swallowed, gagged, and recovered himself. "Them ribs grinding together almost made me puke."

Ridge settled on the seat and picked up the reins. "One of 'em's gonna poke a hole in your lung and you'll drown in your own blood if you ain't careful."

"Quit talking and let's go."

"Why don't we just tell these folks to pass the word and you let me take you back to Doc's?"

"Because I want them to see me sitting here, and because I intend to arrest every Three Fork rider I can find."

"You mean you want *me* to arrest them. I already have Turkey and a couple of others in your jail. Kingman hauled them over there in shackles. Chained to the cell bars with the door locked and chained, too. I stopped outside the jail from out back on my way over here. I heard some hollering and complaining and paused under the window to listen." He chuckled. "There ain't nothing but bars between that cell and all this cold air, and they were mad 'cause after Kingman hauled them in, he refused to light a fire in the stove."

Holding his arms and elbows close to his chest, Runt tried not to laugh. "That's a start, but sure as shootin', if I'm laying back there in a room, somebody's gonna try and come in to finish the job Son started. If I die, I don't intend to do it on an undertaker's table. I plan to go out here." He paused to wipe the corners of his mouth under the great mustache.

Ridge watched him check those fingers for blood.

There was none, and Runt seemed to perk up. "The more people see me alive and kicking, the better chance we have of cutting Three Fork's chances of killing me and, in the process, what's left of their hold on this town, though you've burned a right smart of it down."

"I'm still mad, and there may be more before I'm done."

Ridge twitched the reins on the single mule hitched to the buggy. It stepped forward, dislodging the coach gun lying across Runt's lap. The marshal grunted in pain as Ridge reached out with a forefinger and shoved the barrel a little more ahead of them, so that if it went off, his right knee wouldn't turn into scrap meat.

The fires down the street had mostly burned themselves down from roaring infernos to a sea of flickering coals that ate away at the planks and timbers still standing. Exhausted men had backed away to rest, while more than a few women brought water and food. Some of the women had joined in to fight the fire, swinging water buckets, and many of them had their long skirts tucked into waistbands or belts to keep the hems out of the mud and water.

"Stop here, Ranger." Runt pointed.

With his coat open and the shoulder holster clearly visible, Ridge reined in the mule, and Runt's coarse, gravelly voice rose over dozens of discussions and disagreements. "Good work, folks."

Like filings to a magnet, the people closed in on Runt. Ridge crossed his arms to listen, keeping his right hands close to the Colt riding on his chest.

A woman stepped forward, her face streaked with sweat and soot, and put a gentle hand on Runt's leg. "We were told you'd been killed by that Texas Ranger everyone's looking for."

"Quit looking. He's right here and he wasn't the one who shot me."

"How do you know that?"

"Because I was looking right at him, and the shot hit me in the back. I'd show it to you, but it'd hurt too much."

Another person called from the back. "I heard you were dead."

"Still might be if this wound in my back don't heal up. The pain's about to kill me now."

A rough-looking character pointed his finger. "That Ranger's no friend of yours. He's damned near burned down half the town."

"Only Barlow property, and he's looking for Son, who we believe shot me."

"Even if it's Barlow property, he can't go around setting it on fire." The same man turned his pointing finger into a fist. "That's against the law!"

"You're right, but from what I've heard, this man's been trying to stay alive, because those of you who weren't fighting the fire intended to try to kill him. I want you all to hear me now: Anyone who tries to interfere with this man, this Texas Ranger, or who supports anyone intending to do him harm, will have to deal with me. Hands off of him, you hear?"

More townspeople had gathered behind those surrounding the buggy, and Runt noticed. "Those of you who just showed up, talk with these around me and find out what's going on. But the short of it is that I'm alive, and it wasn't this man, here, who shot me. We're going on down the street to pass the word that I'm looking for Son Barlow, who's accused of attempted murder, and there will be no vigilante law here in my town. No posse, no armed groups, no nothing."

The talk had drained Runt. He leaned back. "Take us down the street."

"You think you can keep doing this?"

"Until I pass out."

"You can't do that until we hit the end of town and everyone knows. Anyone sees you slumped over next to me and they're gonna fill me full of holes."

"Then you better keep me awake."

CHAPTER 49

"You move and I'll blow you off that seat."

The snow was back, hard as the first time, and a hard-looking man in a big hat seemed to step out of nowhere from behind a lacy curtain of falling flakes. Hands full of reins, Ridge met the stranger's gaze and didn't let go of either. "Runt."

The marshal opened his eyes to see a florid-faced gent pointing a double-barreled ten-gauge at Ridge. He'd closed his eyes for a moment to gather strength. "Matt, if you pull that trigger, you're liable to get some of that shot on me."

"You're alive?"

"Of course I'm alive. I'm talking to you, ain't I?"

"You riding up there with your eyes closed, I thought you were dead and this feller had you propped up beside him for some reason." The stranger tilted his head, thinking. "I've talked to ten people, and they all say you're dead, and then me and a couple of men warming up over there by the burned-out saloon saw you with this feller and one said you're the one who caused all this. You all right, Runt?"

"I wish people would quit asking me that. No, I ain't all right. I been shot in the back and I'm hurtin' and I'm tired of telling the same thing over and over, but I'm still alive and kicking, and we'd both appreciate it if you'd lower that scattergun." He drew a shallow breath.

Apparently unsure what to do, the threat under a hat the size of a sombrero lowered the shotgun.

Runt flicked a hand. "Ridge, this here's Matt Larson. County sheriff."

"I took you for a store clerk, or maybe a carpenter."

"I ain't neither, but I'd appreciate it if you'd sit there for a minute and let me and Runt talk through this."

"Be glad to, but I'm tired of shotguns pointing my way. Could you get your finger away from those triggers and find somewhere else for those muzzles to threaten?"

Larson lowered the shotgun and peered from under his wide brim, which had collected considerable snow. "Runt, what'n hell's going on? I rode into a town that's half burned down and hear you're dead and everybody with a shooting iron's looking for the one who did it."

It was Ridge who spoke up. "So you got my telegram?"

"What telegram?"

"The one I had sent."

"I've been on the road for days. I holed up in an old soddy out of town while the storm blew itself out, so no, I don't know a thing." He glanced up at the sky. "It looks like the snow's back, though, so I intend to get me a room at the hotel when we're finished here."

Runt winced at the pain in his back. "So, why *are* you here?"

"Traveling through. I had business close by and stopped for a visit. I wanted to see how the town was growing, too. It looks to me like y'all have taken a step or two back since the last time I rode through."

"It'll be just fine as soon as this range war's over."

"A range war here in *town*?"

"Looks like this is the place where it's come to a head." Ridge moved his coat so the sheriff could see the badge. "I'm a Texas Ranger. Came here to arrest a wanted murderer named Clyde McPeak and wound up on the wrong end of darn near every gun in town."

Satisfied there was no danger coming from that quarter, the sheriff rested the double-barrel in the crook of his arm. "What can I do to help?"

Ridge chinned at the marshal. "We need to get this hard-headed dishrag on a bed somewhere and then deal with the Barlows."

"Who're they?"

"The ones who started this, and I believe one of them shot Runt."

The little marshal leaned his weight on Ridge, sighed, and passed out.

Ridge put one arm around his shoulders like he was a sleepy toddler. "Sheriff Larson, I sure am glad you're here."

CHAPTER 50

Tugging his hat into place as was his habit every time he walked outside, old man Barlow stomped out on the hotel's porch to find a world of fresh white he hadn't expected. The sky was growing lighter when he went inside and he fully expected the sun to be peeking out with water melting off the roof.

Instead, again snow fell so thick it obscured the town, but not the line of men spread out facing him. With their backs to the hotel, Three Fork men were using their horses as shields. Not a word passed between them and the cowboys facing them, looking as calm as if they were examining a herd of cattle.

Bracketed by Son and Judd behind him, Barlow studied the scene until his eyes rested on Drake Hutchins, sitting above the standoff on a big Appaloosa stud. Knowing what to expect, he looked to the side of the rancher and saw his right-hand man, Wes Callahan, smoking a cigar as if he didn't have a care in the world.

Hutchins rode closer. "Barlow."

The old man shrugged his shoulders to set the coat

higher on his neck. "I didn't expect to see you boys here."

"We've been looking for you. I hear that there's some trouble here in town, something about a Texas Ranger, and that Maggie's in trouble."

Barlow started to speak and Hutchins held up a gloved hand. "I know. She's fine. We saw her and the little one run out of here a few minutes ago. A feller who goes by the name of Seminole Sam and my top hand Zeke's walking her home, and I suspect he'll be back with a story to tell before long."

"It won't be one I was involved in."

"We'll see about that." Hutchins raised a finger to his hat. "Howdy, Son."

He didn't have to ask any more questions. Calling out Son was as good as saying to all those around them that he had all the answers.

Somewhat shaken to find himself in the middle of a standoff, Barlow played for time to think what to do next. "Why're y'all squared off with my boys here? They don't look too relaxed."

Hutchins shrugged. "They all gunned up when we got here. I just want to talk to you."

Barlow's face brightened. "Hell yeah. There's a pretty nice bar in here, the only one in town now that that Ranger burned down the Red River. It ain't big enough for *all* our boys, but why don't you come inside and let's talk?"

"Never did like to talk business in falling weather." Hutchins swung down and held up his reins to Wes.

His gray-haired partner chuckled and ignored the

offer. He stepped down, too. "I figure Son, and maybe
Judd, there, might want to join you, so I'd like to hear
what everyone has to say, too."

One of the Oarlock riders reached out and took both
sets of reins. He turned his mount and walked the horses
away from the standoff at a slow pace, proving that he
wasn't concerned about being shot from behind.

Seeing him, the others did the same, turning their
backs to the Three Fork men. Leaving their bosses
Hutchins and Wes, they put considerable distance between them and others before stopping to face them
and wait.

Barlow remained where he was, and because he
didn't move, Son and Judd did the same. "I'll swan, you
two look ready to fight, Drake."

Hutchins stopped where he was. "I don't see much
space between y'all to pass through, and I don't intend
to stand on the steps to wait for you to move. And while
I'm on the subject, I'm not in the habit, nor will I ever
be, to look up at any man to talk. Are we doing this
here, or inside over a glass of whiskey?"

The look in Barlow's eyes changed and he seemed to
settle into the floorboards. "No man talks to me like
that, and you're mighty sure of yourself, with your men
and horses so far away. I can shoot you now and this
will be over before the echo fades."

Wes nodded, as if Barlow had offered up some pro-
found observation. "Kinda figured you for that kind of
man, so if you'd care to look over your right shoulder,
you'll see our boy Zeke, there, with a rifle pointed at the
three of you."

The arrogant expression on the elder Barlow's face evaporated. He glanced to the side to exchange looks with Judd, while Son licked his lips and took half a step back. "I-I-I thought you said he took Maggie back to her place."

"Thought he did." Wes chewed the stub of his cigar, which had gone out. "You can't trust your people to do their jobs these days, can you, Jim?"

Apparently annoyed that Son had spoken, the old rancher crossed his arms and stepped back. With the way cleared, either by consent or the Winchester pointing at them from behind, Hutchins climbed the steps, followed by Wes.

CHAPTER 51

Five tense men crossed the lobby under the frightened eye of the desk clerk, who waited until they entered the small bar to follow. Since they were in the lead, Wes passed two tables before taking the third that was furthest back. He circled around and sat with his back to the wall. Hutchins settled into place with his left side against the table, to keep his gun hand free.

Their choices forced Barlow and Judd to take the remaining two chairs with their backs to the bar, leaving Son to either sit alone or sit at the nearest table. Irritated, he drug one across the floorboards with a wail of wood on wood and placed it on a corner, still out of the circle but forcing himself inside.

The desk clerk picked up a rag as he passed the bar and leaned in to wipe off the table. Barlow waved him back. "We don't need it wiped."

"I'm the only one here today. The bartender either decided not to come in because of the weather or he's out fighting those fires."

"I don't care one way or the other," Barlow said. "Just bring us a bottle and some glasses."

"And a light." Wes held up the stub of his cigar. "I'm out of matches."

Barlow leaned back in his chair, obviously a man used to being in charge. "So, you're here looking for me."

"I went by your place, thinking you might be there."

"My man run you off?"

"If you're talking about the one with the gimp leg, he's a friendly sort of feller. In fact, after we talked, he's coming to work for us."

Barlow grinned. "That's a good joke on us."

There was something in that smile that Hutchins didn't like. "You don't look too upset."

"Hey, riders come and go. Not all of 'em will stay for the brand, but I always figured Clyde would stick."

"Was that his name? He was so anxious to work for us that he didn't say."

The desk clerk came back with a bottle and five glasses. Sitting them on the table, he backed away. "Y'all help yourselves. There's more back there if you need it, but I have to get back to the desk. I'll just put this on your bill, Mr. Barlow."

"Overrun with business, are you?" Son tried to sound like the others but failed.

"Shut up, boy." Barlow poured himself a glass and put the bottle back down. "Let's get down to brass tacks here. I own most of this town—"

"Used to," Wes interrupted and filled his glass. He poured one for Hutchins and put the bottle back down. "Not much left with your name on it."

"All right. I still have the lots, and most of those that ain't built on. The bank burned, but I bought one of the best safes made in St. Louis. It's guaranteed through a fire, so the money inside'll be just fine. By summer, I'll have rebuilt and be back in business. I own all the land on both sides of where the railroad tracks will be, so I'll be set. The only thing left to negotiate is your ranch."

Barlow took a long swallow of whiskey and placed a hand on his stomach. He sat there for a long moment before continuing. "I'll buy you out, pay good money and promise to hire all your men if they want to stay."

Drake Hutchin's gunsight eyes narrowed even more. "That won't be happening."

Barlow's smile vanished. "How about I kill you here and now?"

As if the comment was a weak joke, a slight smile curled the corners of Wes's mouth. "You'll try."

"Look." Hutchins held out a hand to steady every-one. "If we get to shooting in here, or out there, a lot of our men will get killed, if not wounded. I have cowboys on my payroll, not gun hands, and none of 'em deserve that, so we need to figure another way around this."

Judd placed both hands on his thighs and stood up. "I say we ride out of town a ways and settle this where nobody can see, or interfere."

"What do you mean by that?" Hutchins looked up. "And if you remember what I said out there on the steps, I don't like looking up at a man. Sit back down." He paused for emphasis. "Now."

"Nope. I believe I'm about to take both ranches over myself, so I won't have to deal with old farts like you."

Stunned at the announcement, those around the table

took a moment to process what he'd just said. In the next instant, guns appeared, pointing in all directions.

Drake Hutchins saw something in Son's eyes he didn't like. His pistol seemed to leap into his hands, steady on the younger Barlow.

Wes seemed to just shift his position and the Colt snicked when he cocked the hammer and pointed it at Jim Barlow from under the table.

Barlow's own pistol was aimed at Judd, who did nothing but stand there. "I hope I heard you wrong."

Judd spread his hands and stepped back, taking some of the tension with him. "Nope. There's that big cottonwood a mile east of town. The snow's not too deep or falling too hard we can't meet there. Let's settle this out of town and be done with it."

Barlow opened his mouth to speak, but Son cut him off. "I'll be there. I don't know what you think you can do, but you're not taking this ranch."

"Not much threat from a pup who needs to stay under the porch." Judd addressed Hutchins and Wes Callahan. "Y'all might want to come, too. Let's finish this after I'm done with Barlow. I'm gonna take the whole place anyway, so why not get it done today?"

Still holding his Colt on Barlow, the gun hidden by the table, Wes took the cigar from the corner of his mouth. "Settle it now. Here. I'm ready to dance."

"No. Any shooting in this town will draw that Ranger and townspeople." Barlow made sure his hands were in view of all. "There'll be a lot of questions asked, and maybe charges filed. Anything happens out of town is between men, with no law to be involved."

Hutchins softly slapped the table with his free hand and rose. "This is way out of hand. Gentlemen, y'all can fight amongst yourselves and kill all you want. I don't want any of my boys hurt. Like I said, I didn't hire gunmen, I hired men to work cows. Wes and I are walking out of here and going back to the ranch while y'all do what you want to. I'll deal with the survivors later."

Wes stood, his Colt still leveled on Barlow and Judd. They both showed surprise that he held the gun on them without their knowing it. "I'm with Drake here, but y'all do me a favor and wait until the weather warms up. Makes it easier to dig graves."

Drake Hutchins walked out of the bar without looking back. Keeping his pistol level, Wes backed out of the door before turning around. The danger wasn't over yet, though. Three Fork gunmen waited outside and faced the two ranchers as they stepped outside, but Zeke, who was their ace in the hole, hadn't moved from the corner of the building.

The Colt in his hand, Wes appeared on the porch, saw Zeke, and nodded. "We're going."

Zeke waved at the Oarlock men who'd moved closer to the hotel to see through the heavy snow that was coating everyone with fresh powder. Ready for anything, they rode closer, their horses breaking through the new snow, hooves squeaking with every step.

Hutchins stopped when he saw two men with Zeke. Both wore badges. One he immediately recognized as Sheriff Matt Larson and the double-barreled ten-gauge held casually but angled in their general direction.

"Well, I reckon these badges are why it was so quiet out here while we were having that drink inside."

"Howdy, Drake. We came to arrest Son and Judd Frazier. I hear they're inside."

"Go ahead on, if you want to. They're inside, but we're leaving before the shooting starts. Heading back to the ranch."

Old man Barlow came out behind them and paused. "Matt, I hope you're not here for me, too."

"Nope, for Judd and your boy. We're taking them both into custody for kidnapping, murder, and accessory."

"Who's that with you?"

Ridge spoke up. "Tisdale. Texas Ranger."

"Ah, you're the one who caused all this trouble. Well, you and I will talk later, but take 'em both, if you can. I'm done with the two of 'em." He turned to the Oarlock boss. "And Drake, when y'all get back to the ranch, tell McPeak I'll have him horsewhipped if I ever see him again."

"I don't work for you, Barlow. Tell him yourself when you see him."

The Ranger raised an eyebrow. "McPeak? Clyde McPeak?"

Drake Hutchins nodded. "That's him."

"Well, Mr. Hutchins, I'll be out with the warrant I have in my saddlebags. McPeak is wanted for murder and theft."

He sighed. "Come on, then. Zeke, you best come with us while these two lawmen keep an eye on things.

We'll be looking for you, Sheriff Larson, and you, too, Mr. Ranger."

They mounted their horses as Barlow aimed a finger at Drake Hutchins. "Just so's you'll know. I'll be sleeping in your ranch house this time next year."

"We'll see about that."

CHAPTER 52

Two sets of riders went their separate ways as Ridge Tisdale and Sheriff Larson pushed into the Reynolds Hotel, weapons at the ready.

The desk clerk threw up his hands. "I swear. More guns. Y'all aren't here for rooms, are you?"

Ridge kept his Colt pointed at the doorway leading into the saloon. "Bar back there?"

"It is."

"Judd and Son Barlow in it?"

"They were a few minutes ago." The desk clerk tried to save a little face. "Go on back and look if you want to. I don't care."

The lawmen followed their pistols into the small, dimly lit room, which was empty. Noting the whiskey bottle and five glasses, Ridge angled himself to look behind the bar, expecting one or both of the men to pop up and start shooting.

"Nobody back here."

Holstering his revolver, Ridge returned to the lobby. "Did they come through here? If you've misled us, I'm putting shackles on you."

"No, sir! I thought they were back there, same as you."

Sheriff Larson joined them. "They must have heard us out front. They went out through a window and closed it behind them to gain some time. I looked out, but I can't see a damned thing except fresh tracks going around the back."

Frustrated, Ridge tilted his hat back. "What's out there?"

"Nothing." The desk clerk shrugged. "A little shed is all, for horses. We have some hay back there."

Larson rested the shotgun over his shoulder. "Where do you think those two went?"

"Well, there's a footpath that leads straight to Nellie's, and the town's beyond that. I can't say anything else because I didn't see it."

Larson shifted from foot to foot, considering the situation at hand. "If they have horses nearby, they're gone. Could have mixed in with the rest of the Three Fork bunch and lit out for their ranch."

Thinking about his buckskin in the livery at the far end of town, Ridge shook his head. "Well, if they did, we won't catch them tonight."

Larson took off his big hat, revealing a white head bald as an egg. He slapped it against his thigh in disgust and replaced it. "What do we do now?"

Ridge's gaze rested on the ledger, open on the counter. "I've done all I can do today." He picked up the polished pen with a steel point, dipped the point in the inkwell, and wrote his name.

Finished, he looked up at the desk clerk. "Mister, what's your name?"

"Robert Henry."

"Well, Mr. Two First Names, I want the two best rooms in the house for me and my friend here. We're staying the night."

"I don't have any vacancies."

"I don't hear or see anyone, which is strange to me."

"Those staying here went to fight fires, or watch."

Ridge simply stared at the man, waiting him out.

"Well, I do have the room Mr. Barlow has reserved. Since he . . . slipped away . . . I suspect it'll be empty. It's a large room with stream heat. I can bring up another bed so you can have two."

"That'll be fine. While you do that, the sheriff and I will be in the bar, having a drink and getting acquainted."

The desk clerk smiled and nodded.

Ridge waved his hand. "Get to moving on that other bed."

The startled man jumped to the task. "Yes, sir."

Ridge and Sheriff Larson went into the bar and sat at the table holding the bottle and glasses. With their backs to the door, they waited for their room to be ready as the snow piled up once again outside.

CHAPTER 53

Judd and Son left the Reynolds Hotel on foot, heading for the safety of numbers in town. They'd been close to killing each other in the bar, but when they heard the Ranger and county sheriff outside, they postponed the fight for another day.

Cutting around behind the building and across the open lot to Nellie's Place was easier than Son imagined. Though two large groups of men had just left the hotel and headed in different directions, the snow was falling so hard, even if they'd been seen, no one could have identified them.

They pushed on past the entertainment parlor and down the street. Two saddled horses tied in front of the cooper's shop were all they needed. Swinging into the saddles, they slowly walked them down the street, which was fast emptying of traffic in the storm.

The sun was only minutes from setting and the darkness would be their friend.

Judd finally noticed how closely Son was watching him and laughed. "Easy there, boy. Take a deep breath before you get the dizzies."

"You said you were going to kill us all and take the ranch."

"Did you see that old man, Wes?"

"Of course I saw him. The man had a Colt pointed at us."

"Yep, and he was holding it before I said a word. I saw it was aimed at your daddy and I hoped I could start the dance and he'd shoot. With your old man out of the way, the ranch is ours. I had no intention of drawing on those two old coots; they're tougher'n boot leather. I just wanted out of there."

Like his late friend Russ, Son had always trusted Judd . . . up to that day . . . and he felt his anger slipping away. "You're not going to meet anyone under that cottonwood tree outside of town?"

"Hell no. I was just puffing up for a minute."

"But now Dad knows our plan."

"He's always known we'd inherit the ranch."

"*We?*"

"You know what I mean. You. It wouldn't hurt none to hurry it all up, but you heard the old man. He's convinced he's dying. Didn't you see him rub his gut after he took that drink?"

"He's been doing that for years."

"Yep, I think what he's been dealing with on his insides has built to where he's on the downhill slide."

"Then we just wait."

"One thing we can't wait on is those two lawmen." They passed close to a pair of other riders coming in their direction. The horsemen had their hats pulled down against the snow, and Son simply waved a finger in greeting as they passed. "They'll be along right behind us."

"I thought about that. I say we find a place to lay up for a while and then ride on out to the ranch and slip in on the old man before daylight, when he's sleeping." Judd pursed his lips, thinking aloud. "A pillow over his face will do the job. You'll be the boss of the outfit, and we collect the boys and ride straight to the Oarlock.

"We hit them before they know what's happening and wipe 'em all out. We take it over and there ain't no law out this far that's powerful enough to do anything about it. Worse comes to worst, we lay for them somewhere and end the problem."

"I know a place for the night," Son said. "Follow me." They turned between two buildings and crossed an empty lot to a dark house sitting at the far edge of town.

"Who owns this?"

"The bank, which means me. A couple lived here for a while, until they lost a child when a horse kicked it in the head in the pen out back. There's a little milk shed where we can stash these horses until morning."

"Now you're using your noodle."

"I use it more than you expect. When we have both of these ranches, and the rail line goes in, we won't have to drive stock to the market anymore. That was my idea. That's why we bought up all that land north of town. We'll load up our cattle right here and ship them straight out. Judd, we'll rename this place Barlowsville and be as rich as the Vanderbilts and won't need to own a single train."

CHAPTER 54

When Judd woke up at midnight, another foot of snow was on the ground. They'd built a fire in the potbellied stove sitting in the middle of the house that kept the worst of the chill away. He rolled out from under a ragged quilt left behind by the previous owners.

Son slept on a corn shuck mattress a few feet away. Judd considered shooting him to end one problem, but he lay there so long thinking about it he changed his mind and came up with another plan.

He rose, stretched, and saw his breath. "Son. Wake up."

"I've been awake since you rolled over." He sat up, slipped his pistol into its holster, and rose.

Judd felt a shiver run down his spine. Son had slept all night with the revolver in his fist. This boy required more watching than he thought. "We need to get started if we're going to be at the ranch before daylight."

Coats buttoned to the neck and chewing on strips of jerky, they kicked through the new snow to the little milk shed and led out their stolen horses. The town was dark and quiet, with only a couple of windows glowing from either fireplaces or lamps turned low.

Letting Judd take the lead, Son spoke up after they'd been riding for half an hour. "I have no idea where we are. You sure this is the way to the ranch?"

Just like old man Barlow, Judd snorted in disgust. "Of course it is. You see that line of hackberries over there?"

"No. All I see is snow on the ground and more coming down every minute."

"The trees are there all right. It's that draw leading northeast. We go this way for a while. If you look hard on the ground, you'll see where the snow's been kicked up. That was your daddy and his men passing by earlier."

"I've never been good at finding my way at night. Can't track, neither."

Judd swallowed his loathing. He'd let the younger man hang on his coattails like the old man ordered, but his stupidity was wearing on the top-hand-turned-gunman. "You're learning."

"You think so?"

"Sure. Look how you've acted in all this. Hell, boy, you even fought *me*. You'll be a man someday yet."

"It'll be a fine thing, having you as my right-hand man once we take over."

"I agree with that."

They rode in silence for the next hour, suffering the cold and falling snow. The ground rose, telling Judd they were still on the right path. Despite what he'd told Son, finding his way in the dark, fighting the snowstorm that had already dumped more than two feet on top of what was already there, was a challenge.

A couple of times he thought they'd missed certain landmarks such as a thick grove of bare-limbed cottonwood trees, a long, skinny growth of leafless shin oaks, and one particular live oak still wearing its summer leaves, which had been marking an old Comanche war trail for two hundred years.

His spirit lifted when they reached the wide, spreading branches of the tree that rose thirty feet in the air before swooping down and resting their weight on the ground. Live oaks didn't lose their leaves until the spring, and the snow had collected into a thick roof protecting the ground below.

Ducking his head below a limb thick as his horse, Judd rode through an opening into a dark cave floored with dirt and compost mulch that seemed warmer than the air they'd been riding through. Son came in behind him, and they sat their stolen mounts for a while, letting the animals rest.

"I told you we were on the trail."

Son's soft voice came from near pitch-black. "I can't see a thing, but this is that big war oak for sure."

"We're almost there. So, do you have a plan for what to do when we get to the house?"

"I've been thinking on that. He won't have a watchman set, not in this weather. Everything will be dark and all the boys asleep in the bunkhouse. W-w-we keep it simple." He paused, gathering himself. "We ride up to the house, slip inside, and the two of us put a pillow over his head. Our weight'll keep him down; just don't let him reach that Colt he keeps beside the bed."

"Fine. I'll hold his arms and you handle the pillow."

"Right. When it's done, we wake up the boys and tell them he died in his sleep."

"Good. We call 'em in to look, and you tell them there's a new boss in charge of the Three Fork. Once you're done, I tell them the rest of the plan."

"What's that?"

"We saddle up and ride straight for the Oarlock. It should be the same there as here. All quiet and snowed in, even though it'll be light when we get there. We surround the place and have a couple of the boys slip into the barn for insurance."

Caught up in the story, Son picked up the idea. "I'll take some more into the house and we kill Hutchins and Callahan."

Judd cut him off. "I want to shoot Callahan myself. I hate that insolent reprobate."

"Then the rest of the boys pour it on the bunkhouse, and when they find out both their bosses are dead, they'll come out with their hands up."

"If they don't and I'm right about the guy, we have McPeak inside and he's liable to shoot a few in the back." Judd's voice rose in excitement. "They'll give up for sure then."

Son smiled in the darkness. "And then the Three Fork ranch will have doubled in size and we'll own everything within a hundred and fifty miles in any direction."

CHAPTER 55

The snow had stopped falling by the time Judd and Son reached the Three Fork ranch. It was still dark, but there was enough glow off the nearly three feet of white fluff to make out the house, barn, and bunkhouse.

As they expected, only a wisp of smoke came from the chimney and bunkhouse stovepipe, indicating those inside were still asleep. Circling to come in from the opposite side of the barn, they reined up in front of the house. Dismounting, they tied the horses to the hitching post out front and stepped carefully onto the porch.

Son breathed a cloud of vapor through his open mouth as he carefully lifted the latch on the house. Just as he'd expected, it was unlocked. Barlow never locked a door in his life, and that arrogance made it easier to get inside.

They entered the warm, dark living area, moving with care even though both of them were intimately familiar with everything inside. The sound of snoring reached them, and Judd reached out to pat Son on the shoulder.

It was a touch of satisfaction, brotherhood, and to calm them both down.

The door to Barlow's ground-floor bedroom was partially open. Judd sat on the horsehair sofa and pulled off his boots. Throwing them aside, he ripped off his coat and hung it and his hat on a peg beside the door.

Still in his hat and coat, and fearing the hinges would creak, Son sucked in his stomach and slipped inside without touching the door. He paused, feeling Judd do the same.

Judd joined him and they split up, Son going to the left side of the bed and Judd splitting off to the right. Sleeping on his back, the old man had knocked his feather pillow to the floor. Son picked it up and leaned forward. There was barely enough light coming through the single frosted window for Judd to see.

Son's voice was as soft as the goose down in his hands. "Now."

He pushed the pillow onto his father's face and pressed down with all his weight, feeling Judd fall on the old man's arms.

At least that was what he'd expected. Instead, the flash of a gunshot illuminated the room, the explosion loud enough to feel. The flash of light revealed Judd was the shooter, and his pistol was aimed at Son. The slug punched a large hole in his chest, and the younger Barlow stumbled back. Another shot lit the room, the gun in Judd's hand, and old man Barlow's empty holster hanging on the bedpost.

As Son backed against the wall and slumped to the floor with both legs spread out before him and blood leaking from two holes in his heart, Judd hurried around to the dying man. He plucked the Colt from Son's holster as, at the same time, old man Barlow gained enough awareness to reach for the holster and find his revolver gone.

Hearing someone rustling on the opposite side of the bed, Barlow twisted around on one elbow, gasping for breath. "What the hell?"

Judd shot him in the head, and Barlow fell back on his lumpy cotton mattress, limp and already dead. Dropping Son's pistol to the floor beside him, Judd pitched the old man's pistol onto the bed and rushed into the living room.

He thumbed a match to light and touched the flame to an oil lamp. Looking out, he saw a similar light come on in the bunkhouse. Then another added to the brightness. Someone opened the door and peered out, looking for the source of the gunshots.

Shouts reached his ears that were ringing from the shots in the room. He rushed into Son's room and moved a box full of rocks in the corner, noting that the old man had lied about throwing away everything in there. Son's collection of fragile bird nests, collected grasses, and even a hornet's nest was still intact.

Using his fingertips, a loose floorboard came up, revealing a packet of papers. Sliding the board back into place, he returned to the living room and stuck the packet into a cabinet.

He turned up the wick and fully opened the door into

the death room. One of the brand riders, Claude, shouted from outside, "Coming in, Mr. Barlow!"

The door slammed open and Claude stood there in pants and an undershirt full of holes, a Walker Colt in his hand. Behind him came another member of their crew, Caleb, and then the others pushed inside, all carrying guns and looking for trouble.

"Easy, boys." Judd held his lamp high. "It's all over. Mr. Barlow and Son are dead. Light a couple more lamps."

Caleb used a match from a bowl on the table and added more light. Someone else lit a third, and soon the living area was bright.

Claude looked toward Barlow's bedroom. "What happened?"

Acting shaken, Judd pointed with his free hand. "Me and Son got in from town a few minutes ago. We didn't want to wake you boys up, so I was going to roll up here in front of the fireplace, and I thought Son was headed to his room.

"The next thing I heard, there was shooting. By the time I made a light, it was quiet. I hollered, but nobody answered. When I looked into the boss's room, Son's sitting on the other side of the bed, shot to pieces with his chin on his chest. Mr. Barlow's dead in the middle of his bed."

Caleb went to the door and looked inside. "They're both dead all right."

The living room was filled with Barlow men, all carrying guns. Some looked confused, others frightened.

Claude picked up one of the lamps and joined Caleb. Together, they went into the bedroom and, after a few minutes, came back outside.

Claude returned without the lamp. Others stuck their heads into the bedroom. Claude shook his head. "What do you think happened, Judd?"

He was about to give his version of the story, which had Son apparently trying to smother his dad when the old man shot him and Son then drew down on him.

But Caleb spoke up. "I tell you what I see. I bet Son went in to wake his old man up and tell him y'all were back, and the old man roused up from a dead sleep and shot him twice. I might've done the same if I was sleeping hard. Son must have reacted on instinct and fired back."

Seeing the wisdom of keeping his mouth shut, Judd sat at the table and put his head in his hands. His shaking was real, and his reaction drew sympathy from those around him.

A bearded gun hand recruited out of Paris, Texas, sat across from him. "I got some coffee cooking, as soon as that stove heats up. What do we do now?"

Judd looked up. "Well, Harvey, as soon as it's light, somebody needs to ride into town to let Runt or Sheriff Larson know what happened. I'd find Larson first, since this is out of the town limits. Somebody can tell that Ranger, if they've a mind to."

The room full of cowboys and hired gunfighters waited, almost completely silent.

"Most folks won't give a damn."

Caleb spoke up. "Who inherits the ranch now that they're gone?"

Judd waited to see if anyone would speak.

A young cowboy in an unbuttoned shirt and a weather-beaten hat looked around the room. "Is there any next of kin?"

Judd shook his head. "I've been with this outfit the longest. Mr. Barlow didn't have anybody else. Everyone he left behind is dead."

"I wonder if there's a will, then."

"Yep." Judd pointed at a cabinet. "Mr. Barlow showed it to me and Son a year or so ago."

Claude opened the cabinet and found a sheaf of papers tied together with a ribbon. He came back and sat down, untying the slender piece of red material. "Some of these look like deeds or legal papers with Mr. Barlow's name on them." The top document seemed official and bore the words LAST WILL AND TESTAMENT. "There's no seal on this."

"Open it up, then."

Lacing his fingers on the table, Judd listened as Claude, one of the few men there who could read, unfolded the document and studied the single sheet of paper. "This is dated two months ago. It's Mr. Barlow's will all right."

As he read it to himself, several of the men shifted and moved around them, anxious to hear what was in the paper. The look on Claude's face went from curious, to a frown, to surprise. He lowered the page. "This says that there being no relatives, this entire ranch goes to Judd Fletcher."

Someone behind him spoke up. "Is it signed?"

Claude returned to the document. "It is. James L. Barlow. It's his handwriting. There's a couple more papers in here with that exact signature, and it's witnessed by J. T. Buford. I've heard that name. He's a lawyer in Blackjack."

"It's all legal, then. Judd, you're our new boss."

Judd examined his fingers as if they belonged to someone else. It had all come together just as he'd planned. When Barlow was in town two months earlier, and most of the boys were working cows, he'd slipped into the house and put pen to paper, writing the fake document and forging both signatures.

Before Judd came to the Barlow spread, his past was already tainted. He'd made money when he was young forging names on bills of trust and bank checks. When the law got close in Missouri, he'd cleared out and found safer work that wouldn't put him in jail.

Only a month earlier, the lawyer, J. T. Buford, was found dead in a Fort Worth alley down in Hell's Half Acre, just another victim of robbery in the rough and dangerous cattle town. It didn't pay to go visit the girls down there in the toughest place in Texas.

The plan wasn't recent, though. The new owner of the Three Fork ranch had been grooming Son for just such an event for over a year, confident that he'd be able to manipulate the younger Barlow into doing something stupid. It had been his hope that the old man would disown his son and run him off. With Son gone,

Judd planned to do what Son recommended, smother Barlow with his pillow so it would look as if he'd died in his sleep.

In fact, it was Judd who'd put that pillow idea into Son's head weeks earlier.

Funny how an idea can stick in a feller's mind.

"Well, Boss." Caleb slapped Judd on the shoulder. "What do we do now?"

"Were you boys in line with what Barlow had in mind? Taking the Oarlock away from Hutchins?"

"That's why we hired on, though we might need to talk about how much he offered. A little more cash wouldn't hurt."

The others milled, nodded, and looked hopeful.

"I'll double it. How's that?"

Claude's smile went from ear to ear. "Does all this have to be filed in town?"

"It will, but this paper's as good as gold."

Claude looked toward the bedroom door. "We can't bury them right now, as hard as the ground's froze. We can put them in the barn until the doctor and the undertaker come out and take a look."

"Good idea." Judd was surprised at how easy it was to manipulate such men. "Leave the bedroom as it is, but we can wrap them in sheets before we take 'em out. Sheriff Larson'll want to look, and then with Doc's death certificate, it'll all be legal. By that time, we'll have forced Hutchins off his place."

"Hutchins won't give up easy. He'll go to the governor over anything we try, especially if Sheriff Larson squares off with us."

"Then we'll beat him at that game, too. Somebody bring me a pen and paper."

Curious, Claude found the items and slid them in front of Judd. "What are these for?"

"I'm writing this to the governor, saying that Hutchins has been stealing our cattle, shooting at our men, and trying to force the Three Fork out of business. The pressure got to be so much that Mr. Barlow wasn't doing well. He was dying, in fact, and all he wanted was to save the ranch. He's gone now, and we want justice. If we're lucky, the governor will deputize you, Claude, and we can form . . ."

He thought for a moment, pretending to come up with a new name.

"The Blackjack Stockmen's Association, charged with ending this egregious attack on a ranch that has just signed an agreement with the Texas Pacific Railroad to ship cattle from here."

He grinned at the men gathered around him. "Gentlemen, welcome to the newly formed Blackjack Cattle Ranch."

CHAPTER 56

It was full daylight when Wes Callahan poured two cups of coffee strong enough to float a horseshoe. He carried one to Drake Hutchins, who was backed up to the fireplace, warming himself before pulling on his boots.

Over the years, Wes took over the cooking duties, preferring to eat something that was cooked properly instead of raw or burned to a crisp. The last time Drake fried a steak, it was so tough Wes threatened to replace the sole of his boot with it.

The same with coffee. Drake boiled it until the coffee didn't need a cup but stood up on its own. Wes let the pot come to a boil, added a palm full of grounds, and let it set for a few minutes. He even added a sprinkle of salt, if it was available, to cut down on the bitterness.

Drake took the enameled cup. "Much obliged."

"Stopped snowing. Sun's up."

"I knew that while you were still snoring."

Rather than continue a years'-long argument, Wes pulled a suspender into place and walked to the front window. Since Drake was the first one up, he'd stoked the fire, and the interior was comfortable. "The boys are up, too. I suspect they're anxious to get to work. We ain't done a productive thing on this place since it clouded up a few days ago."

Drake blew across the surface of his mug and took a tentative sip. Seeing it was cool enough, he drew in a big swallow of the bitter liquid. "I added too much coffee this morning. It tastes like yours."

"Then I coulda had it made this morning and enjoyed a cup before you ever swung your lazy feet to the floor." He took a sip. "Tastes fine to me. Send the boys out to see if the stock all froze to death. We can't get a good head count till the snow melts, but at least we'll see how they fared."

"It wasn't a blizzard, so I imagine they all buried up in the brush and stayed there. They'll be hungry, though, and it won't be hard to find them on the short grass up by Parvin Branch, I suspect."

The bunkhouse was at a slight angle to the main house and Wes saw the door open. "At least the boys are alive. I see one of 'em standing there, looking out. Can't tell who it is, but I hope he has better manners than to take a leak right there where he's standing."

At that moment, two figures carrying rifles crossed in front of the window and rushed up the steps. Wes frowned at the same time that a loud crack came from outside and the cowboy who'd just stepped outside fell back into the bunkhouse, his booted feet out in the snow. The window in front of Wes exploded inward and the slug buried itself in the mantel a foot from Drake.

Always armed, Wes snatched the revolver from his

holster at the same time a figure shoved through the door. Only four feet away, Wes put two holes in the intruder, and the second man fell back, scrambling across the porch and out of sight.

Hutchins broke for his pistol in the holster hanging on a nearby peg as a fusillade finished taking out the window and punched holes in things all around the room. At the same time, a volley aimed at the bunkhouse chewed splinters in the walls.

Drake snatched up his pistol and the two experienced frontiersmen rushed to the front exterior wall. The big house was originally a log cabin they'd walled years earlier with planks, and no slug could penetrate the thick wood. Glancing out, he saw an army spread out and hiding behind anything that would give them cover. Each gunshot was followed by a puff of smoke.

"Three Fork men!"

Wes holstered his Colt and snatched up a Henry leaning behind a door. Staying back inside the room and out of sight, he went to work with the big rifle, calmly shooting at men like someone plinking cans off a fence rail.

The boys in the bunkhouse finally gathered their wits and fired back through shooting ports built there for that exact purpose back in the Comanche days. Cold and still, the air held puffs of gun smoke that floated in place, barely drifting at all.

Wes shifted his position and fired again so that his shots weren't predictable or coming from the same place. "I told you we shoulda kept them ports here instead of covering them up."

"We'll argue about that later." Drake aimed and fired. He fired again and then went to the gun rack and grabbed a Sharps and two boxes of bullets. He pitched the 45-70s to Wes and loaded the buffalo rifle.

Shouldering the big .50 caliber, he lined up on a man who kept peeking around the edge of the springhouse. "They're about to see what happened at Adobe Walls."

Wes chuckled and jacked a fresh round into the Henry's magazine.

CHAPTER 57

Texas Ranger Ridge Tisdale was looking out the hotel's frosty front windows, drinking coffee in the hotel parlor from a thick mug, when Sheriff Larson came down the stairs. "This is the first time I've seen the sun in a week."

"It's not really up, just glowing pretty bright through the clouds."

"I like to dream." Ridge swallowed. "When was the last time you've seen snow this deep?"

A wagon rolled past, leaving hub-deep tracks behind. "Never here in Texas. I've seen it deeper up in the mountains."

After being stuck inside by bad weather for days, people were moving around, despite the early hour. It almost looked normal, unless one stood under the overhang out front and looked down the street. The still smoldering coals prevented the snow from collecting on the four lots, leaving ugly black blots like rotten teeth in an otherwise white smile.

"Where'd you get the coffee?"

Ridge used the cup to sweep behind him. "There's some on the potbelly in the bar."

Sheriff Larson got his own and joined the Ranger. "What's your plan for today?"

"Probably same as yours."

"Ride out to the Barlow ranch and arrest Son and Judd."

"If they went home last night. I'll ask around if anyone's seen them, but it's either them, or wait a day and go out this morning to collect Clyde McPeak."

"You said that yesterday. For what?"

"Murder, east of Paris. Town called Blossom Prairie."

"Don't they have a county sheriff?"

"They do, but McPeak killed the daughter of a sitting judge in Austin."

"That explains it."

"It does." Ridge took another sip and lowered the mug when he saw Seminole Sam walking their way. "Here comes someone you need to meet."

Larson stepped up beside Ridge to see the big man coming down the road. Sam stepped onto the porch, stomped the snow off his feet, and went inside. "Gentlemen, all is quiet over in Nellie's. I went down to check on Maggie and little Jo, and they're fine. Miss Nell sent me over to help you, Mr. Tisdale. Said you might need me today since you're going to arrest McPeak."

"You know him?"

"Yes, sir, he was a pretty good customer when he first came to town, but we haven't seen him in a good long while. Figured you might need a hand, or someone who recognizes him. He's a big man, too. Might need someone who knows how to use his fists."

Ridge finished the last of his coffee. "Well, then. Since we have the use of a professional pugilist, I think we should take advantage of our opportunity. I was just gonna shoot him and be done with it."

Sheriff Larson shrugged. "Might as well start there, before we go get Son Barlow and that shootist of his. I'd like to wrap all this up today, if we can."

Winter in Texas can change within the matter of an hour. The deep cold that had supported such a snowfall had moved east, leaving bright, sunny skies that immediately set out to melt it all as soon as possible.

The three of them rode out of a town filled with the sounds of dripping water, sloshing hooves in muddy slush, and the soft underbeat of a living community. Well rested, Ridge's buckskin, Rebel, set out full of energy, pricking his ears forward and kicking at the fluff with his forelegs.

The only trails they found were made by animals. Rabbits, squirrels, and deer had already been out, criss-crossing the snow with random tracks. Sam pointed. "You can see where they rode through late last night."

Ridge squinted at the fresh coating of snow, finally seeing the irregular surface that looked different than the undisturbed prairie. "I'm not sure I would have stayed on the road without you, Sam."

"Well, sir, my ancestors were pretty good trackers, and I learned a bit when I was a kid."

"Not exactly good training for a man with your job."

Sam threw back his head and laughed. "Everything we learn in life winds up being valuable at some point."

A variety of bushes and scrub trees thickened, then spread out to be almost nonexistent for long periods of time before crowding in again. Leafless Blackjack oaks, bare mesquite trees, and the multibranched cholla cactus poked up through the snow. Cedars also grew in profusion, and Sam pointed at a thick green growth that was defined by two large trees.

A wide gap forked off from the wagon road. "This takes us to the ranch. See where Mr. Hutchins and his men splintered off and headed northwest?"

"You mean that snow there that looks less smooth?"

"That's right." Sam looked up, judging the position of the sun. "About another mile or so to the ranch house."

They came to a low-water crossing that was invisible beneath the snow. Sam let his horse study what was ahead of them. It could hear the trickle of invisible water below. Satisfied by something no human could understand, it took a tentative step that reassured the gelding. It minced across and continued, followed by the other two.

"Just up this ridge." Sam pointed at the same time a scattering of soft pops reached their ears.

As one, Ridge and Sheriff Larson kicked their mounts past Sam and spurred them forward. Excited by the demeanor of their riders, the horses pricked their ears and moved fast to the crest of a low rise.

Down below was a picturesque view of a wide valley. Three buildings, in an odd bent line like the stars in the

Big Dipper's handle, looked homey and inviting, with smoke coming from two chimneys on the house and the same number of stovepipes rising from a building attached to what Ridge took for a bunkhouse.

Ridge reined up and took in the scene as gunfire rattled and crackled down below from both attackers and defenders. To his right and a couple of hundred yards from the house was a cluster of saddled horses, tied to a variety of brushy, bare-branched trees. A wide track leading eastward was evidence of where they came from.

Their riders were scattered around the house and barn, taking cover behind anything they could find that would turn bullets. Smoke from their rifles floated in the still air, drifting slowly away. Keeping up a steady fire, they maneuvered toward the house, leaving thin, crooked trails in the snow.

A still body was sprawled half in, half out of the bunkhouse, preventing the door from closing. As he watched, someone tried to reach the dead man and drag him back inside but was driven undercover from the sheer number of slugs.

Smoke puffed from inside the house, followed by a huge boom, and a figure fell near what looked like a springhouse to disappear into the snow. The ranch's defenders were giving as good as they got.

"I bet them are Barlow riders." Sam slid a rifle from his scabbard. "I'm gonna take care of them horses. Maybe they won't be so inclined to fight if they don't have a way to get gone when this is over. I'll come in behind when y'all do whatever it is you think is right."

Without waiting for comments, the big Seminole

reined his horse toward a thicket of mesquites that would provide cover until he got close. Spurring his mount, he disappeared in a cloud of flying white chunks and fresh powder.

Ridge checked the loads from a borrowed rifle. His Henry was gone, left in front of the bakery. He already missed it, and the range it provided. He hoped the sights on the Winchester were right.

Sheriff Larson left his rifle in the scabbard. "They're gonna turn them guns on us the minute we get there."

"They will. But my hope is the boys in there will realize what's happening when those Barlow men quit shooting at them and we can get 'em in a crossfire."

The firing intensified below and then receded.

"All this to arrest a man named Clyde." Ridge spurred his horse and let him pick his way down the shallow slope. All the attackers' attention was on the ranch buildings, and they didn't see the Ranger until one of them, behind a stack of split wood, threw up his arms and fell sideways.

The flat report of a rifle behind him told Ridge the sheriff was good at long shots.

Ridge saw the man nearest him stare downward, perplexed. When he looked around for an explanation, he saw the Texas Ranger bearing down on him at a dead run, pistol blazing. A bullet whizzed past, missing him by several inches, and he leveled the Colt at a bundled-up cowboy behind a stacked rock wall separating the house from a split-rail corral.

The man rested his arm on the top of the wall and aimed. A bullet from the house shattered a rock only inches from him and the startled shooter fell back out of sight. Other bullets snapped through the air, but Ridge was focused on the one who'd just disappeared.

He rode straight to the wall and through a hail of bullets to lean over the four-foot barricade and shoot the man lying prone on the ground, checking his arm for wounds. The point-blank shot ended that threat, and Ridge switched the Colt to his left hand. Drawing the spare he took from Son, he fired at a target on his right, and then at a man on the left who'd worked himself up close to the house.

A rattle of shots from the barn blended into a volley from the attackers as they turned to face still another threat as Sheriff Larson galloped up with a pistol in his hand. He triggered a round at a young Barlow rider who rose, stumbled, and fell sideways.

"Let's get outta here!"

The shout came from a bearded cowboy who rose from behind a springhouse and charged back the way they came. A second man bolted up like a rabbit from behind a bush and joined him at a dead run. Following the trail someone had made through the knee-high snow, both dropped and were still a second before two rifle reports reached Ridge.

He didn't need to look to know Seminole Sam had worked his way down to cut off their escape.

CHAPTER 58

"They're fighting back harder than I expected," Judd Fletcher panted, though they'd done nothing but creep up through the snow and take cover. His face was red with the cold and exertion.

He and Caleb were crouched behind a snow-covered wagon that was in turn partially protected by an L-shaped stacked rock wall. Caleb risked a peek around the little sod house. "Most of the fire's coming from the bunkhouse. One or two guns in the barn, though, but those old men in the house are tough."

Judd waved at those he could see. "Pour it on the bunkhouse." He thought aloud. "We tighten it down there, the barn will be next."

"We've already lost some guns."

"Huh?"

"I said, we've already lost several men."

"We're gonna lose more." Judd shot three quick times at the bunkhouse and ducked back out of sight at the same time another of his men slid to stop beside him.

"I'm going to take a couple of boys and set fire to the back of the house."

Judd wondered what the man's name was. "Do what you want."

The man jumped up and waved at two others shooting from behind a mesquite fence. He shot four times fast with his pistol and broke from cover. "Come with me!"

A slug folded him in two and he dropped into the snow.

Wes looked up to see someone riding straight at them, shooting as fast as he could pull the trigger. The horses' hooves threw up white clods and a spray of powdered snow as he charged in.

"Who the hell is that?"

A terrified voice shouted over the gunfire, "Let's get out of here!"

Judd whirled to see two of his men struggling through the snow, running back the way they came. They folded immediately before the report of a rifle came from behind them.

He whirled around to Caleb. "What do we do?"

"You're asking me? You're the boss."

"Then keep shooting!"

CHAPTER 59

As Ridge looked around for another target, a big Sharps opened up from the house and an attacker close by threw up his hands and flew backward as the heavy slug blew out his chest. A steady stream of bullets came from the direction of the Barlow horses.

The moment he registered it was Sam, two riderless horses raced into view, terrified of the gunfire. He figured the big Seminole had cut the picket line and scattered all their mounts.

The fire that had been concentrated on the bunkhouse slackened as the thunderstruck assassins took stock of their new situation.

Someone shouted, "They're behind us!"

"Don't let up on 'em!"

"Take that bunkhouse!" Judd's voice that ordered them to advance came from behind the springhouse.

Sheriff Larson arrived, followed by a spray of snow and ice clods. Leaving his horse to look less suspicious, he swung around behind the sod house, firing the pistol in his hand as fast as he could. They were fighting like Comanches, and their erratic tactics unnerved the attackers.

Ridge wheeled his horse and took in after him, following the roan's tracks. Three men were huddled against the wall, and all of them shot back as they passed. In their excitement, neither the lawmen nor their foes were injured.

Ridge and Larson raced around a mesquite post corral and spurred their horses until they were behind the barn. Out of sight, they reined up and thumbed shells into their pistols.

Heart beating like a drum, Ridge glanced around, thankful for the first time for the snow. There wasn't a track in sight, telling him no one had yet tried to circle around. "You hurt?"

Larson raised his arm and used the muzzle of his hot pistol to point. "Round went through my coat sleeve. Felt the heat of the slug as it passed."

"We can't go back around that way. They'll be watching, and this time we won't have surprise on our side."

"I saw Sam working his way toward them."

"A couple broke that way and he mowed 'em down." Ridge paused as the buffalo gun boomed again. He grinned. "I don't know who's behind that monster, but I'm gonna kiss him when this is all over."

"They can't stand much more of this."

"Split up." Ridge pointed at the barn. "Go around that way and come out between the barn and the house. I'll circle the house and cut back into our tracks again.

With luck, they'll think I'm someone new. It might shake them up some."

Larson nodded. "Meet you in the middle."

Spurring the roan, he reined in between the buildings, firing as fast as he could cock the pistol in his hand. As Ridge raced around, he caught sight of Larson's roan going down, kicking all the way.

He wheeled Rebel around and went right in behind the sheriff. Larson landed hard, but came up and rolled behind the dying horse. Seeing he could do nothing, Ridge rode between the sheriff and the sod house, hoping to draw fire until Larson could regain his feet.

Immediately realizing Ridge's plan, Larson grabbed his rifle and rose, charging as fast as he could run for the house. He was up on the porch in a flash and the door opened. The sheriff disappeared at the same time a bullet slapped the cantle of his saddle, and Rebel suddenly had his own ideas about being in a hailstorm.

The buckskin planted his feet and whirled, ducked back behind the barn, and ran over a gunman with a splint on one leg. He couldn't dodge fast enough and went down under the horses' hooves. The man's hat flew off, revealing curly blond hair.

He wasn't through. Maybe it was because of the splint on his leg and he couldn't maneuver fast, but the blonde's hand came up full of pistol and he fired. The bullet punched a hole through the brim of Ridge's hat and he reined Rebel on top of the shooter.

Feeling the man under his hooves, Rebel jerked left, and Ridge fired downward into the hatless man's chest. Still not out of the fight, the man's hand rose again and Ridge shot him again, and again.

CHAPTER 60

"Man down outside!" Wes threw a round and missed. "He's coming in!"

Despite the fire directed at the house, Drake Hutchins rushed across the room and opened the door. A lanky figure in a big hat fell into the room and rolled out of the way as Drake slammed the door.

"Is that you, Matt?"

Sheriff Larson quickly regained his feet and whirled to meet any threat following him inside. "It is. Ranger Tisdale's still out there."

Well back from the windows and calm, as if taking target practice, Wes jacked another round into his rifle, shifted his position, and fired again. "I was wondering who y'all were."

Two rounds came through the window and buried themselves on the far side. Drake and Larson jumped and ducked against the heavily fortified wall. Drake shoved another thumb-sized shell into the Sharp's hot chamber.

The firing slacked off for a moment, and Wes busted

open the cardboard box of ammunition. He thumbed fresh rounds into the Henry. "I've had enough of this."

Drake nodded. "How many'd y'all hit out there?"

"Not enough, but we've all taken a toll."

Three quick rounds came from one location. Wes again shifted so he could see. "Was there three of y'all?"

"Yep." Larson nodded. "Seminole Sam."

Drake barked a laugh. "I didn't know that big Indian ever left Nellie's."

"He's much of a man. Circled around behind where these guys left their horses and run 'em off. Sounds like he's got them in a crossfire."

"I saw a couple of horses flash past out there. They can't get away now." Wes jacked the lever and shoved in the last shell. "I don't know about you two, but these ain't Comanches."

"You intend to go charging out there?"
They won't be expecting it, and I don't favor a"
                                                    ".siege

Sheriff Larson froze and pointed out the window. "Look at that!"

It was Ridge Tisdale on foot and with a pistol in each hand, walking out there alone, big as you please and shooting like the devil himself was pulling the triggers.

CHAPTER 61

Seeing Seminole Sam move into position on the far side of the ranch yard, Ridge left Rebel behind the barn and walked around into the wide-open space bracketed by the three buildings, the corral, the springhouse, and the stacked rock wall.

Sam shouldered his rifle and fired, then fired again, fast.

When the attackers turned to face that threat, Ridge advanced like a man walking into a rattlesnake den. He fired left and right, sometimes connecting but most times missing. The return fire was sparse. He emptied the spare pistol in his left hand, and like a man shooting prairie dogs, shoved the Colt into the shoulder holster without hurry.

"People! I'm Ridge Tisdale, Texas Ranger." He shook the empties out of his pistol and reloaded from the shells in his gun belt. Standing alone in the snow, he seemed twice as tall as his six-foot height and alone as a bull pine on the Llano Estacado. "If you horses' asses don't put down your weapons, me and Sheriff Larson are going to kill every damned one of you. Throw up your hands and you'll live."

Finished loading the first revolver, he stuck it into the holster on his belt and commenced reloading the Colt. Gunshots echoed from the buildings and bullets whizzed past. "I mean what I say!"

A figure rose from behind a sawbuck and the stack of cut logs beside it. Taking careful aim, he fired and missed. Ridge's Colt bucked, and the man fell backward. Ridge walked even farther into the open.

"I've done told you what's gonna happen. Who's next?"

The ranch house door opened and the three men came out, guns ready. A shirtless, gray-haired man in suspenders over his underwear separated himself from the others. "Somebody else take a shot at me, please. I'm just about mad."

A flurry of shots came from behind the rock wall, and Sam's rifle answered from behind the ranch. One survivor jumped up, threw a shot at the house, and took off running. The gray-haired man with the Henry cut him down.

They heard men talking, and a rustle of bodies came from behind the springhouse. Three figures rushed forward and took cover between it and a wagon pulled up close to the rock wall. They'd found the only place with protection on almost all sides. The little fort kept Ridge and the others from seeing them clearly.

The bunkhouse door opened and a small army of armed, furious cowboys poured through and spread out.

Sheriff Larson stepped off the porch as Zeke left the pack of cowboys and joined the lawmen.

Larson spoke loud, a sound of authority. "You men see this? You're way outnumbered and we'll kill you all if you don't surrender."

"You'll hang us anyway!" None of them could see the speaker, but his voice wasn't scared in the least. It carried the resigned tone of someone with nothing left to lose.

Larson walked over close to Ridge. "This is Sheriff Larson. Me and this man here swore to uphold the law. We'll take you in. There'll be a jury trial. That's all I can promise."

"*Then* we'll hang."

Zeke, who'd been fighting from the bunkhouse, spoke up. "Judd? Is that you?"

The three Barlow men were huddled out of sight behind the deep snow. "It is."

"Where's old man Barlow?"

"He's dead."

"Son?"

"Dead too."

Ridge spoke up. "They laying out there?"

Judd chuckled. "Shot each other to death early this morning."

"So, why're *you* here?"

"The will Barlow left behind says the ranch is mine."

"So?"

"I plan to own this one, too."

Drake Hutchins waved an arm. "Look around you, boy. There's only three or what, four, of you left."

"Mister, I don't see one of my men there, so that tells me I have a man with a rifle somewhere around here pointed right at Zeke there. He's my ace in the hole. Clyde! When I tell you, shoot that one with the tall hat there."

The yard was silent as they all waited for the gunshot.

Ridge tired of the game. "I'm shaking at the knees here."

"Clyde!"

The name dawned on Ridge. "Clyde *McPeak*?"

Drake spoke softly. "That's the Barlow man I hired yesterday."

"He was in the barn this morning," Zeke said. "He got up early and went out to feed. Can't do much more with that splint on his leg."

"Blond-headed? Broken leg?" Ridge called across the yard. "He's dead. I just killed him behind the barn. Boys, you're out of choices."

All was quiet for a full minute while Judd considered his options. "I have an idea."

"What's that?"

"Ranger, since you're the one started all this, how about you and me meet out in the open right here. We draw. The winner walks away."

"You still won't have the ranch. That dream's dead as far as you're concerned."

"I might. We'll work that out when you're dead. If it don't, I don't care. I'll start over just like I did here."

"Fine, then. Come out."

Sheriff Larson frowned at Ridge. "That the stupidest thing I've ever heard."

Sam's voice rumbled low and full of danger. "Mr. Tisdale, before y'all square off, you need to know that Judd and Son kidnapped Miss Maggie and her little one."

Ridge felt that coal relight deep inside his chest, and he had to hold himself back for just a few more moments.

"Coming out!" Judd stepped into the open.

"Y'all stand down." Ridge turned to the hands. "You boys, too. This is my fight now. You heard our deal."

Judd picked his way out of their little fort and walked out into the open. Taking off his coat, he pitched it into the snow, revealing the pistol in his holster. Two more steps later, he planted his feet, fingers wiggling.

His insolent smile was the final nail in the man's coffin. "Holster that Colt and let's get to it."

"No." Ridge raised the pistol still in his hand and shot Judd in the chest. The shocked man stepped back and rested his hand on the butt still in the holster. His other hand went to the hole in his shirt.

Ridge shot him again, and they watched the dead man fall backward.

"There ain't no such thing as a fair fight." He swung the muzzle toward the others. "So, the rest of y'all that rode for Barlow best stand up and raise your hands or die here and now."

Like prairie dogs, five men stood from behind their various hiding places. Hands in the air, they waited as the Oarlock men rushed forward and made sure they were completely disarmed.

Sheriff Larson shook his head. "I never saw such a thing."

Patting his almost bare chest, Wes Callahan gave up trying to find a cigar. "That's the same thing I woulda done. Good work, Ranger."

Ridge Tisdale slid the Colt back into his holster. "I despise a murderer."

He turned to Zeke. "While I'm all riled up, Zeke, I want you to get on that bag of bones you're riding and hie on to town and marry Maggie today. I want that done before the week is out."

Licking his lips, Zeke looked from Ridge to his boss. "Mr. Hutchins, I believe I'll do that. I'm done cowboying."

The old man smiled. "You weren't much count anyway, stringing off over there every chance you got, so good riddance."

Seminole Sam walked up with a rifle in his arms and a wide smile on his face. "Morning, Mr. Wes, Mr. Hutchins."

Hutchins looked the big man up and down. "You know anything about cattle, or horses?"

"A little. Raised on a farm up in the territories."

"You have a job?"

Wes grinned. "He works for Nell. Fighting man."

"Want to work for us?" Hutchins asked. "The size of this spread just doubled, and you look like a man I can count on."

"No, sir, but thank you. I like sleeping late and staying up all night in the presence of attractive women.

And I don't fancy being out in weather, neither. Sir, I'm inherently lazy, but if and whenever you need me again, just send word and I'll be out here in a shake."

Wes drew a long breath. "Well, that was entertaining, though we lost a couple of boys. Reminds me of when we were fighting Comanches. But you know, Drake, I think I'll ride back into town with Sam here, and see where he works."

"You've been there before," Hutchins said.

"Not lately." Wes turned to Ridge. "And what about you? Care to stay and have breakfast with the boys?"

Ridge shook his head. "No, but thanks, anyway. My business is done in Blackjack, but I'll take McPeak with me, to save you the digging of one grave in this frozen ground."

Zeke and Sam helped him load the body onto one of the Barlow horses, and Ridge paused. "Here." He dug Jo's madstone from his pocket and gave it to Zeke. "I believe someone's looking for this. She'll hug your neck when you give it back to her, and listen, you take care of Maggie or I'll come back here and get her."

"You don't have to worry about that," Zeke met his eyes, understanding each other, and they shook.

"Sam." Ridge took his big hand.

"Yes, sir."

"Thanks, and tell Nell I'll send her a telegram when that line's back up. I'll take the train back up to see her when it comes through."

Ridge swung into the saddle with a creak of cold leather, took the reins of the horse bearing McPeak's body, and headed back east as the sun peeked through the clouds and glistened off the snow like a world of tiny diamonds.

It was little payment for what had been done, and as he passed the town of Blackjack without stopping, Ridge soon enjoyed the melting of it.

**TURN THE PAGE
FOR A SPELLBINDING PREVIEW!**

**Meet Tomahawk Callahan, wagon master.
His bullets hurt.**

It's the ultimate Wild West showdown
between a small-time wagoner and a big-city rail boss—
on a deadly collision course—in this blazing new
series from the best-selling Johnstones.

WILL THIS BE . . . THE LAST WAGON TRAIN?

A new railroad line is coming to Hansen's Bend—
and the Old West will never be the same.
Especially for the Callahans. They've been running
the local wagon train outfit for years.
But now a pompous rail boss named Arbuckle
wants to put them out of business.
This big-city weasel mocks the Callahans'
"slow-poke" wagons—and bets he can finish
laying track all the way to the end of the line
before the Callahans' wagon train even makes it over
the mountains. Callahan accepts the challenge—
and gets gunned down before it even starts. . . .

But the contest isn't over. The wagoner's son,
Luke "Tomahawk" Callahan, has returned to
Hansen's Bend after five years as an army scout.
He knows nothing about the rail boss's challenge
or his father's murder—until he sees the
newspaper headline: "The Last Wagon Train?"
The pretty lady journalist who wrote it wants to ride
along and follow this story to the end.
And, of course, Tomahawk wants to defend his
father's honor and avenge his death.
But Arbuckle has sent his henchmen to sabotage
the wagon train to make sure Tomahawk
and his wagons are dead on arrival . . .

National Best-selling Authors
William W. Johnstone
and J. A. Johnstone

THE LAST WAGON TRAIN

On sale now, wherever Pinnacle Books are sold.

Live Free. Read Hard.
www.williamjohnstone.net
Visit us at www.kensingtonbooks.com

CHAPTER 1

They would have just let the Indians go if not for the prospector.

A team of mule skinners out of Deadwood and angling northwest to Montana had found him along a creek when they'd stopped to water the animals. He was a mess, all beat up, shoes gone, and scalped, which was how they'd known it was Indians. One of the freight drivers recognized the prospector as Henry Jakes. A mule and the man's Spencer rifle were missing. The mule skinners took the body to the nearest marshal, who sent a telegram to the blue coats at Fort Keogh.

Lieutenant W. P. Clark hadn't been happy. The Northern Cheyenne trouble was supposed to be over, but there were always rogue groups, and a murdered white man wasn't something he could ignore. A green second lieutenant named Foster and a dozen equally green troopers were all he could spare.

After careful consideration, Clark couldn't in good conscience send out all those inexperienced men without somebody who actually knew what he was doing.

He called Master Sergeant Isiah Parks into his office.

Parks snapped to attention, throwing out his barrel chest. He was a beefy, florid-faced man with red hair now streaked with gray, forty-five years old, twenty-two of which had been spent in the army. He'd taken a Confederate bayonet to his left buttock at Bull Run and had only in recent years developed a sense of humor about the scar. He sported new stripes on his blue sleeve, three up and three down.

"At ease, Sergeant," Clark said. "How would you like to escort our young Mr. Foster on a little nature walk?"

"My pleasure, sir."

"You understand what's expected?"

"Noses wiped and diapers changed," Parks said. "Bring the lieutenant back relatively undamaged."

Clark hid a smile. "That's not how I'd put it if Mr. Foster's in earshot, but yes, you have the basic idea. I suppose I should send an experienced scout with you. Is Mort Whittaker still in camp?"

"Beggin' your pardon, sir, but Tom would be my suggestion," Parks said. "He's at that saloon he likes so much, and it's on the way. If we leave early enough, we can pick him up before he gets started."

Tom referred to Luke Callahan. Tom was short for Tomahawk, which was what all the men called him. Lieutenant Clark had never worked with the man, but he trusted the sergeant's judgment.

"Okay, then," Clark said. "You know what to do. Get started."

* * *

Luke "Tomahawk" Callahan sat at a corner table in Shakey's Place, a low-ceilinged, ramshackle saloon inside a squat log structure along a muddy road between Fort Keogh and the rest of the world. A traveler wouldn't have known it was called Shakey's Place if he just happened by. One either knew Gil Shakey, or one didn't. The shutters were closed against the cold, what with winter clinging and spring slow to develop in the first week of April. The only light in the place came from three lanterns and a modest blaze in the stone fireplace.

Callahan tossed two cards on the table and kept three. The two horse soldiers, a lanky corporal and a short private with a bushy mustache, had already thrown their cards down in disgust, wishing they could have their antes back.

That left the slicker.

Or, at least, *slicker* was how Tomahawk Callahan thought of the man. He had *back East* written all over him, talked educated. He wore a dark suit with a red waistcoat, some kind of tight pattern in the fabric that was hard to make out in the saloon's dim light. A gold chain disappeared into the waistcoat pocket, and presumably there was an expensive watch in there. Gold cufflinks. Bowler hat cocked at a jaunty angle. He smoked a thin cigar. Callahan was no expert on fine tobacco, but the cigar smelled good, so it was probably expensive, too. Mustache and beard well trimmed. No dirt under his fingernails. He told everyone he'd recently been let go from the railroad and was on his way to anywhere else.

The slicker's eyes flicked back and forth between his cards and Callahan. He licked his lips. Nervous.

Or maybe just *pretending* to be nervous. Callahan had learned early on you played the man as much as you played the cards.

He wondered how he must look to the slicker. Tall and rangy, five days of black stubble on his square jaw, beat-up buckskin jacket, battered old brown hat hanging on the back of his chair. A Colt Peacemaker hung on his right hip.

Luke didn't see a gun on the slicker's hip. The man was either too trusting or hadn't been West long enough.

The slicker looked at his cards again and then at the pot. A lot of money there, a sizable pot for so early in the day. It wasn't quite lunchtime.

"I seem to be facing a conundrum." The slicker looked at Callahan. "I beg your pardon, *conundrum* means—"

"A confusing or difficult problem," Callahan said. "I know."

"See, you've only taken two cards, so I'm forced to infer the three you have left are good ones," the slicker mused. "Whereas, I'd planned to take three cards."

A child could see the man was stalling, running his mouth just to see if Callahan would blink or flinch or give anything away.

"I didn't mean to *imply* anything specific about my cards," Callahan said. "You are, of course, welcome to *infer* as you like."

The man laughed. "Sorry. I guess that was pretty clumsy. I noticed you haven't looked at your new cards yet."

"I don't have to yet." Callahan had learned he couldn't give away anything about his cards if he didn't know what they were. If the slicker folded, then it wouldn't matter. If Callahan had to bet, he'd look at his cards then.

The slicker grinned as if amused. "Not even curious?"

Callahan shrugged. He could wait all day.

The slicker threw down two cards. The corporal dealt him two new ones. The slicker looked at them, face blank.

Callahan picked up his cards, forcing himself not to hurry. He held them low and squeezed them out one at a time, seeing his original cards first—three nines. He squeezed the next one. Jack of spades. No help.

He scooted the final card out from behind the rest with his thumb.

The fourth nine.

It was difficult to keep his mouth from quirking into a smile, but Callahan managed to maintain a blank expression. Luck was on his side. Callahan had won a few hands, small amounts of money, but he'd just gotten the best hand of the day right when the pot was the biggest. A bet too big would scare the man off.

Callahan tossed his chips onto the pile, not enough to confirm to the slicker he had a winning hand, but enough to make him pause and think.

"Well." The slicker pushed his bowler back on his head and wiped his forehead. "I can't legitimately claim to have a very strong hand. Having said that, it chagrins to let that sizable pot go without a look at your cards."

Callahan smiled. "It's a conundrum."

The slicker laughed and tossed in his chips. "Call."

Callahan laid down his cards.

The corporal whistled.

The slicker leaned over the cards and frowned. "Four nines. That figures."

He tossed in his cards.

Callahan scooped the chips toward him, allowing his poker face to finally drop in favor of a pleased grin.

The corporal pushed away from the table and motioned for the private to follow him. "That's all for me. Come on, Del, let's get a beer."

The slicker said, "I'd love a chance back at all that money I just lost, but I suppose I'd better not dig my hole any deeper."

A shrug from Callahan, not quite apologetic. "Some days you get the cards. Other days, the other fella has the luck."

"Well, I'd like to prove I'm not a poor sport at least. Let me buy you a whiskey."

"I'll buy you *two* whiskeys if I can get one of them cigars," Callahan said. "Smells good."

"That seems a fair trade." The slicker stuck out his hand. "Ronald Parsons."

Callahan shook. "Tomahawk Callahan."

"Tomahawk?"

"Long story."

Parsons patted his jacket pocket, a thoughtful look crossing his face. "You know what. I don't have any cigars on me. I'm pretty sure I have more in my saddlebags. Follow me. I'll set you up. I need some air, anyway.

It's too close in here with all the shutters closed. My horse is out back."

Callahan stood, gathered the chips. "Let me cash these in. I'll meet you out there."

He took the chips to the man behind the bar, Gil Shakey, a man barely as tall as he was wide with a bald head and a drooping mustache that looked like he was letting a squirrel live rent free on his face.

Callahan cashed in his chips and pocketed the money, then stepped out the back door, and a cold wind hit him at once. He grumbled. Tomahawk Callahan had already had his fill of winter. Spring was taking its own sweet time getting here. He went to where Parsons had his horse tied and stood politely, waiting. They were the only two out back. Most people tied their horses out front. Probably, Parsons had come up from the southern trail, and he'd seen the back door first.

Parsons went from one saddlebag to another. "Apologies. I'm sure I have a few more of those stogies stashed somewhere."

"It's okay if you don't. I'll still stand you a whiskey for good intentions." Callahan wasn't keen to linger any longer in the biting wind. The cigar was rapidly losing its attraction.

"No, no. Just a moment."

It was a bit early in the day to start on the whiskey, but now Callahan figured he'd need it just to warm up.

"*Voila!*" Parsons came out of the saddlebag with a small, wooden box in his hand. He opened it and fished out one of the cigars, then handed it to Callahan.

Callahan stuck it in his mouth. "Obliged. I'll light it inside, and we'll get our drinks."

"Thank you, but I'll need to drink quickly," Parsons said. "I should have been on my way to Bozeman long before now." He pointed. "Is that the best way to go?"

Callahan turned to look where he was pointing. "You can go that way, but it's not the fastest route. If you angle south a bit—"

Pain exploded at the base of Callahan's skull, white lights and stars flashing in his eyes a brief moment before everything went dark.

CHAPTER 2

Callahan came awake with a start, sputtering and spitting and freezing cold. He wiped water from his eyes, looking around, trying to remember where he was and how he'd gotten there.

He looked up into the grinning face of Isiah Parks. The sergeant held a bucket in his hands. "Looks like you started on the whiskey a bit early even for you."

Callahan checked his pockets. All of his money—including the poker winnings—was gone. He stood, spitting a string of curses.

Parks frowned. "Problem?"

"I've been robbed." Callahan touched the sore spot at the base of his skull with three fingertips. Tender, but he'd be okay. "He hit me."

"Who did?"

"Ronald Parsons . . . if that's even his name."

Callahan squinted up at the sun. He'd been out at least an hour. He cursed again, scanning the ground. Too many hoofprints. People came and went all the time to the saloon. Parsons had said he was headed to Bozeman, but, of course, that was a lie. If Callahan followed the wrong trail for half a day, that would only increase the slicker's head start.

He went back inside Shakey's Saloon, asked everyone within if they knew anything about Ronald Parsons or where he might be headed, but nobody had any useful information.

"Some bad luck," Sergeant Parks said. "Sorry, Tom."

"Dirty son of a . . . If I ever see him again, there'll be nothing left of him, I can tell you that. He didn't take my six-gun and knife, at least," Callahan said.

"Good, because you'll need 'em," Parks said. "That's why I come looking for you." Parks briefly explained the expedition with Lieutenant Foster to find the rogue Cheyenne.

"Huh." Callahan scratched his head, thinking it over. "I guess I'm in no position now to turn down a paying job. Okay, Sarge, just let me change into some dry clothes."

They angled southeast toward the spot where the prospector had been found. Callahan rode his painted horse next to Parks, the dozen cavalrymen riding two-by-two behind them. They were traveling known roads, so Callahan's skill as a scout wouldn't be needed yet. Foster rode out front, and Callahan sized up the man.

He was the worst possible combination of everything that made for a rotten officer. He was fresh out of West Point, which meant he probably thought he already knew everything, even though he'd been west of the Mississippi for less than a month. He was appallingly young, which didn't make him a bad person or stupid, but experience counted for a lot out here, and Lieutenant Horace Foster didn't have any. What he did have was a perfectly clean and pressed uniform and the shiniest buttons Callahan had ever seen.

We'll see how long that lasts.

Callahan chastised himself. His opinion was based on young officers he'd met before. Every man deserved a chance to be a blank page. Let Foster write his own story, then Callahan would judge.

They spent the night on a knoll overlooking the road. The troopers were green, according to Parks, but they went about the business of making camp, hobbling the horses, preparing dinner, and setting sentries in a professional manner.

Later that evening, Foster approached Callahan near the campfire, a folded newspaper under one arm. "Callahan? We left Fort Keogh in a hurry and haven't had a chance to meet officially. I'm Second Lieutenant Horace Foster."

"Lieutenant." Callahan shook his hand. "I usually answer to Tom or Tomahawk, but Callahan works, too."

"I understand you have people back in Missouri." He handed Callahan the newspaper. "That issue of the *Post-Dispatch* is only a week old. I've finished it, if you'd like a look."

"Obliged for that." He took the paper and angled it to catch the firelight. A headline caught his eye. THE LAST WAGON TRAIN? Curious. He folded the newspaper and stashed it inside his jacket. "I'll read it when I have better light. Thanks again."

"Well, I'm going to sleep," Foster said. "Early day tomorrow."

They set out the next morning just as dawn was humping up red-orange from the horizon. It warmed soon after, and Callahan wondered if spring had finally made an appearance. By midafternoon, they'd made it to the place where the mule skinners had found the dead prospector.

Callahan dismounted next to Foster. "Lieutenant, keep the men back, will you?"

Foster twisted in the saddle. "You men hold position."

Callahan approached the creek, taking it slow and stepping carefully. He knew the area, knew the little trickle was called Gibson's Creek, although he had no idea who Gibson was. The mule skinners who'd found the body had made Callahan's job harder, both men and horses tromping all over the scene. At least it hadn't snowed or rained. He found a churned up piece of ground on the other side that he suspected as the location of the murder—lots of boot prints and moccasin prints, both in all different directions, like maybe the prospector had put up a fight, and of course, why wouldn't he? Callahan tried to imagine them pushing and shoving and stepping every which way.

He slowly made an ever-widening circle from the spot until he found what he was looking for, a trail made by moccasined feet, trudging single file away from the creek, going north. They'd gone single file, which made it tougher to determine how many.

"Wait here!" he called back to the troopers.

He followed the trail a quarter mile to see if the Indians continued on foot or if they'd tied horses somewhere. No hoofprints, but he spotted a muddy patch of ground that gave him pause. Tracks came in from another direction to intersect the trail he'd been following. He examined the ground for a while and drew a conclusion.

Callahan guessed maybe two or three Cheyenne had ambushed the prospector. They left the scene of the crime and had met another group, a little larger. Then all of them left together, the trail going north.

Callahan went back to the blue coats and took his horse by the reins. "We'll need to walk a ways. I don't want to lose the trail."

"Sergeant, have the men dismount," Foster said.

Parks shouted the order back to the troops.

"How many?" Foster asked.

"Can't be certain," Callahan told him. "A half dozen at least. More maybe."

"More like maybe eight or ten? Or more like fifty?"

Callahan chuckled. "Not fifty. Not a war party. And they're not mounted."

"That's something at least."

They crossed the creek and followed Callahan into the forest, staying back about ten yards to give him room to work. Callahan kept his eyes on the ground, but his mind worked as he followed the trail. It had been his experience that Indians were like anyone else in most respects. Some were good, others bad. Some smart and some stupid.

Callahan wondered if these were stupid Indians. Why kill the prospector? For a mule and a rifle? They surely knew that would bring the blue coats. And they were on foot, so they didn't have the option of a quick getaway. Something wasn't adding up, but there was only so much a man could glean from footprints in the mud.

The forest thinned, then cleared, and Callahan found himself looking across open ground. His attention was drawn east to a rocky formation atop a low hill. A thin tendril of smoke rose from the top. He followed the trail another half mile to confirm it angled toward the hill.

Callahan waited for Foster to catch up and pointed out the smoke.

Foster grinned. "They're making it easy for us."

"They're probably cooking the prospector's mule," Isiah Parks commented offhandedly.

The lieutenant found the notion distasteful, if his expression was any indication.

Callahan mounted his horse. "Well, we found them. Now the hard part."

"I suppose we go up and get them," Foster said.

Callahan shook his head. "Nope."

Foster frowned. "What is it you suppose we're doing out here, Mr. Callahan?"

"I know we've got a job to do, Lieutenant. I just mean we can't go charging up that hill," Callahan said.

"Explain."

"First, they're going to see us coming, maybe have seen us already," Callahan said. "That means they'll have time to decide. Fight or run. Except they can't run, and they know it. They can sneak down the other side of the hill, but on foot, we'd ride them down easy. That means they have no choice but to dig in, shooting down on us from good cover."

"They might wait until nightfall," Parks said. "Then try to sneak away. They might even scatter."

"They might," Callahan agreed.

"Then what are we supposed to do?" Foster asked.

"Let's get closer," Callahan said. "Make *sure* they see us, so they know they're in it deep."

"And then?"

"Then I go up there," Callahan said.

He spurred his horse forward, and the others followed.

They called a halt just out of rifle range, and Callahan dismounted to search his saddlebags. He came out with an Indian tomahawk and stuck it in his belt. He checked the load on his Peacemaker, then dropped it back in the holster. He pulled his Henry rifle from the saddle sheath and checked it, fifteen .44 rimfire shells and one in the chamber.

He mounted again and put the Henry across the saddle in front of him. "Wait here. Keep your eyes open. Everything I said might be wrong. They might try to run, so be ready."

"What do you figure to do up there all by yourself?" Foster asked.

"I guess we'll see." Callahan spurred his horse to a gallop.

He reached the foot of the hill without getting shot and dismounted. He didn't bother tying the horse to anything. It was a good animal and wouldn't wander off. He took his time looking for the best way up and soon found the path the Indians had used. He put his rifle on his shoulder, holding it casually, hoping he was conveying the right demeanor. *I'm ready for trouble, but not looking for it.*

Callahan headed up the hill.

He kept his eyes and ears open but also turned his thoughts back to the two groups of Indians. Callahan had a hunch. If he was wrong, it might get him killed.

About halfway up, the path took him through a cluster of boulders. Some instinct put Callahan on alert, and he crouched through, rifle up and ready. He came out the other side of the cluster, paused, looked left and right. Nothing to see.

He lowered the rifle and let out the breath he'd been holding.

Callahan heard the all-too-familiar sound of a lever action sliding a shell into a rifle chamber. He muttered a curse under his breath. *Caught like some fool greenhorn.*

He turned slowly, eyes going up. Four Indians in buckskin stood on the big boulder above, three pointing rifles down at him. The fourth was older, gray streaks in his braided hair. He held his rifle in the crook of his arm, a dour expression on his face.

"Looks like you got the drop on me," Callahan said.

The older Indian's eyes fell to the tomahawk in Callahan's belt. "Where did you get that, white man? Did you take it off a dead brave?" His English was good.

"It was given to me by Dull Knife," Callahan said.

The Indians stirred, shooting glances at each other. They recognized the name, as Callahan had hoped.

"Why?" asked the one in charge.

"I saved his nephew's life."

The Indians exchanged words, then the one with gray in his hair said, "So you saved Laughing Otter's life?"

"His name's Walks with the Wind," Callahan said. "And he's got big ears."

A sly smile. "Perhaps you speak the truth after all."

"Where are the others?" Callahan asked.

The Indian's smile faded. "There are no others."

Callahan considered his next words carefully. "You left a trail, and the trail told a story. Some Indians killed a prospector along Gibson's Creek. These Indians met some others and then they traveled together to this hill. I seek the end to the story. You've seen the blue coats below?"

"We've seen them."

"The story ends one of two ways," Callahan explained. "The blue coats take all the Cheyenne here, and all are punished for the murder. Or the blue coats take only the killer. Help me write the best ending to this story."

"Why did you come up here alone?"

"What would happen if all the blue coats came at once?"

The Indian thought about it. "A bad ending to the story for all."

Callahan nodded. "My name's Callahan."

"I am called Slow River," the Indian said.

"And those at the top of the hill?" Callahan asked.

"Tall Elk. He is the one who killed the prospector," Slow River said. "His brother Bright Pony is with him."

"Dull Knife has already made peace," Callahan said. "There's talk your people won't be sent south again. Some of the Cheyenne like Little Wolf have even started working as scouts for the blue coats. There's no reason to begin trouble anew. Give the blue coats Tall Elk for the prospector."

Slow River thought long about it but shook his head. "I warned Tall Elk it was foolish to kill the prospector. It would bring the blue coats. And now that very thing has come to pass. But I am Cheyenne. Tall Elk is Cheyenne. It goes against my heart to give him to the blue coats. Still, I know the blue coats will not rest until there is justice for the dead prospector. Fetch him yourself, if you will, Callahan. We will not stand in your way."

Callahan looked up the mountain, then back at Slow River. "Can I call up the troopers to help me?"

"There is not trust for that yet," Slow River said. "You must go alone, Callahan. The story is in your hands. Write the best ending you can."